The WINDS *of* REDEMPTION

Books by Marilyn V. King

The Winds of Love
The Winds of Grace
The Winds of Courage
The Winds of Promise

Hearts of Home
Isabel's Song

Anthologies
The Letter
A Hobo's Thanksgiving
Everybody Out Here Comes A Train!

Children's Book
Tony Finds A Home

The
WINDS *of* REDEMPTION

Book Four

MARILYN V. KING

CROWN LEAF PUBLISHING

The Winds of Redemption
Published by Crown Leaf Publishing, functions only as book publisher. As such, the ultimate design, content, editorial accuracy, and views expressed or implied in this work are those of the author.

Unless otherwise noted, all scriptures quotations are taken from the King James Version of the Bible.

This is a work of fiction. Names, characters, incidents, and dialogues are products of the author's imagination and are not to be construed as real. Any resemblance to actual events or persons, living or dead, is entirely coincidental.

ISBN: 978-0-9967258-1-1 Trade paperback
Library of Congress Catalog Card Number:

Cover design by Ken Raney

Printed in the United States of America
2017–First Edition

123120253

THIS BOOK IS dedicated to my brothers and sisters,
Verdean, Rene, John, Theresa, David, and Bob
for all the years of fun memories and good times.
And for your generous support.

ACKNOWLEDGMENTS

MY SINCEREST THANKS to my critique groups, The Romancers: Roberta Smith, Liz Pye, Loralie Palotta and Ann Minor helped my facts, points of view, storyline, and tenses straight.

Many thanks to my editors, Jenny Margotta and Molly Jo Realy. Your insight was both educational and invaluable. I could not have produced such a fine piece of work without you.

To Roberta, for your expertise in finalizing the last stages of my work. You have been a generous, heartfelt friend.

My love and gratitude go out to my husband, Bob, who has been my backbone, advisor, and ear throughout the building of this book. His willingness to research and edit the book is much appreciated.

NOTE TO THE READER

THE JAMAICAN SLAVE revolt–which lasted from 1831 to 1838–brought turbulent years that irrevocably changed the lives of slaves and plantation owners along the Caribbean Coast. Old traditions crumbled and the philosophy that had kept everyone–prominent, poor white, and servant–in their places vanished.

In the effort to accurately portray the era in which this historical fiction is set; I have used certain terms in this work that are offensive to me personally and which are no longer prevalent in today's speech and attitudes. This is true regarding the men and women held in slavery on the plantations described in this novel as it moves to the South in early America. Please know that when terms like *darky, blackie, coloreds,* and *Negro* are used, they are reflective of this time frame and not meant as any offense to the African-American people. Terms that referred to slaves that were also common in the period, but which were the most offensive, are not used in this novel.

Though I find the period in which I wrote this story fascinating, I find the treatment of human beings as slaves' repellant, and I believe God created all men as equal in His eyes. May the day come when humans treat each other with grace and see each other for who we are and not by the color of our skin. For I believe this is what God intended.

In His Grip,
Marilyn King

ONE

Cooper Riverfront, Charleston, South Carolina
10 September 1848

IT HAD BEEN hot and humid the past three days, and once again, seventeen-year-old Kit Bartholomew stood on the wharf, gazing over the bay at the vast number of ships. Some were docked near the riverfront, but several of the vessels were anchored farther out. She shielded her eyes against the bright sun and narrowed her vision in search of her uncle's ship, the *Sea Baron*. The vessel would bring her cousin Damaris to spend the next few weeks at River Oak.

"Do you see anything, Father?" She leaned forward, one hand holding a small felt hat decorated with silk flowers that spilled from the crown to the edge of the turned-up brim.

"No, I don't see Denzel's ship. I'm beginning to wonder if you women have the right date for their arrival. It's been three days, and no sign of them."

"Damaris wrote that they should arrive on September seventh. I have her letter right here." Kit patted her black felt reticule and stared at her father's smoky gray eyes. "The waiting time hasn't been wasted time," she said in a thick Southern drawl. "You've managed to accomplish much while we've been in town."

"That's true. I needed to see Captain Butler Wilder about the latest export of our rice. He seems to think there will be greater demand for it next year. More countries are buying the rice than ever before."

Kit watched her father as he spoke. Cameron Bartholomew blinked sharply in the midmorning sun. Tall and robust for his fifty-one years, he possessed a regal air. People said it was his thick black hair flecked with gray, penetrating gray eyes, and strong jaw—an unusual and striking combination–that commanded attention. He gazed one more time at the boats bobbing and swaying in the water. "We'll come back tomorrow. Surely, the *Sea Baron* will be here then."

Cameron placed his hand on his daughter's back to steer her away from the crowded wharf that smelled of oily fish and horse droppings. The congested pier was bustling with activity despite the morning heat.

Kit wished the *Sea Baron* had already arrived. It had been seven long years since she'd last seen Damaris. But despite the long-awaited reunion, letters had crossed the ocean continuously. The cousins, born a month apart, were now young women of seventeen years. That alone drew them together. Kit knew she'd matured dramatically in the past seven years. Would she recognize her cousin?

Just as she and her father turned toward the busy traffic of buggies and carriages, wagons and carts, her father looked over his shoulder and said, "Wait."

Kit glanced back to see what he was looking at and spied the *Savannah Rose* gliding into port between ships and longboats, making its way slowly, her massive sails being lowered by seamen scurrying about and calling orders as the great vessel smoothly slid into place along the dock.

"Well, look who's here." Kit smiled. "Captain Drew Harding. That's what I call good timing."

"It's a good thing we waited a bit longer." Cameron squared his shoulders. "I believe I'll pay him a visit. Care to join me?"

Kit's taffeta walking dress with several layers of skirts beneath had become increasingly warm in the bright sun. This was the third day she'd worn the burnt-orange dress with three flounces, all trimmed with black shirring. Grace, her mother, had said the burnt orange was a nice contrast to her coal-black tresses and encouraged her to wear the gown, despite the warm weather. But at the moment, she would give anything to shed the matching, form-fitted jacket, beneath which she wore a white lace blouse trimmed with delicate, tiny bows. It would be far more comfortable if they were out of the hot sun.

"You go on, Father. I'll wait with Nate in the carriage." The family's carriage rested at the side of the road. Their stableman, Nate, sat up front as he waited.

"Are you sure? I may be a while. I'm sure Captain Harding will have refreshments to cool us."

"I'm fine. I'll wait." She wrinkled her nose. "I've been perspiring like a pig. I'll not embarrass myself in the company of the Hardings if you don't mind."

"All right. I won't be long."

Cameron Bartholomew was soon lost in the crowd as he wove in and out among the throng of people. Kit watched until she lost sight of him, then she turned to look once more at the bay filled with ships. Would Damaris and her family arrive tomorrow?

Standing there, she felt a pair of eyes on her and looked up at the stern of the *Savannah Rose* to see a handsome young man peering down at her. Having arrived on Uncle Drew's ship, she was surprised she hadn't seen him before. Had Captain Harding hired new men to work his merchant ship? Not one to shy away, Kit met the man's gaze. He cocked a grin and gave a slight wave of his hand. A second look told her he was quite good looking, with brawny skin kissed by the sun.

She deliberately looked away, aware that the man was far too brazen. Looking out at the sparkling water, she pretended to take interest in the loading and unloading of the vessel. Still, she felt the man's eyes had not wavered. Really? Who was he?

Curiosity got the better of her, and she glanced up at the stern again. That's when it dawned on her who the rogue with admiration in his eyes really was. Jackson Harding, the captain's son! Why hadn't she noticed him before? Could that truly be him? He had grown from a gangly, thin boy to a broad-shouldered man who appeared to be in his twenties. She had to think a moment about how old he really was. Why, she'd known him nearly all her life. They'd ridden horses together, even raced their mounts a few times. The Bartholomews and the Hardings had traditionally spent their summers together ever since she could remember.

In the past, she hadn't given Jackson the time of day, other than to take up his offer to go horseback riding, and thinking about it, she didn't recall his ever making much of her except to spar with the horses. But he hadn't joined the Harding family for the past four years. At his parents' demand, he'd gone to college. Kit hadn't missed him. To her, Jackson was just one of the boys.

"Kit?"

She looked over to see her father frowning.

"I've called your name three times. Are you all right?"

"Of course, Father. I must have been lost in thought. You're back already?"

"Captain Harding has invited us to lunch with him in his cabin."

Kit hardly caught a word he said as she looked back at the dashing man who still eyed her from the stern. His elbows rested casually on the ship's rails, and the soft breeze ruffled his brown hair.

"Kit!"

She spun around. "Yes, Father?"

"What has gotten into you? You haven't heard a word I've said."

"Sorry, sir, I heard you. We're to have lunch with the captain." She lifted her skirt to follow her father to the *Savannah Rose.* "I'm ready if you are."

Cameron looked up at the ship and then at his daughter. "Drew brought his sons on this voyage."

"I see." When she looked up, Jackson averted his gaze as if he were unaware she existed. Kit lifted her chin, and a small smile spread across her face. She could play that game too. He hadn't existed in her mind before. He certainly didn't have to now. A gust of hot wind tugged at her hat, and she quickly lifted a hand to hold it in place.

"The wind's picking up. You'll lose your hat if we don't hurry along," her father cautioned.

Kit slipped her hand in the crook of her father's arm and let him lead the way. The sounds around them were familiar. The clattering of horses' hooves and carriage wheels on the cobbled road filled the air. She never tired of visiting the riverfront. Just before they neared Drew's boat, Kit looked up once more to see that Jackson was no longer at the rail.

Stevedores went up and down the gangplank, carrying crates and barrels and calling out to one another. She kept pace with her father as they moved up to the main deck. Captain Harding waited at the top and opened his arms wide.

Kit flew into his arms. "It is so good to see you, Uncle Drew."

"Welcome to the *Savannah Rose*, young lady." His smile was contagious as he led them to his cabin.

"Did Camille travel with you this time?" Kit looked past the door.

"No. She and Rosamond stayed home. They've had the seamstress sewing nonstop for Rosa's new wardrobe for this school year."

"How long will you be in Charleston?" Cameron asked as they stepped into Harding's cabin.

"Four days at the least. The rice—or the Carolina Gold, I should say—keeps us busy. The merchant business has never been better." Captain Harding pulled out a chair for Kit. "How's your mother?"

"She's well, thank you. She stayed home with the girls and Willie. Our seamstress has had to take up residency, what with the four of us girls needing new gowns for the season." Kit placed her hands in her lap. "Did you know Uncle Denzel, Damaris, and the rest of the family are due here any day?"

"That's what your father said." Drew gazed at her. "You have grown into a beautiful young woman since I last saw you. Where has the time gone?" His eyes sparkled.

"Uncle Drew, you must stop that. You and Aunt Camille were at River Oak last fall. I haven't changed that much." Kit gave him a quirky grin, then swallowed as she glanced out the cabin door. "Father says you've brought the boys with you this trip."

"Boys?" He laughed. "I suppose you could say that about Jackson's brothers. Woodrow is now seventeen, and Spencer is fifteen. They're a lot of help, but Jackson—can you believe he's twenty-three—has become a strong young man and my right hand. I'm sure you'll see him before you leave the ship."

Just then, a sailor arrived at the door with a tray of food. "Your lunch, sir."

"Set the tray on the table," Drew said, standing to one side.

A second sailor arrived with a pitcher and a tray of mugs. He set the mugs on the table and filled each one to the brim with cool, refreshing water.

"You may leave us," Captain Harding told the crewmen.

The sailors took their leave, but as the humidity was high, the captain kept the cabin door open, hoping to catch a stray breeze. Kit wished to remove her jacket but said nothing. Instead, she picked up a mug and took a sip of the water. She leaned back and watched as Captain Harding and her father whiled away the next hour with much talk about the rice industry.

Finally, to Kit's relief, her father said, "We should head back to the hotel. Kit looks as if she's about to wilt."

"Do I, Father? I apologize. I must admit, all these layers are too much for this heat." She blew a puff of hair off her forehead.

Within the hour, they left the ship. To Kit's disappointment, Jackson had not made an appearance. Would he come out to River Oak before the *Savannah Rose* left port?

TWO

KINDRA TALMAZE WIPED at the sweat trickling down her neck as she stood pressed between Cuffee and a hundred other slaves. The three-day journey from Virginia to Charleston had taken its toll on her and the other passengers. Crammed with slaves, the steamer moved downriver, the paddles churning the brown waters while slave men and women stood inhumanely on their feet for the thirty-six-hour journey. They huddled together as if they were cattle headed for the slaughter. The only thing that kept Kindra from falling from exhaustion was the slaves holding her up with their hot bodies pressing against her.

Her feet ached and her stomach growled. Rations for the trip had been passed over the heads of the slaves in several wide straw baskets. Some were filled with chunks of dry bread, and more baskets held a variety of old fruits. Each slave was to take their portion and pass the baskets along. The problem was that those standing at the back of the steamship only got the remains of crumbs or fruit that were better thrown overboard.

At times, Kindra fell back against Cuffee's chest, near tears and delirium. How could anyone expect a person to stand this long?

"Charleston, South Carolina!" bellowed the steamship captain. "Get ready to deport!"

The guide responsible for escorting the slaves safely to their destination stood before the crowd. "Be prepared to move slowly down the ramp at our arrival," he called out. "You will be met by Mister Morrow. He will see to you until you are auctioned off."

The steamer whistle tooted three times, and the boat swayed in the waters as it moved toward the riverfront on the Cooper River. It was late afternoon, and the weather had cooled slightly. The paddleboat moored at the pier with a final jerk, and the slaves jerked as well, working to keep their footing.

Cuffee's hand clamped Kindra's shoulder to steady her. She closed her eyes and waited for what was to come. Slowly, the slaves disembarked. As the men, women, and children moved forward, the pressure of cramped bodies began to loosen, and Kindra took in a deep breath. At the end of the gangplank, a tall, barrel-chested man sorted the slaves into two groups. Kindra felt a stab of fear. Would she be separated from Cuffee?

She sniffed cigar smoke, the smell of horse flesh, and unbathed bodies. When she swallowed, she felt headachy and nauseous. Her world was spinning out of control.

Slowly and methodically, the slaves moved forward. Kindra watched as she neared the slanted gangplank, clutching her brown skirt as it came her turn to step forward.

"Over here!" Mister Morrow pointed her to a small group. Tentatively, she did as she was told and joined Lolly and Effie in the crowd. Having spent the past five years living in their cabin at White Stone Manor, at least she was not stranded among people she didn't know.

Lolly's hand went to Kindra's shoulder and gave it a squeeze.

"You! Over there!"

Kindra looked up to see Cuffee following her, but Mister Morrow cracked his whip, the tip slicing a line in the dirt. "Did I tell you to follow that blackie?"

Cuffee stopped dead in his tracks and jerked his head to look at the slaver. "No, suh, you didn't."

Mister Morrow's man strode over to Cuffee and pointed to the other side of the grounds. "You belong over there." He pulled on Cuffee's arm and steered him to stand a good ten feet away with a second group of slaves.

"Cuffee!" Kindra gasped. Her hand went to her mouth, and she waited for his eyes to meet hers. When they did, he shook his head slightly, a message not to fight it. They held each other's gaze. Her gut twisted, and tears brimmed in her eyes. She lifted her chin, and stood straight, steeling herself for what was to come. Today would be the end of their journey together.

Striking a stern and exaggerated posture, Mister Morrow examined the scraggly slaves. He carried the bullwhip under his arm and tapped the handle repeatedly in the palm of his hand. "A sturdy back," he said, examining a young Negro man. He lifted chins of young girls and turned young boys around, lifting their tattered shirts to inspect their backs. "No scars. That's good."

Kindra watched with curiosity as Morrow approached her. When he stood in front of her, she didn't flinch, nor did she look away.

He grasped her face. "When a white man comes, keep your eyes down." His lips curled then thinned into a straight line. "Always keep your eyes down. Learn to talk your masters' talk and obey their rules. You'll never again walk free. You'll never again see where you came from. That's how it be."

By now, Kindra knew he wasn't only talking to her but to the rest of the slaves as well. He looked down at her with hard eyes. "Do you understand?"

"Yes, sir," she replied in a near whisper.

"What's that you said?"

"Yes, sir," she said again, this time loud enough to please him.

"Good!" He held her at arm's length and examined her stature, her face, and her hair. He turned her around, untucked her white blouse, and lifted it to look at her back. "A small scar by your shoulder blade. Was that from an accident, or did you have it coming with a whip?"

"I fell, sir." The answer was half right.

"I 'spect that be so. A whip would have done more damage." He dropped the hem of her blouse. "I need to know before you stand before the bidders." He turned her around to face him and put a thick finger under her chin, lifting her face. "You're a looker. You'll bring me a good price."

When Morrow walked on to examine the other slaves, Kindra glanced at Cuffee. He held her gaze with lips clamped together. If she knew anything about the man, she knew his fists were clenched. She couldn't see his hands, as another man stood in front, hiding them. But she didn't need to see—she knew. It was her turn to give him a slight shake of the head.

"All right!" barked a guard. "Back on the steamer. The rest of you are headed for Beaufort."

Kindra watched the second group climb up the gangplank. Cuffee didn't look back; he just kept going. "Goodbye, Cuffee," Kindra whispered.

Lolly's hand went to Kindra's shoulder again, and she squeezed it as she had before. Kindra turned her head and rested her chin on Lolly's hand. When she looked up, the last of the slaves had re-boarded the steamer, and the gangplank had been raised into place. She watched the steamship captain grab a red rope looped above his head. He pulled the chain three times, making the whistle blow three shrill blasts. A steam cloud burst from the smokestacks, and the steamer chugged away from the wharf.

"Follow me!" called Morrow. His aides pushed the slaves into a single line. When the slaves were ready, they slowly made their way past the townspeople gawking at them and down the road to a long warehouse. It wasn't until they were being pushed and prodded down the dusty path that Kindra noticed the guards held clubs and muskets to keep them in line.

She clamped her teeth and moved with the others as if they were a herd of cattle. She drowned out the sounds of scoffers yelling at them and instead tried to remember the faces of her family. Her brood would no longer be small children. The first three would now be in their teens, and Cyrus, her youngest, would be eleven. He probably had grown several inches since she had last seen him. She smiled at the thought. Damaris would be a lovely young woman of seventeen, Zeddie fifteen, and little Piper thirteen. Would she even recognize her children if she saw them?

Desperately lonely, Kindra wanted to wrap her arms around herself, close her eyes, and dream of Denzel. But the rope tied at her wrist didn't allow this simple gesture, and she had to keep her eyes on the line in front of her.

"Stop!" Morrow called out. At once, the line of slaves stopped walking. The tattered group stood before a long wooden structure. The building was old and weathered, with a row of double doors spaced every twelve feet. "Put the women and girls in here," he commanded, opening one set of double doors that creaked loudly as they scraped the ground. "The men and boys go down at the end."

For the next few minutes, the women were prodded inside the dust-filled building. As Kindra was pushed through the opening, her eyes had to adjust to the dim lighting filtering in through half-inch gaps between the boards that made up the walls. There were holes in the roof that allowed more light. It looked like the building was an abandoned stable.

After the ropes were cut off their wrists, the women were shoved into cubicles. The wide swinging door in each space scraped the floor as the guard slammed it shut and locked it.

Kindra was shoved into one of the cubicles with other women. Taking stock of her surroundings, she saw that the floor was covered with stale hay. Two narrow, wooden benches sat against the far wall. She shivered and hugged herself. Behind her, a dull voice said, "Well, at least they done kept us together."

Kindra spun around to see Lolly and Effie. "Thank God, they didn't separate us." She hugged the older woman first and then pulled Effie into her arms.

"It be one small thing to be grateful for," Lolly said. "They already done take my Asa and Suzanne. I be fearful all those years and justa hopin' that never happen." She wiped her cheek and looked at her daughter Effie, who was now a young woman herself. Lolly opened her arms, and mother and daughter held each other for a long time.

Hands free, Kindra looked at their meager surroundings. Above the two benches, there was a high, narrow window with bars on it. A milking stool sat near the door. Other than that, the small space was empty.

"I wonder how long we'll have to be in here," Effie said, pushing out of her mother's arms.

"I thought I heard one of the guards say something 'bout the auction bein' Saturday. So, we'll be here three days, at least," Lolly said.

Kindra sat on the bench. Her stomach growled, and she felt she could sleep for a year. "Have a seat. We've been on our feet for three days. This feels almost like heaven, getting off of them," she said. She kicked off a worn shoe and massaged her toes.

The women found places to sit and did the same. Effie smiled tiredly. "If I weren't so worn out, I'd rub yer feet, Mama."

"Don't you even think about it, little missy. I'm doin' fine by myself."

"What do we do now?" Kindra yawned.

"Ain't nothin' to do but wait. Wait and sleep. Sleep and wait," Lolly said grim-faced.

A half hour later, the three women found a spot on the hay-covered floor. Effie curled up in her mother's arms. Kindra lay facing the wood-slatted wall.

Her mind wandered to the fact that she was in Charleston, South Carolina. This was the city where her sister, Grace Bartholomew, had been born and raised. It was here that Grace had learned her father was not dead, and from here she had sailed the Atlantic Ocean to find him in Jamaica. And it was then that Kindra had discovered she had a white sister. They shared the same father, Phillip Cooper.

Cameron had said he had found land upriver from Charleston. He built River Oak on that land. Her pulse picked up. She was closer to Grace and Camp than she'd been in the past five years. What were the chances of Cameron coming to the auction and finding her? She tried to still the trembling of her body.

Her mind played back to the day she had boarded the steamship in Jamestown. The captain had told her that two men were looking for her. It had to have been Cameron and Denzel. Just knowing this lifted her spirits. There was hope again. If all went well, she would see her beloved Denzel soon.

The scratchy hay crackled under her as she tried to get comfortable. She closed her eyes and let her mind wander to beautiful Barbados. Tropical flowers filled the air with a sweet perfume. This time, her children met her on the lawn in front of the Great House. Denzel strode up behind them and opened his arms wide. As her tired body sank into slumber, she stepped into his arms and let him embrace her. The smell of his body filled her nostrils, and his strong arms protected her. *I'm coming home, my beloved. Please wait for me.*

THREE

WITH HANDS CLASPED to her chest, Kit stood in front of her father as they watched the *Sea Baron* glide into the bay and work its way to the docks. "They're here!" She felt a thrill and smiled up at her father. "They're finally here!" She stood on tiptoe and waved at the ship, hoping to see a return wave as the large vessel moved closer. Then she saw it. A hand went into the air and waved. Kit started walking, picking up her pace to reach the point where the ship would moor.

"Kit, wait up!" Cameron called.

"Sorry, Father." She turned on the wooden pier ripe with the smell of scaly fish and buckets of tar and impatiently watched as he strode toward her. The dark green water lapped against the wharf in a steady motion from the ships that crowded the pier. Stevedores moved past, their shoulders burdened with crates and boxes.

Cameron took her elbow. "They'll be lowering the gangplank over here." He escorted her to the edge of the dock, where they watched the gangway lower with a loud creak and a shudder. Sailors moved down the ramp, carrying cargo on their shoulders. Kit walked up the crowded ramp to where she could see Uncle Denzel, Damaris, and the rest of her cousins waving frantically, broad smiles on their faces.

When Kit and Cameron reached the main deck, she broke loose and ran into Damaris's arms. "You're finally here! What took you so long?" Kit stepped back at arm's length and looked her cousin over. "Oh, dear, you look absolutely frazzled after having sailed for nearly a month across the sea."

"Truly, I feel like I'm about to wilt in this dress," Damaris said. She pointed to the plain cotton dress she was wearing and continued, "We remembered to dress down for our arrival. I borrowed a couple of dresses from the women in the colored district. What do you think?" She turned around, holding out her brown, worn skirt with her fingertips.

"You could pass as my slave for sure!" Kit laughed softly. "Well, let me really look at you." She gently touched Damaris's shoulder to turn her cousin around again. "You did well. But tell me, did you bring a gown for our fall party?"

"I did. I brought two, and they nearly filled one trunk to the brim." Damaris stared at Kit for a long moment. "I've waited such a long time for this day. It's so good to see you." Her brown eyes shimmered with a glint of tears.

"Oh, Damaris." Kit took hold of her hands. "We have so much catching up to do. There is only so much one can say in a letter, and then it takes weeks for it to arrive."

Kit looked over to see their fathers in deep conversation. It was apparent they were just as happy for the reunion. Though one was an African man and the other an Englishman, the two had grown up like brothers on Cooper's Landing in Jamaica. It wasn't until now that Kit realized her other cousins stood at attention, waiting to be noticed. They, too, were dressed in worn and tattered clothing for the charade they'd play during the trip out of town. She opened her arms wide. "Come here, all of you!"

Fifteen-year-old Zeddie gave a shy smile as he stepped into Kit's arms. After a brief hug, she gently pushed him back. "Look how tall you are, and look at those eyes! Zeddie Talmaze, you're growing more handsome as the days go by."

Zeddie hung his head and looked over the rail of the ship as if he'd rather jump ship than stand there being appraised.

But Kit had already moved on to thirteen-year-old Piper. "You've grown too. Bella Grace and Sunny will be happy to see you. Do you remember them?"

Piper smiled shyly. "I do, some. It's been a long time."

Kit held Piper's hands and twirled her around. "That faded purple dress brings out your dark eyes. But you look as if you're about to wilt."

"I am. Is there somewhere we can stand in the shade?"

"Oh, honey, we're going back to the hotel today," Kit said in her thick southern accent. "There's a row of quarters behind King's Hotel for servants. Unfortunately, you'll be staying there, as they don't allow servants in the main hotel. We'll bring you something to eat, and they have the best lemonade. That'll cool you. But first I must reacquaint myself with this young man." She pulled Cyrus forward and ruffled his hair. He immediately jumped out of her reach, and his hand went up to straighten his short curly hair.

"Do you remember me?" Kit smiled.

"Yes, ma'am."

Kit's hands flew to her hips. "Ma'am? I'll have you know I'm the same age as your sister." She feigned a frown and wrinkled her brows. "How old are you, Cyrus?"

"Eleven."

"Well, I can see that you and Zeddie are both going to be tall like your father." She looked at his dark eyes and grinned. "Let's see if we can get our fathers to take us to the hotel and out of this hot sun." Kit fanned herself as she led the small group across the deck.

Cameron and Denzel watched them approach. "Are you ready to go?" Cameron asked.

"We are," Kit said. "If we stand in this heat much longer, you'll have to mop us up."

"We can continue our conversation over lunch. Let's get this brood off the ship," Cameron said.

As the group turned to leave, Captain Austin Kincade strode across the deck and put out a hand. Cameron took it, and the two shook with a firm grip.

"Cap'n!" came a booming voice across the deck. "You 'bout ready for the trunks to be loaded?"

"Yes, Barnabas, but before we do, come here."

The large black man, clothed in a tattered, faded shirt that barely covered his bulging muscles and blue straps that buckled to his black breeches, had a shiny, bald head. He lumbered across the deck to where the three of them stood and towered like a giant in their midst. His size could have been intimidating if it weren't for the kindest chocolate eyes looking down on them.

"Barnabas, it's been a while since you've seen Cameron Bartholomew."

"How do, suh. It be a pleasure, fer sure." He held out a massive hand. "We brung up the family's baggage and trunks, an' we can load 'em anytime yer ready."

"You can have the men load the wagon. We'll only be a moment," Denzel said.

"When will we go to River Oak?" Zeddie asked.

"In the morning. I have a few supplies to pick up before we travel back to the plantation. And besides, if we leave now, we wouldn't arrive before dark."

A wagon waited behind the carriage. Some supplies sat on the wooden floor, but there was plenty of room for the family's luggage. While the girls found a seat in the carriage, the men saw to it that all of the baggage and trunks were stacked in and around the supplies.

A wagon had been rented for Denzel's family. They would ride the short trip to the King's Hotel for the evening, and Cameron would return it to the blacksmith before they traveled into Charleston.

Seated in the coach with Damaris, Kit looked out the window of the carriage to see her father shove his wide-brimmed hat off his forehead and wipe the sweat off his brow. Then his hands went to his hips and he gazed at something across the road. As Kit watched, Cameron grabbed Denzel's arm and the two men crossed the street to a sign posted on a high fence.

"What are you looking at?" Damaris asked.

"Them." Kit pointed out the window.

Damaris leaned over her to see out the window. "Is that a slave auction sign?"

"I think so."

Damaris reached for the door handle on her side.

"Wait, Damaris. If it's anything worth checking out, they'll tell us."

Damaris leaned back and closed her eyes. "I've dreamed so many times that one day we'll find Mama."

Kit's hand went to her cousin's. "Me, too, Damaris. Father goes to nearly all the auctions in the hope of finding her. We won't give up."

"My dad plans to hunt for her while we're here." Damaris squeezed Kit's hand back and opened her eyes.

"I know. That's all father has talked about for the last few days. They're counting on this trip to find Aunt Kindra so you can all go home as a family."

"I truly hope that happens." A tear slipped from Damaris's eye, and she wiped it away. She looked out the window again. "Here they come."

Kit watched the men stride back to the carriage.

"Are you ready?" Cameron asked.

"What did that sign say?" Kit pointed.

"There's to be a slave auction Saturday."

"Will we wait until then to see if Aunt Kindra is here?"

"We're going to take all of you to the hotel, and then Denzel and I are going to the warehouse to see if she's there."

"Can I come with you?" Damaris asked.

"No," Cameron said. "It's no place for a woman. And with your dark skin, I wouldn't risk it."

Damaris looked defeated.

Denzel reached for her hand to help her out of the coach. "You girls can talk later. For now, you have to ride back in the wagon with the rest of us."

Damaris leaned over and kissed Kit's cheek. "We'll see you in a few moments."

"I'm so sorry it has to be this way. I'd give anything for you to stay."

"Don't give it a thought. We were told before we left on the trip that the southern states are very strict about darkies. I can play the game. It's worth it to see you again." Damaris gave a genuine smile. "Meet you at the hotel." She disappeared behind the carriage.

"All right, Father." Kit leaned back on the lonely seat. "I'm ready."

After settling the children at the hotel and the slave quarters, Denzel and Cameron walked the five blocks to the warehouse. Denzel had changed into the customary, worn, and dirty work clothes of a slave. He wore the breeches and shirt when traveling with Cameron. It wouldn't do to be caught looking uppity.

When they came to the long-weathered building, several buggies were parked alongside the road and up against the warehouse. Plantation owners and high-society men alike stood in circles, smoking pipes and cigars. Other men were on their way through the open double doors to inspect the slaves that would be up for auction the coming weekend.

"Stay close and slightly behind," Cameron reminded Denzel.

"Yes, suh," Denzel replied.

The two men chuckled, and Cameron quirked a grin.

"I sure hope we find Kindra today." Denzel's voice, low and husky, carried over the hum of men's muffled voices inside.

"Me, too, buddy. Let's go."

Hired guards stood at posts at opposite ends of the warehouse. When Cameron and Denzel approached the building's rough exterior, Cameron asked, "Where are the women?"

The guard looked at Cameron, then at Denzel, and frowned. Denzel lowered his eyes and stepped just behind Camp.

"You don't mind if I bring my slave man with me, do you?" Camp asked.

"It's not customary to let the slaves walk through and see the pickings. He can wait outside," the guard said gruffly.

"I don't think I want to do that. He's, my man. He stays with me."

Just then, Mister Morrow walked up to where they stood. "Mister Bartholomew. Good to see you this fine day." He reached out a hand to Cameron's and shook it. "We have some quality shipments this time. Some strong bucks on the backside and a few choice women in here. Take your time looking." He rocked on his heels and puffed his cigar.

"Your guard has reservations about my slave coming with me," Cameron said.

"You're a good buyer. You can take him with you." Mister Morrow scowled at the guard and flicked the ashes from his cigar.

"Go on ahead." The guard spat a wad of brown tobacco onto the ground.

"Mind your manners, Jed. It's folks like Mister Bartholomew who keep you employed."

Jed just stared at Denzel, working his jaw.

"Go on," Mister Morrow said. "No one will give you any trouble." He glared at Jed, shoved his cigar in his mouth, and walked away.

"Follow me," Cameron told Denzel.

The two men stepped inside the warehouse and walked down the dusty aisle that led past small compartments of slaves. The doors to each compartment were open, and the slaves sat on benches, their hands tied together. They looked up wide-eyed when Cameron and Denzel went from one stall to the next and peered in. Some women were heavy-set, others were thin as a post, but they all had frightened eyes. Each time the two men entered a small area closed off by high walls, they asked, "Is there a woman by the name of Kindra here?"

Each time the answer was, "No."

Cameron and Denzel continued through the stale-smelling cubicles, looking in each with hope in their hearts that Kindra would be found sitting among the women and girls. Each time they asked if she was among them. Always the answer was, "No." At long last, they came to the final stall, still with no sign of Kindra. Disheartened, they went out to the yard and breathed in the fresh air. "Well, Denzel, she's not with this group. I guess we can go to River Oak. There's another auction in Beaufort on Saturday. Maybe we'll find her there."

Denzel's shoulders slumped, and his face looked weary. "Do you think we'll ever find her?"

"I sure hope so, my friend." Cameron laid a hand on Denzel's shoulder and squeezed it. I sure hope so."

FOUR

KINDRA LEFT THE outhouse with a guard's hand clamped around her upper arm. The bright sun nearly blinded her after all the hours in the stable. She and the guard rounded the corner of the old building, and he led her back to the compartment she shared with Lolly and Effie. Men's eyes widened as she passed them, and a shiver ran through her. Some of the plantation owners looked as if they couldn't wait to get their hands on her. She lowered her eyes and stared at her worn black shoes.

At last, the small area she shared with the women came into view. The guard pushed her down on the bench and retied the rope on her wrists. He looked at the three women and said, "Why so downcast? You won't be here fer long. All these plantation owners got big estates. Far's, I know, they got better accommodations than this here horse stall." He turned and walked away.

"There sure has been a lot o' men tramplin' about this place. I can't hardly breathe with all the dust they be kickin' up," Lolly said.

"Mama, I hate how they be lookin' at us." Effie stared at her tied hands. "Tell Kindra 'bout them men who come lookin' fer her."

"Has someone come looking for me while I was gone?"

Both women stared at Kindra and then at each other. "Well, there be two men who come by before you come back. One was a black-haired man with silver streaks. He asked if you were with us," Lolly said.

Kindra's heart nearly leapt from her chest. "And did you tell him I was here?"

"Why, course' I didn't. I be protecting you from them no-good-for-nuthins!"

"Lolly . . . was there a black man with him?"

"Well, yes. He be a good-looker, followin' his massa close behind. He seemed more desperate to look in our room than that gent who came askin' 'bout you."

Tears flooded Kindra's eyes. She couldn't breathe. She wanted to shake Lolly's teeth out of her head. Instead, she whispered loudly, "That was my husband, Denzel." Her lips trembled, and she could hardly sit a moment longer. She stood, grasped the rough wooden doorjamb, and stared out at the men walking by. She sniffed, and her head throbbed as she leaned against the opening. *How could she have missed them? She had only been gone a moment!* She swung around and stared at the two women who shrank back in shock. "That was my beloved looking for me." Tears streamed down her face, and she lifted her hands to wipe them away.

"Oh, Kindra. I never thought about that man bein' yer husband. Those men looked in so expectantly that I jist thought of them like alla the rest of the plantation owners who jist be waitin' to do our women. It never occurred to me that it might be yer man." Lolly shook her head sorrowfully. "Maybe they'll come to the auction Saturday and see you then."

"Just knowing they're still looking for me gives me hope." Kindra's stomach flinched. She had to sit down. "Please, Lord, please send Denzel back to find me."

The next morning, Denzel's family settled into the crude wagon. Kit handed them a basket with boiled eggs, warm toast, and fresh fruit. "This will hold you over until lunchtime. Father says you only have to ride in the wagon for an hour."

"You go on and get in that fancy carriage." Denzel grinned, giving Kit a teasing look. "We be jist fine back heah."

"Uncle Denzel, you're not funny. I hate what the city folks think." She laid a hand on his. "But I must say, you sure can play the part."

"It came in handy plenty o' times. Saved my hide fo' sho'."

Kit narrowed her eyes at her uncle and shook her head. "See you all in an hour." She waved at them and went up to the carriage. Once seated, she crossed her arms over her chest and closed her eyes. She'd rest until they came to John's Island, where the family would be reunited and ride back to River Oak together.

It was midmorning when Cameron and Denzel returned the rented wagon to the blacksmiths. When they returned to their waiting families, everyone was eager to continue their journey. Nate helped Kit and Damaris step into the carriage, followed by the rest of the group, one at a time.

Kit patted the seat next to her as she slid to the door. "Sit by me, Damaris. We've a long ride back to the house, but it will give us plenty of time to catch up on everything." Damaris scooted in next to Kit, her expression drawn. She had become quiet after her father returned from the warehouse with no news of her mother. Kit took hold of her cousin's hand and squeezed it. "I know you miss your mother terribly. You can't give up. The men will find her. You wait and see."

Damaris looked over and gave her a small smile. "I'm certainly counting on it this trip."

"Make room for me," Piper said as she nudged Damaris's elbow. She slid over to make room for Cyrus. Once he settled in, the four had little room to move.

"Maybe I should ride in the wagon with the driver back there." Cyrus adjusted his shoulders for comfort.

Denzel moved across the leather seat and glanced at his son. "That'd be a long ride on the buckboard."

"I don't care. At least I could breathe."

Cameron, Denzel, and Zeddie climbed in last, sitting across from the four. Zeddie sat between the two men. Denzel seemed preoccupied as he glanced out the window.

Cyrus piped up once more. "Can I ride in the wagon, Pop?"

The carriage lurched forward as the horses began to trot away from the stable. Denzel reached up and knocked on the ceiling with three hard thumps. The rig stopped at once, and Nate called back, "Is somethin' wrong, Mastah Camp?"

Denzel called out the window, "Hold up, Nate. Cyrus is going to jump out and ride in the wagon."

"Yes, suh. I wait."

"Thanks, Dad." Cyrus quickly opened the door and stepped onto the road. "Enjoy the ride." He closed the door and disappeared.

"That was mighty nice of him to give us room to breathe," Damaris said, tucking her skirts under her as she moved over. "Now tell me, Kit, what have you been up to the past seven years?"

An hour later, the passengers in the carriage were quiet, the swaying of the rig lulling them to sleep. Damaris leaned into Kit and lay her head on her shoulder. They linked pinkies and softly laughed before sleeping the rest of the way.

"Whoa there!" Nate called out, and the coach rolled to a stop. Damaris leaned forward and looked out the window at the beautiful Great House. "Oh my, your home is just delightful!"

The door flew open, and Nate stepped down to help the passengers out. Servants began to spill out of the house, and a few men from the slave district approached to give a hand with the luggage, trunks, and supplies.

Damaris, still in the carriage, looked curiously at the two-story white house with a porch surrounding the front and sides. Twin stairs led up to it from the left and the right, joining in the middle to continue to the large porch.

"Mama said you oversaw all the construction of the house, Uncle Camp. I haven't even seen the inside, and I'm already impressed," Damaris said.

"Thank you, honey. Your Aunt Grace loves her home."

Damaris eagerly followed Kit as she slid out of her seat and took Nate's hand. The yard was filling fast with a commotion of welcome from family and servants. Damaris looked for Aunt Grace. Before long, she spotted her hurrying down the stairs, skirts in hand and a smile beaming on her face.

"Welcome home!" Grace kissed Camp's cheek and held out her arms. "Come here, Damaris. Let me look at you."

Damaris flew into her arms. "I've missed you so!"

"And we've missed all of you. Why, you're not a little girl anymore." Grace's brows pinched together as she smiled and tears brimmed in her eyes. "You're the spitting image of your mother. Your eyes are a beautiful brown, but other than that . . ." She hugged Damaris again. "Your mama would be so proud."

Bella Grace, Sunny, and Will waited at a distance for their chance to get reacquainted. And Maddie stood waiting on the steps, looking down on the crowd. Soon, laughter and talk filled the air.

"Come into the house. The cooks will have your supper shortly, and the servants will bring in your luggage," Grace said over the family's excitement.

A tall field hand, holding the bulky luggage under both arms, looked for instructions. "Where do you want these, Massa Camp?"

Damaris watched the young man in dark breeches, and a faded brown shirt. Acutely aware of his broad shoulders and strong hands, she thought he was handsome in a starkly rough way. His nose was broad, and his lips were thick. A five o'clock shadow deepened his serious manner. He looked out of eyes that seemed to have seen more in his twenty-some years than most should have experienced. But in that moment, Damaris felt he was a wise man for his years. And until now, she hadn't realized he was watching her with the same curious look. She cleared her throat and said, "Those pieces are mine." She pointed to the three large cases. "They'll go up to Kit's chamber."

A small smile formed on his lips as he nodded. "Yes'm." He broke away from the crowd and took the stairs two at a time.

Damaris was fully aware of him and couldn't take her eyes off his glistening dark arms as he carried her luggage. She hadn't realized she was staring after him until she heard Kit's soft voice.

"Damaris?"

She spun around. "Yes. What can we do to help?"

"Nothing, silly girl. I thought we lost you for a moment." Kit smiled knowingly.

Damaris leaned her head close to Kit's and whispered, "Who is he?"

"He's one of the field hands. He's Cuffee and Tabitha's son."

"And his name?"

"Solomon." Kit looked up. "And here he comes now. Don't stare, you silly goose."

Damaris kept her back to the stairs and watched as Solomon passed them and moved out to the front porch to retrieve more luggage. He didn't look back.

Her heartbeat quickened, and she felt a little dizzy. *What's come over me? Surely not him.*

Before Damaris could pursue that thought further, Gemma came out of the kitchen with the other cooks. "Y'all come sit down. Your suppah's ready." A smile spread across her face, showing white, shiny teeth.

The family congregated around the table and everyone found a seat, but Damaris had to look out the door just one more time before the field hand walked away. She stepped onto the front porch and looked to where several men carried crates to the barn. Solomon was holding what looked to be one of the heaviest loads. He glanced back at Damaris, and she quickly lowered her chin and smiled.

A broad smile lit up his face, and he turned toward the barn.

"Damaris?" Aunt Grace came to the door. "Aren't you hungry, dear?"

"Coming. And yes, I'm famished." Damaris glanced back one more time to look at the tall field hand. Somehow, she knew she'd have trouble falling asleep tonight. She'd never seen such a striking man as this one. But what was she thinking? He was a slave, and she came from a wealthy family. Nothing could truly come of anything between them.

"Damaris!" called a voice.

"Coming!"

FIVE

AFTER SUPPER, KIT and Damaris went upstairs to Kit's bedchamber. There, sitting squarely in the middle of the floor, was Damaris's brown trunk with three tapestry bags piled on top.

"Oh, Solomon," Kit breathed and looked at Damaris. "He should have set your trunk against the wall."

"Can we push it over there?" Damaris pointed at an empty spot between the chifforobe and the vanity.

"I don't see why not. Let's try."

The two girls pushed and shoved until the chest was against the wall. No sooner had they accomplished their mission than Hedy, Grace's chambermaid, appeared at the door. "Your mother sent me up to see if you need any help unpacking."

"Yes, Hedy. Let's move my clothes to the left in the wardrobe closet and make room for Damaris's dresses."

"We'll leave my gowns in the chest until the party. You won't have an inch of room in the closet otherwise." Damaris lifted a carpetbag. "I do, however, have a few dresses we can hang up."

They took their time putting Damaris's clothes and toiletries away for the three-week stay. Before they'd finished, Bella Grace, Piper, Sunny, and Maddie barged into the room and plunked down on Kit's double bed. Voices bubbled through the air.

"Piper, who are you rooming with?" Damaris asked.

"Sunny. She has the loveliest room, and her bed is so soft. Have you seen it?"

"No, I haven't, but it's good you're settled in."

"I assume Cyrus and Zeddie will share Will's room," Kit said.

Hedy placed her hands on her hips, looking around the bedchamber. "Yes'm, Miss Kit. Mastah Camp done brought up another bed for the two boys to share. It's a bit cramped in Will's room, but the boys don't care about floor space. It's the outdoors they'll be spendin' most their time." Hedy waved a hand as if to shove that thought aside. She pulled another dress out of the valise and held up the coral-colored day garment. "This be fine, Damaris."

Laughter and chatter continued to fill the room as Hedy excused herself to go downstairs until the girls were ready for bed. The younger girls carried on with giggles and antics while they watched their older sisters share in small talk.

"All right, everyone, shoo! It's time for bed." Kit waved the younger girls out of her room.

Moments later, Hedy appeared again and laid out the girls' nightgowns. She unbuttoned the tiny row of buttons on the backs of their dresses and hung them up after removing them. She pulled the pins out of Kit's crow-black hair, letting it fall to her shoulders and down her back.

"Oh, Kit. Your hair is beautiful," Damaris said, fingering the silky strands.

"It be one of her finest assets." Hedy smiled, running the brush through Kit's hair. When she finished, she gestured for Damaris to sit on the small stool before the vanity. She pulled out the pins and fluffed the torrential curls that bounced around Damaris's shoulders. Carefully, she combed the ebony hair, and when she was done, Damaris's tresses fanned the shoulders of her white nightgown.

"Now, if you excuse me, ladies, yer mama be needin' me next." Hedy set the comb down and stared at the girls. "I don't know when it happened, but you two grew up."

The girls looked at each other and smiled as Hedy left the room. Damaris's brow puckered. "What happened to you?" Her slim finger traced a scar above Kit's eyebrow and down the side of her jaw.

Kit reared back, and her face reddened. "I'd hoped it wasn't noticeable." Her hand went to the side of her face, tracing her brow, and just below her left ear.

Damaris leaned forward and removed Kit's finger. "And another scar here. Kit, what happened?"

"I went horseback riding and jumped the north fence in the back of our property. I've done it a hundred times if I've done it once, but that time Dandy jumped higher than I was used to, and I lost my balance."

"The fall must have been bad." Damaris frowned slightly and took hold of Kit's hand.

"It was. I fell against a large rock where a nearby limb had fallen. I guess the branch scratched a gash in my neck. I fell unconscious. When Dandy arrived at the house without me, Father put out a search party. There I was, lying on a patch of ivy next to the rock and not knowing what had happened."

"Kit, you could have died!"

"That's what Father said. They sent for the wagon and hauled me back to the house, afraid I might have broken a bone somewhere in my body. But all I broke was my pride. Fortunately, this was the worst of it."

"How old were you when that happened?"

"Fourteen."

"Well, you can hardly see the scar. If we weren't sitting so close and with the light shining on it just so, I wouldn't have noticed it."

"That's what Mother says. Of course, I'm always aware of it."

"Your hair hides the scar on your jaw." Damaris raised Kit's hand and kissed the top of it. "I'm so glad you're all right."

The girls hugged, then sat in chairs by the window, looking down at the vast lawn. By now, the stars were twinkling in a black carpet of sky, and the moon cast a yellow ribbon on the river beyond.

Damaris blushed and smiled slightly, a sure sign that her mind had traveled beyond the soft glow of the room.

"What are you thinking?" Kit asked.

"Your field hand, Solomon. He came to the carriage and stepped forward. He was about to offer his hand to help us climb to the ground, but Uncle Camp told him he'd take it from there." Damaris laughed softly. "Solomon looked as if he was about to run."

"He *is* handsome in a rough kind of way, but his exterior can be frightening."

Damaris nodded, and a light shone in her dark eyes.

"He's a slave, Damaris. He'll never be anything more than that."

"I know." Damaris lowered her eyes, and then a second later she raised them again and asked, "Do you have a beau? You haven't said a word in the letters."

"No. Adam Sparrow lives up the river. I've known him all my life." Kit looked at her hand and then at Damaris. "He's a big flirt and always has been. But to be honest, I have no suitor."

"I find that hard to believe, Kit. I would think the men would be scrambling for your hand."

Kit quirked a smile and shook her head. "A few have shown up at the front door, but Father turned them away."

"You'll never find a man to marry at that rate."

"I don't mind. I watched a couple of them ride away as I was standing at my window. I'm grateful my father sent them away."

The girls laughed softly, as the hour was late.

"Hmm." Damaris placed her hands in the folds of her nightgown. "No one has come calling at Kindra Hall. Yet, considering that my parents are colored plantation owners, I suppose that is to be expected. There aren't too many Negroes who own plantations in Barbados." She stepped to the window and leaned her forehead on the glass pane. Below, she could see the carriage lane. "You said Cuffee is Solomon's father. I've heard that name before."

Kit cleared her throat and hesitated. "He used to be our grandfather's slave. Then he got mixed up with something with Aunt Tia. My parents won't talk about it. The next thing they knew, Cuffee disappeared for a long time. Mother brought his wife and children here when she left Cooper's Landing. And ever since, the family's been with us. I've watched Cuffee's children grow up."

Damaris blushed again.

Kit raised a brow. "Did Solomon catch your eye?"

Damaris lowered her chin and smiled. "I'm afraid so."

Early the next morning, a wagon sat out front of the Great House. Servants bustled about, packing camping gear for their master's three-day journey. Inside the house, Gemma worked up a sweat seeing to the meals for the trip. Her voice could be heard over Penny's and Mama Jezelee's. "Now make sure there's plenty of food. Camp be saying he gonna take young Solomon along with them. You know how the men be. They always have an empty stomach."

Damaris's ears perked up at the mention of Solomon. From where she sat, she glanced out the dining room window. Several men came and went from around the wagon, but for now, she didn't see any sign of the handsome field hand.

Penny's voice could be heard from the kitchen and interrupted Damaris's thoughts, and she listened as the cook's helper said, "If they find Kindra and bring her back with them, they'll need enough food for four people on the ride back."

The kitchen door was propped open with a red brick, and the cooks came and went with an air of importance as they prepared the meal for the journey. Damaris watched Penny place a large bowl of fried chicken into the picnic basket. Then she covered it with a white towel. Mama Jezelee set a tin coffee pot, plates, cups, and utensils into a box on the table. She hummed a tune as she worked.

Damaris continued to watch, barely taking a bite of her breakfast. Gemma's eyes strayed to her, and she stopped what she was doing. She wiped her sweaty face with the hem of her apron and stepped into the dining room. "Why ain't you eatin' your food, Miss Damaris?"

"I guess I'm not hungry." In truth, her insides gnawed at her. All this running around to prepare for the trip was about her father and Uncle Camp hoping to find her mother at the slave auction in Beaufort. Would they find her? It had been seven years since she'd last seen her mother. The memory of the marauders taking her away continued to haunt her. All she wanted was to see her father and uncle bring her mother back.

"Now, I'm thinking you be worried about your mama." Gemma's thick hands went to her hips while her brows creased. She pulled out a chair next to Damaris. "Am I right?"

Damaris wasn't prepared for the cook's next move. The old woman took hold of her hand and massaged it while she spoke. "Do you believe our Mastah on high be watchin' and carin' 'bout everythin' goin' on around us?"

Damaris swallowed, and her throat grew tight. Tears stung her eyes. "Y-yes, I do. It's just . . ."

"Just what?"

"It's just that He let them take my mother away."

Gemma threw her arms around Damaris's shoulders and rocked her. "When we's weak, He be strong. The good Lawd never expected us to carry our burdens alone. He be sayin', 'Come to me those who are weary and heavy-laden, and I will give you rest.' He's wantin' you to give that burden 'bout your mama to Him."

Damaris basked in the cook's wise words and tried to let her rock her fears away. "I hope they find her."

"Course' you do, honey. You been waitin' nearly half your lifetime for your mama to come back." She pulled her apron up and wiped Damaris's face. "We don't always understand why things happen the way they do. It's times like these we have to trust God. He's the only one who knows what's goin' on with your mama and can help her." Gemma patted her hand. "Now pull yourself together."

Damaris smiled and straightened her skirts. "I will."

Gemma returned to the kitchen to continue giving orders and packing food. Damaris stared out the window just in time to see Solomon stride up to the wagon and drop something into the back of it.

Damaris was so caught up in watching Solomon that she failed to hear Aunt Grace come in from the front porch, and she was startled when Grace spoke to her. "Well, they'll be leaving in a moment. Do you want to tell your father goodbye?" Grace asked.

Kit had followed Aunt Grace into the room, and the gleam in Kit's eye brightened when she tilted her head toward the front yard. "You'd better hurry. They're about to leave."

Damaris quickly rose and went outside to the front porch to look down at the activity. Jake barked continuously and wagged his tail. He seemed happy to have company in the yard. She sailed down the steps to the left, and when she came to the ground, she searched for her father. When he went around the backside of the wagon with Solomon by his side, Damaris hesitated, "I came to wish you Godspeed." She kept her eyes from straying to Solomon and gave her father a hug. When she stepped back, she noticed

Solomon had moved away, but his eyes held a look of subdued admiration. It surprised her and gave her more courage. She lifted a hand and waved to him as well, but then stepped quickly away.

"All right, men. Jump in. We're burning daylight," Cameron said.

Aunt Grace and the girls fanned about Uncle Camp while Denzel's children did the same to him. She watched Zeddie shake her father's hand. "I'll keep watch while you're gone."

"I know you will, son. I'm counting on you."

The men stepped into the wagon. Uncle Camp and her father sat up front. Solomon climbed into the back and leaned against a thick roll of canvas. Damaris watched with the others as the wooden buckboard rolled out of the long drive and turned west down the main road that led to Fields Landing. From there, they would take the fork in the road to the right and continue to Beaufort.

No sooner had the wagon disappeared down the lane than the *River Belle* steamboat floated to the dock at the end of the yard and tooted three shrill whistles.

"Good heavens!" Aunt Grace said. "We've got to get your lunches out of the house. Will, tell the steamship captain the girls are coming." Aunt Grace lifted her skirts and went up the steep porch steps with ease, with the girls following her. Moments later, Bella Grace, Sunny, and Maddie came out of the house with their lunch baskets.

"Hurry, girls. You can't hold up the boat. He's got to pick up other students along the river."

The girls blew kisses and ran down the sloped lawn. As Damaris stood near the house with Aunt Grace and Kit, her aunt said, "We used to have the children tutored here at the house, since we live too far from the school. But the captain announced he'd pick them up if we wanted to send them along with the other children downriver." She stared at the red paddles of the steamship as it rounded the bend. "The girls wanted to go to school in town. It's been a blessing in disguise."

Damaris looked over to see Grace standing with her arms folded across her chest and a trickle of sweat working its way down her brow. "Let's go into the house, Aunt Grace. You look like you need to sit down."

Grace held Damaris's eyes before they walked up the lawn. "Your father and your uncle are going to bring your mother home one of these days. You wait and see."

"Are you trying to encourage me or yourself, Aunt Grace?"

"I think both of us." She hooked her hand in the crook of Damaris's arm and pulled her along. "Let's take a brief rest, and then we need to freshen up. I believe Lauren Sparrow is coming to visit this afternoon."

Damaris looked back at the yard. All was quiet.

Please come home, Mama.

SIX

TODAY!
PUBLIC AUCTION OF
SLAVES
PRIME NEGROES
INCLUDING
2 SPECIAL AND CHOICE
FEMALES
A MORE DESIRABLE LIST OF
NEGROES CAN NOWHERE BE FOUND
JAMES S. MORROW

KINDRA WATCHED AS ten coloreds stood on the platform—eight men and two women. Lolly and Effie held hands, fear in their eyes as they stared over the heads of the crowd below. The men wore ankle chains, but Lolly and Effie were unshackled. A brash, stocky white man in a loose-fitting blue shirt stood before the darkies, his booming voice calling out as he tried to jack up the price of the men and women.

It was mid-September in Charleston, and the sun beat down in a steady heat that seemed to bake the land as if it were in a hot oven. A throng of nearly seventy people stood around the raised platform up the road from the Cooper River. The men in the fray were of every category, tall or short, rough or fancy, some dressed as if they were ready to attend a business meeting, some looking as if they'd just come from the plantation fields. They were the best and the worst Charleston and the neighboring towns had to offer. The sea's salt air washed over the cluster of people and drifted in and out with the breeze. The men stood in uneven rows, gaping at the slaves as the sun baked them to a crisp.

Kindra waited along with the other slaves under a lean-to. It gave little relief from the heat, but the shade kept the sun from beating down on her black curls. It felt strange, standing in the crowd of slaves without Cuffee. She had no idea where the steamship had taken him. It didn't matter. He was gone, and she'd likely never see the gentle man again. The hope of seeing Cuffee reunited with his wife and family had faded when the boat drifted around the river bend and out of sight.

It had been three days since he'd gone. She'd heard talk from the loose tongues of the guards that the boat took a load of darkies up the river to a town called Beaufort. Had Cuffee been sold yet, or was today the day he would reach his new destination?

The auctioneer sold off the medium-sized men first. Flat-chested and with thin arms, none of them sold for a large sum of money. Then the auctioneer called up the next man. "See these arms," he said. "Look at his muscles and thighs. He has a strong back—all the things you want in a hard-working field hand. Somebody give me an opening price for this strong buck! I won't listen to a low bid for this darky. This is a good hand. You can see that for yourselves."

Shouts went out as the men in the throng topped each other's bids.

"Nine hundred dollars!" Bellowed a well-dressed man.

A murmur ran through the crowd.

"Can I get a higher bid for this healthy darky?"

The murmuring was silenced.

"Sold!" said the auctioneer as the muscled man stepped off the platform. Blue-shirt pointed to a stout woman and waved her up onto the stand.

"Now, just look at her," he said, turning the red-scarved woman around. She's a bit older than some of the women you'll see today, but she will put a good meal on your table. I'm told she's one of the best cooks in all of Virginia. What'll you start the bid at for your next delicious meal?"

And so, the bidding went as one slave after another stepped onto the platform to be sold like animals. Finally, only one more Negro stood between Kindra and the blue-shirted man. She wiped the sweat from her brow and brushed her dark curls. She gripped the folds of her brown skirt and watched as the auctioneer finished with the last Negro, shoved him off the stage, and turned to her. She quickly stared at her worn black shoes and felt a tremor run through her.

An aide clamped her upper arm and guided her up the three steps to stand in front of the onlookers.

"Now look at this bronze-skinned woman. Her clothes are filthy and tattered, but she is obviously made of quality material. A unique slave this one is. She speaks English, not Gullah, as the Africans commonly do here. I'm told she is originally from the Caribbean coast and of mixed race. This silky-skinned darky is from quality breeding, too."

Mister Morrow jumped up on the platform beside her. "Turn around," he said. "Nice and slow."

Kindra's knees felt weak as she did what she was told. When she faced the fray again, her hands clamped before her, she glanced at the spectators' faces. Were Cameron and Denzel in the mix, waiting to bid for her?

The buzzing in her ears drowned out the sounds of rising voices and the auctioneer's as she scanned the men and women whose hands were raised as they called out their bids. She looked and looked, but none was the familiar face of her beloved or of her brother-in-law. Disheartened, she resigned herself to her fate. Today wasn't the day she would go home. Today would mark the day of a new journey, one she had no control over. As her stomach twisted in fear, she looked up and listened.

"Now look at this one," said Mister Morrow. He pushed her forward another step. "She's straight from the house of Mister and Mrs. Winfield Abrams from Whitestone Manor in Richmond, Virginia. Her name's Kindra, and she was their housekeeper."

Kindra watched the townspeople study her, the women gauging her worth, the men's eyes moving up and down her body. She felt as if bugs crawled over her arms and legs and up her back. She hated the way the men stared at her, as if their wives were somewhere else rather than standing beside them. Why should a man have the right to scrutinize a woman this way? Why could he look her over as if she were a prized horse? Her stomach turned, and the heat that burned down on her black curls sizzled like the heat in her veins.

Several unsavory remarks flew through the air. Kindra cringed, her fingers tightening on the folds of her skirt.

"Stop!" Mister Morrow's voice boomed over the crowd.

The people's laughter died away. "She's a well-bred woman and clean," he said. "She has only one scar." He turned her around so that her back faced the knot of people and lifted her blouse. The murmurs hummed as the spectators stared at her smooth skin marred by the singular scar near her shoulder blade. Mister Morrow dropped her shirt and turned her to face the crowd again. "That was not from a whippin'! That's from an accident on her travels through the jungle. I got papers to prove it. She got sold when her master died. Their daughter didn't want to continue working on the cotton plantation, as she already had a life in the city.

The townspeople nodded with understanding.

"Who'll start the bid?" The auctioneer stepped forward as Mister Morrow gleamed at Kindra and walked off the platform, hands in his pockets.

"I'll go seven hundred," said a man.

"Make it nine," said a second man.

"Twelve," hollered a third.

A rustle ran through the crowd. "Fourteen," came a bid.

Sweat trickling down her brow, Kindra watched the people in frustration. *Why wasn't Cameron here to save her?*

"Sixteen hundred."

"You're not wanting her for housekeeping!" Someone yelled out.

The onlookers roared. Kindra felt hot tears brimming in her eyes. She waited and wished for all the world for a familiar face to stop the taunting crowd from their rude sentiments. Yet she knew she was left to stand alone. Who would make the final bid that set the fate of her destination? Would the master be as cruel as the Abrams had been, or would she find a home with a bit of kindness? Kindra closed her eyes on the latter thought. So far, she had no reason to believe people in America were kind, except for her sister and her family.

"Nineteen hundred."

Kindra glanced up. This new bidder was a medium-sized man with gold-colored hair and wearing a gray hat to match his gray jacket. His brows creased, and his eyes dared anyone to cross him. The bidding stopped. The prominent man strolled toward the platform with a determined gait.

When the people stepped aside to let him pass, Kindra saw a mixture of grudge and dislike in their eyes. Another man with red hair and a red beard walked beside him, this one tall and broad-shouldered. The second man wore a hat, too, but it was a wide-brimmed straw hat, faded yellow and looking as if it had too many days in the sun. "Anyone else have a bid?" he shouted at the mob as he reached the platform. A disgruntled rumble coursed through the crowd, but he faced the agitated group, his stance daring them to bid against the man who stood beside him.

"It's Lawrence Bridger!" somebody called. "From Ash Haven Plantation."

Kindra stared at the shorter man's back as he faced the townspeople, his golden hair cut neatly above his collar and waved over his ears. He looked to be in his mid-forties. He hadn't come to her stall with the other curious plantation owners. It didn't matter. None of this mattered. She was a pawn waiting for the next move.

The auctioneer tried to raise the stakes. "Are we goin' to give her up at such a bargain to Lawrence Bridger? Let him walk in at the last minute and steal her away?"

"Be gone with you!" shouted a man from the back. "He's got more money than the governor! If he wants her, we don't stand a chance. We all know that."

Kindra stilled herself. Who was this man who caused the crowd to take a step back? She clamped her jaw and waited.

"Sold!" yelled the auctioneer. "To Lawrence Bridger of Ash Haven!"

The auctioneer pointed to his left, and Kindra moved off the stage and down the steps. Lawrence Bridger and his overseer moved to her side, and she waited. Red's eyes roamed over her body. She wanted to spit on his boots and tell him to stop gaping at her. It wouldn't do any good, she knew, and she didn't dare. All it would get her was a lashing. She'd been stung enough for one day. She clamped her jaw tighter.

"You look well enough," Red said. "Not sickly like some of the lot." His voice was deep and cut through the crowd's noise.

Kindra didn't speak; she only glared at the man. It wasn't until now that she realized the owner had stepped away. When Red kept his gaze on her, she looked away.

"We'll be ridin' out of here soon's the master pays up," he told her. "And you'd be wise to keep those green eyes to the ground. He won't put up with any sass."

Kindra bit her lips and kept her head turned away from the tall man.

Red took her chin and jerked her face up. "Did you hear what I said?"

"I'm not deaf. I heard you."

"We'll have to get you settled at Ash Haven. You've been married, I reckon," Red said. "I don't suppose one such as you doesn't have some family along the way."

Kindra thought of Denzel and of her children. Her heart ached for them. But she didn't want to talk about her precious family to this man.

"Well?"

"I'm married. My husband's name is Denzel."

"Never heard of him. Where's he now?"

"Looking for me." She held Red's gaze.

"Won't do him no good, and chances are he's been bought up already by some other plantation."

"You're wrong. My man's free."

"Free? How's that?"

"My father freed him."

"Now you're talkin' in circles. You sayin' your father be a plantation owner?"

"He was. He owned a sugar plantation in Jamaica, where I met and married Denzel."

"So, your father . . . he's a white man?" He chuckled and slid a finger up her arm. "That accounts for your coloring. He had his way with one of the slave women."

Kindra jerked her arm away. She looked at the people coming and going. Carts and wagons had started to move away from the auction square. Most had one or more slaves sitting in the back. Kindra shut her ears to anything else the overseer had to say. It wouldn't be long before she was loaded into the back of a buckboard like a sack of goods.

Red grabbed her chin again, rougher this time, his eyes searing into hers and daring her to pull away.

She ground her teeth and waited.

"You belong to Lawrence Bridger now. I oversee Ash Haven for him.

You do what we tell you, and you'll do well. You pull any sass, it'll go hard on you."

Kindra glared back, but her stomach was in a knot. Red's tone left no doubt that he meant what he said. He didn't have to worry, though. She'd learned long ago to do her work and keep to herself. She wasn't looking for trouble—but it had a way of finding her.

After Bridger settled up and paid for his slaves, the three of them walked to a shaded spot where five slaves were chained and waiting. "This here's Bart Odell, my overseer. He'll be seeing to you when we arrive at Ash Haven," Bridger said.

Bart grabbed the chain wrapped around a tree and held it together with a lock. He unlocked the chain, and it rattled to the ground. He picked it up and yanked the men forward. Once they reached the wagon, they all climbed in, the overseer and Bridger up front on the wooden bench, Kindra leaning against a bag of seed in the back.

Lord, give me strength to go through this valley. You said when we are weak, You are strong. I rest in Your love and compassion. I don't know how You're going to do it, but I believe You will rescue me and return me to my family.

It was the noon hour, and the sun was high in the sky. The wagon jostled over the cobbled streets as they headed out of town. Kindra closed her eyes and let the sounds of the city and the birds flying overhead rest her soul. She would sleep for now. She would need her strength when she arrived at Ash Haven. Would she get along with the new mistress of the house? Only time would tell.

River Oak, Fields Landing

The *River Belle's* whistle interrupted the quiet afternoon as it rounded the bend and slowed to stop in front of River Oak. Bella Grace took hold of Amy Sparrow's hand. "You're getting off with us. Your mother should still be here."

"I know." Amy gathered her lunch pail and waited in line with Bella,

Sunny, and Maddie. Once the gangplank was lowered, the four girls hurried off the steamer and turned to wave at the captain. "Goodbye! We'll see you tomorrow!"

In answer, the captain pulled on the red rope hanging by his head. The paddleboat's whistle shrilled three times.

"It's been such a warm day. I'm hoping we can convince the girls to have a picnic on the blankets near the pond," Bella said, leading the way up the sloped lawn. To her delight, she found Kit, Damaris, Florence Sparrow, and Charice Seward sitting languidly on a quilt on the grass.

Amy looked at the older girls, then back at Bella. "How did they know you wished to sit on the lawn?"

Bella winked. "It was already planned this morning. I overheard Kit telling Damaris that your mother and Florence were coming. Kit's been waiting to see your sister for over a week. All she can talk about is the Fall Coming-Out party and what she'll wear. I must say I'm surprised to see Charice here. Kit hadn't said anything about her."

"Your mother and Blanche have become friends. It makes sense to have her daughters over, doesn't it?"

"You're right, but had I known Charice was here, I'd have invited Emma over, too." Bella blew her bangs off her forehead as she watched the *River Belle* disappear around the bend.

When the small group reached the quilted blanket on the lawn, they found Kit and the three other girls eating maple cookies and talking softly.

Florence looked up and squinted. "How was school?"

"It was fine. We have a test tomorrow, so I can only sit out here for a while, and then I've got to study," Bella said. "Have you decided what you'll wear to the party?"

Kit yawned and said lazily, "We're planning a trip into town. We want to look at fabric and pick out patterns. It's up to Mother to send for the seamstress and get the gowns started. You might want to join us. You'll need a gown too."

Bella looked at Florence, seeing her long auburn tresses highlighted by the sun's rays. She was Kit's best friend, except for Damaris. And at the moment, Kit leaned her head on Florence's shoulder. Charice sat on the other side of Florence, a wistful look on her face.

"Your sister's been a nervous wreck, planning her gown," Florence said. "I told her Adam didn't give a hoot what she wore. But she doesn't listen to me." A twinkle lit her eyes, giving away Florence's fun in teasing Kit.

Charice's cheeks glowed red at the mention of Adam, and her eyes narrowed on Kit. The change in her attitude was not lost on Bella. Did she have her heart set on Adam, too?

"I'll have you know, Miss Florence Sparrow, I'm not choosing my gown for Adam. I'm choosing my gown for me and the guests attending the coming-out party. The four of us," Kit stopped to look at Damaris as well as Florence and Charice, "will never have another opportunity like this again."

"You don't fool me, Kit. There are times divine providence needs a little human intervention."

"Horsefeathers!" Bella laughed. "Since when did Kit need intervention to get Adam's attention? He nearly trips over himself every time he sees her."

Laughter and giggles spilled across the lawn as Kit's face turned a fiery red. Charice didn't join in the laughter, but no one seemed to notice. Instead, she slid away from Florence and balled her fist in her lap.

"Stop it, all of you," Kit demanded. "I never said I liked Adam Sparrow. Now let's drop it!"

All the girls closed their mouths and looked at each other, only to break out into fits of laughter again. Bella held her stomach as tears streamed down her cheeks. "You're going to have to do a better job of convincing us, Kit, because . . . look who's coming."

Kit looked toward the road by the riverbank. Sure, as the sun was shining, Adam Sparrow was riding up to River Oak on a bay horse. Kit jumped to her feet, hiked her skirts above her shoes, and stomped off toward the house while the girls tumbled over each other in hilarious laughter.

Charice sat up straight and ran a hand over her blonde curls. She, too, looked like she wanted to escape the scene. Instead, she sat there eyeing Adam, a rosy tint in her cheeks.

Adam rode up and stopped before the group of girls. "What's so funny?" He lifted his brows as he looked past them to the fast-striding, raven-haired Kit, who'd reached the porch and disappeared inside the house with a resounding slam of the front door. "What's gotten into her?"

The air filled with shrieking laughter as Adam dismounted and headed for the house. "Women! Who can understand them?"

SEVEN

THE MORNING WAS a flurry of activity as the women and girls in the Great House readied themselves for the excursion to Fields Landing for a full day of shopping.

Grace popped her head into Kit's bedchamber. "Are you two about ready? It won't be long before Lauren and the girls arrive." She glanced at Kit's simple day dress and frowned. "You aren't planning to wear that old thing to town, are you? You've a dozen more suitable garments for the outing." Grace crossed the floor and opened the chifforobe.

"Mama." Kit tilted her head to Damaris. "Have you forgotten our talk?"

Grace looked at her niece and clamped a hand over her mouth. "Oh, for heaven's sake. How foolish of me. I'd completely forgotten we'd gone over what you'd wear today." She glanced at the worn dress Damaris had donned, the same dress she'd arrived in from the ship. "I so wish all of this charade weren't necessary. You're too beautiful to wear rags to town."

"Maybe I should stay here, Aunt Grace." Damaris's shoulders slumped.

"Nonsense." Kit hugged her. "You'll do no such thing. Think of it as a game. Nobody will know this simple *darky* is of noble blood. You are the most special person I know. You have to come."

"All right." Damaris gently pushed Kit away with a crooked smile. "Am I goin' ta be yer slave girl?"

Kit fell back on the bed, holding her stomach, and giggled. "Oh, Damaris. You did that just perfectly." She sat up and pulled a stern look. "That's what you'll have to do while we're in the shop."

"I can do it."

Kit slid off the bed. "Thank you. We'll have a wonderful time despite those snooty people."

"Of course we will," Damaris quipped in her honey tone.

"Are you sure you're okay with this?" Grace asked, hating to put her niece in a situation she'd never faced before. Damaris had been protected from the public in Barbados.

"I don't mind, Aunt Grace. Gram explained all of this to us before we left home. If wearing these rags lets me visit you, so be it." She held out the tattered brown skirt and curtsied with a dimpled grin.

Kit turned to her mother. "That's why I picked out my plainest dress. If she has to dress down, so will I." Kit hooked an arm through Damaris's. "Having said that, I believe we're ready."

"All right. Meet me downstairs. Nate's bringing the carriage around."

During the next half hour, the house was a bustle of noise as the girls came down to the foyer. Blueboy and Rosey, the Bartholomew's bluebirds, joined in the merriment with chirping and singing.

Kit moved across the sitting room and peeked at the birds in the large brass birdcage. "You will be darlings while we're away, won't you?"

Blueboy tweeted a trill chirp and jumped from the swing dangling from the center of the cage. He stepped sideways on the low perch and poked his beak through the narrow bars.

"You're a pretty boy," Kit said, as she rubbed his orange belly with a slim finger. Rosey cocked her head and flew to the abandoned swing. Her black, beady eyes watched Kit as she trilled a song, too. "We shan't be long." Kit turned at the sound of the cooks in the foyer.

"Now, you know you won't be dining in none of them fancy restaurants in town. They ain't gonna allow Piper and Damaris in." Gemma's eyes shone knowingly. "But don't you worry none 'bout that. We put together a much finer meal and packed it in these baskets." She held up two wicker picnic totes. "There ought to be more than enough for all of you and some left over."

"Thank you, Gemma." Kit kissed the old woman's cheek. "I feel sorry for those sour people. They won't be eating as good a meal as we will. But then, it serves them right."

Gemma's dark eyes gleamed. "You be too kind, young lady."

Grace watched her oldest daughter with pride. Kit was coming into her own. Still, as she watched everybody, a low-grade throb ached at the base of her head. She massaged the back of her neck for only a moment, not wanting to draw attention to herself.

Jake, the family's black and white collie, started barking and ran down the porch steps to the front drive.

"I believe Lauren has arrived. Come on, girls, let's not keep her waiting." Grace herded the girls out the front door like a mother goose.

"I'll take those for you," Will said, relieving Grace of the food baskets.

"You and Zeddie stay out of trouble while we're gone," Grace said, glad to hand the heavy baskets to her son. She took a deep breath and fanned herself.

"Don't worry. I'm taking the boat upstream to the Sparrows'. Rory's found a good fishing pond. We'll be spending the day there. Hopefully, we'll get a good catch and have a fish fry for supper."

"Does Gemma know you're going? She'll want to pack a lunch for you boys, too."

Zeddie rounded the house with three poles and a green canvas pouch. "I got us some worms from the kitchen garden."

Cyrus followed close behind with a gunnysack slung over his arm. "Think we need more than this for the catch?"

"That'll be fine, bud." Will ruffled Cyrus's curly locks.

The young boy jumped back and combed it in place with his fingers. "How come everyone wants to muss my hair?"

Will didn't answer. Instead, he leaned forward and kissed Grace's cheek, then waved for his cousins to follow as he strode toward the dock, where the boat bobbed in the water.

"Well," Grace said as she walked over to Lauren's carriage. Florence and Amy sat in the seat opposite their mother. "It looks as if everyone's got their day planned out."

"Good morning, Grace. You looked flushed," Lauren said.

"It's been a busy morning, what with getting the girls fed and back upstairs to get dressed. But we're ready now, and that's what counts." Grace gazed at both coaches. Their open carriage was parked in front of the Sparrows' rig. "How do you want to split up the girls?"

Lauren stepped to the ground with the help of her driver and put a hand up to stop Amy from descending. "Let's have the three older girls ride with us in your carriage and the five younger girls ride in ours."

"That'll work." Grace stepped back as the driver helped Florence to the ground. "All right, girls, come on. Bella, Sunny, Piper!" The young teens quickly moved to the yellow rig, leaving Maddie standing on the lawn, a disgruntled look on her face. "You, too!" Grace waved her youngest daughter forward. The frown quickly changed to a grin as nine-year-old Maddie scooted onto the leather seat. "Now mind your manners and keep your hands inside the carriage. No horsing around!" Grace said.

"We will," the girls chorused.

Grace blew a wayward strand of hair off her forehead and felt a tingle of excitement course through her. She couldn't remember having an outing like this since they'd moved to River Oak. She glanced up at the partially clouded sky. "Hmm," she mused. "This day could go one of two ways. I hope the sun comes out."

"What'd you say?" Kit's dark eyes shone brightly as she sat between Damaris and Florence.

Nate helped Grace into the coach, and she slid onto the seat. "I said, I'm looking for the sunshine to slide out from behind those gray clouds." She gave Lauren a weary smile and brushed a trickle of sweat from her brow.

"It's been this way for three days. It's going to be fine." Kit sat back and glanced at Grace. "Are you all right, Mother?"

"I couldn't be better. This is going to be a splendid day." She closed her eyes for a second. If only I didn't feel so hot, and this nagging headache would cease. Did I overdo it this morning? If I didn't know better, I'd think I might have a fever coming on.

The two carriages rolled into Fields Landing by mid-morning. The gray clouds continued to threaten above them. Still, the day was hot and humid, but no one in the coach seemed to notice.

"Where shall we begin?" Kit asked as the carriage slowed to a stop alongside the curb of the busy street.

"There are only two dry goods stores here, one across the street from the other. Let's start with Miss Reed's Dry Goods, and then we can try the other."

Grace turned to Nate. "There is a row of trees down the lane. You and Hakim might want to park the rigs there. Come looking for us in a couple of hours."

"Yes'm, Miz Grace. That'll be fine." Nate helped the women from their carriage, while Hakim, the Sparrows' driver, assisted the young girls. Moments later, the two rigs rattled down the cobbled road, leaving the party of women to shop.

There were several stores and businesses on both sides of the street. Damaris watched the pedestrians who crowded the boardwalk in front of the shops. Her eyes automatically searched each face of the black women who followed their mistresses, carrying bundles of packages in their arms. Wherever she went, Damaris always watched the people, especially the darkies, in hopes of finding her mother. She didn't look for Kindra in a beautiful dress like she had worn at home in Barbados. She looked for a middle-aged woman in an old worn-out dress, one a slave woman would be seen in.

She had hoped to go with her father and Uncle Camp to the slave auction in Beaufort, but they wouldn't hear of it. Uncle Camp was adamant that she stay at River Oak with the rest of the women and wait. It was no place for a free black woman, he told her. And yet her mama was a free black woman who'd been sold as a slave. That her mother had been served this dreadful fate was more than she could bear to think about.

"Damaris?"

"Huh?"

"Your mind is a mile away. We're going across the street. Come on." Kit pulled on her cousin's arm.

As the women wove their way across the busy road, they had to stop a half-dozen times to avoid getting run over. The streets were filled with a constant flow of traffic. Wagons, mule-carts, and pedestrians crowded the thoroughfare. Damaris didn't miss the hard stares slanted her way. She held her chin up, determined to ignore the rude gestures as she kept her pace with the family.

Moments later, the women filled the narrow aisles at Miss Reed's. Several gown-covered mannequins displayed the popular fashions of the day. There were several hat stands holding every type of hat a woman could want, sitting on the counter. There was large, flowing straw hats decorated with plumes of feathers and flowers clustered near the crown. Then there were smart little hats with black or white veils to hide a woman's eyes. Damaris reached a hand to a blue-feathered, dainty one.

"Don't you dare!" came a loud retort from a woman behind the counter. "You'd best get on back to your mistress. And keep your fingers off the merchandise." The clerk's eyes narrowed on her.

"Yes'm," Damaris said and swallowed. She looked over her shoulder at Kit.

Kit hooked her hand in the crook of Damaris's arm. "Come over here, dear. Help me find the material I need for my gown." She gave the clerk a sharp look.

The shop grew noisy with the young girls straying to look at all the pretties on other aisles. A moment later, Mrs. Reed shrieked, "Get your hand off those slippers!"

Kit, Damaris, and the rest of the older women flew to the back of the store. There stood Piper, holding a pair of white-satin shoes in her dark hands. She bent to set the shoes back on the shelf.

"Stop right there, you little weasel." Mrs. Reed's eyes fired at the young black girl and then at Grace. "You're going to have to pay for those shoes, Mrs. Bartholomew. I can't sell them now." Her eyes bore into Grace's.

"That's nonsense, Hilda, and you know it. She didn't hurt those shoes." Grace turned the dainty slippers with satin ties in her hands. "They're not blemished."

"I can't sell them," the woman repeated as she looked over the heads of the customers.

Damaris looked back to see several dour-looking female customers with their noses raised in the air. They had stopped shopping to watch the exchange between Grace and the shop owner.

Grace took a deep breath, her face bright red, and marched over to the counter, setting the shoes down. "Write them up." She turned to the women in her party. "After I pay for these perfectly good shoes, we'll be going across the street to Mrs. Flynn's shop. I don't see anything I want here!"

All the girls filed out of the dry goods store and waited on the boardwalk as Grace paid for the shoes. Piper's chin lowered as she joined the others.

"Don't let that old woman ruin your day, Piper. She doesn't know good manners." Damaris drew her sister to her and clamped her arms over her shoulder.

"Sorry," Piper said in a small voice.

"You didn't do anything wrong. You forgot we're supposed to be acting like slaves. We can't touch anything in the stores," Damaris said.

"Then why'd we come?" Piper asked.

"To be with the family."

Piper slowly looked up. "Is that how the people treat Mama?"

Damaris looked at Piper's eyes. They were brimming with tears. "I'm afraid so."

Amy and Sunny each hooked an arm at Piper's elbows and drew her away from Damaris. "We didn't want to leave you at the house by yourself," Sunny said. "Now come on, you ninny. Stay with us."

Grace came out of the shop with a brown box. She lifted the package and pointed it at Bella. "I don't think all is lost. I believe these will fit you."

Bella Grace's eyes grew big. "Really? I love them!"

"Thanks to your cousin, we've made our first purchase for the day." Grace shrugged. "You would have needed the shoes anyway."

A distant rumble rolled in the sky. All eyes looked upward. "Oh, no. Hurry, girls. We've got to pick out your patterns before the day gets out of hand." Grace led the way across the road.

Damaris watched as the family threaded their way across the road again. If she didn't know better, she would have thought Grace looked a little flushed.

The bell tinkled as they flooded into Mrs. Flynn's shop. This time, as the women and girls perused the fabric, patterns, and fancy lace gloves, Piper stuck like glue to Sunny and Amy, keeping her fingers locked behind her back. Damaris's heart sank. Everything in the shop begged to be touched. She found herself locking her own fingers behind her back as well.

The bell tinkled as more customers filed into the dry goods store. Two older women spoke freely as they admired the fabric and tried on hats. When one looked Damaris's way, she frowned and whispered to the woman on her left, loudly enough for Damaris to hear, "We best watch that little nigger girl. They'll steal you blind if you don't keep an eye on them."

Damaris's ears burned hot, and she inched closer to Kit.

The next hour was spent looking over the fabric, ribbons, and patterns. When they had exhausted nearly every inch of the store, Grace waited while the clerk tallied up her purchases.

"Who's that darky you got with you?" Mrs. Flynn asked Kit.

"She's my . . ."

"Don't matter, young lady. Your mothers just paid for these dry goods. You'd best give them to your servant girl to carry." Mrs. Flynn handed the first of three brown packages to Kit.

Kit's lips thinned. "Here you go." She handed the package to Damaris.

Mrs. Flynn's gaze strayed to the young girls roaming the aisles.

"Piper," Damaris called. "Come help carry the packages."

Piper's eyes questioned her as she did as she was told. She held the large brown bag and waited.

"Come with me. We'll wait outside," Damaris said.

Piper looked relieved. She lifted a hand to wave at Sunny and Amy and quickly moved through the door. Moments later, the two sisters stood on the boardwalk, waiting. The sky was growing darker, and a deep roll of thunder drummed overhead.

Damaris looked up in time to see Nate running their way. "Is Miz Grace 'bout done shopping? I think we're in fer some rain!"

"They're coming shortly. Bring the rigs."

"Yes, ma'am!" Nate grabbed one of the packages from Damaris and then held onto his hat as he hoofed it down the lane.

No sooner had he left than big plops of rain began to fall. First, just a couple of splatters hit the boardwalk, the brown paper, and their heads. Then a few more. Within a minute, a torrent of rain filled the air, blurring the buildings across the road.

Damaris opened the door to the dry goods store, sending the bell tinkling a warning. She looked at the counter at the front of the shop. Mrs. Flynn was handing a large brown package to Grace and another to Lauren with a bright smile on her face. She looked past them at Damaris and frowned. "You're dripping water on my floors! Outside!"

"Is it raining?" Grace asked as she walked through the aisle.

"It's pouring, Aunt Grace!"

"Oh, my word! We should have brought the coach," Grace said as the women rushed out of the store.

The carriage rolled up in front of them, and Nate climbed down to help the women into the rig. Damaris looked over to see Hakim doing the same.

"There's a covered bridge down the road some. We'd best park under there until the rain lets up," Nate said.

"Good. We'll eat lunch while we wait it out," Grace said.

Soon, the two carriages were parked under a red-covered bridge that spanned a bubbling creek. By then, everyone was soaked to the bone.

"Who would have known the day was going to turn out like this?" Kit asked. She covered the brown package of fabric on the floorboards under her skirts. Lauren and Grace did the same.

"Well, let's eat," Grace said. "Nate, bring out the food."

"Yes'm." He hurried to the back of the carriage and opened a compartment that hid the food baskets. No one talked while they ate their sandwiches. Rain drummed on the roof of the bridge. It sounded like a squadron of soldiers marching overhead. All eyes were on the road beyond, where mud puddles were forming.

Damaris watched her aunt. She wasn't eating. "Aunt Grace. Are you all right?"

"Of course, I am." Grace waved a hand and smiled weakly.

Lauren Sparrow looked at Grace and put a hand to her forehead. "You're burning up!"

"I'm fine. Really, I am," Grace said. But she was noticeably shaking as if she were chilled.

Damaris didn't think it was from the rain or the cool breeze. "Is there a blanket in the cubby?" she asked.

"I think so." Nate opened the compartment behind the rig again, and he held up a brown wool blanket. "Look what we have here!" He walked back to where Grace sat and tucked it around her. "Miz Grace. I don't think you been tellin' us the truth. I don't think you be feelin' well at all."

"I am a little cold," she confessed.

Kit moved over and laid the back of her hand on her mother's cheek. "Mama! You *are* burning up!"

"No, honey. I'm cold." Grace closed her eyes and drew the wool blanket closer up her shoulders.

Kit looked at Damaris and then Florence. "As soon as this rain lets up, we've got to get Mother home."

But the rain didn't let up for some time. The girls in the Sparrows' carriage finished their lunch and got out to watch the water flow under the bridge. Their voices echoed inside the covered bridge.

"Maddie!" Bella hollered. "Don't lean so far over the rail! You could fall into that rushing water, and we'd lose you forever."

Maddie stepped off the lower rung of the rail alongside the bridge. "I wouldn't have fallen, Bella." Her arms went over her chest, and her bottom lip went out.

Forty-five minutes passed before the rain finally stopped. The younger girls climbed back into the Sparrows' carriage, and the two rigs rolled down the lane. Not a one of them said a word.

"Good Lord," Damaris prayed out loud. "Please keep the rain from pouring down on us the rest of the way. We need to get Aunt Grace home!"

EIGHT

THE RAINFALL HAD delayed the carriages, and it was late afternoon when they arrived at River Oak. Kit was relieved to see the Great House as the horses trotted into the long drive.

"Hurry, girls." Lauren admonished. "We need to get Grace into the house."

She didn't sound panicked, but something in her voice propelled Kit into action. "Mother's slept the whole way. I hope we can wake her up." She gently placed a hand on her mother's shoulder.

Lightning crackled in the sky, followed by a tremble of thunder. This sent a reminder that they didn't have a minute to waste.

"We've got to get your mother inside," Lauren repeated, a worried crease across her brow. "Florence, get the girls and packages out of the carriages."

"Of course, Mother." Florence stepped down from her side of the coach and ran back to the Sparrows' rig.

"Nate!" Kit called. "Come help me!"

Grace lay limp against the carriage seat. Her face was flushed a deep red, and her teeth chattered as she continued to sleep under the wool blanket.

"What can I do?" Damaris asked, moving out of the carriage and standing a few feet away.

"Run and get Zeek," Kit said, leaning over her mother and pulling the blanket off.

Damaris lifted her skirts and ran to the porch. "Zeek!" she called out. "Zeek, we need you!"

Zeek opened the front door and poked his head out. "Someone callin' my name?"

"We need you down here!" Damaris bellowed.

The old butler scurried down and assessed the situation as he reached the rigs.

"We gots to carry Miz Grace up to her bedchamber," Nate instructed. "She done got sick 'fore we left town."

Lauren and the girls had climbed out of the carriage to allow room for Nate to climb in and maneuver Grace into his arms. Now, before Zeek could step forward, Cato and Amos came around the side of the house. "What's going on?"

Nate stepped awkwardly to the ground with Grace in his arms. "Miz Grace is out."

Amos moved in. "We'll take her from here." He hooked his arms under Grace's shoulders and relieved the stableman of his burden. Cato discreetly picked up her lower body, and the two men swiftly carried her up the porch stairs.

Zeek raced ahead and opened the door wide. "Careful with the Missus. She be burnin' up like she be in a furnace."

The two men ascended the stairs with Kit, Damaris, and Lauren following.

Hearing the commotion, Hedy looked down from the landing, frowning. "What's wrong with Miz Grace?"

"Mama's sick," Kit said, lifting her skirts as she climbed the last step and followed close on Amos's heels. "Pull the covers back on her bed."

"Yes'm, Miss Kit. I be doin' that." Hedy flew down the hall.

The women started down the east wing. When they came into her mother's bedchamber, Kit instructed the men to lay Grace on the bed gently. After doing so, they stood back with grim faces.

"Thank you," Kit said. "Now I need you to go after Doctor Moab."

"Yes'm." Amos and Cato quickly walked away. They would have to find the doctor in the slave district, where he lived among the field hands as a slave himself.

She looked up to see Nate, Zeek, and the girls standing in the doorway. "You can all go about your business," Kit waved. "There's nothing you can do here." She looked over at Lauren and Damaris. "Help me get Mother out of her wet clothes and into something dry."

Hedy had been wringing her hands at the foot of the bed. At the mention of dry clothes, she went to the wardrobe and pulled out a soft white nightgown. "We'll put her in her nightclothes, Miss Kit."

Not once had Grace opened her eyes as the men carried her into the house. Now that she was changed, her eyes remained closed, but she thrashed her head on the pillow and moaned softly.

Thunder rolled and the skies darkened. Kit watched Lauren with a grateful heart as her mother's friend lit the lantern and closed the curtains. Another rumble of thunder reverberated overhead. "Lauren, you'd better get home before it starts raining. We can take it from here."

"I know you can." Lauren hovered over Grace and touched her arm. "Send for me if you need me."

"Of course," Kit said.

After Lauren left, Kit and Damaris stayed with Grace. They stood on each side of the bed, staring down at her. Her breathing was shallow, her face a deep red. Flecks of sweat beaded her brow.

"What do you think has made her so sick?" Damaris whispered.

"I don't know." Kit brushed the tendrils off her mother's slick forehead.

Gemma appeared at the door, breathing hard. "Lauren told me 'bout your mama." She crossed the floor and carefully laid a hand on Grace's cheek. "I don't like the looks of her," she whispered.

"What do you mean?" Kit asked.

"If'n I didn't know better, she lookin' like she's got the fever," Gemma murmured.

"She's been burning up the whole ride home," Kit said.

"I ain't talking 'bout any ole fever, Kit. I'm talking 'bout that nasty yellow fever."

"Yellow fever? This isn't the time of year for it."

"Yellow fever doesn't care what time o' year it is. She might have had a low grade of the fever and is only just now showing signs of it."

Kit knelt by the side of the bed. She clung to her mother's hand and looked up at Gemma. "What are we going to do? We can't lose her!"

"What we're going to do is send up a lot of prayer and let Doctor Moab take care of her," Gemma said. She'd just spoken his name when the doctor came through the door.

At the sound of his footsteps on the hardwood floor, the four women looked his way. Kit stood and moved away as he walked over to examine her mother. Damaris slipped her hand into Kit's and squeezed it. "She's going to be all right."

Doctor Moab confirmed their worst fears. Grace had yellow fever. Kit stared down at her mother, alarmed that the dreaded virus had found its way into the Great House but grateful that her mother slept. Kit settled into a chair next to the bed and looked on as the doctor woke her mother and gave her the first dose of medicine. It was going to be a long night. Given time and good doses of quinine, Grace could recover.

"She could get the fever again from time to time, but never as intense as this first attack," Doc said. "What matters now is getting her through the first few days."

Kit stared at her mother, filled with dread over the fearful news. Her father was due home tomorrow, possibly with the joyful news they'd found Kindra. Oh, how life played a tug of war with the human soul. She bent her head in prayer. *Dear Lord, don't take my mother now.*

Early the next morning, Kit entered the sitting room where her mother's secretary sat near the window in the south wall. She glanced out in time to see Jackson Harding ride up in the drumming rain. He sat straight in the saddle, his jacket soaked, and water dripping from his wide-brimmed hat. He looked altogether too handsome, seated in the saddle, so tall and lean and whipcord strong; one tanned arm rested on his leg, while sinewy fingers gripped the reins.

As she watched, he dismounted and threw the reins over the post near the steps. Kit drew back from the window, annoyed that her heart tripped at the sight of him. She hadn't expected him to arrive at River Oak without Captain Harding and his brothers. What was he doing out in this wretched weather? A moment later, she heard a loud rap at the front door and moved to the entrance as Zeek opened the door.

Jackson's tall frame entered the foyer, a dark look on his face. "Is your father home?"

"No. He and Denzel went to Beaufort to look for Kindra," Kit said in her smooth southern drawl. "Is something wrong?" Their eyes met, and she felt a slight flush warm her cheeks.

Jackson lowered his gaze and lifted his wet hat off his head. He combed his fingers through his damp hair. "My father has seen Kindra."

The statement smacked Kit full force. "Wh-what did you say?" She turned toward the stairs, ready to take the flight two steps at a time.

"Wait!" His deep voice reverberated in the foyer. "Where are you going?"

"I have to tell Damaris. She's here, and she's been waiting seven years for this wonderful news."

"Don't you want to know the rest before you go sashaying up the stairs?" Kit heard a hint of annoyance in his tone.

"Not until I bring Damaris down here." She held up her index finger. "Please wait." Kit lifted her skirts and ran. The last time she'd seen Damaris, she had been taking a nap on her bed.

The banging door roused Damaris out of her sleep. "What's all the noise about?"

"Captain Harding's seen your mother. Jackson's downstairs right now and has all the details." Kit stood at the side of the bed, grinning at Damaris.

Damaris stared back wide-eyed. "What did you say?" She slid out of bed. "Is he going to take us to her?" Fully dressed but barefoot, she started for the door.

"He didn't say."

The two girls sailed down the stairs. Damaris nearly slid into Jackson when she stepped off the last step. "Is it true?"

"I'm not the one who's seen her." Jackson's lips turned up with amusement. "Dad was in town, purchasing supplies this morning. He saw her riding in the back of a wagon."

"Can you take us to her?" Damaris interrupted him.

"Uh, no."

"Kindra's in Charleston?" Kit could hardly grapple with the sheer truth of it.

"It appears so." Jackson stared down at her with the bluest eyes. "My father was on foot, but he tried to see which way the wagon went. He lost sight of her when the wagon turned off the main thoroughfare two blocks down the road. He said he set the box of supplies down and ran. When he reached the corner, the wagon was gone."

"But he found her," Damaris insisted, pushing her way forward. "Tell me he found her." Her pinched expression as she searched Jackson's face clearly showed her anxiety.

"Did he?" Kit felt unnerved that this man seemed to take his time as he drew out the details.

"I'm getting to that." He looked at Damaris and then at Kit. For a breathless moment, their gazes held. Kit couldn't have looked away if she wanted to.

Jackson held his hat in his hands, fingering the brim. Kit stared up at Jackson's gold-brown hair, slicked back and damp from the rain. Today was the first time she'd seen him up close in four years. She didn't know when he'd finished college, but seeing him now, she realized she'd missed him.

Kit's cheeks burned when she realized he was watching her with a glint in his eyes. Her finger went to the scar above her left eyebrow and slid down below her earlobe.

It was Jackson who broke the glance. He slapped his hat against his pant leg, sending drops of water to the hardwood floor. He didn't seem to notice.

"Tell me!" Damaris pulled on Jackson's sleeve. "Where's my mother?"

He pulled out of Damaris's grip, and his hand went up to still her.

Kit looked out the front door, seeing rain drip from the eaves. "My father and Uncle Denzel won't be home until tomorrow. Of course, they'll return empty-handed."

"Of course," Jackson said.

"D-did your father ask who'd purchased my aunt?" Kit sputtered, feeling like a ninny. It was difficult to break eye contact with him. She rubbed the scar over her left eye out of habit.

Damaris crossed her arms, and impatience showed on her face. "Are you tongue-tied? Where's my mother?"

"Yes, go on with your story. You said your father saw Kindra, and yet we know nothing at all." Kit's excitement at the news of Captain Harding seeing Aunt Kindra was beginning to edge on irritation.

"The auctioneer was gone when Father went back to the square, so he rented a horse and rode out of town. He said he went quite a ways, but there's a fork in the road. When he didn't see her, he went back to town and combed the neighborhoods." Jackson shrugged. "She's somewhere in the area. We just don't know where."

Damaris looked at Jackson before pacing. "How could your father have seen my mother and let her get out of his sight?"

"He tried to find her." Jackson shrugged.

"That's utterly frustrating," Kit said. "All right. I'll tell my father when he arrives home." She glanced into the dining room, remembering her manners. "Will you stay and have lunch before you ride back to Charleston?" It was all she could do to keep from staring at his handsome face. She clutched her skirts and waited.

Jackson looked over his shoulder toward the dining room and then returned his gaze to Kit's. For one horrible moment, she feared he might read her feelings in her eyes.

"Thank you, but no. I told Father I'd give you the message and return right away. We should have left for the Caribbean coast this morning, but several sails need mending. We're going to stay a couple of days longer to repair them while we're in port. He needs my help."

Kit thought the hat in his hands was going to be crumpled if he didn't stop turning and pinching it. "Maybe you and your father can come for dinner while you're in town," Kit said, her face heating up again.

Jackson's blue eyes roamed over her face, but he gave no indication of his emotions. The glint she'd seen in his eyes only moments ago was gone. "I'll relay that message to my father." He paused and stared down at her as if he wanted to say something more, but he turned for the front door and stepped out onto the porch. He replaced his hat and peered down at her. "Maybe I'll see you again before we sail." He touched the brim and nodded to Damaris and then to Kit.

Kit closed the door and stared at Damaris. "Your mother's in Charleston!" The two girls hugged each other and joined hands. Tears brimmed in Damaris's eyes. "I can't believe the captain lost sight of her. Do you think we'll ever bring her home?"

The wild thumping in Kit's heart slowed to a halt. "I don't know. Jackson said Captain Harding saw her riding away in someone's wagon. I don't know if we can get her back or not."

"We won't know if we don't try," Damaris said in an urgent tone.

"That's the truth of it. Let's not dampen the news with a wet rag. We've got to have faith that we can bring her home." Kit clasped Damaris's hands again.

Before the girls could say anything more, Gemma came through the kitchen door with a plate of sandwiches. "Y'all better sit down here, your lunch is awaiting." She set the plate on the sideboard. "I need to get you all fed and then tend to your mother." Gemma stood at the base of the stairs and called up, "You boys best git down here iffen you want to git fed."

Will, Zeddie, and Cyrus stomped down to the landing and filed noisily into the dining room.

"I'll be right there," Kit said. "I'm going to rustle up the rest of the girls and get them down here." She took the stairs with light steps as her mind went to the handsome man who'd stood in the foyer only moments before. She would have to put him out of her mind for the moment. She had more pressing matters to think about. Kindra was in Charleston! She had to tell her mother!

Jackson stepped off the porch and loosened the reins from the post. Seeing the saddle was wet, he reached into his back pocket, pulled out a handkerchief, and quickly wiped it dry. He mounted the sorrel and nudged the horse's flank with the heels of his boots. When he reached the road, he glanced back at the Great House. The rain had let up, and slivers of sunlight peeked through the oak trees and fell across the lawn.

His mind played over the past few minutes he'd spent inside that house. He hadn't expected to run into Kit. He'd come to see Cameron. He wasn't disappointed, however, as he remembered how her hair was mussed, delightfully so, and fell over her shoulders. Something stirred inside him. Her dark gray eyes had lifted to his, and he'd seen a faint embarrassment, mingled with something else. A warm glow accompanied the lovely flush to her cheeks. He'd taken in her crow-black hair and the soft contour of her face. If she hadn't drawn attention to the scar on her brow, he wouldn't have noticed. He wondered how she'd obtained the pale jagged line that traveled near her eye.

He turned, clicked his tongue, and the horse trotted down the lane. The break in the rain would let him make good time on the road. An odd sensation rippled through him, and he wondered at his feelings. Never in his twenty years had a person gotten under his skin so quickly. Her face floated in his mind. He was utterly captivated by this woman. The sound of her southern drawl flowed over him like warm honey. He knew he'd be better off if he wiped the thought of her from his mind before he did something he'd regret. Jackson dug his heels into the horse. He needed to get back to town. Sails needed mending before the *Savannah Rose* left port. He didn't have time for a woman in his life right now; his father was training him to be a merchant captain. He would be spending more time out to sea than he would on dry land. That wasn't a way to court a woman.

He clamped his jaw and kicked the horse. No matter how fast he rode, he couldn't shake the thoughts of her raven hair and the light in her smoldering eyes. "Lord, have mercy," he groaned. "What am I getting myself into?"

NINE

Beaufort, South Carolina

GUILT RIDDLED CUFFEE as he stumbled along the path that led to the auction square. His bloody ankles were shackled with iron braces, and a metal collar choked him as he moved slowly along behind the chain gang of slaves. Each slave's movement affected the rest in line. If one stumbled and fell, the rest of the men and women would jerk forward, and their metal collars would dig into their necks.

Scores of people moved up and down the riverfront of Beaufort, some walking, some riding in wagons or carriages. Using canvas tarps to shield from the sun, street vendors sold an assortment of vegetables, fruits, and fish of all kinds, or Cuffee's favorites: homemade pies and jars of canned jelly.

His mouth watered at the thought of warm apple pie. He could almost taste it now, with the spicy scent of cinnamon and apples tormenting his senses as it drifted across the road. He hadn't had such a delectable treat as this in more than fifteen years. He turned his head and paid attention to the downtrodden lad in front of him.

His thoughts came back to Kindra. He both missed and worried about her. That's where the guilt came in. Far too often, he thought of Kindra instead of his beautiful wife, Tabitha. He rationalized that he was concerned for Kindra's welfare. Was she being treated humanely, or would she fall into the hands of a cruel slave master?

He also reasoned Cameron and Grace were fair masters. Tabitha and his children were in safe hands. Grateful, he breathed a prayer of thanks. His family would live the life of slaves, but they would be cared for as if they were Camp's own.

Truth was, he had grown to love Kindra more than a friend. How could he not? He'd protected her for five years. He'd held her in his arms at night while she cried herself to sleep. Though they had not consummated their marriage at Whitestone, he'd taken it upon himself to be the head of their relationship, one that she often reminded him was just a ruse. She had no power over his heart. Neither did he.

The man ahead of him jerked forward, pulling on Cuffee's neck collar. It brought him out of his reverie. He shoved the thoughts of Kindra and Tabitha out of his mind. An iron gate swung wide, and the slaves were herded through the walkway.

Hands free, Cuffee clenched his jaw and his fist. Two more steps and he would enter the auction square, where nearly a hundred aristocratic men eyed the line with anticipation. A guard pointed to a wall where the slaves would stand and wait until the bidding began. Cuffee stood in the second row, his eyes staring straight ahead, his mind drowning out the low rumble of voices and calls of obscenities.

The primary crops in South Carolina were rice and cotton. Would he work on a dreaded cotton plantation again? He hoped not. He had learned the method of growing rice. The work on that crop appealed to him. It didn't matter. Fate would have its way.

He'd heard the steamboat captain talking to one of the crewmen. He said Charleston was a day's ride from Beaufort. If Denzel and Camp had gone all the way to Virginia in search of Kindra, it wasn't far-fetched to believe they would come to Beaufort to search for her here. Then again, they may have already found her in Charleston. The slave auctions were being held on the same day. His heart sank. There was no reason for Camp to show up in Beaufort. He resigned himself to the fact that not only would he not see Camp, but he wouldn't see Tabitha for a long, long time. Too many years had passed. Did she even think of him anymore?

Cameron set the coffee pot aside and put out the fire as Solomon rolled up the camping gear. It was all he could do to keep Denzel at bay as they finished breaking camp. He stretched to get the kinks out of his back and limbs after a rough night on the hard-caked ground. If he had traveled on his own, he would have slept in an inn on the way, but having two Negroes with him, the inn would not let them in. There was no other recourse but to bring a tent and sleep alongside the road. Gemma had packed more than enough food for the men, and they ate well on the trip. He poured one more cup of coffee.

Denzel sat on a boulder, lacing his boots. "So, what do you think, Camp?"

"About?"

"Do you think we'll find Kindra at the auction?" Denzel pulled his pant legs down over his boots and stood.

"I hope so." Cameron's heart ached for his brother-in-law. He watched Solomon put the rolled tarp in the back of the wagon and come back for the utensils. While loading the kettle and plates in the box, Cameron said, "You know that when we get to the auction square, you and Solomon will have to wait in the wagon."

Denzel gave Cameron a sharp stare. "I can't just sit out in the wagon without seein' for myself if Kindra is in the line-up."

"You have to, Denzel. They don't allow black servants inside the auction square. Strict rules."

Denzel swore under his breath.

"If she's there, I'll bring her out as quickly as I can."

"I know that." Denzel groaned. "It's been over seven years since she's been gone."

Cameron laid a hand on Denzel's shoulder. "You've been served more pain than should be allowed. I can't even imagine what you're going through."

Denzel looked up. "Thanks, my friend."

"Let's get going. It'll take us half an hour to roll into town."

The Bartholomew wagon rattled on the cobbled streets. Posing as Cameron's servant, Denzel took the reins. Solomon rode in the back again and watched the pedestrians and people in carriages, being careful not to give away his hatred for the business of buying and selling slaves. If he had his way, all of this nonsense would be done away with.

Solomon thought of Kindra, Damaris's mother, whom he had admired since his childhood. He had been ten when she married Denzel, and fond memories of her filled him with warm thoughts. She was good to the slave women, always showing interest in their way of life. Never in a million years would he have thought there would come a day that Kindra would have a daughter who would fill his mind. When Damaris showed up at River Oak, her beauty and grace shook his world. He saw her shy smile in everything he did, whether working in the rice barns or out in the fields, hoeing weeds. It was all he could do to put the ebony-skinned beauty out of his mind. He leaned back and watched traffic, letting his mind trail to Damaris and wondering how he'd find the nerve to speak to her. To talk to her, he would when the time was right.

Denzel pulled the wagon ahead of the iron gate. Solomon rested his arm on the box beside him and gazed inside the auction square. Against the far wall stood two long rows of men and women. Each of the slaves had shackles on their ankles, and a chain hung between them at their necks. Solomon's jaw clamped tight, and he cracked his knuckles in irritation.

Out of curiosity, he looked at the face of each slave, particularly the women. He'd heard plenty of talk about Kindra. He knew she was a beauty. His eyes scanned the women now, but as he looked at each one, it was clear that Kindra wasn't with this group.

Still, he combed the faces until he caught sight of one man. He froze. He jerked to his knees and clamped his hands on the side of the wagon.

Camp had climbed down from the wagon and was giving the two men orders. "Stay put, both of you. I'll return shortly." He gave Solomon a questioning look. "What's wrong, Solomon? Did you see her?" Cameron swung around and looked at the slaves.

"No, Massa. I don't see Kindra, but I do see somebody I ain't seen since I was a boy."

"Your daddy?" Cameron walked a few steps toward the gate, placing his fists on his hips. He looked back at Solomon. "By gum, it's Cuffee!"

Denzel approached Cameron. "You're not kidding. That's Cuffee all right."

Hard stares from the men inside the gate reminded Solomon why he'd stay put. "Denzel," he called. When Denzel glanced back at him, he took another step toward the gate. Solomon continued, "You better git over here by the wagon. Those men be lookin' like they're huntin' for a lynchin'!"

Cameron patted Denzel on the shoulder. "Go on. Wait for me. I don't see your wife."

Denzel's shoulders sagged as he retraced his steps and climbed back up into the front seat. Disappointment penetrated the air around him, and the silence was loud.

Solomon felt sorry for him, but at the moment, he couldn't take his eyes off the man in chains. He hadn't seen his father since he was a young boy. And there he was, big as life for all the world to see, standing pitifully with a metal collar around his neck like a dog.

Sweat poured down Solomon's neck as he sat in the hot sun, watching one slave after another stand on the auction block. Bids flew through the air as prominent men hollered the sums they were willing to pay for the African people.

A half hour later, his father was unshackled and led to the platform. Solomon's emotions ran amok inside him. He was both glad and angry to see his father.

Cameron stepped into the crowd and joined in the bidding. Would he outbid the others to win his father back?

"Six hundred!" called one man.

Six-fifty!" called another.

"Eight hundred!" Cameron called.

"Nine hundred!" called a man in a black bow tie.

Solomon's attention grew as he watched the bidding continue. His father was not a tall man, but he was straight-backed and muscular. He saw taut muscles in his forearms and beneath the thin layer of material of his shirt sleeves. Funny, as a child, he'd always imagined his father as a tall man. Seeing him now, a medium-sized man, he realized he'd been wrong. But he looked strong as an ox.

"One thousand!" Bellowed a man.

"Let me show you this man's back," called the auctioneer. "You'll not see a lash or scar on this one. He'll be a loyal servant. Someone give me a decent bid!"

"Eleven hundred!" said another.

Solomon watched with anticipation, but every muscle in his body tensed. "Come on, Massa Camp!"

"He won't let the others take your Pappy," Denzel said.

"How high do you think he'll go?"

"Until he wins," Denzel said nonchalantly.

"Thirteen hundred!" Black Tie called out.

"Fifteen!" Cameron topped him.

"Sixteen!"

"Sixteen-fifty!" Cameron said in an even tone.

"Eighteen!" A new voice joined the bidding.

The cluster of bidders looked back to see a man in a cream-colored suit, holding a bamboo cane.

"Nineteen!" said Black Tie.

"Nineteen-fifty!" The cane waved in the air.

"Two thousand!" Cameron said.

"What's he worth to you?" asked the man with the cane.

"Does it matter?" asked Cameron. By now, he'd slipped his hands into his pockets and looked as nonchalant as if bidding for a Sunday pie.

"It might," said Mister Cane.

Cameron shrugged and waited.

"Don't give up on my Pa!" Solomon said. He leaned over the rail of the wagon, raised an arm in the air, and made a fist.

"Sit down, boy!" Denzel said, giving him a harsh look. "Camp's workin' the crowd. Be still."

Solomon's stomach was tied in a knot. He moved back, but he kept his eyes on the auction.

"Twenty-two hundred!" said Black Tie.

"Twenty-five!" said Cameron.

A low rumble stirred in the crowd. All eyes went to the man in the cream-colored suit and then to Black Tie.

"Can I get twenty-five fifty?" called the auctioneer.

Cuffee looked at Cameron as if he'd seen a ghost. He didn't smile. He didn't frown. He just stared with a look Solomon couldn't gauge.

The unmerciful sun rose high, and sweat trickled down Cuffee's forehead. The front of his shirt was damp. But he stood steady and looked out over the crowd. His gaze traveled over the heads of the men until he made eye contact with Solomon. Solomon rose on his knees. He swallowed hard and held his breath as he gazed at the man. Did his father know he was looking at his own flesh and blood?

"Don't let this man get the last bid!" cried the auctioneer. "You can do one better."

But the throng began to shuffle and hum, and the men shook their heads. One called out, "Let him have the blackie!"

"Going once! Going twice! "Sold!" The auctioneer cracked the gavel on the table and stood back.

Cuffee's shoulders sagged in relief, and he stared at Cameron before looking at the wagon.

"It's me, Father," Solomon whispered.

"What'd I tell you?" Denzel said and slapped him on the back.

It was several minutes before Cameron signed the papers, paid up, and walked out the gate with Cuffee in tow. Once they walked past the gate, Cuffee turned to him. They spoke a few words and shook hands, then Cameron turned the man toward the wagon and pointed.

Cuffee stopped and gaped. The two men walked across the walkway, and Cuffee stood at the back of the wagon. "Solomon?"

"That's me." Solomon scooted out of the rig and stood in front of his father, whose eyes brimmed with tears.

The two men threw their arms around each other and slapped each other on the back. "It's been seventeen years," Cuffee said, filled with both thanksgiving and disbelief.

"I'm aware of that," Solomon said in a low voice.

"You're a grown man."

"I'm twenty-two."

"You look older than that, my son."

Cuffee ran a thick hand over his face. “I can’t believe you’re all standing here. That I’m here with you.” He looked up at Denzel, who hadn’t climbed down from his seat.

“Truth is,” said Cameron, “we came to this auction looking for Kindra. Instead, we found you. We’ve got a long ride home. We'd better get goin’.”

“Not yet,” Cuffee said, walking around the side of the wagon.

Denzel looked down, his dull eyes revealing disappointment at not finding Kindra's name written on his face.

Cuffee gave him a steady gaze. “I’ve seen Kindra.”

Denzel sat straight. “What are you talkin’ about?”

“She was on the same plantation I was on in Virginia.”

“What?” Denzel climbed down and stood before him. “Go on.”

“We both got sold off, Morgan Blissmore’s ship to the Abrams at Whitestone. It was a cotton plantation.” Cuffee held back from saying more. The hungry look in Denzel’s eyes said everything a man needed to know—he lived for the day he’d see Kindra again.

“We were there in Virginia, searching for her. No one seemed to know anything about her.” He swiped his face with an agitated hand. “Is she all right? Is she still there?” Denzel’s hands shot out, and he shook Cuffee.

“Last time I saw her, she looked fine. The Abrams were killed by one of their servants. Their daughter didn’t want to take over the plantation. She sold all of the slaves to a man who loaded us up in a paddleboat and took us downriver.”

“Go on!” Denzel said desperately.

“She was on the steamboat as far as Charleston. She was taken off, along with some of the other slaves. The rest of us went on to Beaufort.”

“Charleston?” Denzel looked wildly at Cameron.

“Yes. That’s where I last seen her.” Cuffee eyed the man before him. What would he do if he found out he and Kindra had been forced to marry? He couldn’t think about that now.

Denzel had a crazed look in his eyes. “We’ve got to get back to Charleston!” he told Cameron. “We’re wasting time!”

“Well, let’s go,” Cameron said.

They climbed into the wagon, and Solomon leaned against the canvas tarp, eyeing his father. Cuffee moved in beside him and leaned against the bundle of blankets. His hand clamped his son's strong arm. "It's good to see you, my son."

"Yes," Solomon said.

Denzel cracked the reins, and the wagon jerked away from the side of the road. As the rig moved away from the auction square, relief washed over Cuffee. His tall son looked strong as a bear. "How is your mother?" he asked, hoping she was alive and well.

"Mother is a strong woman." Solomon gave him a level gaze. "She's had to be to raise six children by herself."

Cuffee breathed in a long sigh. "There's so much to tell you—to tell your mother." He looked away at the buildings on the sides of the road as the wagon moved into the line of traffic.

"She'll want to hear everything, Father. She's waited a long time."

Cuffee nodded but didn't speak again for a long while. His thoughts went to Kindra. *She won't want to hear everything. It would break her heart.*

TEN

GRACE OPENED HER eyes after midnight to find Kit slumped over in a chair near her bed, the lamp turned low. Her body ached, and even though the blankets were tucked under her chin, she felt chilled to the bone.

Her breathing was stilted, with a dryness in her throat that felt like sandpaper. Turning her face into the pillow to stifle the cough, she hacked and coughed as the thrumming pain in her head intensified. "Oh," she moaned. "Water."

Kit jumped out of the chair and hovered. "You're awake."

"Y-yes. I need water." Grace coughed again and again until a nauseous wave came over her and she grew colder.

"Hold on, Mother." Kit moved to the pitcher on the nightstand and poured water into a crystal tumbler. She slid an arm under her mother's neck and raised her from her pillow. She tilted the glass to her lips, letting the cool water slide refreshingly down her throat.

Grace pulled away after drinking nearly half the glass. "That's good. So good."

"Do you need more?" Kit asked.

"No, honey," Grace said weakly. "Is the window open? I feel so cold."

Kit frowned and placed the back of her hand on her cheek. "You're burning up again. Maybe I should go after Doctor Moab."

Grace grabbed her arm. "Don't leave me just yet."

"All right." Kit placed the glass on the nightstand and then sat on the edge of the bed. She brushed the damp strands of loose curls off Grace's forehead.

"What time is it?"

"I don't know. Around three in the morning."

"Have I slept the day away?"

"You've slept two days away." Kit smiled warmly.

"Oh, dear. I don't remember anything after leaving town."

"You've been very sick. But you're getting the best of care. Doctor Moab has hardly left your side."

"Why? I can't be that sick." Grace started to rise from her pillow.

Kit gently pushed her back. "You are very sick," she repeated. "You've contracted yellow fever."

"What?" The effort to speak constricted Grace's throat, and she coughed and coughed until she nearly gagged.

Kit jumped up and poured another glass of water. Once the hacking ceased, Kit tilted the tumbler to her lips again.

The cool liquid felt wonderful. Grace touched Kit's hand to tip the glass forward and swallowed the rest of the water. Exhausted from so small a feat as drinking, she fell against the pillow and felt the room spin around her. The pain in her head pulsated. "Oh, Kit. How did this happen? The yellow fever at River Oak has been over and done with for nearly a month."

"Doctor Moab said that even though yellow fever had its seasonal run, sometimes the infected mosquitoes aren't all gone. If they bite someone, they'll contract the disease, yet it won't show up for several weeks. In your case, that is true. We spent half the summer at Pelican Island to avoid this awful disease, but somehow, you've been bitten by a mosquito."

"How long?" Grace asked through a dry mouth.

"How long?" Kit's brows furrowed. "Since you've been sick?"

"No. How long will I be sick?"

Kit looked down at her hands before she spoke. "Two weeks with good treatment. Doctor Moab has been prescribing quinine for you. He said the first week is the worst."

"So many of our people have died from yellow fever." Sweat slicked her brow, and Grace slid a hand from beneath the covers to wipe it away. She quickly put it back under the bedclothes as the chills wracked her body and her teeth chattered.

"Oh, Mama. It's dreadful that you're going through this. We're all praying for you. You're too strong to let it take you."

Grace nodded, and tears slid down her temples. "I'm scared."

"I know. We all are. But that won't keep us from fighting the good fight of faith to battle against this evil disease."

Kit's thumb traveled across Grace's forehead. It felt comforting to feel her daughter's touch, and she closed her eyes. The room was quiet for a long moment, and then Grace's eyes snapped open. "Has your father come home?"

"No. They should return sometime today."

"That's good. I hope they found Kindra. I want so desperately to see her."

"Mama," Kit said in a tone that alerted Grace that something was up. She fought through the foggy haze of fever for an answer.

"What?"

"They won't find Aunt Kindra in Beaufort."

"You can't know that."

"Yes, I do."

"How could you know such a thing?" Her voice felt raspy as a toad. "Tell me, do you know where she is?"

"Captain Harding saw her yesterday."

"In Charleston?"

"Yes." Kit laid a hand on her arm. "Jackson came by yesterday afternoon. He said his father saw Kindra riding on the back of a wagon." A small smile played on Kit's lips.

Did Grace see a rosy blush on her daughter's face? She would pursue that thought later. For now, she'd concentrate on the news that Kindra was in Charleston. "How did your father and Denzel miss her at the warehouse?" she voiced her thought.

"I don't know. Father said they combed the building. That's why it came as a surprise when Jackson said Kindra's in Charleston."

"So." A dryness filled Grace's throat again, and she started hacking.

Kit poured another small glass of water and brought it to her mother's lips.

After a good swallow, Grace waited to speak, letting the water coat her throat. "I feel so weak."

"You should rest, Mother." Kit stood.

"Wait." Grace closed her eyes to get her bearings. The room was spinning, and the pounding in her head was excruciating.

Kit laid a soft hand on her forehead. "You're still burning up. I should go after the doctor."

"First, tell me," Grace took a shallow breath. "Did Captain Harding see where Kindra went?"

Kit shook her head sadly. "No. He ran to follow the wagon. But he lost sight of it."

"She's in Charleston," Grace said, the drug of sleep consuming her. "We'll find her."

It was well past eleven the next night when Kit heard a clatter of hooves coming into the long drive. She rolled over and grabbed Damaris's arm. They're here!"

It was clear she wasn't the only one to hear her father's arrival. The sound of running feet thundered past her bedchamber. When she swung open her door, Will, Zeddie, and Cyrus were at the top of the landing, ready to scramble down the stairs.

"Quiet! You'll wake Mother!" Kit whispered loudly as she and Damaris joined them.

Another door flew open, and Bella, rubbing her eyes, stumbled out of her room. "Father's here!"

The group padded barefoot down the stairs and out onto the porch in anticipation. Damaris broke away from Kit, Zeddie on her heels.

"We've found Mother!" she said, running up to the wagon.

"Captain Harding's seen her in Charleston," Zeddie said, standing on the side where his father sat.

"Whoa! Not everybody at once," Denzel called out as he climbed down. He looked at Damaris, stunned. "Captain Harding's seen your mother?"

"Yes. Jackson came by yesterday to tell us the good news. We've got to go after her."

Denzel looked frantic as Damaris stood on the graveled drive. Kit's heart went out to him. "Where'd he see her?" Denzel grasped her shoulder.

"On the road, leaving town by the riverfront." Zeddie stepped up and spoke before his sister could respond.

"That's not telling me much. Did he see where she went after she left town? Did he see who'd taken her?" His hands went to the top of his head, and he swore under his breath.

Kit walked up and stood beside her father, who had climbed down and joined the small party on the opposite side of the wagon.

Denzel walked in a small circle and then kicked at a rock at the edge of the driveway. "Who's got her, Damaris?"

"We don't know," Damaris groaned. "Captain Harding was on foot when he saw Mother riding in the back of a wagon. He said he ran to catch up to it, but the road was busy and he lost sight of her."

Denzel stared at her. "How could that have happened?" he barked. "My wife is seen riding on a wagon down the road, and he lost sight of her?"

"Dad," Zeddie said.

"Shut up!" Denzel hollered.

"Denzel." Cameron stepped closer.

"This is preposterous! My wife has been gone for more than seven years. We just spent the last two days going in the opposite direction in search of her when she was right under our noses right here in Charleston! And who do we come home with? Cuffee!"

Kit stared at the back of the wagon to see Solomon and Cuffee standing silent—and stiff as two poles. She'd never seen Cuffee before, but she'd heard plenty about him.

Denzel broke the silence. "We have to go back to Charleston. We've got to find my wife."

Cameron's hand went up. "I'm in total agreement. But we can't go tonight. Everybody's asleep in town. Not to mention it's a four-hour ride. We need to put the horses in the stable and get them food and water. We'll start fresh in the morning."

Damaris and her siblings huddled together as they watched their father and Camp. Piper leaned into Damaris, her eyes big. "Is Daddy going to bring Mama home?"

"We hope so. First, they have to find her."

Cameron spoke up. "We don't know who purchased her. It won't do us any good to look for her without some direction as to where we're going." Cameron reached his side. "Come on, Denzel. We'll go first thing in the morning. Get some rest. You're going to need it."

"How can I sleep tonight? I have to go!"

"In the morning, my friend. We can't do anything until then."

Denzel looked at him with thunder in his eyes. "All right," he conceded. "But I won't be sleeping tonight. This is more than I can bear."

Damaris moved to Denzel's side and hugged him. Zeddie laid a hand on his father's shoulder.

"Okay, everybody, back into the house," Cameron said. "I've got to get Cuffee settled at his place, and then I'll be in."

Kit watched the men with her stomach in a knot. Cuffee stood by the wagon, a look of anxiety on his face. Solomon leaned against a tree, seeming to keep his distance.

"You're right, Camp." Denzel broke the silence. "Let Cuffee see his wife and children. I'm going to the house."

As the group turned back to the house, Kit remained by her father's side. "Father?" When Cameron turned to look at her, Kit continued, "There's more news waiting for you in the house."

"What kind of news?"

"Mother. She's got yellow fever."

The commotion in the front drive woke Nate and Tungo. Both men walked up to the wagon.

"Nate, take the horses to the stable," Cameron said. "Tungo, we've got a new field hand who needs to get settled. But there's not much to do, seeing as how he's Solomon's father."

Tungo's eyes lit up at the news. "This be Cuffee? I done hear that name a few times."

Cuffee waited at his son's side. Solomon hadn't said much on the eleven-hour ride home. It seemed his son was deep in thought. It was just as well, Cuffee thought. There was something about being in Cameron's care that gave his spirit a restful feeling. So much so that he could hardly keep his eyes open, it was almost as if the years of wishing and waiting to get back home to his wife and family had come crushing down on him. Deep relief consumed him. Now that he was here, he was eager to see Tabitha and the rest of his children. He reached out to Tungo and the two shook hands.

"I'm going into the house," Cameron said. "Tungo, you take it from here."

"Yessuh," Tungo said. He turned to Cuffee, "This be yer first time in Fields Landing?"

"This is my first time in South Carolina. I spent five years in Virginia." He looked over at his son, who seemed eager to reach their shack ahead of the two men. "So, yes, it's my first time here."

By the time Cuffee reached the steps of the white clapboard shack, the door was open and a kerosene lamp had been lit.

"This be yer home," Tungo said, slapping him on the back. "Welcome home." The tall overseer walked away, leaving Cuffee to go into the house and see his family for the first time in seventeen years before he set one foot on the steps, a patter of feet clambered in the small house.

Tabitha, wearing a worn, cream-colored cotton nightgown, hair mussed from sleep, was the first to stand at the front door. Somehow, this wasn't how Cuffee had imagined he'd see his wife when they met again. But the nightclothes made her look soft, and he wanted to take her in his arms.

Tabitha stared down at him in disbelief. "Cuffee?"

"That's me." He waited, his heart thumping in his chest.

She flew down the steps to stand in front of him. She stopped just short of throwing her arms around him, seeming a bit unsure. "I almost forgot what you looked like," she said.

Cuffee had always dreamed that, on the day they saw each other again, his beautiful Tabitha would fly into his arms. Yet here she stood, staring at him with an emotion he couldn't read. Was she shy after all these years? Was she angry?

She touched his arm gently and turned to look at their children, who'd filed out of the house. Only three of them stood on the ground. The moon slanted a silvery light over the family as if to shine a spotlight on Cuffee's homecoming. The soft beam let him see their faces.

Nothing prepared him for the reaction he felt when he saw his children.

When he'd been smuggled by Morgan Blissmore seventeen years ago, the children had been small. Now they were grown adults. His two oldest daughters were missing. "The older girls?" He looked at Tabitha.

"Lilly and Anna have their own homes. They're married and both have babies," Tabitha said proudly.

While Solomon stood behind his siblings, Tabitha took the arm of one tall son and said, "This is Cabeto. He's twenty-five now."

Cabeto stared at him for a short moment before he stepped forward and stretched out a hand.

"Cabeto!" Cuffee took his son's hand and pulled him to his chest. He hugged him hard, a powerful surge of emotion running through him. "It's good to see you, my son!"

When Cabeto stood back and looked him in the eye, he smiled broadly. "Welcome home, Father."

A teenage boy stood watching them with a look Cuffee couldn't read. He opened his arms, and the boy stepped up to him, but he did not hug his father. "I'm Toby."

"Toby." Cuffee echoed the name. "A good, strong name for one such as you." Cuffee stared at his son, whom he'd never seen before. Tabitha had been expecting him when Cuffee had been smuggled away. He hardly knew what to say. Finally, he broke the silence. "I should have been there when you were born. And I would have if I could."

"Mama told me the story many times, how the slavers took you away. Is that true?"

"Your mama wouldn't lie to you. It's true. We'll sit down and I'll tell you everything."

Toby nodded and looked over his shoulder at his sister. "Tisha."

A young woman stepped forward. She looked just like her mother. "Tisha. You were the baby of the family when I left."

She smiled shyly.

"Come here," Cuffee kissed his daughter on the cheek and held her at arm's length. "You must have been a great help to your mother."

Tisha nodded.

"It's late," Tabitha said. "You all go to bed. I want to spend a moment alone with your father."

The children nodded and walked back into the house.

"I don't know my children anymore. They're all grown into adults," Cuffee said, a sad regret consuming him.

"You've been gone a long time," Tabitha said, keeping her distance.

"Don't I know it. I hope you'll let me tell you my story before you judge me."

"I haven't judged you, Cuffee. I've only waited half my life for you to return."

"Come here," he said, throwing his arms around his wife. "We'll spend the rest of our lives making up for lost time. Just you wait and see."

"That sounds good to me." Tabitha pulled his head down and kissed him softly. When they broke the kiss, she said, "Come into the house. I've waited a long time for you to come home. I won't be alone tonight. God has heard my prayers." She took his hand and together they stepped through the front door of their home.

Thank You, Lord. It's good to be home!

ELEVEN

CAMERON TOOK THE stairs two at a time, passing Gemma on her way down with a tray of tea. "Your wife be asleep, Mastah Camp." She kept going, looking weary as a dog left out in the rain.

"Thanks, Gemma. I'll look in on her." He hurried down the east wing to their bedchamber and opened the door. Grace lay in their bed, her face flushed, and a low moan on her lips.

Cameron stepped quietly and knelt beside her. Her chest rose and fell with her shallow breaths. He placed his hand on her forehead. *Oh, Lord, she's burning up!* He gazed at her for a long moment, not wanting to leave.

She stirred, tossed her head, and coughed. Her hand flew to her throat, and she coughed some more.

Cameron eyed the water pitcher and the small glass in front of it. *Should I wake her?*

The coughing stopped, and Grace moaned softly. She looked like an angel with her long auburn curls spread out on the pillow.

"Lord," he whispered. "I'm asking that You heal my wife. I couldn't bear it if You took her away from me."

Beads of sweat gathered on Grace's brow. He dipped a rag in the bowl of cool water on the nightstand and wrung it out. Then he folded the cloth and gently placed it on her forehead. She jerked away, and the rag slipped onto the pillow. He quickly picked it up and laid the cloth on her damp skin again. This time, she didn't move.

Taking a deep breath, he stood and looked around the room. He wanted to stay by Grace's side but didn't think it wise to sleep next to her. He was too weary to try sleeping in the chair; he needed to lie down. He strode to a guest room and tugged the bedding off the bed, carried the bundle back to their room, and laid it on the floor. He removed a pillow from next to Grace and dropped it at the head of the blankets.

For another long moment, Cameron watched her. Sometimes she moaned, sometimes she coughed. He shook his head, weary from the long trip from Beaufort, and distraught to learn they'd missed Kindra while in Charleston, and now he was fearful for his wife, who fought for her life.

Feeling as if the world were crumbling down around him, he went to the chair and pulled off his boots and breeches. He crawled under the blankets and lay on his back, staring at the ceiling and listening to the sounds of Grace's shallow breathing. *I humbly ask You to heal my wife, Dear Lord.* Finally, he slept, while uncertainties raged in his dreams.

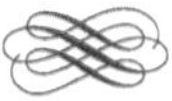

Cameron awoke to rustling sounds. For a moment, he couldn't recall why he was on the floor.

"Mornin'," said Doctor Moab.

"Morning," Cameron said, getting to his feet and grabbing his britches. He quickly dressed and stood by Grace's bed. He watched Doctor Moab gently touch her neck, and the scene from the night before came back to him. Kindra was in Charleston, and he'd promised Denzel they'd go after her.

Grace's eyes flew open. She looked at him and smiled weakly. "Hello, stranger." Her voice croaked.

Cameron went to the opposite side of the bed and sat down. He took her hand and massaged it. "Hello, beautiful."

She closed her eyes and smiled.

"How is she?"

"She's very sick," Dr. Moab said gravely." But your Grace is a strong woman. I expect her to pull through this."

Cameron took a deep breath. This was the best thing he'd heard in days.

"I'm not sayin' she out o' the dark, yet," Moab said as he poured liquid from a brown bottle into a spoon and helped Grace take it.

"I understand." Cameron squeezed Grace's hand and spoke to her gently. "You've got the best doctor in all of South Carolina. You'll beat this."

"I know," Grace said in a small, raspy voice. "I have to be here for all of you."

"And you will." He slid off the bed.

"I'll leave you two to talk," the doctor said. "I have a couple of stray cases on the top side o' this yellow fever. Even tho it didn't rampage through River Oak this summer, it worked its way into the settlement and took hold of a few later than usual." He turned to the door. "I'll be back later this mornin'. Stay in bed and rest, Miz Grace."

"Yes, doctor," Grace scratched out. She looked at Cameron. "Drew saw Kindra."

"Damaris told us as much last night. I promised Denzel we'd go to Charleston this morning to search for her, but that was before I learned you were sick."

"You must go after her," Grace said fiercely.

"I can't leave you now."

"You have to help Denzel find her. I won't sleep a wink, knowing she's in Charleston."

Cameron felt the heat radiating from her brow as he kissed her forehead. "You still have a high fever."

"Gemma and the doctor are taking good care of me. Kit has hardly left my side. It will be a relief knowing you are looking for my sister. I want you to go."

Cameron reached down and pulled Grace into his arms. "You have to get well. I need you."

When Cameron and Denzel rode into Charleston just before noon, the wharf bustled with the usual activity. They stopped in front of a building on the waterfront, jumped down, and strode to a door which read: "J. Janzen Slave Auctioneer." Mister Janzen was the only one who could help them discover where Kindra had been taken, and they hoped to find him in his office.

Cameron tried the doorknob, but it was locked. "No one's here. Now what?"

Denzel's brows furrowed. "I don't know. I hate to think we rode all this way for nuthin'." He shook his head. "I hadn't expected to find everyone gone." He took off his hat and brushed it against his pants.

They looked up and down the road. "The auction square is across the street. Maybe there's a sign that can give us some information," Cameron said.

"Let's take a look." Denzel kept stride with Cameron as they threaded their way through the traffic. When they reached the other side, they came to a sign posted on a billboard outside the gate.

TODAY!
PUBLIC AUCTION OF
SLAVES
PRIME NEGROES
INCLUDING
2 SPECIAL AND CHOICE
FEMALES
A MORE DESIRABLE LIST OF
NEGROES CAN NOWHERE BE FOUND
JAMES S. MORROW

Denzel swore under his breath. "I can't believe we missed seeing Kindra before this auction." He worked his jaw as if agitated.

"We'll find her," Cameron said, not quite believing himself.

Denzel grasped the top of the poster and ripped it from the wall, tearing the parchment in a wide swath down the middle, leaving the outer paper still attached. The gaping hole exposed the wooden board behind it. He wadded the paper in a ball and tossed it in the street just as a horse and buggy went by—the horse's hooves trod the paper.

Cameron sucked in his breath. "What do you think you're doing? You're going to get us both in trouble!" He swung his hat off and combed his hair back with his fingers as he looked up and down the street. Luckily, no one seemed to have noticed what Denzel had done. Cameron wasn't sure he wouldn't have done the same thing himself, but then he could have gotten away with it. He pushed Denzel away from the wall, and the two of them continued walking. Seeing the rage in his brother-in-law's eyes, Cameron placed a hand on Denzel's shoulder. "Come on," he tugged on Denzel's arm. "Let's go back to the wagon."

To his surprise, Cameron saw Captains Kincade and Harding striding up the boardwalk. Behind them were Kincade's first mate, Barnabas, and Harding's first mate, Jamie.

"What a pleasure to find you here," Kincade said. "We're on our way to The King's Inn for lunch. Will you join us?"

The storm in Denzel's eyes stopped the captain from saying more. Denzel nailed a glaring stare at Drew. "I understand you saw Kindra." His words sounded more like an accusation than a question.

"Yes, I did—"

"Why didn't you stop them?"

"I tried. When I realized it was your wife . . ."

"You could have saved her!" Denzel roared. He jumped forward, clamped his hands around Drew's neck, and knocked him to the ground, then straddled Drew's body and pummeled him.

"Hey!" Cameron shot forward to pull Denzel off, but Barnabas's giant form jumped in front of him and lifted Denzel off the captain.

"Massa, you gots to get a hold of yerself!" Barnabas said as he threw his arms around Denzel's chest and pinned him in a vice grip. "You can't be beatin' on the captain. They's folks watchin' you. You keep it up, they be lookin' fo' a lynchin'!"

"Let me go!" Denzel growled as he kicked and pulled to get out of Barnabas's hold.

"Not until you stop fightin', suh."

Harding got up, dusted his wide-brimmed hat, and pinned his hazel eyes on Denzel. He wiped the blood from his mouth with the back of his arm and swayed. "You think it didn't kill me that I couldn't catch up with the wagon?" He stumbled forward until he was inches from Denzel's face. "I would have done anything to find her. I wanted to. I searched the city and countryside for hours. She was gone, Denzel. Flat gone! My gut ached that one moment she was there and the next she was gone. I hated myself for letting her out of my sight. But I couldn't find her!" He slammed his hat against his pant leg. "I'm sorry for that. And as long as we're in port, I will keep my eyes and ears open."

Denzel clenched his teeth and stared at Harding while he spoke. Then his shoulders slumped and he hung his head. Barnabas released his grip, and Denzel walked away with his hands on his hips and heaved.

The other men looked first at each other and then at Denzel's back.

Finally, Denzel turned with tears brimming. "Sorry, Drew. I shouldn't have attacked you." He visibly swallowed and looked away again.

"You're forgiven, friend." Drew approached Denzel and placed a hand on his shoulder. “We’ll find her, pal. We won’t give up.”

Denzel nodded and looked at the traffic.

“Let’s say we take them up on lunch at the King’s Inn,” Cameron suggested, “then we can work up a plan to find Kindra. All right?”

Denzel nodded again and bit his lip.

“Come on.” Drew threw his arm over Denzel’s shoulder. “I’m hungry.”

“Y’all seem to be forgetting something,” Denzel said, and tilted his head to the Inn up the boardwalk. “They won’t be lettin’ Barnabas and me into their establishment.”

“They have tables outside in the back for coloreds,” Cameron said. “We’ll join you there.”

“You’d do that for us?” Barnabas’s eyes grew round.

“Of course. Let’s go.”

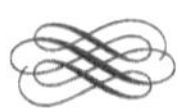

The six men poured out of the café, ready to go their separate ways. They had learned Mister Janzen had been in town only for the auction. He had a home on the outskirts of the city.

“There’s a sign in front of his home,” The King’s Inn owner told them. “It’s red-bricked and lined with holly berry bushes inside the black iron fencing.”

“Well, let us know what happens.” Captain Harding shook hands with Cameron. “We’ll be in port a few more days. We have several sails in bad repair. I’ve got the crew working on them, and my boys, too. It never hurts to let them learn all the workings of a ship.”

“Come out for dinner before you leave,” Cameron said. “Although I have to warn you, Grace is sick with yellow fever.”

Denzel’s head jerked to look at Cameron. “Grace is sick?”

“Yes. I hated leaving her, but she wouldn’t have it, me staying at River Oak when there was a chance of finding Kindra.”

Denzel hung his head again and walked away from the men. He pulled off his hat and threw it on the ground. “I’m more of a fool than I realized! First, I pound on Drew. And now I find out Grace is fighting for her life while you’re out here looking for my wife.” He snatched up his hat before a pedestrian could kick it aside. "God, forgive me," he said as he looked up at the sky.

"You're being too hard on yourself, Denzel," Cameron said. "We all understand your frustration and need to find Kindra. We want that too."

Cameron turned to Drew. "If you can, ride out to River Oak. I'd like to see you before you sail."

"Will do." Drew and Jamie waved goodbye and disappeared into the throng of people.

Kincade folded his arms over his chest and looked at Denzel. "May I have a word with you?"

"Certainly."

"We'll be sailing in the morning. When do you want us to return?"

"Come back in two months. That'll give me time to find my wife."

Kincade and Barnabas stalled.

"If there's anything I can do, I will," Kincade said.

"Thank you, Captain. There's not much you can do at sea. Be back in eight weeks. I hope to have my bride by then."

"Yes, sir." Kincade touched the brim of his hat before he and Barnabas strode back to the dock.

Cameron and Denzel looked up the road that led out of town. "I guess our next order of business is to check out Mister Janzen's place," Cameron said. "Let's go."

As the wagon rattled over the cobbled stones in the busy street, Cameron held the reins loosely in his hand. Denzel sat beside him but said nothing.

Cameron had more on his mind than Kindra at the moment. He feared for Grace's life. It didn't matter that the threat of the disease should have left the plantation. It had taken one last bite at his wife. Yet he and Denzel had to exhaust every avenue in hunting for Kindra before they returned to River Oak. *Hold on, honey. I'll get there as soon as I can!*

The wagon rolled to a stop. "You wait here." Cameron set the brake.

"What? I'm coming with you."

"No, you're not. Mister Janzen won't tell me anything if you're standing there. You forget you're a darky in his eyes."

Denzel blew out a long sigh. "All right."

"I'll be right back." Cameron opened the iron gate, walked up to the porch, and knocked on the thick white door. A few seconds later, a black man opened it.

"What can I do for you, suh?" the man asked.

"I'm here to see Mister Janzen."

"May I ask who's calling?"

"Cameron Bartholomew of River Oak."

"Please wait." The door closed, and Cameron glanced over the manicured lawns and flower gardens while he rocked on his heels in anticipation of seeing the auctioneer.

A moment later, the door opened again, and the butler waved him inside. Mister Janzen came to the foyer with a gleam in his eyes. "Mister Bartholomew, how good to see you. Right this way." He waved Cameron into the parlor and then spoke to the maid. "Bring us some coffee and your fresh-baked molasses cookies."

"Yes, suh." She disappeared while the butler remained at attention at the entrance to the parlor.

"That'll be all, Beckett."

"Yes, suh." The butler turned and walked away. Cameron knew the man wouldn't go far—the slave had been trained to stay in earshot in case he was needed.

"What can I do for you?" Mister Janzen asked as he waved Cameron to the stuffed chair across from his and waited for him to sit. "Are you in need of more field hands or servants? We've got another shipment that'll arrive in a couple of weeks." He grinned and twisted the ends of his handlebar mustache.

"No. I don't need any workers at the moment." Cameron leaned with his elbows on his knees. "I've come to ask about a female slave you sold this last weekend." He eyed the man, who dropped his hands to his lap.

"A female slave? We sold seven women last Saturday. Would it be the cook? She sold for a handsome price, given that she had a reputation for cooking the best meals in the territory."

"No. I have pretty fine cooks at River Oak. I'm talking about the middle-aged woman with a lighter complexion."

Mister Janzen grinned and nodded. "I know which darky you're talking about. She was a beauty—as some would say—for a Negress. Kindra's her name?"

"That's the woman." Cameron held his breath.

"She sold to a plantation owner."

"Can you tell me who this man is?"

"No, sir. Strict rules. If you weren't there in the crowd to see who purchased her, I can't disclose who bought her."

Cameron tilted his head. "I don't understand. If I were there, it wouldn't have been confidential."

"That's true. However, I learned a long time ago that when folks come looking for a slave I've sold, it usually means there's more to it than just wanting to buy. What stake do you have with this darky?"

The tables had turned on Cameron, and he looked at the man's shiny black boots before he answered. "I knew her before."

"Ahh," Mister Janzen smiled broadly. "A clandestine encounter with the pretty ones is not unusual. But you're too late. The owner paid a pretty penny for her. Beyond that, he's a hard man to counter. When he gets his way, he won't let anyone talk him out of it." Mister Janzen pushed out of his chair. "You're out of luck. The woman's sold and that's that."

"If you could just . . ."

"Is there anything else I can do for you, sir?"

"No. Nothing more. If you should change your mind about Kindra, you know where to find me."

"Yes, Mister Bartholomew. A fine estate you have in Fields Landing. One of the best. Like I said, we'll have another shipment arriving in a couple of weeks. We may have a pretty little Negress show up with that lot." He smiled wickedly.

"You misunderstand, sir. I'm not looking for her for myself."

"Of course not." Janzen twisted his mustache again. "Who might be interested if not you?"

"No one you know, sir. Thank you for your time." Cameron turned and stopped, reaching for a wad of bills from his pocket. "Can I talk you into giving it a second thought?"

Mister Janzen looked at the bills in Cameron's hand. He licked his lips, and his cheeks grew ruddy, but his eyes blazed hard when he looked Cameron in the eye. "Good day, Mister Bartholomew."

Cameron put the money back in his pocket and touched the brim of his hat. "Good day." Just then, the maid walked into the foyer with a silver tray. Two mugs of coffee and a plate of cookies were placed in the center. Cameron took two cookies off the plate. "Thank you, miss." He turned and walked out the door.

Denzel stood in the buckboard when Cameron came through the gate. "Well? Did he tell you where we can find Kindra?"

Cameron climbed up into the seat and gave him a cookie. "No. He's as stubborn as a jackass. 'Rules,' he said. If we weren't there at the auction, they don't disclose who bought her."

Denzel issued a scalding stream of words. "Is she in town or on a plantation?"

"That much I know." Cameron ignored the derogatory tone in Denzel's voice. "A plantation."

"Well, that's a start," Denzel grumbled.

"Hardly. There are too many plantations and too many square miles to search. We'll have to hire a couple of agents to scout out the area until they find her."

"Hire somebody?"

"I want to find Kindra, too, my friend. But I've got a rice plantation to run and a sick wife at home. I need to be there a good portion of the time."

Denzel slumped in his seat as Cameron unwound the reins from the brake post. The wagon moved out into the road, jostling the buckboard as they went. Cameron felt dissatisfaction emanate from Denzel's side of the seat. He ached for the man but didn't know what else to do. Hiring agents seemed the best way to go about it for now.

A long while later, Denzel spoke up. "Thank you, Camp, for all you've done. I know I can't go tromping on any plantations in this area, or I'll end up working one of those fields myself." He sat up straight. "Let's hire those men, like you said. She's here somewhere. They'll find her."

"There you go, and you're right. We'll find her.

TWELVE

Charleston, South Carolina

KINDRA CLAMPED HER fingers tightly against the rough boards of the wagon as she rode with the three men and two teenage boys. Her feet dangled just above the dirt road. The men moved in farther and leaned against the sides and the back of the jiggling vehicle, their arms crossed over their chests and resigned looks on their faces.

Supplies crowded them even more. She'd intended to doze on the way to Ash Haven, as she had hardly slept a wink the night before, but then it occurred to her to keep her eyes and ears open while on the ride. What if Cameron and Denzel were on the way? If she saw them, could she get their attention?

Kindra watched the busy city of Charleston fade as the wagon rolled along the potholed road. How would Denzel find her once she was settled at the plantation? Her heart plummeted. All through the night, she had prayed God would intervene and send Cameron and her husband to the auction. Now here she was, traveling away from town, a newly purchased slave headed to Ash Haven. She heard someone say the plantation grew cotton. Would she be required to work the fields as she'd done at Whitestone?

The callous voice of the overseer driving them to their destination carried over the air to where she sat trying to drown him out. "That little nigger girl you just bought is sure gonna bring in some good-looking babies. Whew, doggie!"

Master Bridger chuckled but talked too low for Kindra to hear. She dug her fingers into the wood until they burned with pain. *I won't be providing your plantation with babies*, she told herself. *I'm not a victim, just you wait and see. You might have paid a handsome sum for me, but I'm strong enough to resist your power.* She loosened her grip and relaxed her shoulders. Her love for Denzel made her stronger.

One of the slave men leaned her way. "Don't be listenin' to dem folks."

"I'm not," she said. "It's just fool talk they're saying. Nobody has control over me."

"Don't you go talkin' foolish, either," the slave warned.

She stared the man in the eye, a man she'd traveled with from Whitestone. All the men who rode with her were familiar with her ways, and they'd seen her in action before. "Now, have I ever given any of you cause to worry about me?"

The men jabbed each other with their elbows and laughed.

"What's goin' on back there!" barked Red.

The men grew silent, but the gleam in their eyes as they looked at each other and then at Kindra said differently. She turned back to watch the countryside roll away. They came to a fork in the lane, the horses veered to the left, and a half hour later, the wagon pulled up to a row of shanties.

"Hold up!" Red called to the horses.

"Get out, all of you!" Bart said.

"I'm going up to the house," Bridger said. "Take care of the darkies." He strode to where Kindra stepped off the back of the wagon. "You're coming with me."

"What?" Bart walked over. "I thought she was replacin' old Sally?"

"You thought wrong. Phoebe wants the new slave up at the house."

"Phoebe ain't seen the new slave," Bart grumbled under his breath.

"You got a problem?"

"No, sir."

"I didn't think so." Bridger grabbed Kindra's elbow and shoved her forward. "Get up to the house and be quick about it. I'm hungry. Nelly should have lunch waiting for me."

Kindra kept pace with the new master. Though he was handsome enough, the man hadn't smiled once during the whole ordeal. Even now, as they strode to the house, his brows were furrowed as if something beyond the business at hand needled him.

They soon came to the back steps of the house, and the door flew open. "Welcome home, Massa Bridger. Watcha got here?"

"Step aside, Nelly. I've brought the new downstairs maid for my wife. Is she up?"

Kindra listened intently, doing her best to get a feel for the way of things at Ash Haven. It was well past noon, so why had he asked if the mistress was up? She gazed at the plump cook, who wore a soiled white apron over her brown dress.

Nelly wiped her hands on a dish towel and waved it in the air. "I ain't seen the missus this morning. Mary has." She turned to a bean-pole of a woman, nearly six feet tall.

The woman towered over the others as she stepped up. "You need somethin', suh?"

Lawrence Bridger looked as if he were about to explode, his face reddening three shades darker. "Is the mistress up?"

Kindra was surprised at his even tone. She'd expected an outburst, but he'd taken a long breath before he asked about the mistress.

"Yer wife be up, Massa. But she hasn't left her chambers. Shall I fetch her?"

Bridger swiped his face with a handkerchief and rubbed his eyes with stiff fingers before he pinched the bridge of his nose. He walked to the dining room, looked around, hands on his hips, then raised a hand and walked back into the kitchen. "Nelly, show this nigger the downstairs rooms. Then show her where to find the cleaning supplies." He marched out of the kitchen, his footsteps echoing on the hardwood floors as he entered the foyer and climbed the stairs.

Kindra felt heat race up her neck and over her scalp. She couldn't recall anyone calling her such an abrasive name, even at Whitestone. She looked at the cooks and waited. Somewhere in the recesses of the house above, she heard pounding on a door. Did he have to knock to see the mistress?

Nelly shook her head and mumbled something under her breath. After the quick downstairs tour, they returned to the kitchen, where a door led to a pantry closet full of cleaning tools. Light from the outer room allowed Kindra to see rows of shelves, some filled with rags and brushes, buckets, and enamel bowls. Aprons hung from hooks, and mops and brooms leaned against the far wall.

Nelly plucked an apron off a hook. “Put this on.” As Kindra took the apron and tied it to her waist, the cook continued. “This be where you get your cleaning supplies. It’s up to you to put everything back where you found it. Massa expects everythin’ to be orderly. If he comes in and finds things layin’ where they don’t belong, you pay the fiddler for that.” She turned and walked out the back door.

Kindra followed close on her heels and looked where Nelly pointed. “That be the well. That’s where you be gettin’ yer water to mop the floors. Massa wants that done with hot water.” Nelly led her to the outer kitchen. “There be the woodstove. It’s up to you to stoke it with wood and get a fire goin’. Once you get the flames lickin’ up the sides o’ the stove, then set yer bucket o’ water to heatin’ up. Then you can mop the downstairs.” She lifted a finger. “Always start with the dining room first. He don’t like it if dinner’s late cause he waitin’ on floors to dry.”

Something told Kindra the new masters would be much like those at Whitestone. Her heart hit the flagstone floor, and she cleared her throat. “Anything else I should know?”

“Have you ever worked as a housekeeper before?”

“Yes, that was my last job before the owner sold us.”

“How come yer massa sold ya?”

Kindra felt heat rise up her neck again, remembering that awful day not so long ago. “He and the missus died.”

“Well, how did they sell ya if they be dead, child!”

“Their daughter inherited the plantation and all of us slaves. She didn’t want the plantation or us. She sold everything.”

“Well, ain’t that somethin’!” Her belly shook as she laughed. “Ain’t that all our dreams? We be wishin’ somethin’ bad be happenin’ to the master, too.” Her dark liquid eyes lit up. But then she sobered. “That wouldn’t be so bad if it happen to the massa at Ash Haven. But you gonna learn different ’bout the mistress. That is, iffen you git to meet her.”

“Why wouldn’t I meet the mistress?”

“She don’t come outta her bedchamber much these days. She be complainin’ ’bout headaches most all the time.” Nelly headed for the doorway. “You likely know more about yer job than I can tell ya. You best git at it before the day's gone."

"Should I heat the stove before I start sweeping?"

Nelly stopped dead in her tracks. "You sho' got yerself a fine way o' talkin'. Real refined like."

"Is that bad?"

"Where did you learn to talk like that?"

Kindra clutched the apron between her hands. "I, I . . ."

"Never mind . . ."

"What?"

"Massa don't say yer name."

"Kindra."

"That be a fine name, too. All right, git to work." Nelly walked to the house without looking back.

Kindra eyed the woodstove. Before long, she had a fire burning inside and a metal bucket full of water sitting on top. "I'd best start with the dining room," she mused. "Then I can tackle the others."

As the day wore on, she met the all-around servant, August, who did odd jobs for the women. She wondered if he would light the woodstove tomorrow if she asked him. Then she met the butler, Rufus, who was also Master Bridger's valet. He watched her with a nonchalant air.

An older woman came through the back door, carrying a wicker basket full of folded linens and towels. She stopped short of going to the hall closet and set the basket down. "You must be the new maid all the men be talkin' 'bout." She held out her hand.

"My name's Kindra." Kindra shook the woman's frail but warm hand.

"I'm Tamar. And all I do is laundry. Laundry be done day in and day out. The folks don't care if the bedding be touched or not. Every week I strip them beds that never a soul be seein'. I haul that bedding to the washroom. Course," her eyes lit up as if she had a secret. "Some o' the rooms ain't got a soul who live in 'em, but come mornin', it sho' look like somebody usin' 'em." She shook her head and picked up the heavy basket. "You'll git the feel o' things 'round here soon enough."

The day had seemed to go on forever, but one thing had really surprised her. When she stopped for a bite of food with the cooks in a small room off the kitchen, she couldn't believe her eyes. All the servants were seated at a table with food before them.

"Your mistress doesn't mind if you eat in the house?"

The servants looked at each other and then back at her. Some smiled, some looked downcast. Matthias, the stableman, whom she learned was also the carriage driver, bowed his head. All of the servants followed suit.

"Dear God, we be thankful for Your bounty. And we be thankful for the new maid who has joined us. Keep us safe in Your lovin' arms. Amen."

A murmur of "Amen" went around the table. Matthias looked at her with sorrowful eyes. "I take it you come from a master who don't share his food with the help."

"We had to wait till the end of the day and eat with the field hands," Kindra said, eyeing the warm stew on her plate and the bowl of biscuits at the center of the table. The clatter of spoons and talk filled the room as she asked, "Do you eat together every day?"

A woman answered. "You best quit talkin' and git to eatin'. The answer's 'yes,' we eat together every day, but they don't take to us lollygaggin' while we're at it."

"Sophy!" Nelly said. "She be new here. It's all right if she asks a few questions."

Sophy shrugged. "Suit yerself."

Kindra eyed the upstairs maid. Everything about her was well put together. She had a slim nose and thin lips, unlike the rest of the servants, who had broad noses and thick lips. Her hair was silky smooth and placed in a bun. Her body was slim and her height agreeable for one who'd been handed the gift of beauty, but her attitude stank.

After Kindra returned to work, she didn't stop thinking about Sophy. She swept and dusted the rooms without thought to her work. She didn't make it to the study before Nelly approached.

"Put yer cleanin' stuff away. Sammy's waitin' at the back door to show you to yer cabin."

When Kindra entered the kitchen, the cooks were bringing in a meal from the outer kitchen. Standing aside at the door, a tall middle-aged man waited for her. His eyes lit up when he saw her.

She went to the pantry and put her apron on a hook, ran her hands down her skirts, and took a deep breath. *What kind of living quarters await me here?* She stepped outside. “I’m ready.”

The slave district reminded her of Whitestone. Just like back there, many of the shacks held several families. Sometimes there were only two people per family, and the overseer wouldn’t let two or three people take up a shanty to themselves. Blankets were stacked against the walls by day, but at night, as many as eight to ten people filled the floors. Some shacks had two rooms. That allowed more people to share the shanty.

Kindra looked around the room where Sammy had delivered her. Several couples apparently lived there, along with an older man and a young teenage girl.

“My name’s Abraham,” said the old man. “I’m the oldest here, as you can see.” He looked at a young girl who eyed Kindra curiously. “This here’s Deborah.”

“Hello, Deborah. I’m Kindra. Do you mind if I put my blanket next to yours?”

The girl shook her head and pulled her blanket over.

“I sleep by the door,” Abraham said in a deep voice. “If we git comp’ny, I be the first to know.”

Sammy still stood at the door, eyeing Kindra. “Well, good night,” he told her. “It looks like you found a spot to sleep jist fine.”

“Thank you.” Kindra waved goodnight. The door closed, and everyone found their places. The fire crackled in the fireplace, sending warmth across the floor. Kindra heard Deborah’s soft snore beside her. She watched flames lick up the side of the charcoal stones. Loneliness crept inside her spirit. She was on a new plantation with people she didn’t know. At Whitestone, Cuffee had been there to lighten the blow. Tonight, she was all alone. *Dear God, You know where I am, even though my soul feels empty. Help me to fall asleep among these strangers, and I ask that You walk with me each day.*

And Lord, please send Denzel to find me. Tears slid down her cheeks as she watched the fire dance. The crackle and sparks continued as her lids grew heavy. This was the time of day she always loved. This is when she'd visit her family in her dreams. She curled up on her side and let slumber take over. *Come find me, Denzel. I'm waiting for you.*

THIRTEEN

Ash Haven Plantation, Charleston, South Carolina

"KINDRA, WAKE UP! You goin' to be late fer work!"

Kindra's eyes fluttered open, and she sat up swiftly as consciousness broke over her. She focused her vision on the crowded room. It was still dark outside, but a kerosene lamp was lit, throwing weak light across the floor.

The others were stretching and yawning as they rolled up their bedding. Kindra gazed at Deborah. "Thank you. I might have slept the day away if you hadn't awakened me." She wiped her eyes and gave the young girl a groggy smile.

"I 'spect you would do the same fer me if I slept in." She returned the smile but lowered her lids. "We best git movin'. Bart don't put up with us arrivin' late in the fields."

Kindra pulled on her worn shoes and tied them as she spoke. "Is it harvesting time?"

"It is. Cotton bolls sprung open 'bout a week ago." Deborah looked at the tips of her fingers.

Kindra laid a soft hand on the teenage girl's arm. "I came from a cotton plantation. I know how hard the work is. I'm sorry."

"There ain't no cause fer you to be sorry. You ain't pushin' us out in those fields." Her words were curt, but she eyed Kindra hungrily as if she needed a mother's touch.

Kindra withdrew her hand and rolled to her feet. Her skirts were rumpled, and she knew her hair was worse. Running a hand down her dress, she did her best to brush away the wrinkles and glanced around the dark room for a wall mirror. Seeing none, she said, "I'll plait your hair if you'll braid mine."

Deborah's eyes lit up. "I'm real good at doin' hair. Have a seat."

Kindra sat on a rickety chair and folded her hands on her lap. Deborah set to work combing her fingers through her hair. When the girl was done, Kindra grasped the braid and wound it into a tight bun atop her head. She reached inside her blouse and unclipped a hairpin she'd hidden there.

Deborah's eyes lit up again, and she crooked a smile. "You be full o' surprises. I 'spose we women have to find the means fer keepin' our hairpins safe."

Patting the sides of her hair, Kindra felt a little more put together. She eyed the girl's hair. It puffed out every which way as if the girl had had a fright. She stood and pointed to the chair. "Your turn."

"We's got to be quick about it. The sun's comin' up."

"I've had a little practice at this myself." Kindra deftly plaited the wayward hair into a single braid.

One by one, the slaves opened the door and stepped outside, each taking turns looking at them as Deborah sat straight as a pole. She began to fidget and stared back at the couples.

One woman stopped and locked her eyes on Kindra. "You sho' didn't waste no time settlin' in with our bunch. I guess you'll do jist fine." She patted Deborah's shoulder and filed out of the house with the others.

Kindra's stomach growled. "Do the slaves get breakfast?"

"Not till later in the morning. I don't know how it is up at the house."

"Do you want your hair pinned up?"

"That won't be necessary." Deborah stood and looked as if she ought to bolt out the door, but she turned swiftly and gave Kindra a quick hug. "I be seein' you tonight." The girl flew out the door and marched up the lane, tagging along behind old Abraham, who seemed to be waiting up for her. He lifted a hand and waved.

Kindra waved back and strode toward the Great House, wondering what the day would hold. She entered the back door and found the kitchen was alive. Nelly and Mary talked as they prepared breakfast.

"Morning!" Kindra moved toward the cleaning closet. She quickly tied her apron on and came back out with the mop over her shoulder and the bucket in her hand. She headed to the back as Nelly called, "Breakfast be ready in an hour. We feed the massa and the missus first, then the servants join in the back dining room like we did yesterday."

"All right." Kindra set her pail down and leaned the mop against the wall. "I suppose I ought to mop after breakfast."

"That's right." Nelly dipped a large spoon into a bowl and stirred it once before she scooped a heaping spoon of pancake batter onto the hot grease in the cast-iron skillet. The batter sizzled, sputtered, and bubbled as it cooked. Kindra watched the batter just long enough to see the pancake browning before Nelly flipped it over with a wide spatula. "Massa Bridger sho' like his pancakes toasty brown," she said and tilted her head toward the inner rooms. "You could git to work by startin' with the sittin' room. Git it swept and dusted. By then, we should be ready for our breakfast."

Kindra looked at the mop and bucket and decided to take Nelly up on her suggestion.

"You can leave it there. Ain't nobody gonna steal it," Nelly chuckled.

The sitting room was nicely furnished with a rich sense of interior design. Flowered armchairs and a sofa made it feel comfortable. Lamps with stained-glass shades and porcelain vases were placed on smooth wooden tables on each end of the couch. Kindra lost track of time as she cleaned, and she jumped when she saw Master Bridger watching her from the doorway.

"I'm sorry. I didn't know you were here." She swept a tendril off her forehead and hugged the broom to her chest. She didn't care for the light in the master's blue eyes.

"I've been standing here for the past five minutes."

"Did you need something, sir?"

His eyes roamed over her and lit up again, but just as quickly, his brows furrowed. "No. Not at the moment. Proceed." He turned and walked out of the room.

By mid-afternoon, Kindra was cleaning the master's study. She was surprised to find he kept his letters on the top of his desk, but she guessed it was unlikely any of the servants could read. As she straightened the pile, she looked to see if the butler was anywhere near the study. She hadn't read anything in so long, and now curiosity had her in its grip. She lifted a cream-colored parchment off the desk and began to read what appeared to be a legal document.

"What you doin'?"

Kindra dropped the paper and twirled around to find Sophy standing in the doorway. "I . . . I was moving the papers so I could dust," she stammered. She could see from Sophy's wary eyes that she hadn't fooled the upstairs maid one bit.

"You git caught with that paper in yer hand, Massa sends you out to the overseer. You don't want that. He'll beat the livin' daylight outta you."

Kindra asked, "You ever wish you could read all those funny marks on the paper?"

"No. Nevah. And you best git that notion outta yer head." Sophy gazed at her long and hard, then walked out.

Why had she come to the study? As far as Kindra knew, the woman's job was upstairs. Kindra went to work dusting the chairs' legs. Had she fooled Sophy into believing she couldn't read? She glanced once more at the document while she moved it aside to dust the table top. It looked like a business letter. She slowed her movements to read: Baxter & Steward, Attorney at Law.

I suppose when one had a plantation the size of this estate, one would need an attorney to keep legal matters in place. She moved on to shake the curtains and beat the dust out of them. Standing at the window, she glanced out at the acres and acres of cotton fields. Every row was manned by men, women, and children who picked the bolls and stuffed them in their shoulder bags. Though her body ached from non-stop work, she was grateful to be working inside the house.

Her mind traveled thousands of miles away to the lush island of Barbados. Visions of large-leafed tobacco fields filled her mind. She could smell the spicy tang of the dried leaves in the curing barn, and she could hear the slaves singing their soulful songs. *When Lord? When will I get to go home?*

Sophy rapped on the mistress's bedchamber door but didn't wait for a reply. She stepped into the room, head held high.

Phoebe sat against her fluffy pillows in bed, a photo frame in her hand.

She scowled and rubbed her temple with two fingers. "What brings you to my room this time of day? You know better than to intrude on my privacy." She set the frame face down on the coverlet and clamped her hands together.

"Massa done bought another maid fer the house."

"Of course he did. I sent him to do so." Phoebe looked annoyed.

"I jist found her in the massa's study, snoopin' 'round his desk. She be holdin' one o' them fancy papers and readin' it." Sophy straightened her shoulders, her nose in the air, sure her message would alert the mistress that she had trouble in the house. She hoped the news would send that prissy new woman out to see Bart, their overseer. A darky readin' white folk's business was cause enough for a good lashing. Maybe this would get that beauty out of the house and into the fields. She didn't need competition here at Ash Haven. All the servants knew Massa Bridger favored her over the others, especially in the wee hours of the night. She had already caught the master watching that woman while she was cleaning the sitting room. The sooner the mistress sends her to the cotton fields, the better.

Phoebe's head jerked up, her eyes wide. "Can she read?"

"She say she wishin' so. Truth be, she holdin' that paper like she readin' it." She stepped back, hoping her mission had worked. "I be warnin' the twit to keep Massa's papers outta her hands if she don't want no whippin."

"Send her here."

"Ma'am?"

"Do as I say, Sophy. Send her to my room."

"Yes'm, Miz Phoebe." Sophy curtsied and slipped merrily out of the room. She wished she could be a mouse in the mistress's pocket. The new maid was surely in for a browbeating. She found Kindra in the sunroom, wiping a cloth over a large vase. "Miss Phoebe wantin' to see you."

Kindra looked up with dismay. "You told on me?"

"I did. Now don't keep the mistress waitin'. And don't take up too much of her time, she's havin' another one of her migraines."

Kindra set her cleaning cloth in the bucket and straightened her shoulders. She slipped past Sophy and went quietly up the stairs, not once looking back.

Sophy watched the elegant slave climb the stairs and muttered to herself. "She sho' don't be actin' like one o' us. She be climbin' those stairs in a stately manner, carryin' herself like she thinks she somebody. If I don't know bettah, that woman ain't always been a slave." She glanced at the top of the stairs where Kindra had disappeared. "I best be keepin' an eye on that one. If anyone can find dirt on her, it be me."

Kindra rapped lightly on the door and lifted her chin for what was to come.

"Come in," came a soft voice.

She entered the mistress's sitting chamber. The room was delightfully decorated in soothing hues. The settee and armchairs were covered in a creamy white with dual shades of blue and floral designs. She stepped farther into the room and glanced to her left. The bedchamber door was open, and she saw the soft hues of a cream-colored quilt and beige chairs to the side.

Phoebe gazed out the window, her back to Kindra. She wore a pale blue gown, and her shiny brown hair was swept up neatly into a loose bun. Tendrils of curls fell down her neck and over her temples. The woman was thin and willowy, exuding elegance.

"You wanted to see me, Miss?"

Phoebe turned around and eyed her for a long moment. A mixture of emotions played on the woman's face. "Sophy said you can read."

Kindra opened her mouth and then shut it. She couldn't lie to the new mistress, but dare she tell the truth? "I can, some."

"How is it that you're a darky, and you can read?"

"My mother was African, but my father was English."

Phoebe's shoulders raised, and her brows grew together. "That doesn't answer my question. There are always illegitimate darkies born to their white masters, but that doesn't give them the right to read."

Kindra held her breath. *How much of my past should I disclose?* "It's a long story, ma'am, but I wasn't always a slave."

"Really?" Phoebe's shoulders relaxed, and she gave a little smile. "I want to learn more about your past, but for now, you may be worth more to me than all the slaves on this plantation. Come, sit down." She gestured to the blue-flowered settee.

Stunned, Kindra crossed the floor and sat on the sofa, placing her hands on her lap. Wary that this could be a trap, she held her shoulders stiff and waited.

Phoebe shut the door and sat beside her. "I have a secret I've never told anyone except my husband."

Kindra watched the color deepen on Phoebe's cheeks.

"I can't read."

Kindra's head jerked up. "What do you mean you can't read? You're a white woman. I . . ."

Phoebe's finger went to her lips, and she swallowed. "I used to be able to read. It seems that though I come from a wealthy family and have brought a fortune to this plantation, this did not allow me to escape the inevitable. I haven't been able to maintain my vision. You see . . . as time goes by, my eyes have become worse." She shrugged. "Oh, I can see the usual things, but when it comes to small print on letters or books, all I see is a blur."

"I'm sorry to hear that. Have you seen an eye doctor?"

"No. Call it pride, but I don't want to wear spectacles, and that's what the doctor would recommend."

"I don't understand. If you can't read . . ."

"You will do that for me. You read well, don't you?"

Kindra's shoulders slumped, and she resigned herself to telling the truth. "Very well, ma'am."

"Good. My husband will be gone tomorrow. I will bring the letters and documents he has left on his desk into my study across the hall. We will take each one and go through them."

"Yes, ma'am. But why not just ask him to read them to you?"

Phoebe shook her head vehemently. "No. He's been too secretive. He's up to something." She waved the thought away. "I plan to find out what it is."

"Oh." Kindra eyed the slim woman beside her. Was this why she was having migraines?

Phoebe flashed a narrow eye at Kindra. "You speak well for a darky."

"As I said, my father was an Englishman."

"And he schooled you?"

"Yes, Cameron and I."

"Who's Cameron?"

"My father's adopted son."

"Well, I can see you have loads of stories to share with me. I want to hear everything. For now, you're dismissed. When Master Bridger's carriage drives away in the morning, come see me. We'll get started."

"Yes, ma'am."

Kindra stepped out of the house that evening and strode to the slave shanties, a million questions going through her head. *What have I gotten myself into?*

FOURTEEN

FROM HER WINDOW, Phoebe watched the carriage carrying her husband drive away. She clutched her fists to her sides and turned to face Sophy when she came into the room. "I'm going downstairs for breakfast. Get me dressed."

"You must be feeling a heap bettah if you goin' downstairs."

"Yes. The migraines eased off last evening, and I'm feeling quite well. Now fetch me the green plaid skirt and a white blouse. I have a busy day ahead of me."

"Lordy, Miz Phoebe, you really do feel bettah."

Phoebe's hand flew up. "Quit wasting my time with your chatter."

"Yes'm." Sophy opened the wardrobe, shoved gowns aside, and pulled out the plaid skirt in forest green and black. Lying it carefully on the bed, she opened the other side of the wardrobe and searched until she found the starched white top the mistress preferred.

A few minutes later, dressed and with her hair styled atop her head, Phoebe stepped outside the bedchamber and looked down the long corridor for the first time in weeks. It felt good to be out and about the mansion. She heard sounds below and gracefully descended the stairs.

Rufus greeted her with a bow. "Why, good mornin', Miz Phoebe. You be lookin' refreshed as a sparrow on a spring day."

"Thank you, Rufus." With her shoulders lifted a little higher, she nodded and went on to the dining room. Pots and pans clanged and dishes rattled as the cooks scurried to prepare breakfast. When she pushed the door open and entered the large kitchen, both cooks stopped dead away and looked at her.

"Well, goodness gracious," Mary said. "Good mornin', Miz Phoebe.

You all dressed and lookin' as though you're on a mission!" She smiled widely and her eyes lit up.

"Will you be havin' yer breakfast downstairs this mornin'?" Nelly smiled as she wiped her hands with a towel.

"I will. Is it about ready?" Warmth filled Phoebe's heart for her slaves. She had always treated them with respect, and in return, they did the same.

"We'll have yer meal on the table in two shakes of a lamb's tail," Nelly said. "You jist sit yerself, and we'll bring it right out."

"Thank you." Phoebe went to the dining room and walked around the table, arms crossed over her chest. She noticed movement in the sitting room and looked to see Kindra polishing the fireplace mantle.

The fireplace held a few embers, and the room was chilled. Kindra worked carefully, lifting porcelain figurines as she ran a dust rag over their surfaces. After a moment, she looked over her shoulder and jumped. "I didn't see you, Miss Phoebe." She set the figurine on the mantle and folded her hands. "You're up. You must be feeling better." Her gaze went to the window facing the front drive. "I see Master Bridger has gone."

"Yes. We have the day to ourselves," Phoebe said in a low voice. "I will send for you after you've had breakfast."

"All right."

"Carry on." Phoebe went back to the dining room and sat at the head of the long table. A sideboard decorated with vases and a silver tea set was centered along one wall. Oil paintings of fruit bowls and flowers hung on the walls. Pale blue satin drapes partially covered the leaded window panes, and small tables with figurines sat on each side of the entrance. The room was large and airy and should have been used often to entertain guests, but it had been far too long since she and her husband had done so. As time wore on, they didn't sit together here. He went his way, and she went hers.

They'd grown apart; his evenings were spent at gambling houses. She had entertained herself with reading in the evenings, that is, until the pages had begun to blur. Straining to read had given her such terrible migraines that she gave up the hobby. Instead, she resorted to going to bed early and sleeping the nights away.

"Here you go." Nelly brushed the door aside with her hip and carried a plate of scrambled eggs and fruit to Phoebe. "Will you be having coffee or hot tea?"

"Coffee will do."

"I'll be right back." She pushed through the door again, and it swung behind her.

Phoebe snapped the white napkin open and placed it on her lap. She bowed her head and said grace. When finished, she set to work on her meal. When Kindra came out of the sitting room a few minutes later, cleaning tools in hand, Phoebe barely looked at her. Instead, she moved into the sunroom, retrieved her journal, and went to her sitting room. There, she slid onto the soft sofa and rang the bell on the table.

"You rang?" Mary asked.

"Bring me a cup of hot tea, and while you're at it, tell Rufus I need him. It's chilly in here."

"Right away, Miss."

The fire had burned down to hot embers, not nearly enough to make her warm. She cupped her elbows while she waited.

Rufus entered the room and asked, "You needin' me, Miz Phoebe?"

"I'm chilled to the bone. Please feed the fire."

"Of course." Rufus shoved another piece of wood onto the fire grate. After a moment, he stood and watched the flames lick higher. "That ought to warm the room some."

"Thank you. You may leave."

"Yes'm."

Phoebe felt so chilled she wished she could crawl into the flames. The coldness came from within, she knew. The distance between her and Lawrence had become icy and now seeped into her bones. Silence filled the room, broken only by the crackling embers. She stared into the fire, determined that today was the day she'd start to set things right. There was much to find out, and she'd put it off for far too long. It was time to discover the secrets in this house. Glancing at the journal, she wrote a to-do list in large letters. When finished, she rang the bell again. "Yes'm, Miss Phoebe?" Nelly asked.

"Bring the tea to my study."

"Yes'm."

Phoebe went into her husband's study and stared at the letters and documents strewn on top of the mahogany desk. She smiled ruefully at how careless Lawrence had been to leave them there. One by one, she picked up the parchments and crisp papers and stacked them until she had a bundle of papers in her hand. She opened the middle drawer and found a couple of small envelopes that had been unsealed. She collected those, too. When done, she hugged the stack to her chest and glanced around the room. It had been far too long since she'd set foot here, but after today, she would visit often. She'd let Lawrence think he had the upper hand, but she was ready to retake control of her affairs.

She climbed the stairs. With no one else in the hall, she opened the door to her study and hid the letters in a desk drawer. Brushing her hands together and stepping out of the room, she glanced in the guest room and saw Sophy fluffing the pillows. "Have you seen the new maid reading any more letters?" She wanted the chambermaid to think she was at odds with Kindra. She couldn't afford for the persnickety maid to guess the real reason for the time spent with her.

"No, ma'am." Sophy's eyes brightened. "Shall I go downstairs and watch her?"

"I want to speak with her again. Send her to my office."

"Yes, ma'am, right away, ma'am."

"I want no one on the upper floors while I speak with her. You'll stay downstairs until I summon you."

"Of course." Sophy's shoulders lifted merrily, and she sailed downstairs.

Phoebe heard the maid's footsteps on the hardwood floor as she walked down the hall below. Why was she so eager to see the new maid harassed? Generally, the darkies looked out for one another. Sophy was up to something, and until she knew what it was, she'd keep her eyes and ears open. Could she trust her chambermaid? Was she the one who crept through the halls at night after all the lamps were out?

She'd heard footsteps many nights, and she knew something was going on. Fearful of what she'd find, she would hug the sheets to her chin, listen to the floor creak and the soft closing of a door down the hall. Part of her didn't want to know the truth. Instead, she'd closed her eyes and tried to drown out the sounds of the night. Now she was ready to put an end to it and ready to get her life back. Only in her late thirties, she still had a lot of living to do.

Activity in the Bridger house seemed normal from the vantage point of the average eye, and what the servants didn't know, Kindra intended to keep secret. She couldn't afford for Sophy or anyone else to discover she could read. That knowledge could send her to the whipping post. How the mistress would keep this to herself, she didn't know, but Kindra's stomach had been in knots ever since she left the Great House the night before.

Before breakfast, she had watched Lawrence Bridger walk out of the house, dressed in a fine gray suit and carrying a small overnight bag. She knew it wouldn't be long before the mistress called for her. Now, when she stepped into the study, she found the desk was swept clean of all letters and documents. Had Phoebe been here?

Interrupting her thoughts, Sophy walked up behind her and said in a stiff voice, "The mistress be seein' you in her study. She says you bettah be quick about it, too." She glared harshly at Kindra.

Kindra slipped past the brittle maid, jutted out her chin, and ascended the stairs. When she reached the landing, Phoebe waved her into the room and shut the door. "Have a seat."

Two chairs sat before the desk, and all of Master Bridger's mail was laid out on the desktop. Kindra felt her skin tingle as she looked at Phoebe. There was no turning back now. Whatever they found would likely change the course of the mistress's life.

Phoebe lifted a parchment that appeared to be a legal document. "Start reading."

There were three letters from Lawrence Bridger's attorneys, Baxter & Steward. The documents thanked him for coming by and listed several requirements: medical proof that Mrs. Bridger was not of sound mind and could not make decisions for herself, proof of the deed to the property at Ash Haven, and the signatures of parties with access to the holdings at their bank.

"Well," Phoebe said breathlessly. "He's been busy, hasn't he?" She brushed her skirts nervously and leaned toward another letter. "Read this one."

Kindra held the letter.

My Dearest Lawrence,

I enjoyed the dinner last week. You are quite the gentleman. I would like very much to see you again. Perhaps we can go horse riding or have a picnic by the river. My parents will be taking a short trip to Georgia in the near future, and I will have the estate to myself. There are too many rooms in the house alone. If this interests you, please send a post.

Your dearest,

Candace Bigsby

Phoebe looked stunned. "So, he has a lover, does he?" She clamped her jaw tightly and looked at Kindra. "I'm not surprised. I've had my suspicions for some time now." Even so, tears rimmed her eyes, and she brushed them away.

"I'm sorry, Miss Phoebe. No woman should ever have to endure this kind of treatment." Kindra looked kindly at her. She wanted to reach out but kept her hands in her lap.

After reading many more letters, Phoebe looked at the envelopes and letters they'd gone through. "There's one more letter, and we'll be done." She shoved a note to Kindra. It looked as if someone with little education had written it.

Dear Mister Bridger,

I got your message. There's a discrepancy in the fee. I don't come cheap. If you want the job done right, you'll pay the price. I will wait for further notice.

E. M.

Kindra looked up with furrowed brows. "What is this?"

Phoebe leaned forward and eyed the chicken scratch. "I don't know. The message is vague, but it sounds as if my husband is hiring this person to do something, possibly illegal, for a handsome price."

Kindra felt she understood the note better than her mistress. "I think it's more than that."

"What?" The color drained from Phoebe's face.

"I'm afraid to voice what I make of it."

"You will tell me."

Kindra swallowed the lump in her throat. "This sounds like your husband has hired someone to . . . to . . . ." She lowered her lids and stared at the scrawny writing.

Phoebe's face paled as white as the parchment she held. "Would he kill me to get his hands on all my holdings?"

Kindra gently touched the mistress's arm to steady her. "I don't know the man."

"I shouldn't have married him. My father warned me not to." Phoebe dropped the letter on the desk.

Kindra held her tongue.

"When I married Lawrence, I brought with me a large fortune. My father gave me Ash Haven as part of our wedding gift, as he and Mother were getting on in years and wanted to enjoy the rest of their days free of obligations. It was a wonderful gift, and I promised Father we'd continue to make profits from the cotton crops." Phoebe dabbed at her eyes with a lacy handkerchief. "It wasn't long before I realized we were losing money at the bank at a rapid pace. Though the account was originally in my name, I had added my husband."

She shook her head, and the veins in her neck looked strained. "When I met him, he was so charming and debonair. He said all the right things to make a woman swoon." She shook her head. "I fell for all his tricks. After we married, I soon learned he was a gambler and a cheat." She licked her lips and massaged her temples as if her migraine had returned. "I couldn't tell my father that my husband was draining our finances dry, not to mention he had no interest in the plantation. He's left it all to the new overseer, whom I'm not sure I can trust at all."

Kindra patiently held her tongue and listened.

"Over time, I realized if I were to save the plantation, I had to take charge of the money at the bank. I retracted his signature and told the manager they were not to release any more funds to him. Lawrence was so angry. We fought for hours after he found out. But when I agreed to give him a handsome allowance, he seemed to accept it."

"But now he's getting even with you," Kindra said.

"It looks as if that's the case. He never has enough money. He throws it away at the gambling tables and, apparently, on other women."

Kindra laid the note on the table and waited.

Phoebe straightened. "We need to see Mister Croft, my attorney. I will fight Lawrence all the way. If he is trying to steal my father's plantation, he'll lose."

"It's good you already have a lawyer."

"Of course, I do. Mister Croft has been my attorney for many years. He handles all my legal affairs for the cotton plantation and the house."

"He's only your attorney and not Master Bridger's?"

"Yes." Phoebe held her hands in her lap. "I suppose I knew long ago this day would come. I didn't trust Lawrence."

"From the documents here, it looks like the master has started proceedings, but his lawyers can do nothing without all the information they've requested. You may be able to beat him at his own tricks."

Phoebe looked Kindra in the eye. "You're not like any darky I've ever met. You're intelligent and exude self-assurance. There's more to you than what meets the eye."

"Miss Phoebe, you'd be surprised if you knew where I come from." Kindra clamped her hands together and raised her head. "We both have sorely walked a path no woman should ever travel."

"You will go with me to town. You can tell me your story on the way." She opened the door. "We'll be leaving within the hour."

"I'll be ready."

The carriage pulled up in front of Croft & Zimmerman, Attorneys at Law. The driver opened the door. "Here we are, Mrs. Bridger." He reached out a hand to assist her.

"Thank you." Phoebe stepped out and turned to Kindra. "You'll come with me."

The driver stepped back as Kindra stepped to the ground.

The two women walked into the attorney's office and stopped in a mahogany-paneled room where a middle-aged clerk sat behind his desk. "May I help you?" He glanced from Phoebe to Kindra and frowned.

"I'm here to see Mister Croft if he has a moment."

"Certainly." The clerk disappeared behind a polished door. Moments later, he reappeared with Mister Croft on his heels.

"Mrs. Bridger, it's a pleasure to see you again." The attorney reached out and shook Phoebe's hand, then glanced at Kindra with brows raised. "Your slave woman can wait outside while we attend to business."

"She will come with me." Phoebe stood straighter.

"I beg your pardon?"

"I said my servant will come with me."

"We don't allow nig . . ."

"I suppose I shall have to take my business elsewhere, Mister Croft." Phoebe twirled toward the door.

"No, no." The lawyer jumped forward and touched her shoulder as his face turned three shades of red. "That won't be necessary. She can come with you."

"Very well then." Phoebe hooked her hand in the crook of Kindra's arm, and the two women marched into the attorney's office.

Kindra felt her skin prickle as the desk clerk and the attorney scowled at her. As she took the chair next to Phoebe in front of the large desk, she fought the urge to keep her eyes on her hands in her lap.

Mister Croft sat down and bridged his fingers. "How can I help you today?"

"Mister Bridger has given me cause to believe I need to draw up papers denying him the rights to the funds in the bank, proceeds from the cotton plantation, and anything tied to Ash Haven." She handed him the documents she and Kindra had found earlier that morning.

Kindra watched Phoebe sit straight as a pole, her hands clamped together and her feet firmly planted on the floor. She was a picture of composed perfection. But it was all for show. The migraines persisted, and after the shocking blow Phoebe had encountered just that morning, her nerves must undoubtedly be a wreck. She admired the mistress for her calm, collected demeanor.

Mister Croft silently read the request from Mister Bridger's attorneys and scribbled something on the paper before him. He looked up. "You are aware, of course, that your husband legally has control of Ash Haven. It doesn't matter that your parents gave you the plantation and the slaves as a wedding gift."

"But the plantation belonged to my father before he gave it to us. Wouldn't that make a difference?"

"As a matter of fact, no."

Phoebe's lips thinned, and she shook her head. "This is wrong, Mister Croft. There's no way Lawrence should have control of Ash Haven."

From the looks of these documents, he apparently doesn't realize the control he holds on the land. I find it curious his attorney hasn't informed him of such."

"Well, better that he doesn't know. I want to fight it, Mister Croft. I want to fight for my land in court."

"It would be a waste of time, not to mention the fees involved."

Phoebe reared back and stared at the attorney. "I beg your pardon?"

"Ma'am?"

"Fighting for my father's property would not be a waste of time, and I am not concerned about the fees."

Mister Croft wiped his hand over his face and looked Phoebe in the eye. "All right. I will draw up the papers. Mister Bridger will have to be served to appear in court." He tapped his pencil on the polished desk as if deep in thought.

"Is there anything else you need to proceed?" Phoebe clutched her purse tightly in her lap.

"You can't have him served as long as he lives in the same home as you."

"Oh." Phoebe glanced at Kindra and then back to the attorney. "Then I will return when Lawrence has moved out."

"I don't want to speak out of line . . . but has . . ."

"No. He hasn't said a word about moving out." Phoebe's chin went up. "But he will."

Mister Croft visibly swallowed. "Anything else?"

"Yes. I'm filing for divorce."

The attorney leaned back in his chair and pulled a handkerchief out of his pants pocket. He wiped his brow and then behind his neck. The announcement seemed to unnerve him. "Are you sure you want to do that, Mrs. Bridger?"

Phoebe leaned forward. "I've never been surer of anything in my life."

He scribbled on the paper again and laid the pencil down. "I will have the papers drawn up this week. That is the one thing you can do without reservations . . . on the grounds of drunkenness, insanity, or desertion, and of course, adultery."

"I understand. For the most part, he fits all of the above."

"Then I'll draw up the divorce papers." He leaned back, picked up the pencil, and twisted it in his fingers.

"I don't want any of this revealed to my husband until I'm ready."

"Yes, of course, Mrs. Bridger." Mister Croft held her eye. "Once you've signed the papers, we can set a court date."

"That will be fine." Phoebe stood. "Until then."

"Until then." Mister Croft shoved his chair back and escorted Phoebe to the door. Kindra followed at a safe distance behind.

Once outside, Phoebe said, "Mister Croft can be trying at times, but he's a good lawyer."

"I wouldn't trust him, Miss Phoebe."

The women climbed into the coach. Once the rig started rolling, Phoebe leaned back and turned to Kindra. "Now tell me about your past."

Kindra spent the ride back to Ash Haven telling the mistress all about Denzel and her children, Kindra Hall, and Barbados. Before she finished her story, Mistress Phoebe understood that Kindra, too, was a mistress of her own plantation. Kindra took a breath. "All I've wanted these past seven years is to return home to my family and to my plantation." She brushed away a tear.

Phoebe had gazed out of the window as she listened to Kindra's story. When Kindra finished, she looked at her for a long moment. "You are my slave. You belong to me. I intend to keep you." She looked out the window again as the rig bounced along the cobbled road.

Kindra swallowed, and a shiver ran down her back. At that moment, hopelessness knocked on the door of her heart.

Once they arrived at the house, Phoebe handed her husband's mail to Kindra. "Put these back on Lawrence's desk. See to it that it looks as though nothing has been disturbed."

"Right away, Miss." Kindra clutched the stack of mail that could very well indict the master's demise. When she entered his study, she placed the envelopes and documents onto his desk as she remembered them.

When evening came, she left the house and strode toward the shanties. She watched the field hands work their way back, too. Did anyone at Ash Haven have any idea the plantation was in a world of trouble? Did they know the two people who ran their lives were barely hanging on by a thread?

"Lord, have mercy," she sighed. "If only I could get back home to the solace of my family, where our life was peaceful and where secrets don't exist."

She had seen a light shine in Phoebe's eyes as she told the woman everything there was to know about her. It appeared the mistress felt a kindred spirit toward her, but she said she would never release Kindra from slavery. *She needs me right now,* Kindra thought. *She needs my eyes. Lord, keep me safe under the shadow of Your wings. And if it be Your will, send Denzel to find me.*

FIFTEEN

River Oak, Fields Landing, South Carolina

THE FEVER HADN'T taken a firm hold on River Oak this year. The Bartholomews had lost a couple of slaves and thanked the good Lord for sparing the rest that summer. Now, here lay Grace in and out of consciousness, burning up with fever. Kit threw herself into nursing her mother, her mind numb to personal danger. She knew the disease could kill her, but what mattered was doing all she could to help her mother get well.

Kit spent most of her waking hours sponging her mother's brow with a wet cloth. Gemma daily carried out and washed the bedclothes that Grace's sweaty body had soiled, and she tried to get Grace to swallow soup when she could.

Now, nearly two weeks since Grace had taken ill, Kit sat in the chair and read while her mother slept. It was in the wee hours of the morning, while the rain pummeled the world outside, that she caught a slight movement as her mother awoke.

"Kit?" Grace croaked.

Kit set the book on the nightstand and went to the bedside. "You're awake. How do you feel?"

"Sluggish . . . like mush." A weak smile formed on Grace's lips. "Is your father home?"

"No, he and Uncle Denzel are still searching for Aunt Kindra. But you should try to go back to sleep, Mother. It's the middle of the night."

"Oh." Grace turned her head to look at the windows. Kit did too. Deep black was all she saw, along with the reflection of the kerosene lamp, flickering a dim light. Outside, the rain dribbled down the pane. Kit looked at the clock. It was two in the morning.

"I feel as if I've been sleeping my life away."

"You're getting the rest your body desperately needs."

"I need to use the water closet. Can you help me up?"

"Of course." Kit turned down the bedcovers and reached her arm under her mother's neck to lift her.

"Oh!" Grace moaned and clasped her fingers on Kit's arm. "The room is spinning."

"Just sit still a moment until you get your bearings," Kit said, holding her steady.

A moment later, her mother dropped one leg off the bed and scooted to place her other foot on the floor. Kit pulled her to her feet and steadied her until she felt confident enough to stand without falling.

"Oh, Kit. How did this happen to me?"

"I don't know, but we're going to get you through it."

With slow steps, she walked her mother into the bathroom. They only had to go a few feet inside the door to reach the chamber chair, with a white metal pot beneath it. Kit guided Grace until she was safely seated.

"Oh, my," Grace said, looking as if she were trying to still herself. "My head is swimming, but it feels good to be out of bed."

Kit stood close by as Grace sat on the chair. Several moments later, she guided her mother back to bed.

"Let me sit here a moment. I'm not ready to lie down."

"All right," Kit said, keeping a vigilant eye on her mother.

"I hope your father and Denzel bring Kindra home tomorrow."

"Me, too, Mama. It's been hard on Damaris. She cried herself to sleep tonight."

"Poor dear. I can't imagine what she's going through."

"I can't either." Kit looked at her frail mother. She couldn't stand the thought of life without her. "I love you, Mother."

Grace looked up with tears in her eyes. "I love you too, Kit. You're such a good daughter."

Kit hugged her mother and felt the clammy sweat on her skin. "You should lie down. I'll put the covers over you."

"I suppose you're right." Grace yawned. "I'm beginning to feel cold."

Once Kit had her mother settled, she sat on the edge of the bed and watched her.

"I have something I want you to do," Grace said.

"What's that?"

"I want you to send for Mrs. Unruh. We have to begin the gowns for your coming-out party."

"No, Mama. I can't possibly consider such a selfish deed."

"Is it selfish to help me keep my mind off this horrible headache?"

"Of course not."

"Then do as I say," Grace said. She took a breath and swallowed. "Send a note to Mrs. Unruh and tell her we're ready for her to make the dresses."

Kit bit her bottom lip. "This seems so frivolous when there is the pressing matter of getting you well."

Grace took Kit's hand. "I choose to believe this is just a short drawback. Doctor Moab said I'm getting better. I have to get rid of these headaches. I won't let this fever consume me."

The rain pitter-pattered against the house, and dribbles of water slid down the window as they gazed at each other.

"All right, Mama. I'll send for the seamstress, but I'm not doing it for me."

"Thank you, dear."

Kit watched as her mother's hand slipped to the side of the bed, and her brows furrowed. When Grace's eyes closed and a soft moan escaped her lips, Kit quietly stood and pulled the coverlet under her mother's chin. A moment later, she heard a soft snore; Grace's breathing seemed regular. Kit kissed her fingers, laid them on her mother's head, then lifted her chin and left the room. If her mother wanted to see the seamstress, she would make sure Mrs. Unruh came.

At mid-afternoon the next day, the sound of wagon wheels filled the front drive. The family had kept themselves busy inside the house as the rains continued to fall. But at the sound of the wagon, they ran onto the front porch to see if Kindra was with the men.

Damaris stepped forward and peered over the porch rail. "She's not with them." Her tone was despondent, and Kit slipped an arm around her waist.

"Maybe they have news of her."

"Yes. Maybe."

Nate ran out to the drive and took the reins as Denzel and Cameron climbed down and walked to the side steps that led up to the porch. Both men removed their wet hats and beat them against their pant legs before Denzel spoke. "We didn't find her."

"I'm sorry, Father." Damaris broke away from Kit and threw her arms around Denzel.

"You're gonna get your nice dress all wet," Denzel said, pushing her back. "Let me change my clothes, and we'll meet in the parlor. I do have a bit of news about your mama."

Damaris gazed at him with a hopeful look in her eyes. "Will she be coming home?"

"We'll get her home, Damaris. How soon, we don't know."

Zeddie stood behind Damaris, watching the conversation. Kit went to him and threw an arm over his shoulder. "Let's get the men in the house. They need to dry off and change their clothes." She dropped her arm and turned toward the front door. "I'll have the cooks bring out some dessert and hot coffee."

"Thank you, Kit," Cameron said. "All right, everybody, back into the house before we're all as wet as hens!"

In dry clothes and freshened up, Cameron sat on the edge of Grace's bed. She had waited impatiently for him, wanting nothing more than to have him here by her side.

"What did you find out?" she asked weakly.

"It was nothing more than a rabbit chase," he said.

"You didn't find Kindra?"

"No. We have little to go on, but we know she's on a plantation somewhere in the area of Charleston. Nothing more."

"Now what?"

"I've decided to hire some agents to hunt for her. They'll have to scour the countryside. Maybe they can find her."

Grace looked at her husband, relieved to have him home. He was a handsome man even in his fifties. The years had enhanced his good looks. His thick black hair had flecks of white and silver strands intermixed throughout. A two-day growth of beard shadowed his narrow face and cleft chin and down his neck. Lines had deepened the furrows of his brow, and crow's feet lined the sides of his eyes. She relished the changes that had taken place in his features, and she drank in the charcoal-gray eyes that gazed at her now.

"I'm glad you're home." She reached for his hand.

He bent down and kissed her forehead. "I couldn't get here fast enough."

Love for this man swelled inside of her. "I'm not letting you out of my sight for a while."

He brushed the damp curls off her forehead.

His touch was reassuring. "I'm sleepy."

"Get your rest." He kissed her again and laid a rough hand on her cheek.

She smiled inside. The world was sinking away as darkness clutched her in its grip. She heard footsteps fade across the floor before she fell into deep slumber.

Grace's first outburst of pain from the excruciating headache woke Cameron from a deep sleep in the middle of the night. Her skin was inflamed, and she was as red as hot coals as she thrashed unconsciously on her pillow. He rushed to her side and saw her tossed to and fro as her hands clutched her head. Her auburn curls were damp with sweat, and the moan that escaped her throat sent a lick of fear up Cameron's spine. *She's getting worse!*

Pulling on his boots and britches, he left the room and knocked on Kit's chamber door. She opened it and stepped out of the room, wearing a long, white nightgown. "What is it? Is Mother okay?"

"She's burning up! I'm going after Doctor Moab. I need you to sit with her."

"Of course." Kit ran to her mother's room while Cameron dashed down the stairs and out the front door.

The night was cool as he strode quickly past the slaves' bungalows. Soon, he came to Doctor Moab's shack and pounded. Moab jerked the door open and peered out at him.

"Grace has taken a turn for the worse," Cameron said. "Something's terribly wrong with her. You have to come to the house."

"Let me get my bag!"

Cameron didn't wait. Dogs barked as he ran back to the house, leaving the front door open for the doctor. He continued up the stairs as Jake took up the cause of barking with the other dogs. As he reached the top of the stairs, Cameron heard the front door close and the sound of the doctor's heavy footsteps working his way up to the landing.

The kerosene lamp was lit, and Kit soothed her mother as though Grace were a child. "You're going to be all right," she said softly and brushed Grace's wet curls off her forehead with a damp cloth. "The doctor will be here soon, and then you'll be fine."

Cameron watched his daughter with a lump in his throat. He was so proud of the woman Kit had become. She had a gentle heart and a love for her family. He entered the bedchamber and stood by her side. "How is she?"

Kit shook her head, and her eyes were round with fear. "I've never seen her like this."

Doctor Moab moved to the opposite side of the bed and leaned over Grace. She thrashed and moaned, but not once did she open her eyes. She coughed, and the hacking lasted so long that she gagged and vomited on her pillow.

"Oh, Mother!" Kit removed the pillow as quickly as she could. Cameron moved to shove a clean pillow under Grace's head, but Kit's hand went up. "Not yet. We need to clean her hair first."

Kit dipped the cloth in tepid water and wrung it out. She carefully cleaned Grace's hair and crooned as she freshened her mother.

Cameron watched as his wife groaned. "Is she going to be all right?" he asked, his gut in a knot.

Kit removed the blankets as Hedy rushed into the room and went to work. "We've got to take off her nightgown and put on a fresh one," Kit instructed the chambermaid.

Together, Kit and Hedy changed Grace's clothes while she continued to cough and moan. Gemma appeared at the door with a bundle of fresh bedclothes. "I heard the commotion and come runnin'. Figured you'd need me. Mastah Camp, if'n you could move Miss Grace, we could fix her bed."

Cameron carefully picked up his wife. She'd lost weight these last few weeks; it was easy to hold her in his arms. Suddenly, her head fell back and her arms hung lifelessly at her sides. He lifted her limp body close to his heart and kissed her cheek. "Come on, Grace. You've got to pull out of this."

He watched Gemma and Hedy work quickly to pull the sheets tightly across the bed and tuck the long ends under the mattress. They worked in unison to spread the blankets on top, and when finished, Gemma pulled one side down.

Cameron gently laid Grace down and set her head on the fresh pillow. He pulled the blankets over her shivering body and saw her teeth chatter again.

All the while, Doctor Moab stood back with Kit by his side. He held a brown bottle of quinine. Once his patient was settled, he moved to Grace's side and lifted her head, spooning the needed medicine into her mouth. Some dribbled down her cheek, but most of the clear liquid made it past her lips, and she visibly swallowed. "This won't help the coughing, but it will help her body to fight this disease."

The room was silent as Cameron, Kit, and the servants stood by the bed, watching. Minutes passed before the sound of shallow breathing took over, and Grace slept peacefully.

"You all can go to bed," Moab said. "I'll sit with her tonight."

Cameron nodded and placed a hand on the doctor's shoulder. "Thank you, Doctor."

The rest of them filed out of the room, and Cameron gave his wife one last look before he slipped out of the bedchamber and crept silently to the guest room. He sank onto the bed and pulled off his boots, realizing for the first time that his heart was pounding wildly in his chest. He climbed into bed and turned on his side. The moon cast a silver light across the blankets. He stared at the muted round ball in the sky until his eyes grew heavy and the thudding in his chest slowed.

Heal my wife, Lord. I couldn't stand to lose her. Please, God. Heal my wife.

SIXTEEN

DAWN ARRIVED PALE blue and cloudless with a gentle wind blowing from the west. The air held the scent of rice grass cut from the day before. Tungo approached Cuffee as he slipped out of the shanty with Cabeto and Solomon. "I've come to tell you that today you be working with your two sons in the rice fields. Cabeto knows the process well, and he can show you what to do."

"Thank you, suh. I'm familiar with rice growin', but it be some years since I been at it. I could use some learnin' again."

Tungo strode away at a brisk pace, and Cuffee and his sons followed. During the early hours, slaves came out of their shacks and headed for the work sheds. Farther ahead, another slave handed out sickles or what some called "rice hooks" to the men and women who waited in line. Everyone knew where to go when they received their sickles, and they went down the lane to the lower fields and spread out through the rows in the rice paddies.

Cuffee took his rice hook and followed Cabeto past fields where slaves hacked away at the plants. They kept walking until they reached unmanned rows.

"We'll start here," Cabeto said. He and Cuffee looked to Solomon, who hadn't said a word since they'd risen from bed. It seemed a dark cloud hung over him, and he was in no mood to talk.

Cuffee let it be. Whatever was brewing in his son's mind, he would find out later. Now it was time to get back to the business of working, and he would cut as many rice stalks as he could before the sun went down.

"I'll take this row."

"You remember what to do?" Cabeto asked.

"If this be the final dryin' of the fields, we gonna cut them stalks down so's they be ready for threshin'."

Cabeto grinned, leaning his rice hook over his shoulder. "That's right." He turned to Solomon. "You take the next row and I'll go on to the third."

"I'll take the third if you don't mind." Solomon walked away with his sickle over his shoulder. Two rows down, he entered the field and, without looking up, began to cut.

Cabeto shrugged and shook his head. "He's been mighty quiet since you've been home."

"To be expected," Cuffee said. "I think my boy's holdin' a grudge against me for bein' gone."

Cuffee and Cabeto looked at Solomon, bent to the task, already moving steadily along. His sickle crashed against the stems with a meaningful force.

Cabeto looked back at Cuffee. "I think you're right. If that be so, and if he keeps up the pace he's workin', he'll knock some o' that simmerin' outta him."

Cuffee nodded and looked down the long row ahead of him. "We'd better get at it."

"The whistle be blowin' when it's lunch time," Cabeto said.

"All right. See ya then." Cuffee swung his hook and chopped off the first layer of rice. He cut three rows at a time as he worked. His sickle felled the rice about a foot above the ground and laid the stalks back on the stubble. This effectively kept the grain off the moist ground and allowed air to circulate the heads.

After he worked midway down his first set of rows, he set the rice hook down and drew out his worn handkerchief to wipe his brow. He thought he'd kept a good pace with his boys, but when he looked over, he saw Cabeto farther down, and Solomon was about to step onto the road to move to the following field.

He couldn't help wondering what was brewing in Solomon's mind. It sure seemed like thunder and lightning goin' on there. Would his son ever come to understand his father wouldn't have left if he could have helped it? Cuffee shoved the kerchief back in his pocket and bent to the work. He cut and hacked, careful to lay the stalks just so, and moved on at a faster pace. He couldn't let his sons see that his age slowed him down.

As the morning wore on, young boys carrying buckets of water flooded the fields to offer the field hands a drink. Just before noon, the whistle finally blew. Cuffee stood straight, feeling every aching muscle in his body. His hands cramped from grasping the thin rice hook for too many hours. "I'm sure gonna sleep well tonight," he said when Cabeto and Tungo walked up.

"It be hard work. You'll get used to it by the end o' the week," Cabeto said.

Tungo nodded. "We'll let the rice fields lie in the sun for a day to begin curing. The day after tomorrow, we'll bind them into sheaves. Is that how you remember it?"

"It's all comin' back loud and clear as I been cuttin' those stalks. No matter how back-breakin' this work be, I like it better than pickin' cotton." Cuffee gave the men a broad smile and looked around for Solomon. He saw him lift buckets onto poles over a young boy's shoulders and pat the child's head. Solomon looked his way, but only briefly. A scowl remained on his face.

Cuffee hung his head. *Lord, I see my son be hurting. I ask You, mend the rift between us.*

Young boys and girls filled the lanes with baskets of cornpones, baked potatoes, and fried squash. Slaves took one of each and hung around the road to eat their simple lunch. A half hour later, they were all back in the fields.

Cuffee picked up his speed while thoughts of Tabitha filled his mind. His memory went to the night before and how good it had felt to lie in bed next to his wife again. It hadn't taken them long to renew their love for each other. "She sure does have a nice touch," Cuffee whispered to the rice stalks as he worked. He recalled how her hands had caressed his back and clung to his arms. "Been too many years without my Tabitha."

He frowned as his mind traveled to Kindra. Was she all right? Would she be bought and sold to a better plantation owner than at Whitestone? *Protect her, Lord. Let her find peace wherever the wind sends her.*

At long last, the whistle blew the final time, and field hands threaded their way up the lane toward the work sheds. One by one, they handed their tools to the tool master and went home.

Cuffee was eager to get to his shanty and feast his eyes on Tabitha again, but first, he looked for his sons. He found Cabeto close by, but Solomon hung back, deep in conversation with a group of men. "Come on." Cuffee clasped his arm over Cabeto's shoulder. "I bet your mama's got a good meal waitin' for us."

"Massa Camp and his missus give us plenty of food supply, better than some planters in these parts. And you be right, Mama's a good cook."

The two men walked up the lane to the shacks. Smells of cooked chicken and vegetables wafted through the air. The tantalizing scent grew stronger when they reached their shanty. Cabeto moved ahead and opened the door, and the sounds of women and children floated out to them. Eager to join in, Cuffee stepped in and glanced around the room.

"Papa!" His oldest daughter, Lilly, flew into his arms. "Welcome home!" Her belly swelled with child, and she held a toddler on her hip. "Benny, this be your grandfather." Lilly kissed Cuffee's cheek, and her eyes sparkled. "You've been gone most of my life. It sure be good to see you."

Lilly stepped aside, and a younger woman came forward. "Do you remember me?"

"Anna. Of course I do." Cuffee opened his arms wide, and she flew into them. The house filled with noise and laughter while the women finished the meal.

Cuffee bounced Anna's baby on his lap. "She be a chubby little thing." He smiled. It wasn't long before the baby fussed, and Anna took her. She sat on a stool by the wall, her back to them, and nursed the baby. The fussing stopped as the hungry baby ate, but a new sound filled the air, and they all laughed again.

Lilly and Tabitha set the table, and soon they all sat down. The sounds of chairs scraping the floor and of shuffling feet as the family gathered around the table were good for Cuffee's soul. All seemed right except for Solomon. He had not come home to join them. Cuffee looked at the door more than once, his heart descending to reality. All would not be good until he and his son settled what was bothering Solomon.

"So, Father," Lilly said. "We want to know where you've been and how you got here."

"I want to fill you in on that as well." Cuffee looked into the faces of his family and told how Morgan Blissmore had smuggled him away and how the evil captain had tried to make him smuggle other slaves. "But once I was out of Tia's control, I decided it didn't matter what happened to me. I wasn't going to do anything against my will again."

"Then it's true you worked for the massa's wife?" Cabeto asked.

"Mastah Coopah never married that woman. He kept her at the Great House only so his chile be raised in comfort."

"He had feelings for Tia."

Tabitha rolled her eyes.

"I'm not doubtin' Mastah Coopah had feelings for the black panther. But he didn't know she used some of us field hands to help her smuggle slaves off his and other plantations."

"Go on with your story, Father," Anna said.

"After ten years in Blissmore's hands, he and another captain decided to sell me and Miss Kindra to planters here in America."

"I knew Kindra well," Tabitha said with a nostalgic look on her face. "She'd come to our shanties justa wishin' she be one of us so she could marry our overseer, Denzel."

A soft noise made Cuffee look behind him, where he saw Solomon. "Come sit down and join us, son."

Solomon dragged himself to the other side of the table and pulled out a chair. He grimaced and dished food onto his plate.

Cuffee knew they needed to talk. Somehow, he reckoned that wouldn't happen anytime soon.

"So," Cabeto continued, "where were you before you came home?"

"Like I said, the captains decided to sell me and Kindra across the ocean."

"How was it that you and Kindra ended up at the same place?" Tabitha set her spoon on her plate and leaned forward.

"I learned later that one of the captains, Jule Spade, kidnapped her from her plantation. He had a prison compound on the other side of Barbados. The growth was so thick that the huts were hidden well."

"Morgan Blissmore sent me to that jungle compound days before Spade brought Kindra." Cuffee stopped to think back over that terrible day. "They roughed her up badly. I ain't never seen Mastah Coopah's daughter look a sore sight like she was that day."

"Oh, Cuffee." Tabitha bit her lip.

"It was bad. She was there 'bout four days 'fore Denzel showed up. I 'spect he come lookin' for her on his own, but Spade's men captured him and threw him in a cell too."

"But he's been here several times in the past few years, always looking for Kindra. How did he get away, but not you?" Cabeto asked.

"I don't rightly know how he escaped. Blissmore and Spade put me and Kindra on a ship before that happened."

"How did Massa Camp find you?" Lilly asked.

"That's comin'. You see, when Kindra and I sailed across the ocean, Blissmore had a bit of kindness in his heart, as he didn't make her stay in the hold with the rest of us."

"Daddy . . ." Anna said.

Cuffee raised his hand to silence her. He wanted to finish his story. "When we got to Virginia, Blissmore sent us to the slave auction. I kept tellin' Kindra, 'Don't you go lookin' at me, cuz they will split us up.' You see, I thought it was my duty to Mastah Coopah to keep an eye on his daughter."

"Did it work?" Tabitha asked.

"Sure did. When the biddin' was done, Mastah Abrams put us both on the back o' his wagon and carted us off to his cotton plantation at Whitestone."

"Did they mistreat her?" Tabitha asked.

"Some."

"Then you saw her enough to know what was going on in her day-to-day life there." Tabitha leaned back and placed her hands in her lap. "Kindra knew you from Cooper's Landing. Did she run to you for support?"

Cuffee felt a tug of mixed emotions. He had cared what happened to Kindra then, and he cared what happened to her now. But he was grateful to be home with Tabitha and his children. "Tabitha, you have a lot of questions I can't answer right now. I'd rather talk to you alone if it's all right." He looked at his grown children and back to her. He watched her swallow. Was she worried there was more to the story than he was sharing? He clenched his fist under the table. She should be worried. But he wasn't responsible for the last five years with Kindra. The master at Whitestone had made them get married. He reached over and pulled her hand into his. "You are the light of my life. I'm happy we're together again."

"I'm glad you're home too." She swiped at the tears that rolled down her cheeks, leaving two wet trails.

Cuffee looked around the table. They all fixed their eyes on him. The deep scowl on Solomon's face unnerved him. His son shoved a mouthful of food into his mouth, but he kept his gaze on Cuffee.

"You got somethin' you want to say?" Cuffee held his son's dark gaze.

"Not here. Not now." Solomon pushed his chair back and stomped outside. The house shook as he slammed the door.

All eyes flew to Cuffee.

"Don't worry 'bout your brother. All this has been hard on him." Maybe it was time to talk.

Grace sat against her pillow as the doctor felt around her throat. "How do you feel?"

"That terrible headache is gone." She yawned. "And I'm not sore like I have been the last two weeks."

"I believe the quinine helped a good deal, along with the rest you've received."

"I've had more rest than a newborn baby. I'm ready to get up and get on with the demands of the house. I'm afraid to see how much has been neglected since I've been down."

"You may be surprised to find everything has been well taken care of," Doctor Moab said. "Gemma's been in charge. The servants listen to her."

"You said there were others who had taken ill with yellow fever. How are they doing?"

"Tungo's wife, Essie, was sick. She improved, like you. There's a twelve-year-old girl who hasn't fared as well."

"Will she make it?"

"Yes. I believe so. But it's going to take her a little longer. Now, it's my suggestion you stay in bed a day or two longer, Miz Grace." Doctor Moab started toward the door.

"Before you leave, hand me that sketch pad and pencil."

The doctor grinned as he took them off the table. "It's good to see you well enough that you want to draw. I'll look in on you this evening."

When he opened the door, Grace's orange-and-white cat walked into the room and jumped onto the foot of the bed. He gave her a slow blink, curled up on the coverlet, closed his eyes, and wound his tail under his chin.

"Smitty." Grace smiled. Leaning back against the plush pillow, she looked at the blank piece of paper and realized that, often, this was how she felt. Blank. How could she go on in her day-to-day routine when Kindra suffered as a slave in the hands of strangers? Kindra hadn't seen her family in seven years. Was she all right? Was she waiting to be rescued? The fact that Denzel and Cameron hadn't found her was disheartening. Still, Grace had a house to run and children who needed her. She blinked back tears that threatened to fall, bowed her head, and prayed.

Oh, God, have mercy on my sister. Protect her from her enemies and guard her against those who would seek to hurt her. Help us to find her, and give her peace each day.

She breathed a silent "Amen," and picked up her charcoal pencil. She let her hand draw at will, and before long, she had a sketch of Kindra in a lovely gown and with a flower in her hair. Her thoughts drifted to Damaris. Her skin was darker than Kindra's, but she resembled her mother in so many ways. Did she have a secret admiration for Solomon? Grace thought so. Back in the day, Kindra had had a secret admirer. She and Denzel had fled to the barns many times to have a moment together, moments Tia had hated.

And what of Tia? The recent letters gave her the impression the tigress had changed. She'd never dreamed she'd get a letter from Kindra's mother. And yet when she did she sounded more like a kitten than the she-cat Grace remembered. What had gotten into the woman? Was it the loss of Kindra?

Restless, Grace slid her feet to the floor. She sat on the side of the bed and waited to get her bearings. She smiled. It was the first time in two weeks she could sit without the room spinning out of control. She carefully stood and grabbed the bedpost, letting strength infuse her. When she let go, she looked at the bed. Should she climb back in?

There was a slight thump as Smitty jumped off the bed and strolled to the closed door. With a haughty turn of his head, he paused to look at her. "Meow!" It was an imperious call. Grace smiled at the sound and the marked impatience in his tone.

"Do you want out?" She walked to the door and opened it enough to let Smitty through.

He started to walk out and looked back. "Meow!"

"Am I supposed to come too?" She bent down and ran her hand over his soft fur as he purred loudly.

"You go on. I'm not dressed." Grace stood and rubbed her toes on his sleek back, then nudged him out the door. Smitty turned and walked with a stately and unhurried grace into the hallway.

Grace closed the door and looked at the window. The sun was shining high. She couldn't bring herself to lie down again; instead, she crossed the floor slowly and looked down at the front lawn. After the long rains, the world was bright and clean and crisp.

"I can't stay a moment longer cooped up in this room," she said to no one. She pulled the tapestry cord in the corner, rang the bell three times, and waited.

"Miz Grace! You're up!" Hedy entered and crossed the floor, concerned.

"I'm up and I want to get dressed. And please hurry. I need to get downstairs as soon as possible."

"Yes'm, Miz Grace." Hedy flew to the wardrobe and opened it wide.

"Is Kit downstairs?"

"Yes'm."

"I need to summon Mrs. Unruh. The girls need dresses for Kit's coming-out ball."

"Miz Grace? You sure did get some resurrectin' when you got over the fever!"

"Yes, and I've got a lot of living to do. Now button me up. We've got to make up for wasted time."

SEVENTEEN

DAMARIS WRUNG HER hands as she looked out the dining room window at the lazy river sparkling in the setting sun. Faint sounds of pots and pans clanging on the stove came from the kitchen as the cooks prepared the evening meal. She looked out on the lawn, but nobody was there.

She had spent the earlier part of the day with Grace and Kit, going over the guest list for Kit's eighteenth birthday party combined with her coming-out celebration. The house was quiet now, with Mrs. Unruh working quietly in the guest chamber. When Damaris left Mrs. Unruh, the seamstress had been holding straight pins pressed tightly in her lips and a measuring tape stretched around Kit's waist, taking notes as she prepared to make her gown for the upcoming event. It would be a while before Mrs. Unruh would need to take Damaris's measurements, and for that she was glad.

Damaris's mind wandered to the handsome field hand she'd seen a few times around River Oak. She didn't know how long her family would remain at the plantation. If her father found her mother, they would certainly sail for Barbados right away. If that should happen, she would never get to know Solomon, and try as she might, she couldn't get him off her mind. She heard low murmurs turn into laughter and stepped away from the window to glance down the hall. She quickly left the room and stepped onto the porch, feeling the humid evening air against her cheek.

Lifting her hand over her eyes, she gazed toward the colored town. The older women and young children sat on their porch steps, but the field hands were out of sight. They worked down in the lower acreage rice fields, but the sun was receding fast, and they would soon be turning in their tools and heading home for supper.

With decided steps, she picked up her blue skirts and moved down the stairs, continuing until she came to the slave district. She saw those who sat on the steps, but to the right, she also saw several older women sitting in a circle on straw mats. They deftly wove shallow baskets from the piles of sweet grass and palmetto leaves strung between them. Damaris slowed her steps to watch them. "They're beautiful," she said, bending to touch one of the green bowls.

"We be makin' rice baskets fer the workers." One woman lifted her basket for Damaris's inspection. "The field hands be usin' these fer winnowin' the dried rice seeds. They shake them in baskets, which separate the seed that be fallin' from the chaff." She lowered her newly made bowl and lifted a stem from the pile of thick grass. "There neber too many baskets, 'cuz they wear out fast from the hard shakin'." She started her next shallow bowl by making a knot around which the coils of bundled grass began to weave.

Damaris watched the women as the sun continued its descent. They were eager to demonstrate their skills, and though they all used the sweet grass and palmetto leaves to make the shallow baskets, the designs varied.

After several minutes, she reluctantly waved goodbye and continued beyond the housing district to follow a lane that slanted toward the lower fields and rice barns. As she came around a curve in the road, a whole new scene opened up. As far as the eye could see, the rice fields were full of workers. Along the edge were rick-carts with donkeys hitched to them.

The men, women, and young teens worked feverishly to bind bundles of rice stalks into sheaves. They carried the bundles on their shoulders and stacked them into the ricks to cure. Stacked six to eight feet high, the ricks wobbled on the bumpy road as the workers led the donkeys pulling the full carts to the storage barns.

There were too many people to tell which one might be Solomon. The slaves bent over in the crops, and she couldn't see their faces. Feeling foolish for wandering the fields alone, she watched a moment longer before she turned to head back to the house.

Along the way, she glanced to her left and saw the double doors of the barn open wide. She slipped inside and looked around the dark building. A large wagon full of dried sheaves sat to one side. The building was rich with the sweet tang of rice grass. She turned to leave but heard a sound from the far side and stiffened. She wasn't alone. Her heart beat in her ear; she started to step out of the building, but a low voice called to her.

"What are you doing here?"

She'd heard that voice before—when she first arrived. She spun around to face the man she was looking for. "I . . . I . . ."

"Does the mistress know you're out here?"

"N-no."

Solomon wiped his hands with a dirty rag and continued to watch her in the dim light. A slow smile curved his lips.

"I . . . I . . ." *What is wrong with me?* She tried again. "I don't usually wander out alone, but I don't know how long my family will be at River Oak, and I wanted to see you."

His teeth gleamed in the dark. "You been here 'bout a month." Solomon's dark eyes stayed on her as she stood a distance away. "I know, I been countin' every day you here."

She smiled and let her shoulders drop. "Yes, and if Father finds my mother, we will surely go home. She's been gone seven years."

Solomon took a couple of steps closer. "That be a long time."

"Too long." All at once, tears blurred her vision. She hadn't thought that speaking of her mother would bring on such intense emotions. She didn't want that right now. She swiped at her face and turned away.

She turned to see Solomon standing before her. "I'm glad you came."

She caught her breath and gazed into his eyes. *Was he pleased to see her?* The longing in his eyes said he was. She lowered her chin and smiled. "I'm curious what you do out here?" She looked past him to the long, crude tables against the wall.

He glanced over his shoulder. "I tend the sheaves once they've been brought to the rice barns. It won't be long before it's threshing time. Then we'll load the rice to be milled."

Damaris shrugged. "Seeing the donkey carts headed this way, you've a lot to tend to."

"I don't work alone. There be plenty of hands to get the job done." He wiped his hands with the rag again, then dropped it on the back of the wagon. "My name's Solomon." He reached out a work-roughened hand.

“I know.” She slipped her small hand into his. An unexpected tingling surged through her, and she felt warmth slide up her neck. “M-my name’s Damaris.”

He chuckled. “I know.”

She pulled her hand out of his and felt heat singe her skin. “So . . .” A man’s form shadowed the entrance to the barn, and she turned quickly to see who it was.

“Miz Damaris,” Tungo stepped into the building.

She took a step away from Solomon.

“Does Miz Grace know you out here?”

“No. They’re all busy.”

Tungo looked at Solomon with dark eyes. “You need to get back to work.”

“Yes, suh.”

Tungo turned to Damaris and said, “And you need to get back to the Great House.”

“I will.” Damaris looked up at Solomon’s tall frame, wishing for all the world that she could talk to him a moment longer.

Tungo touched the brim of his straw hat and walked out of the barn and out of sight.

“I best go.” Damaris picked up her skirts.

“Wait!” Solomon stepped in front of her.

She stared at his face expectantly, and her heart raced like a runaway horse.

“I shouldn’t ask, but can you take a walk with me this evening after supper?”

Her heart fell to her feet, and she touched his arm. “I would very much like to take a walk with you, but . . .”

“The massa?”

“No. He and my father are in Charleston looking for Mother.”

“Then?”

“Aunt Grace. While they’re gone, she doesn’t allow us out after dark.”

Solomon nodded. “All right.” His shoulders sagged.

“Maybe . . .” Damaris looked out at the twilight as the sun slid behind the forest on the back side of the rice barns.

Solomon's head shot up.

"I may be able to slip out after supper. The women retire early in the evenings to the parlor to read or do needlework. I didn't bring mine with me." She pinched the creases of her blue skirt, knowing she should get back to the house, but she could not make her feet move. Instead, she stared into his eyes, her heart thrumming in her chest. "If you see a candle in the upstairs window, meet me in the garden behind the house."

A smile brightened his face, and his hand clutched her shoulders. "I be lookin' for that candle, Miz Damaris."

"I must go." She fled the barn and walked quickly past the slave shanties. Her heart beat a rhythm in her ears as her feet hit the ground. Did she have the nerve to meet Solomon after supper? Yes, with all her heart!

Captain Drew Harding neared the end of the pier at Cooper River, where the *Savannah Rose* had moored for the past week. He saw a mass of pulleys and ropes had been thrown together in what appeared to be a tangled mess. How his officers and crewmen kept track of them, he didn't know. He'd spent the past twenty-seven years as a merchant captain, sailing the vast seas. He knew how to command a ship, man the helm, and survive the sea, sometimes in the worst conditions, but when it came to replacing a mast, he left that to his crew.

Some of the ropes were tied to mooring piers and pilings next to the ship; others stretched across several piers and were tied to the masts and yardarms of ships berthed on adjoining piers. His crew, some wearing tan-colored coats identifying them as carpenters, were hoisting a new mainmast into place. Drew stopped on the wharf to watch.

His first mate, Jamie, stood on the deck with a megaphone and shouted instructions to several teams of men as they held onto stiff ropes as thick as bedposts. "Heave!" cried Jamie as a throng of men held a rope at waist level.

As Drew neared the ship, the new, coarsely made mast replaced the one that had snapped in two in a storm off the Caribbean coast on their last voyage out.

"Heave!" Jamie bellowed again.

The entire mast slid toward the vacant hole with a swoosh, followed by a loud thump that reverberated throughout the deck as the pole dropped down into the hole. The ship shuddered, and the crew roared in delight as the pole thudded loudly into place.

"Hold to!" several officers shouted simultaneously.

Sailors began to climb the new mast, removing stay ropes and rigging, untangling pull lines, and climbing the front and rear masts, releasing lines and pulleys. Jackson was among the men who shimmied down a pole and planted his feet on the deck.

Going aboard the ship, Drew pulled off his wide-brimmed hat and wiped his forearm across his brow. The day had been nothing short of trouble. First, he'd had to locate canvas to repair the three sails that had torn in the storm. Then there was a mix-up of invoices for the rice cargo he'd arranged with Cameron. The accountant had given Bartholomew's order to the ship captain, who delivered Wendell Seward's supplies. Drew slapped his broad hat on his head and marched up the gangplank. Nothing was going right.

He found Jackson and Woodrow knee deep in canvas, mending the sails. "The new mast is in." Drew knelt on one knee.

"I see," Jackson said, keeping his eye on the thick needle he shoved into the coarse material. "It won't be long before these sails are mended and we'll be back on the sea."

"Dad, are we still going to River Oak before we sail?" Woodrow held the canvas taut as he worked on a long rip. He shoved the triangular needle in on the top side and pulled it out from the bottom. His lips pursed as he pushed the needle back through the next quarter-inch of material and pulled it out again from the top.

"I told Camp we'd ride out for supper before we left. How long before these sails are repaired?"

Jackson looked at the pile of canvas beside him. "We have three to go. I'd say we can have them done in the next two days."

"All right," Drew said. "I'll send a post tomorrow letting the Bartholomews know we're coming." Drew stood and watched his eldest son. Jackson hadn't looked him in the eye once as they spoke. Was he hiding something?

The crew worked hard throughout the rest of the day. The next morning,

Drew found his two sons back at work on the sails. "Good morning. It's early, and you're already at it."

"Yep." Jackson eyed the thick needle in his hand. He flexed his fingers and licked his thumb.

"Let me see your hands," Drew said.

Jackson laid the needle aside and turned his palms up. Woodrow did the same. The tips of both men's fingers were red and blistered. A thin piece of cloth covered Jackson's index finger. He looked up at his father, his jaw taut.

"Tough work," Drew said. "There should be something you can use to protect your fingers."

"We tried one of them thimbles the ladies use for sewing." Woodrow cracked a grin. "Ha!"

"What's so funny?" Drew asked.

"Have you ever tried to stick your finger in one of them contraptions?" Jackson's eyes lit up as if the thought of a woman's thimble was humorous.

"Can't say that I have." Drew smiled down at his sons and felt pride for the two of them. They'd endured blisters, and their fingers were red and cracked, yet they didn't complain. "Your mama does all the sewing at home." Drew quirked a grin.

"She wouldn't be able to do this kind of work." Jackson stood. "It's ruthless." He removed his hat and raked his tawny hair with his fingers. He stretched to get the kinks out of his back before he leaned his arms on the ship's rail and looked over the port.

Drew joined him. "I'm ready to get back on the voyage. The sooner we get out to sea and deliver the cargo, the sooner we get home. I miss your mother."

Jackson looked sideways at his father, a pinched look on his face. "It'll be good to be back, but first I want to visit the Bartholomews." He looked at his blistered fingers as if studying them.

"There wouldn't be a certain pretty little gal out there who's got your attention, would there?"

Jackson hung his head. When he looked up, his neck was red. "She's really something, isn't she?"

"I don't know when it happened, but she grew into a beauty." Drew saw the longing in his son's eyes. "The sea life is hard on a woman."

"I've thought of that. But then, you married Mother. It's worked out for the two of you."

"That's true. They say absence makes the heart grow fonder. With me gone half the time, it seems your mother and I are on a constant honeymoon. But I have to say, it's been hard on her." Drew watched the water between the ships ripple in its murkiness.

"I wouldn't want that for Kit. I wouldn't want her waiting half her life for me to return from a merchant run." Jackson heaved a long sigh. "I just can't get her off my mind." He spat into the water.

"Are you going to leave me to do all the work?" Woodrow cut in.

"No. I'm coming." Jackson gave his father a crooked grin. "You going to send that post this morning?"

"Why don't you and Woodrow take a break. Let's get breakfast at the King's Inn, and then I'll send out the post."

"Breakfast!" Woodrow dropped the canvas and stood. "My stomach's been growling for the last hour. Let's eat."

The three men strode down the gangway to the wharf. Drew followed his sons, trying to keep up. Jackson's tall frame moved ahead of the crowd. Drew had wondered when Kit became a woman, but he had also wondered when Jackson became a man. The two of them might have their share of differences about Jackson's work at sea, but the truth was, he didn't think the two of them had even said two words to each other yet, much less worry about the future. Somehow, Jackson would have to come to terms with whether he could live without Kit. Only time would tell.

Damaris tiptoed down the stairs and through the hall toward the back door. Looking back, she hoped no one would notice her absence. Kit, Bella Grace, and the younger girls sat in the parlor, surrounding Grace. Eager for normal family time, the girls took up their needlepoint by the light of kerosene lamps while Grace read the Godey's Lady's Book to them. Part of Damaris wanted to join the women, but she wanted to see Solomon more, so she feigned wanting to turn in early and, instead, lit the candle and set the brass holder in the window. Would Solomon see the thin flame?

She lifted her gauzy, green gown as she tiptoed out to the garden behind the Great House. Light from the house shone across the lawn, and the yellow haze helped her make her way across the brick walkway. Tall oaks spread their long, black arms over the vast lawn, and in the dark, they appeared daunting. But she knew the path was well lined with benches and flower gardens. She neared a bench and waited, fingers clutching her skirts. Now that she was here, doubt crept in. Would he come?

A shadow moved from behind an oak, and she watched a tall figure move into the pale light streaming from the window. "Solomon!" she whispered.

He moved hesitantly toward her, grasped her elbow gently, and pulled her near the trunk of the tree, out of the yellow light. "I be watching the window when I see the candle." He pulled her near a bush; seemingly unsure they were hidden in the dark. "I didn't waste any time gettin' over here."

She could see the light of his smile and relaxed. "I'm glad you came." Still, she stepped back so she could look up at his face. "I can't stay long."

"Do you think anyone see you sneak out of the house?"

"No." She looked over her shoulder at the closed door. "They're listening to Aunt Grace read."

His large hand took hers, and he pulled her to him. "You 'bout the prettiest thing I ever laid eyes on."

Damaris's heart picked up. "Thank you. I must say, since I saw you that first day I arrived, I haven't been able to get you off my mind." She lowered her eyes and smiled. When she looked up, she jutted her chin out. "That's a brazen thing for a woman to say to a man she hardly knows, but time isn't on my side. I won't always be here."

"I'm glad you said it. Makes me feel real good inside."

Crickets made a chorus of noise. An owl hooted in the darkness, flapped its long wings, and flew to another tree. The two hid behind the Spanish oak, wishing they didn't have to hide. But they came from different worlds. However, for the moment, the night was theirs. Damaris looked back at the dim lights in the window. "I must go."

"Not yet," he pulled her close.

"I will come again. Look for the candle in the window."

He relaxed his hold. "I will look for it every night."

"I won't always be able to come."

"I know, but I will look just the same."

She stood on tiptoe and kissed his rough cheek. "Until then." She raced back to the house. When she reached the door, she turned around. She could barely see his tall form standing against the tree. His hand went up. Hers did too. She opened the door and slipped inside. Her breath came quickly, and her heart pounded in her chest.

She listened for sounds from deep inside the house. Grace was still reading, her southern drawl soothing. Damaris picked up her skirts and tiptoed up the stairs, a smile on her lips. When she reached the top, she looked out the window to the backyard. She found the tree where she and Solomon had stood. He was gone. She leaned her forehead on the cool pane. *Look for my candle, darling, until we meet again.*

EIGHTEEN

"MIZ KIT, IF you don't sit still, I'm never goin' to get yer hair braided!"

Kit fidgeted. "It's been weeks since I've ridden, and today looks perfect outside."

Hedy stared at the girl's reflection in the mirror. "I'm workin' as fast as my fingers can go."

Kit gazed at her long ebony hair. People thought her hair was one of her best features, but right now it would only get in her way. "I prefer braids when I ride. Especially if I put the old black into a run."

"I thought your father told you not to ride so fast." Hedy clicked her tongue.

"I'm not riding Dandy. I'm riding Scimitar."

"And that makes a difference?"

"Of course. Dandy's skittish. I never know what her mood will be when I take her out. Scimitar's getting old. He's more predictable."

Kit glanced at Damaris, who watched them from a chair by the window. She looked lovely in her olive-green day dress with the prim, white lace collar. "I'm asking for the last time, honey, would you like to go riding with me?"

"Go on with you, Kit. I have never cared to ride a horse. I'd slow you down."

"If you won't ride with me, then what are you going to do while I'm gone?"

Damaris smiled mischievously. "I'm going to take a walk around the pond. I've not spent much time on that lovely white bridge, and I have some thinking to do."

Kit waved Hedy's hand away as she swiveled on the padded bench to look at her cousin. "What kind of thinking?"

"Aren't you the nosy one?" Damaris's eyes lit up.

"Pray tell, are you keeping a secret from me?" Kit stared as Damaris wiggled uncomfortably in her chair and cleared her throat.

"Do I not have the right to private thoughts?"

"Yes, you do," Hedy chimed in, then pointed to the mirror as she told Kit, "Turn around so I can finish you up."

Kit rolled her eyes and turned around.

Hedy continued. "Your mama be jist like you when she was your age. She couldn't wait to get Dandy out of the stall and ride like the wind." She worked quickly, plaiting the long black strands of hair with nimble fingers. Giving a final tug, she secured the braid and twisted it into a bun. "There. Now get on out to the stable. I think you have a horse waiting fer you."

"Thanks, Hedy." As Kit slid from the cloth-covered bench, she stopped long enough to give her chambermaid an impulsive hug. "Now let's get my jacket on."

Kit wore a brown-colored riding dress. The front of the skirt had a long row of black velvet buttons. Her shirt was made of white cambric. Hedy held out the short jacket, ornamented with the same black buttons as the skirt and black braided hoops that also served as closures. Kit slid her hands through the sleeves and pulled on her cream-colored gloves while Hedy fetched the matching felt hat with a rolled brim. The back was embellished with tightly rolled ostrich plumes and a ribbon to tie under her chin.

Kit ran her hand down the skirt and whisked out of the room. She'd spent far too much time getting ready when the meadows in the fields were calling her.

"Kit!"

She halted and turned back to the chambermaid. "What now?"

"Your mama wants supper in two hours. That doesn't give you much time."

Kit waved her gloved hand. "I'll be back in time."

"There may be company tonight." Hedy reminded her.

"Are you talking about Captain Harding?"

"Yes'm. Miz Grace done say she got a post from the captain."

Kit stilled herself as she remembered the last time she had seen Jackson. She hadn't known the handsome man was riding out to River Oak from Charleston. Tending to her deathly ill mother for so many days, she hadn't taken any extra measures to look her best. Heat ran up her neck when she remembered his long gaze before he had ridden back to town. Had he felt attraction for her, even when she had looked a fright? Seeing Hedy's smile at her silence, she asked, "Are his sons coming too?"

"That, I don't know. I heard tell the boys be finishin' up mending sails on the ship."

Kit's shoulders relaxed. "I'll be back in time." She threw the words over her shoulder and dashed out the open door. Sailing into the bustling kitchen, she snatched two apples from a bowl.

"You goin' out on yer daddy's horse, Miz Kit?"

"I am." She opened the door to the side yard and went outside.

"Supper be ready in a couple o' hours," Mama Jezelee hollered.

Drawing deep breaths of the spicy fall air, Kit strode to the stables. She glanced toward the double doors of the aged barn and then to the meadows beyond, where a filly and a mare grazed close together. Passing up the stable, she strolled out to the lane and watched the horses chomp the grass. The filly was Dandy's and was sired by Scimitar, her father's horse. She'd paid particular attention to the red filly. The cinnamon-colored horse was a beauty with a white patch on her muzzle, a black mane and tail, and four black socks. Kit stepped onto the first rail of the crude fence and rested her elbows on the wooden planks.

The three-year-old filly pranced around the grounds as if showing off before she finally trotted over to the corral fence, where Kit held out a shiny apple.

"Hello, Ginger."

The filly tossed her mane and snorted before walking up and resting her chest on the top post. She nuzzled Kit and lipped the apple out of her hand, then stepped back. The fruit fell to the ground, and she lowered her muscled neck and chomped on the apple. When done, she raised her head and stared.

Kit reached out a gloved hand to the pretty horse. When the filly stepped back and snorted, Kit laughed. "Oh, now you're playing hard to get."

Ginger nickered softly, then stepped forward and rested her soft nose on

Kit's shoulder. Kit reached out and stroked her. "I'll see you again tomorrow." She kissed Ginger's silky forehead. "Be good, little lady."

Kit turned around and strode toward the stable. When she reached the barn doors, Nate led Scimitar out. "You have him ready!" She was filled with delight as she gazed lovingly over her father's towering black Arabian.

"Of course, Miz Kit. You expected less?" He held the reins for her. Old Nate had cared for the horses ever since she could remember, but now it seemed he was getting older by the minute. His once coal-black hair had streaked with gray. His dark freckles were more pronounced.

"I didn't expect anything less, but I know you've been tending to that new foal the mare delivered yesterday. Thank you for having Scimitar ready." She took hold of the reins and walked the great black out of the stable.

Scimitar had been a gift from her grandfather, Phillip Cooper, to her father in Jamaica. When her parents sailed to South Carolina, they brought all their horses. The black was reaching his prime and, in some ways, reacted as if he were ten years younger. Arabian horses were a hardy breed and lived long, natural lives of up to 30 years. She'd heard that some Arabians lived well into their forties. Familiar with Scimitar's antics whenever she took him out, she believed he'd live a long life.

As she stepped into the stirrup, she glanced back at Nate with a mischievous smile. "I'm going to ride him like a man today. This silly sidesaddle notion is not for me. No one should have to ride a horse like that."

Nate shook his head but smiled. "You've always wanted to do things yer own way, Miz Kit. I'm thinkin', when you be born, God made you special. You don't fit into any mold I ever did see."

Kit stared at the stableman for a long time. "Thanks, Nate. I'm going to take that as a compliment." She sat in the saddle, both feet in the stirrups, and waved at the old man as she and the Arabian headed for the open gate. Once she rode out of the long drive, she turned right and let Scimitar trot. His hooves raised dust in the autumn air. A little farther down the lane was another gate. She leaned forward and lifted the rope. Once inside the pasture, she picked up speed and passed the rest of the horses, who grazed in the meadow. She watched them nibble the lush green grass. It was peaceful out there.

Her father owned hundreds of acres. Over time, she had ridden much of the land and knew the terrain well. These grounds were higher than the rice fields. This side of the plantation was where her father kept their stock, primarily cattle, but some sheep. It was fenced off from the provision fields. A forest bordered the grazing ground, and far beyond the trees was the shore of the Atlantic Ocean.

She wasn't allowed beyond the pasture. The fence near the trees was where she'd jumped Dandy and had fallen off the horse. She shaded her eyes and peered toward the trees. They looked dark in the distance. In another two hours, they would blend into the black night sky. She nudged Scimitar's flanks and galloped the steed in the field, free as a bird. The horses raised their heads to watch them. She leaned forward and put the black Arabian into a run. The beast's hooves drummed the ground as they sped along, horse and human as one, sailing through the meadow.

Moments later, she pulled on the reins to slow Scimitar to a walk. She circled the pasture and let the horse catch his breath. This gave her time to think about herself. She'd be eighteen in another month. Some said that's when a girl became a woman. Indeed, her body had changed dramatically, as evidenced by her slim waist and full bosom. She'd seen the changes more than ever in the past few months, and more than the physical attributes, she'd *felt* something change inside her. Things that mattered before now seemed frivolous, and childish play was a thing of the past. Instead, thoughts of Adam Sparrow and Jackson Harding filled her mind.

Adam had been around all her life. She liked him very much, although she would never let him know. If she told the truth, she cared for him to some degree. In retrospect, she had even considered he might be the man she'd marry one day. Everyone in the Bartholomew and Sparrow families seemed to think so. All of that changed the day Jackson Harding rode up. He was the man who filled her every waking hour and sent Adam Sparrow to the recesses of her mind. And for that, she felt a measure of guilt. She never wanted to hurt him, but she knew Adam wanted more from her than just friendship. She found it easier to evade him until she knew what her heart really wanted. Right now, she didn't know.

A wagon rambled into the front drive, and Grace pushed the white lace curtains aside to peer out. "Captain Harding and his sons are here!" She headed for the front door.

"Good. I'm ready for a long talk with that man." Cameron laid his newspaper aside, joined her on the front porch, and watched as the men climbed down from the buckboard.

"Evening!" Drew said and raised a hand.

"Welcome to River Oak!" Grace stretched her arms toward the men as they climbed the steps.

"Drew." Cameron extended a hand to his friend.

Grace glanced up at Jackson and Spencer. "My lands, you boys have grown. I hardly recognize you anymore." She gathered her skirts. "Come into the house. The food will be ready soon."

They all clomped into the house, their shoes echoing on the hardwood floors. Cameron led them to the parlor. "Have a seat. We've got about an hour before supper's ready."

Willie came to the entrance with a smile. Zeddie and Cyrus stood behind him. "Hi, Spence. We're headed outside." He waved for the younger of the captain's sons to join them.

Woodrow quickly looked at his father.

"Go on, son. They'll ring the bell when supper's on."

"Thanks!" Woodrow wasted no time following the boys out the front door. It slammed shut and rattled the windows.

The adults laughed, but Grace noticed Jackson seemed preoccupied, sitting nervously on the edge of the seat. "Can I get you something to drink?" She glanced his way and then to Drew.

"Coffee sounds fine." Drew nodded.

"Same here," Camp said.

Grace gazed at Jackson, whose hands were clamped on his knees. "No, thanks." He leaned back and strummed his fingers on the arm of the plush chair.

Well, for goodness' sake, Grace thought. *If I didn't know better, I'd think he was a nervous wreck. But that couldn't be possible. Jackson's been in this house at least a dozen times over the years. What could possibly have him tied in knots?* She'd have to give that some thought later, but for now she had guests who needed her attention. She rang the bell and Gemma appeared.

"Yes'm. You folks be needing some refreshments while you wait for supper?"

"Coffee, please."

"Four cups?"

Grace glanced at Jackson.

His hand went up. "No, thanks."

"I be right back." Gemma left the room.

Drew and Cameron wasted no time striking up a conversation. Grace leaned back to listen, but her mind flew to the young man sitting across the room.

Moments later, Bella Grace and the younger girls descended the stairs, their laughter and voices filling the entryway. When they reached the bottom, Bella said, "We're going out to the pond to meet Damaris."

"Supper will be ready soon," Grace reminded them.

"We'll hear the bell." Bella led the small group out of the house, and they tromped noisily on the porch and down the steps.

Jackson watched the girls disappear and looked at Grace. "Where's Kit?"

"Oh, she went horseback riding. She should be along soon."

Jackson nodded, his ears turning red.

It finally dawned on Grace why Jackson was fidgety. "She's out in the west pasture, if you'd like to join her."

His eyes lit. "She won't mind?"

"I can't think why she should. Take a horse if you'd like. I'm sure she'd enjoy the company."

Jackson stood. "I think I'll take you up on that."

"Go on. Nate will fix you up."

"Thank you." Jackson didn't waste another second. He went out the front door and disappeared.

Grace looked at the two men who'd stopped talking long enough to watch the exchange.

"That got him flying out the door," Camp said.

"He's been chomping at the bit to get here," Drew said.

"To see Kit?" Camp asked.

"One and the same." Drew smiled.

"She's not a little girl anymore," Grace said, an uncertain feeling gnawing at her insides. They'd sent invitations for her birthday celebration and coming-out party for this very reason. Kit was coming of age. "Oh, for heaven's sake," she said. "Look at the three of us acting like we never thought this day would arrive." She glanced out the window to see Jackson riding down the long drive at full speed. "I knew this day would come, but truth to tell, it happened entirely too fast."

NINETEEN

KIT, DEEP IN thought, watched the herd of Arabians in the meadow. She rode Scimitar toward the edge of the field. A stand of trees lined the fence and provided the horses with shelter from the elements. Today was a beautifully sunny afternoon, however, and the horses gathered in the center of the field and watched her with pricked ears.

In the distance, she saw someone riding toward her. Who could it be? It wouldn't be her father, as he was assisting Tungo with the rice shipment. Whoever it was, was riding at a brisk trot.

She nudged her horse forward and rode to meet the rider. Scimitar snorted and raised his head at the approaching visitor. She pulled on the reins, and the horse side-stepped. Kit squinted and stared ahead—a man wearing a broad hat rode in the saddle. And then it dawned on her who was coming. The man just ahead on a dappled Arabian mare was Jackson, tall and handsome in the saddle. Halfway through the field, the two met and stopped as their mounts chuffed and stomped the ground.

"Hello." Kit smiled. Heat ran up her neck.

"Hello to you. Have you been out here long?"

"Not really. Is Uncle Drew here?"

"We all are. We've been invited for dinner." Jackson's eyes held hers.

Kit's stomach flipped with him so close. She had to think of something quick to quell the awkward moment. She leaned forward and stroked Scimitar's neck. "How did you find me?"

"Your mother said you were in the west fields. It wasn't hard to find you with that black mount and your raven-black hair."

Kit jerked a hand to her head, feeling the brown felt hat over her tightly braided bun.

His eyes lit up. "I don't need to see your tresses. I remember them well." He leaned an elbow on the saddle horn and watched her lazily.

The way he eyed her sent a thrill up her back that was followed by an awkward silence. What should she say? She couldn't bear the giddy feeling a moment longer, and she turned her horse in the opposite direction, looking over her shoulder. "Want to race?" She didn't wait for an answer. She dug her heels into Scimitar's flanks and leaned forward for the ride, calling out in her strong southern drawl, "Beat you to the creek!" Farther ahead, on the other side of the fence and beyond the trees, was a narrow stretch of water. If one followed the stream, it led to the backside of their property, all the way to the river.

She could hear Jackson spurring his horse in competition. She heeled her horse sharply and crouched down behind the black mane flying in the wind. Kit was lighter on Scimitar than Jackson was on his mare, but she maintained an elegant fluidity on her mount. She relished the breeze flying past as if she had the wings of a bird.

The pair sped along the meadow. Jackson, never one to take a beating well, heeled the horse's left haunch and leaned into the ride. Hoofbeats echoed up the vast fields, and chunks of grass flew behind. This land wasn't new to him; he knew the creek was perhaps a half mile away. He urged his horse to run faster until his mare was nose to tail with Kit's stallion and gaining.

Kit pulled her horse's bridle reins a tad to the right, and Jackson watched her reach up and touch Scimitar's neck. The horse veered right, straight for the high fence that bordered a field with green stubble and a stand of trees beyond. Scimitar drew to the fence at full gallop, lifted his front legs in a practiced motion, and kicked mightily with his rear legs, sailing over the fence with a few inches to spare. They hit hard, jolting Kit's chin near the stallion's head, but she turned her cheek to the right and peered back at the same time. The field was thick with tall grass, and both horse and rider would have tumbled to a sliding halt.

As the range of trees came into view, Jackson, who lacked the skill to jump such a high hurdle, saw Kit and her horse running at full tilt across the field. Clumps of grass showered behind her steed, lifted off the green meadow by the horse's massive hooves.

They both came to the north pasture in a blur. Kit neared the trees, lifted lightly out of the saddle, and leaned forward.

Look at her go! Kit, where'd you learn to ride like that? Jackson watched in awe.

The big Arabian raced on and reached the creek in triumph.

Kit pulled up on her horse, reached down, and stroked its damp neck. Scimitar's sides were billowing as he gasped for air. She pulled off her hat and wiped her forehead with the back of her hand, and giggled. Her gray eyes shone. "That felt good. Thanks for the race. It appears after all these years, I can still best you."

Jackson dismounted and led his horse to the creek's edge. "That you did, Kit. I was never very good at jumping high hurdles. Frightens me if you want to know the truth." He pulled off his broad hat and slapped it against his pant leg.

"Afraid you'd fall?" She brought Scimitar to the cool water and joined Jackson.

"I'm not talking about me, Kit." He walked over to her and touched her left brow. He ran a rough finger down the scar and then cupped her chin, holding it firmly. "I'm talking about you."

She pulled away and looked at the water. "I did fine, didn't I?"

"When's the last time you took that risk?"

She didn't answer but walked to the stream and pulled off her gloves. She tossed them on the grass, along with the felt hat, then went to the edge of the bank and splashed water on her face.

"I didn't mean to embarrass you." He stepped lightly through the damp grass and watched the creek bubbling downstream. The late-afternoon sun cast gold ribbons across the sparkling water.

Kit wiped her face with the sleeve of her jacket and turned to face him. "Is it that visible?" She searched his eyes.

He wanted to throw his arms around her and protect her from ever feeling less than the beautiful woman she'd become. "To tell the truth, I'd forgotten all about that scar until we last met." He took her hand and held it firmly.

"You tend to draw attention to it." He grinned.

She pulled back, but he drew her forward. "Don't. Don't run. Hear me out."

Kit's eyes clung to him, but then she looked away, her face flushed. Something was captivating about her, something all too endearing about the look on her face.

"You're the most beautiful woman I've ever met. Nothing will ever change that, not even this trademark that tells the world how fearless you are." He thumbed her brow and then kissed it.

A small smile broke over her face, and she looked up at him. "Jackson, as far back as I can remember, you've always been my champion." She touched his chest with both hands and fingered the rough material of his shirt. "Why did you come looking for me?"

"You don't know?" He pulled her close.

"Tell me." She smiled up at him.

"Since the last time I rode out here, I've not been able to put you out of my mind." He rubbed her cheek with his thumb.

"And here I thought I was the only one with that problem. You've invaded my every waking moment." She leaned against him, her face upturned. "So what are we going to do about it?"

Jackson's world spun as he bent to kiss her sweet lips. After a long while, he pulled back to drink in her beauty. "I could stay out here forever, but I know that's not possible. Your folks will be looking for us."

"So soon?" Her eyes strayed to the water. "We just got here."

"We shouldn't be here alone. I don't want to soil your reputation."

"Thank you. I must say I feel quite safe with you."

"I'm much obliged, but you shouldn't. You're far too tempting for a man like me." He gave her an amused grin.

"All right. Want to race back?"

"No," he said softly." I want to take our time."

Kit broke away and gathered her hat and gloves. "I'll follow you."

They wove their way through the path in the forest and back onto the west fields. Jackson wanted nothing more than to turn back to the creek and hold her once more. But he was grateful the Bartholomews had allowed him to come alone to find her, and he wouldn't ruin that trust. He wanted more time with the raven-haired southern belle, but he knew he'd have to earn it. In the distance, a bell clanged. "We'd better hurry. Supper's ready."

The house was alive with laughter and talk as Kit and Jackson joined the family.

"Where have you been?" Cameron asked Jackson with a stern look. "I was just about to send a posse out looking for you." He slapped Jackson's back and pointed across the table. "Have a seat over there."

The table was covered in a white-starched tablecloth. Grace's finest silverware was placed beside each china plate. Kit eyed the crystal glasses filled with wine and realized her mother had surely missed having company at River Oak and the past weeks had been trying times, weeks that must have led to some soul-searching. From the looks of the fine spread on the table, her mother was ready to get back to the land of the living and treat each guest special. Before Kit sat down, she kissed her mother's cheek. "The table looks lovely."

"Thank you, Kit. I'm glad you made it back in time. It's been too long since we've had company. Let's make the most of it."

Kit sat between her mother and Bella, looking around the long table. "Goodness, we've not had a full table like this in a while." She looked at her father at the head of the table and Uncle Denzel at the end. Damaris sat across from her and next to Jackson.

"Did you have a nice ride?" Damaris asked with a curious look on her face.

"I did, as a matter of fact." Kit looked at Jackson and kept a straight face.

"Did you race Father's horse?" Bella asked and elbowed her.

Kit looked at her father, whose attention stayed on her. "Ah, yes. I did." Her hand went up. "Scimitar is still a strong horse, given his years. He did very well."

"I'll check on him after supper." Camp winked and looked at the others.

Bringing out a fanfare of food, Gemma, Penny, and Mama Jezelee came through the swinging door from the kitchen, laden with bowls and dishes. On one side of the table sat plates of fried chicken, coleslaw, and sweet potato fritters. On the other side they crowded bowls of sliced peaches, dumplings, sugar peas, mashed potatoes, and a platter of golden biscuits.

The room buzzed until Cameron said, "Bow your heads and I'll say grace. Lord, we thank you for this bounty and for the hands that prepared it."

A round of "Amens" murmured through the room. Food was passed around while conversation resumed.

Everyone filled their plates except Kit, who only dished herself small servings of the scrumptious food. After being at the creek with Jackson, she had lost her appetite. A thought had nagged her much of the ride back. Tonight would be their only time together for a long while. Captain Harding and his sons would soon be sailing to the Caribbean coast. How long would it be before she saw Jackson again? She shoved her vegetables around her plate and felt eyes on her. When she looked up, Jackson held her gaze until the corner of his lip went up.

Laughter and voices came from the small dining room beyond the kitchen, where the younger teens shared a table. An easy feeling filled the house where they were all in one accord. She relished this moment, knowing time had a way of changing their world. She tucked this memory in her heart and picked up her fork.

All was perfect until Kit knocked over her glass of red wine. "Oh!" She gasped and quickly dropped her white napkin over the spill. The puddle of wine seeped through, and Kit groaned. "Oh, dear! I've certainly made a mess!"

Chairs scooted back as everyone went into action. Each one held their napkins out to be of help. The room became a scene of utter confusion as her plate was moved away and more napkins flew to sop up the wine.

"Gemma, come quick!" Grace called as she elbowed her way to Kit's chair. By now, the wine had infused both tablecloth and napkins, bleeding red into the material.

Kit's eyes jumped to Jackson, who restrained his composure for the moment. Heat ran up her neck as she looked at the stained tablecloth. "I'm sorry, Mother. It all looked so lovely."

"Think nothing of it, darling. Accidents happen." Grace looked at the others. "Be seated. We have it under control."

Gemma rushed to Kit's side and picked up the soiled napkins. "I be right back with clean ones." She started to walk out of the dining room but turned. "You want some more of that fine wine?"

Kit bit her bottom lip and looked around the table. It seemed everyone held their breath. "Yes, please."

"Thatta' girl!" Cameron said, and laughter filled the air.

The room grew louder as the men shared stories of past accidents. After dinner, the men moved onto the porch chairs to have a smoke, and Grace led the young women into the parlor, where they broached the subject of Kit's upcoming birthday celebration. "Mrs. Unruh sent a post this afternoon. She'll come by next week for dress fittings."

"She's got them all done?" Bella asked.

"No, of course not. She's started with Kit's and Damaris's. Yours will be next."

"Phooey. Kit always gets hers done first." Bella picked up a sofa pillow and hugged it to herself.

"No, she doesn't," Sunny said. "She did yours first the last time. Maddie and I are always last."

"That's because there's less material to deal with by the time she gets to yours," Grace said. She glanced at the piano. "Sunny, why don't you play a tune for us?"

"All right." Sunny sat on the piano bench and thumbed through the music sheets. Finding one she liked, she placed it on the narrow ledge of the music sheet holder and played the first chord.

Kit and Damaris sat side by side, Damaris's head on Kit's shoulder. They listened quietly as the melody filled the room. Sunny was the only one of the Bartholomew women who had taken an interest in the piano. She learned quickly and saved many a boring night with the songs she played. Music filled the air, and Kit closed her eyes.

Damaris squeezed her arm and whispered, "Did he kiss you?"

Kit lifted her shoulder, nudging Damaris's cheek. "Wouldn't you like to know?"

"He did, didn't he?" She sat up and leaned against Kit. "I want to hear all about it tonight when we go to our room."

Kit opened her eyes and smiled teasingly. "You will, Miss Nosy. And I want to hear all about your rendezvous with Solomon."

Damaris's brows raised, and her eyes gave her away. "How'd you know?"

"Since when do we have a candle in the window?" She elbowed her cousin. "It's so romantic."

Damaris relaxed and laid her chin on Kit's shoulder again. "It is," she said softly. "I'll tell you all about it, too."

A loud burst of laughter floated in from the front porch, and the cool evening air crept in. The spicy scent of cigar smoke filled the air, too. It was all Kit could do to keep her mind on the conversation in the parlor while Jackson sat on the porch with the men.

The bluebirds flitted from perch to swing while Sunny played the piano. Smitty lay on the polished hardwood floor a few feet away, his eyes watching their every movement. His orange and white fur bristled and his tail thumped the floor. The evening wore on until at last the men filed into the parlor.

Sunny played the last key, stood and curtsied, and then sank onto the sofa next to Bella. The room, full of people, continued to buzz.

Drew crossed the floor and reached out a hand to Grace. "Thank you for having us to dinner."

Grace stood and hugged him. "You're always welcome. You don't have to wait for an invitation."

Kit and Jackson stole glances at each other. Her heart sank as the late hour was upon them, and that meant the men were leaving.

"We'll walk you out to the wagon," Cameron said, preceding the men to the door. The young woman stayed put as Grace and Denzel followed the Hardings.

Damaris nudged Kit. "Aren't you going to say goodbye?"

Kit pushed out of the sofa. She didn't need any more coaxing. She quickly stood and found her parents on the carriage lane, talking to Uncle Drew. Jackson stood a few feet away, his eyes searching the front of the house.

She stepped out and saw the glint in his eyes. She picked up her skirts and brushed past the adults to where he stood. A gust of cool air chilled her, and she cupped her elbows with her hands.

Jackson drew her away and spoke in low tones. "We'll be in port for a couple more days. Then we'll be sailing out." He held his hat in his hands and fingered the brim.

"How long before you sail back to Charleston?"

"A month. Your mother sent an invitation to my mother for your coming-out party."

"Camille is coming?"

"I don't think wild horses could keep her away."

"And you?" Kit stepped one foot closer.

"I wouldn't miss it for the world. You'll save me a dance?" His free hand clasped her fingers gently.

"I will." She wanted him to hold her once more, but they didn't dare show affection in front of their families.

Uncle Drew and Woodrow climbed into the wagon. "Jackson, you ready?"

"Yes, sir." Jackson gazed at Kit with warmth in his eyes. "Until then." He placed his hat on his head.

She nodded. "Until then."

He dropped her hand and strode to the wagon, where he stepped onto the wagon wheel and slid onto the bench. He touched the brim of his hat as the horses jerked forward, pulling the wagon out to the long drive.

"They've got a long drive back," Grace said, sliding her arm over Kit's shoulder. "Are you all right?"

"I am." Kit shivered in the cool breeze. "It's going to be a month before they come back."

"A month is a long time. But it'll give you plenty of time to find out where your heart is." She squeezed Kit's shoulders and directed her toward the house.

When Kit looked up at the window, she saw a candle glowing. She smiled. It wasn't likely she'd find Damaris in the room. She was somewhere on the grounds, giving her heart away to a slave, just like her mother had done so many years ago. She hoped Damaris would find true happiness. After many years of pain and hopelessness over the loss of her mother, she deserved a ray of light in the darkness. But was she giving her heart to the wrong man? In another month, she and her family would be sailing back to Barbados. Would she have to leave her heart behind?

Kit glanced down the long drive to the road. Wasn't that what she was doing? Jackson wouldn't remain on dry land for long. The sea was his driving force. He would become a ship merchant just like his father. The four of them were in an awful, love-entwined predicament. And she didn't see any way out of it. *Lord, guide our steps. Set us in the right direction.* She prayed the words, but her heart wasn't in it.

TWENTY

KIT SAT WITH needlepoint in hands. She worked on purple irises, sewing rows of satin stitches for one of the petals while Grace continued to work on her cross-stitch of the pond and gardens. They worked comfortably in each other's presence, with few words needed. After a while Kit looked up from her project and held up the silver needle. "We've been at this for nearly an hour, and I've not seen nor heard a soul in this house." She pushed the threaded needle through the material. "Where is everybody?"

Grace set her needlepoint aside and stretched her neck. "The men and boys are out in the fields, the girls took the boat upriver to see Amy and Florence, and I believe Damaris is upstairs taking a nap, pleading a headache." She smiled softly. "It's not often you and I have time to ourselves. What with all the company, we've hardly spoken two words alone."

"Hmm." Kit glanced toward the stairs. "I hope Damaris feels better after her nap. She's been awfully tense the past couple of days."

"Why so?" Grace picked up her sewing project again.

"She hasn't said." Kit stared out the window toward the slave district. "Maybe she's hating the thought of leaving River Oak at the end of the month."

"I had hoped Denzel and your father would have found Kindra by now. This must weigh heavily on her mind."

"That and Solomon." There, she said it. Sooner or later her parents needed to know that Damaris and Solomon were in love.

"What?" Grace caught her needlepoint before it slid from her lap.

"I've wanted to protect Damaris with her secret, but truth to tell, their relationship has grown. It's all they can do to keep from seeing each other."

"But . . . when? I never see him come around." Her mouth dropped open. "We have to put an end to this right away."

"Mama. Please don't interfere. Let them have their time. She'll be going home soon."

"I will not stand by and let her see him. Her father has entrusted her to our care while they're here."

"Nothing can ever become of it. She'll be going back to Barbados and he's . . . a slave." Kit set her project on the sofa and went to the window. She looked out a long while, her elbows cupped in her hands before she turned back. "I promised Damaris I'd keep her secret."

Grace joined Kit at the window. "How long has this been going on?"

"Since she arrived. It is the only light in her darkness with her mother gone. I'd hate to take that away from her."

"I can't believe this has been going on right before our eyes." Grace pinched the bridge of her nose.

Kit laid a hand on her mother's shoulder. "You've been sick for a while. That has kept you out of the loop of things. So don't be so hard on yourself." Kit rolled her eyes. "Haven't you ever done something you were sure others would be disappointed in before they found out? Besides, it worked for her mother. If Aunt Kindra hadn't fallen in love with Uncle Denzel, Damaris wouldn't be here."

"Yes, but look at all the hard times they've faced, and now your aunt is a slave, and we don't know where she is."

"Father will find her. I believe that, and Uncle Denzel will never give up until Aunt Kindra is home."

"Kit, when I was your age, I thought your Aunt Katy was going to have gray hair within a year of your Grandmother Olivia's death. I wanted to sail to Jamaica to meet my father for the very first time, and Aunt Katy wouldn't hear it. She did everything she could to stop me from sailing, but in those days . . . I was a hardheaded woman." Grace had a far-away look in her eyes. "I sailed to Jamaica and not only met my father, but I met your father too. If I hadn't gone after what I believed I had to do . . ." Her hands went up as she twirled around. "None of this would have happened. And you wouldn't be here."

Kit clutched her mother's shoulders. "Mum's the word?" She held her mother's gaze.

"Oh, Kit." Grace glanced up the stairs and laid a finger on her lips. "I suppose."

"Thank you, Mama." Kit threw her arm around her waist. "She needn't know you know."

The house quiet, Kit hefted her skirts and climbed the stairs to see if Damaris was awake. When she reached the landing, she found the second floor just as silent as the lower. She started to move down the west wing but she saw the guest chamber door cracked open just enough to catch a glimpse of Alice, the upstairs maid sitting on the edge of the bed. Curious, Kit stepped closer and peered in.

She gasped and her hand flew to her mouth! There sat Alice with the peacock journal in her lap. It had been missing for seven years. Had she stolen it from Kit's trunk? From time to time Kit had pulled all of her treasures out of the trunk in hopes of finding the peacock journal and treasure map. Each time she had wondered how the mysterious book and map had disappeared. Never had she considered the housemaid had gone through her personal belongings to steal them.

Heat flared up her neck as she saw the old woman thumb through the pages as if she were trying to read the book. She set it aside and pulled the cloth map out of a drawer by the bed. She held it up and turned it around then suddenly stopped. She lowered the cloth and gazed at the door.

Kit stepped back and held her breath. Ever so quietly, she moved away and turned for her bedchamber, her heart pounding in her chest. *Alice has had the treasure map and peacock book all this time!*

When she looked back, the guest door was closed. *Well, we'll see about that!*

The house came alive at suppertime. The men shuffled into the house with news of the rice nearly ready for shipment. Willie, Zeddie and Cyrus' voices grew loud as they related how one of the blackies had had a tumble with an alligator. "That old alligator lost the battle! The men are building a big ole bonfire while the others are cutting the meat into long strips," Zeddie said. "They'll be eatin' good tonight."

"That happens now and then," Cameron said. "When I first arrived at River Oak, some of the men caught a gator and shot it. They ate good for a week after that. It's pretty tasty if you ask me."

The younger girls filed in, flushed from the afternoon sun and full of news about Florence's and Amy's gowns for the coming out party.

Kit looked around. Damaris and Grace were missing. "Where's Mother?"

"She's upstairs, refreshing herself for supper," Gemma said. "Alice and Hedy getting her dressed and doing her hair."

"I better wake up Damaris."

Slipping past the others, Kit hurried up the stairs and to the guest chamber door. Stepping quietly to her mother's door, she heard the women talking. She returned to the guest chamber and quietly entered. On the table right out in the open lay the peacock journal and the treasure map. She grabbed them up as she looked around the bedchamber before she walked out of the room and closed the door until it clicked. The women could still be heard talking as Kit glanced at her mother's door.

Holding the two items to her chest, she made a quick decision. She wouldn't wake Damaris until she hid the journal and map. She went to the landing and gazed down at the entryway. Could she get down and out of the house before the others saw her? She had to try. Alice would be done with her mother soon, and she didn't want to get caught with the recovered items in her hands.

Lifting her skirts, she tucked the book and map into the waistline of her underskirts. Dropping the hem, she brushed her hand over her stomach and felt the hard lump of the book. Nearly taking the stairs two at a time, she rushed down, flew out the front door, and hit the ground at a run. She could hear Bella Grace calling out. "Where are you going like a bee's in your bonnet?"

Kit stopped and turned around, her arm across her front. "I forgot something in the stable. I'll be right back."

"It can't wait until after supper?"

"No. Go into the house."

Bella shook her golden curls and went inside.

Kit's breath came quickly as she marched to the barn. Once inside, she looked around the musty-smelling stable. "I can't hide these in the house," she mumbled to herself. "But where in heaven's name can I hide them out here?"

She held her skirts as she looked in stalls and in the corner where bales of hay were stacked. "I can't hide them there. Nate will find them." Her heart pounded as the sun dropped behind the horizon. She frantically looked around.

Beyond the stalls stood a tack room. She looked at the closed door and relief washed over her. She heard the horses breathe and chuff at her as she quietly moved to the door and pushed it open. It was dark inside, but she didn't need to light the kerosene lamp. An old chest of drawers held miscellaneous tack. But it also held things that had belonged to Kit when she was a child. Nate never bothered the bottom drawer.

She scraped the rough drawer open and pulled out her old gloves and riding skirt. There were other items that meant nothing to anyone but her. She quickly stuffed the journal and map into the back of the drawer and replaced the gloves and skirt. She stared down at the open drawer. One could not tell there was anything suspicious hidden there. She pushed the drawer closed and stood, then stepped outside the tack room, closed the door, and went to the basket where Nate kept a few apples.

Going to Ginger's stall, Kit held out the apple toward the filly. "How are you, little lady?"

The young horse nudged her hand and took the apple. She backed away and chomped on the fruit. When she finished, she pushed her head over the stall door.

"Can you keep my secret?" Kit petted her velvet nose. A sound interrupted her thoughts at the stable entrance and Kit leaned back to see who'd come to the barn.

Willie stomped in. "Kit!"

"Over here."

"What are you doing?" He came to where she stood.

"I forgot to give Ginger an apple today." She held out her hand and massaged the filly's forehead.

Willie's hands went to his hips. "You and your horses."

"She's not mine. But I wish she were." She gave Ginger a pat on the head and moved away from the stall. "Supper ready?"

"Yes. Dad sent me out to get you."

"Let's not keep them waiting." She moved in front of Willie and walked out into the night air. Up ahead the Great House was lit up in all the windows. "It looks homey, doesn't it?"

"If you say so." Willie strode ahead and kept going.

One would never know that secrets lurked beyond those walls. She picked up her step.

After supper, instead of joining the women in the parlor, Kit went up to her room. Her door stood ajar. Kit moved close and pushed it open. There on the opposite side of the bed stood Alice, shuffling through Kit's belongings in the brown trunk. "Can I help you?"

Alice jerked and pushed to her feet. She looked at Kit with a knowing eye but said nothing. Instead, she walked around the bed and brushed past her as she left the room.

"Alice!" Shaken, Kit watched the maid stomp to the guest bedchamber and close the door. *Good Lord, what am I to do?* She couldn't trust Alice, not after she caught her red-handed. Kit picked up the rest of her belongings and placed them in the trunk. When done, she sat on the lid in the dark. What should she do about Alice? She gazed out the door to the hallway that was dimly lit in golden hues, her mind racing. She couldn't tell her mother the maid was untrustworthy. She too was not to be trusted. Hadn't she found the map those men were after—the ones who'd raided their house?

Would the maid tell her mother about her secret? She got up and paced the floor and then stopped. She looked out the window onto the lawn and the lazy river beyond. She wished she'd never found the book and map, and yet somehow, she believed she should keep them to herself, at least a little longer.

The maid wouldn't tell her mother about the map. She wanted them for herself, Kit reasoned. Her fluttering heart quieted at the thought.

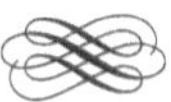

After breakfast Kit returned to her room. It was a wreck. Her drawers, chests, and wardrobe, had been gone through, and her clothes were thrown on the floor. She knew who it must have been.

"Now she's done it!" She marched into a room Alice was cleaning and slammed the door open. The maid drew back, her hands going to her mouth.

"As a housekeeper, your job is to dust the furniture and floors and sometimes tend to my mother. You will stay out of my room! Do you understand?"

"Yes'm, Miz Kit. I do."

"You will return to my room and clean up the mess you made. I want every garment in my drawers and in my wardrobe replaced neatly the way they should be."

Alice clamped her mouth shut, but she bowed her head and crept past Kit to do her bidding. Kit stood at the threshold with her arms crossed and watched the solemn maid as she obediently picked up each item and folded, tucked, stored, and hung the clothing.

When she finished, Alice turned to her. "I be sorry, Miz Kit."

"You should be. From here on out, if I so much as see one thing out of place" Kit pointed her finger at Alice, "you'll be standing on the auction block. I won't put up with your shenanigans again." Although she was whispering, there was no mistaking the tone of her voice.

"Miz Kit?"

"What?"

"Does yer mama knowed what you got?"

"Don't threaten me, Alice. You're walking a tight line."

"Why that book be so important to you?"

Kit stared at the housemaid. "I don't know what you're talking about."

Alice shook her head and waved a hand at her. "I give up. I won't be huntin' fer that fancy book no more." She stepped out of the bedchamber.

"No. You won't." Kit moved into the hallway, shut the door, and watched the maid retreat to her room. She brushed her hands down her skirt.

Why do I want the map and journal? She clamped her jaw. Somehow, she knew they would lead to something important in their lives. They were tied to something she didn't know about. Until she found out what that could be, they'd stay hidden in the barn.

TWENTY-ONE

CUFFEE RAN THE back of his hand over his sweaty face. Memories of Whitestone tumbled over and over and chafed his mind until it was worn raw. With the tail of his shirt, he wiped the grit from his weary eyes.

He had to keep moving. He cut the stems from the rice stalks and laid them carefully aside. From where he stood, he glanced across the fields. Acres of rice fields stood bare, the rice stems cut and bundled for threshing, and waiting to be packed into coopered barrels for shipment. And yet, looking to his right, hundreds of acres of rice waited for the harvest to continue.

All the while, bent to the task with a sickle in hand, his mind roved over the past five years he had spent with Kindra. He felt a kindred spirit for her, and in his own way, he wanted to protect her from her new masters. It haunted him that he didn't know where she'd gone or who had purchased her. He only hoped that her new venture would be better than the plantation they had left.

The news that Captain Drew Harding had seen her riding on the back of a wagon going through town riddled his mind. Was she going to a plantation that would treat her well, or would she be doomed to a fate worse than Whitestone? The worst part of the continual grappling to make sense of it all was that she wasn't his responsibility any longer. He could no longer help her. He needed to come to grips with the fact that he was home with his family and his beautiful wife, Tabitha. He shouldn't be wrestling with thoughts of Kindra. Yet here he was, once again standing in the middle of a rice field, his heart and mind in a quandary.

Guilt riddled him. He hadn't told Tabitha the truth about him and Kindra.

That alone tortured him. He wanted no secrets between him and his wife. He bent and grasped the ripe stems in one hand and brought the sickle near the base with the other. He carefully laid the rice atop the cut base to dry. Tonight, he would put an end to the relentless agony of his soul. He would tell Tabitha the rest of the story. He would tell her what had gone on between him and Kindra. *The truth will set you free*, the Good Book says. He wanted to be free of his raging thoughts. He wanted peace more than anything.

His family had plenty to say about their day's work. Cuffee listened quietly, waiting for the right moment to speak to Tabitha. As his daughters cleared the table, he held his wife's hand, keeping her in her seat. "Let the girls do the work, Mama. You put in a long day in the field. It's yer turn to rest." He squeezed her hand. "Let's go for a walk." He pushed back his chair and pulled her to her feet.

"I haven't taken a walk in such a while. That be soundin' good." Tabitha turned to the girls. "Clean the dishes and then get ready for bed."

"We will, Mama," the girls chimed.

Stepping out into the brisk air, Cuffee said, "It's chilly. I'd better get you a wrap. Wait here." As he stepped back into the house, he noticed Solomon at the table, a grim look on his face.

"Sumthin' wrong?" Cuffee asked.

"Don't be worryin' 'bout me," Solomon said. He drummed his fingers on the tabletop.

Cabeto eyed his brother with a suspicious gleam. "He can't git his mind off the mistress's niece." He shoved Solomon's shoulder.

"That purty girl at the Big House?" Toby asked.

"Ain't none of yer business!" Solomon scooted his chair back, brushed past Cuffee, and stormed out of the house.

Cuffee raised his brows and plucked Tabitha's sweater off the wall peg. He looked back to see his two daughters watching him. "He sho' been moody since I been home. I don't know what to make of it." He didn't wait for a reply. He quickly joined Tabitha at the front of the steps and slid her sweater over her shoulders.

For the first few moments, they walked in silence down the dirt road toward the rice fields. "The men be sayin' there be sightings of a twelve-foot alligator in the swamps. The trees are denser and it be darker over there. I'm not sure we should be walkin' that way at night." Cuffee said.

"You be scarin' me with that kinda talk. Let's walk down by the river," Tabitha said.

Cuffee directed her in the opposite direction, a grin on his lips. "Walkin' with you on the banks of the river sho' sound good to me."

As they passed their shanty, Cuffee looked over his shoulder toward the shadows of the house and the trees lining the road. Nothing moved, but he took a shallow breath.

"Cuffee?" Tabitha looked up at him.

"I thought someone was following us. I must be mistaken."

"Lord have mercy, they's always folks out on the road at night. It's safe here." She walked beside him as if she hadn't a care in the world. Cuffee looked down at his woman, and his heart began to swell. Did she know how much he loved her?

They strolled to the entrance to the slave district and moved down the sloped lawn toward the road that ran parallel to the river. The black velvet sky held a million diamond stars. A huge white disk hung among them, showering the earth with a silvery glow. The water sparkled and quivered in the cool breeze.

"I'm thinkin' you got somethin' important on yer mind." Tabitha looked up at him once they reached the road.

"You asked me 'bout Kindra the other day. I told you we'd talk about that when we're alone."

She stiffened under his arm. "Go on."

"Massa Abrams bought both of us at auction. I didn't want the massa and the overseer to know that Miss Kindra and I knew each other. When we rode in the back of the wagon to the new plantation, I told her not to talk to me."

"Why's that?"

"'Cause then I wouldn't be allowed around her."

"You wanted to be around Miz Kindra?"

"Not the way you be thinkin'."

"I ain't thinkin' anything, but you bettah explain."

"I felt responsible to Massa Cooper."

"You thought Miz Kindra be yer responsibility?"

"That's right."

Tabitha stopped walking. "Did it work?"

Cuffee looked down at her, his gut swirling. "More than I wanted it to."

"What you mean by that?"

"The mistress wanted Miss Kindra married. She be wantin' babies from her."

Tabitha lowered her chin and slid out from under his arm. She stared at the river. "What does that have to do with you?"

"They made me marry Miss Kindra." There, he'd said it. He clamped his hands on Tabitha,'s shoulders as she faltered in her step.

"Y-you married Kindra?"

"I didn't have any choice. We talked about it and agreed to savin' our love fer our spouses. The massa, he don't know we talked it out. She don't want to marry me, no more than I don't want to marry her. But when we be sold to the likes of those people, they say they own our souls."

Tabitha's head hung low.

Cuffee went on. "We never made a marriage bed, Tabitha. I saved myself fer you. She saved herself fer Denzel. We stuck to our agreement all those years."

"Did you sleep with her?"

An iron weight slammed into his gut. "Yes."

Tabitha moved away.

Cuffee let her. "There be people who share our shanty. We couldn't let them tell Massa Abrams we don't sleep together." He turned her to face him. "If one of the slaves in the shanty had told Massa we didn't look married, he would have pulled us out of the house and whipped us in front of all the slaves, and makin' an example of us. We seen more cruelty on that plantation than was human."

A tear trickled down Tabitha's cheek, and Cuffee wiped it away. "I saved my love fer you all those years. There ain't never been anyone besides you."

Tabitha nodded, the moonlight shining on her glistening tears. She walked into his arms and held him tightly.

Relief washed over him and he let out a long breath he hadn't realized he'd been holding. "When I got here and laid eyes on you, I thought my heart would plumb jump outta my chest. You be the best thing my eyes seen in a long time."

Tabitha rested her head on his chest. She still hadn't spoken a word.

"I can't do nuthin' 'bout the past, but I be workin' every day till I be laid to rest to show you that you be the light o' my life."

She looked up and, with both hands, clasped his cheeks and pulled his head down. He tasted her sweet lips. Warm honey coated his insides. He was home.

A limb snapped in a bush nearby. Cuffee's head jerked up to listen. "You hear that?"

Tabitha nodded. "Let's get back to the house."

They strode up the lawn to the slave district, and all the while Cuffee glanced back to the grounds behind him. Who was out there? When they reached the shanty, Tabitha climbed the steps. A dim light shone when she opened the door. Cuffee waited at the base of the steps.

"Are you coming?"

"Not yet. I'll only be a moment." Shadows lurked everywhere. The tall oaks that lined the street had branches that stretched across the lane. Silver light speckled the ground below. Long shadows loomed every which way along the road from the branches above.

Cuffee felt someone behind him and spun around. There stood Solomon with gritted teeth, arms at his sides, hands balled into fists.

Cuffee's chest fell. "Why you hidin' out there, son? Why you listenin' in on our conversation?"

"You shouldn't have come back."

"That's not fer you to say. You forget who we be. We slaves, boy. You got a problem with me bein' here, you best be takin' it to the Massa."

Solomon gave him a stony glare. "I heard what you told Mama. After all these years, you come back and plunge a knife in Mama's heart!" Solomon raised his fist.

"Stop it, Solomon. It hurt yer Mama to hear the truth. But I won't live a lie. I had to tell her what had gone on in my past, so we could move on in our future."

"None of this would have happened if you hadn't of been so eager to do Tia's bidding." His lips curled in disgust.

"Is that what you think? You think I wanted to help that heathen woman smuggle slaves?"

"You helped her, didn't you?" Solomon broke a twig from a limb and threw it across the road.

"Not because I wanted to. I hated it. Every time that woman come fer me, my stomach would sour. I always had high regard for Massa Cooper. She done made me do him wrong."

"Why didn't you tell the massa? You got yerself so caught up in her stunts that when Mama be lyin' in the ditch by the road, givin' birth to Toby, you be long gone! It only be by the grace o' God that she get help from the mistress and the neighbors. Mama and Lily be thrown from the cart in the middle of the night, and all because they be lookin' fer you!"

"What you be sayin', son?"

"I'm sayin' Mama never gave up on you. She be prayin' her heart out every night you be gone. She be prayin' you come home. Here you were, a million miles away and takin' care of Miz Kindra as yer wife!" Tears streamed down Solomon's dark face, and he took a deep breath. He stepped forward, clamped his large hands on Cuffee's shoulder, and shook him. "Don't you be knowin' it be killin' Mama that you married another? All the while, she be prayin' fer you to come home!"

"Git yer hands off me, boy!" Cuffee's hands went up and he threw Solomon off. He pushed him back and shoved a finger in his face. "It weren't like you be thinkin'. We were married in name only. I never touched Miss Kindra." Cuffee scowled. "When Massa Abram forced us to take the vows, we agreed to it so they leave us alone. She kept herself fer Denzel, and I kept myself fer yer mama." Cuffee lifted his chin to stare Solomon in the eye. "And all that time we never know if we ever goin' home!" When Solomon returned Cuffee' look, Cuffee saw revelation dawn in his son's face.

"You didn't love Miz Kindra?"

"No, not like a man loves a woman. I cared about her welfare and we became good friends. But we lived in a shanty full of slaves." He shook his head. “Why am I tellin’ you all this? You been sneakin’ in the bushes and heard it all.”

Solomon shook his head and his hands went to his hips. He stared as if he were looking over the roof of the shanty, his mind working on something. A moment later he laid a gentle hand on Cuffee’s shoulder. “I’m sorry, Dad. You did good.” He walked to the front steps, his shoulders squared and his back straight. He didn’t look back.

Cuffee watched his son disappear inside the house. “He sho’ ain’t no boy anymore. He be a man if ever there be one.” He shook his head and rubbed his chest. “A strong buck at that.” Pride washed over him. He looked past the shanties to the far fields bathed in the moon’s faint light. *I be makin’ up fer lost time with my Tabitha. She deserves better than she’s been dished out. I got a lotta makin’ up to do.*

Captain Drew Harding, Grace, and Cameron sat in the parlor, talking in low tones.

“I didn’t think you’d be back before you sailed,” Grace said, keeping her eyes on Jackson and Kit sitting on the porch swing just past the window. “All those years ago, when I sailed on the *Savannah Rose* to find my father, I never dreamed there would come a day our children would become attracted to each other. They could possibly bind our families together more than they already are.”

“Drew was like family long before we had families of our own,” Cameron said.

“Yes, I know.” Grace smiled, melancholy settling in her soul. “When I met Camille, I understood why Captain Harding couldn’t wait to sail to Jamaica. We quickly became friends.”

Drew stared out the window. “Now my son is sailing in the opposite direction and all for the sake of love.”

“Hmm,” Grace murmured. “Love is a wonderful thing.”

“Let’s just hope nothing happens to spoil things between them. I kinda like the idea of Jackson for a son-in-law,” Cameron said.

Grace started giggling. “Just look at us planning their future.”

Just then, Bella Grace slammed the front door as she walked in from outside.

"Bella!" Grace said. "What's gotten into you?"

"Adam just rode up on his bay. That's what."

The three adults darted glances at each other.

"And I was just getting ready to tell you we'd best get going." Drew stood and started for the foyer.

"Oh, no," Grace moaned. "We'll walk you out."

Disconcerted that Adam Sparrow rode up just when Jackson, his father, and his brother were getting ready to leave, Kit kept her gaze averted from her neighbor. When Jackson was gone, she turned to Adam and raised her chin. "What brings you here?"

Adam looked up at the sky where the moon set the world in its spotlight. It lit the ground around them, and the river mirrored its brightness. "I went to check on the horses in the stable. When I stepped outside, the whole world seemed bright as day. For the life of me, I didn't want to miss this moment, as winter is just around the corner." He gazed lazily at her with a look she didn't want to acknowledge.

"I jumped on my horse and followed the lane down here, hoping to share it with you." His gaze went to the horses trotting down the lane toward Fields Landing. "I didn't know the Hardings were here."

Heat crept up Kit's neck. "They came to say goodbye. They'll be out to sea for a fortnight. Maybe longer."

Adam hadn't dismounted. He sat tall in the saddle, a silhouette against the silver lighting. She couldn't read the expression on his face, but she felt it. He watched her for a long moment.

"Care to take a walk along the river?" Adam asked.

Kit sucked in her breath. That was the last thing she wanted. She had no desire to lead Adam along with false hopes. In her mind, there would never be anything romantic between them. She watched him slide out of the saddle and wrap the reins around the front post. He held out his elbow.

Clamping her teeth tightly, she accepted the gesture and slipped her hand through the crook of his arm. Slowly, they meandered to the riverbank.

Fish swam to the surface and ate water bugs that flitted across the water. Frogs croaked somewhere near the muddy banks, and the peacocks cried out in the distance. She pulled her arm from his and crossed them over her chest as if chilled.

"Are you cold?" Adam stepped closer and drew her into his side, his hand firmly holding her shoulder. "Peaceful, isn't it?"

"Yes. It's peaceful. I don't come to the water's edge often enough at night. There's a quiet beauty here."

"This is what I wanted to share with you. I can't think of anyone else who would understand and appreciate the stark beauty of the land and the river like you do."

Kit pressed her lips together, trying to hold back the tears that suddenly sprang to her eyes. Adam was a good man. He deserved someone who would appreciate and love him for who he was. But her heart wasn't in it. She hated the thought of hurting him. She cleared her throat. "Adam."

"Don't."

"What?"

"Don't say it."

"But . . ."

"Give it some time, please. I see how you look at Jackson and how he looks at you. But he's going to be gone a very long time. I'm here."

"Adam."

"Just think about it, okay? You don't have to rush into anything." He dropped his arm and wiped his face. "As long as I can remember, I have dreamed of you being my girl. And now that you are coming of age . . ." He looked down the lane that was now empty.

"It just happened, Adam. I don't know how. But it did."

"I know. I saw my world inching toward another."

"That's not fair, Adam. I've never done anything to make you think we were an item."

"No, you haven't. Not on purpose anyway."

Kit turned to walk up the lawn. She couldn't do this anymore. She needed to persuade Adam to leave her be.

"Kit."

She stopped walking and felt him coming.

He reached her side. "I'm sorry. I sound like a desperate fool."

"Well, at least you have that right. I've not made a commitment to anyone, and I won't for a while. I've yet to have my coming-out party."

"That's just it. All the single men in Fields Landing and Charleston will be pounding on your front door." He crooked a smile.

They had reached the steps to the front porch.

"Good night, Adam."

He looked as if he wanted to throw his arms around her. Instead, he stepped up to the bay and mounted her. "Goodnight, Kit. Save me a dance at the party." He clicked his tongue, and the horse trotted out of sight down the long drive.

Kit looked up at the candle in her bedroom window. "Lord, have mercy." She lifted her skirts and climbed the steps. "It'll be a while before I can talk to Damaris," she whispered to no one. She stood in the shadows of the porch and looked out at the shining river. If only Jackson could have been the one to walk her to the water's edge. She would have thrown herself into his arms. But he was gone, and would be for a very long time, just as Adam had said. She'd wait for Jackson. She'd wait forever if she had to.

Jackson stood on the main deck and looked around. Up above him, sailors clambered back and forth, balancing on thin ropes, repairing the foresail rigging, and hoisting a new mainsail. His father had gone to his cabin to look at the books. He'd left the details to Jackson. When all the repairs and preparations had been made and final orders given to the first mate, Jamie, Jackson commanded the grapnels released and all canvas set to the wind. The sails caught the breeze and made a jaunty snap. The *Savannah Rose* coursed through the waters as the foamy spray splashed over the bow. Jackson stood at the rail and watched the shore fade away.

They'll be gone for the next few weeks. He wanted nothing more than to deliver the cargo to its destination and return to Charleston. He hadn't cared for Adam Sparrow showing up just as he left River Oak. Didn't he know Kit was spoken for? The ship lifted on a swell and dipped in the valley. He loved how the vessel soared through the waters. But did he love it more than being with Kit? His heart torn, he turned away from the rail and watched the sailors take their places.

Wait for me, Kit. I'll be back as quickly as I can!

TWENTY-TWO

Kindra Hall Plantation, Barbados

"MIZ TIA, DO I see love in the air this evening?" Mayme asked.

A smooth grin played on Tia's face as she sat straight on the vanity chair. "What gives you that notion?"

"I be seein' those blue eyes of yers lookin' a bit brighter these days, and mostly after you and the overseer be takin' a walk."

Tia fingered the folds of her turquoise-colored day dress and played with the idea of admitting her fascination of the foreman. She hadn't planned on falling in love with the man. At first she had resisted him, thinking he was too hard on her. He didn't cower to her harshness as others had. She'd never known a man to be so patient with a woman such as she. Especially those first weeks after she had arrived at Kindra Hall fresh from prison with a heart full of hate.

Little by little, Ebenezer broke through the brick wall she'd built to keep others out. And little by little, she had started to look forward to the wise words that fell from his lips. If she rejected his counsel, it was like water off a duck's back. Nothing seemed to ruffle him. Ebenezer's take on life was solid through and through. He believed a person could turn their life around, and his confidence was contagious. She found herself wanting to hear more of what he had to say. Surprisingly, much of his wisdom came from the Word he'd hidden in his heart. So much so that in recent days she was inclined to search out those truths in Kindra's Bible. The more she searched, the hungrier she found herself to read from the Good Book.

All this time her appreciation and devotion grew for Ebenezer. He was a strong man, inside and out. His square jaw, usually spattered with a day's growth of black and speckled with a hint of gray, always caught her attention. He was a starkly handsome man with nearly black eyes who didn't need her permission to stand his ground. He'd been holding his own long before she arrived. And in some ways, he held a powerful pervasiveness in his attitude with her and others that intrigued her. How could one so kind and gentle appear so strong and powerful? Yes, she'd fallen hard for this man and wondered what the future held for them.

"Miz Tia?" Mayme's voice brought her back to the present.

"I'm sorry, Mayme. You are right. I believe the overseer has thrown the sharp hooks of his fishing line into the muddy waters and pulled me out of the mire. And in doing so, he has helped me clean up my life. I not only owe him my gratitude; I've fallen in love with him to boot."

Mayme brushed Tia's hair away from her face and straight behind and began plaiting it in a rhythm she'd grown used to, working the braid down her back. "Your hair is beautiful, Miz Tia. I remember when you first arrived, how straggly it be. Lookin' at it now, it recover real nice."

"Thank you, Mayme. The gray streak has grown wider on this side, but I don't mind."

When Mayme twisted the end of Tia's hair, she tied a turquoise ribbon to hold it in place. "There you go." She patted Tia's shoulder. "Do you need me for anything else?"

"No, Mayme. I believe I'll sit on the porch a while."

"The day's been a scorcher. I'm thinkin' this evening has brought a bit of cool air."

"Carry on." Tia left her dressing room and gracefully descended the stairs. When she came onto the porch, she found that a tropical trade wind had blown in. She went to the porch rail as she often did and gazed at the moon.

"Everybody in the world sees the moon at night. Is my Kindra looking at the moon too?" She whispered her thought as she often did. She'd learned to talk to God in every circumstance. When she was alone with the vast sky overhead, she imagined it was only she and God with the hundreds of thoughts rippling through her mind. She knew her Father in heaven cared about the smallest details of her life. And when alone, she liked to talk to

Him.

A breeze sailed around her, ruffling her skirts. The tall palm trees in the long driveway bent softly in the current, their fronds feathering to the right and the light of the moon shining on their slick branches in a shimmering glow.

She raised her face and closed her eyes. Bring my daughter home. I have trespassed against her. I so dearly want to ask her forgiveness.

"Good evening." Ebenezer's deep voice broke into the contented spell.

"And good evening to you." Tia left the rail and descended the steps.

"Care to take a walk with me?"

"I'd be delighted to," Tia said. "That moon is yearning for our company."

Ebenezer chuckled and squeezed her hand warmly in his. "I'm sure likin' the change in you, Miz Tia. There be some fine choice words that be hidin' in yer heart far too long."

"Go on with you, Ebenezer." She swung his hand playfully.

Their steps led them where it always did. They left the front walkway and meandered down the long drive. Trees arched overhead, nearly blocking the stars and moon, but when they came to the main road, the sky opened up to them like a black velvet carpet sprinkled with diamonds as far as the eye could see.

After a long silence, Ebenezer asked, "Were you talkin' to Him 'bout Kindra?"

"Yes. You said if I keep knocking on His door, He might answer. I've been pretty pesky lately, knocking every chance I get."

"Don't give up, Tia."

The scent of jasmine filled the warm breeze and Tia took in a deep breath. "Did you know jasmine flowers have always been my favorite?"

"No. You never said."

"Well, they are. In earlier years I'd pluck a jasmine petal and put it in my hair, just so I could smell it all day long."

"That be how God sees you, honey. A gentle flower on this Earth."

Tia stopped walking. Her heart felt as if it were about to burst. "Is it true? Does God love me that much? Has He really forgiven me for all my evil deeds?"

"It's true, Tia. He took those sins and threw them in the deepest seas. His

Book said He won't remember them anymore."

The path blurred in front of her as tears swam in her eyes. "I don't deserve it."

"None of us do," Ebenezer said.

They walked on in silence a while before Ebenezer spoke. "There be a softness about you these days. The harsh Tia done gone and died when you asked Him into your heart. Standing before me is the creature you were meant to be, soft and pretty. Your soul's not black no more. It's white just like them jasmines you be longin' for."

They walked on, Tia's hand in the crook of his arm.

"Would you like to go on a picnic tomorrow?" Eb asked.

"A picnic?" The thought sent a thrill up her back. *What does one bring to a picnic?* "Do you know I've never gone on a picnic—not once in my life."

Astonishment lit up Eb's face. "Surely, you lie."

"I'm done with lying, my love. You forget I was a slave before I became the headmistress at Cooper's Landing."

Ebenezer dropped her hand and strode to the edge of the road. "I remember Massa Cooper. He come here every few months and check on Kindra Hall. He'd come to see for hisself that the tobacco plantation prosperin' like it should." Ebenezer looked up at the sky as if checking to see the stars were still there. He didn't look at her when he said, "You be his mistress then."

Tia swallowed and said quietly, "He made me headmistress of the Great House. I didn't have any choice in the matter. I was full of myself back then. You wouldn't have liked me. Not many people did." Tia crossed the road and reached out for Ebenezer's work-roughened hand. "I had everything a woman could ever need, and yet it was never enough. I was miserable. Simple pleasures such as going on a picnic were the furthest things from my mind." She lifted his hand to her lips. "You have shown me it is the simple things in life that matter." She kissed the top of his hand again. "And I thank you for that."

"So—I be the first person to take you on a picnic?"

A chorus of crickets sang in the trees as they stood there. Frogs croaked in the distant brush. They all seemed to wait for her answer. She swallowed again and looked back at the Great House. The first floor looked homey, all lit up. No one would have guessed that Denzel and his family were gone, leaving a big hole in her heart. She missed them terribly and couldn't wait for the family to come home. Only then would she feel all was right again.

She gazed into Ebenezer's dark eyes. "Yes, you will be the first person to take me on a picnic. Funny thing is, I don't have the foggiest idea what to bring." She leaned her forehead on his and laughed softly.

Ebenezer pulled her close and whispered, "All we need is a blanket to sit on and food to eat."

She grazed her lips across his rough beard and backed up. "That doesn't sound difficult. I can round those items up." She clenched her hands together and raised them to her chest. "I must go in, as it's late and getting cold."

The two of them retraced their steps to the front porch. Tia turned to Ebenezer. "I'll see you tomorrow."

"At noon?"

"That'll be fine." She stepped back into his arms. "Tomorrow then?" With that she turned toward the house and climbed the steps. *A picnic!*

Tia felt a hint of excitement as Mayme finished tying the wine-colored ribbon at the end of her hair. Her tresses hung down her back in a loose braid. "Let's get my dress on."

"This be one of yer nicest day dresses, Miz Tia." Mayme buttoned her up.

"I know. I don't wear it often enough." Tia turned sideways to decide if she should wear it for the day's outing or change. "Is it too much, do you think?"

"Not at all. It be fitting fer such an event. You'll see."

"Enough talk about my dress. Tell Boaz to send for the stableman to bring the wagon around to the front of the house. He can leave it there. I believe Ebenezer will want to drive."

"Yes'm. I be tellin' him right away." Mayme left the room.

Tia stood before the mirror and squared her shoulders, and then she pulled in her tummy. *Was her dress too much?* She shook her head. Why am

I acting like a school girl going to a dance, instead of the old hag that I am? Why, look at that gray streak in my hair. Look at those wrinkles at the corners of my eyes. My youthfulness has faded like ashes in the wind. She smiled warmly and allowed her shoulders to relax. "That man coming for me today, he knows all about my features. He doesn't seem to care. Not only that, he's learned all about my evil ways and he's shown more love and forgiveness than anyone on God's green Earth." She chuckled and shook her head. "I'm one lucky woman." She looked out the window and up at the blue sky scattered with clouds. "Lord, did You have a hand in that?" Seeing Abner bringing the wagon to the front of the house, Tia turned from the window, scooped up the colorful quilt, and descended the stairs.

Boaz waited at attention near the foyer. She held out the quilt to him. "Put this in the back of the wagon. And if you see Ebenezer, tell him I'll be out directly."

"Yes'm."

The noise and laughter in the kitchen drew her attention there. She pushed the swinging door and entered the bustling room with suspicion that much of the tittering was likely about her. When she stepped in, the room grew quiet.

Louiza came forward. "You jist 'bout ready for yer outing today?" A gleam showed in her brown eyes.

"As ready as I can be. Have you packed our lunch in the basket?"

"Yes'm. I think you'll be pleased as punch."

Tia eyed Louiza's shiny face. "What did you put in there?" She lifted the corner of the white dish towel and peeked in.

"Jist some sandwiches, fruit, and a bottle of wine." Louiza held her hands in front of her and rocked on her heels. "Is there anything else you'd like?"

Clara waved a hand in the air and fussed with the towel, covering the food again. "We put napkins in there, along with Kindra's fine china and a couple o' crystal glasses. We made eaten' yer fruit easy too, by slicin' the mango and puttin it in bowls."

"Thank you, Clara, Louiza. Boaz is taking the quilt to the wagon." Tia clenched the folds of her dress. "I don't mind telling you this is my first picnic."

Clara and Louiza hugged her. "You'll do fine, Miz Tia. Jist think on relaxin' in the sun. You never know if you get a chance to do this again."

A sharp vision of Kindra being dragged away in the mud flashed through her mind. She closed her eyes and pinched the bridge of her nose.

"You all right?" Louiza held Tia's shoulders to steady her.

"Yes. Yes I'm fine. I just need to remember to take every day one day at a time. And like you said, learn to relax."

Netty came into the kitchen. "Ebenezer waitin' by the wagon, Miz Tia."

"I'll carry this out for you." Louiza picked up the bulky picnic basket and led the way.

As Tia sat up on the wooden bench with Ebenezer, she looked back to see Boaz, Netty, and Louiza standing on the porch and waving at them. It warmed her heart to see the smiles on the house servants' faces. She felt forgiveness in so many areas of her life. Could it really be that easy?

Once the wagon rolled out to the main road, Ebenezer began to whistle a tune. He seemed to be in good spirits today, and Tia listened attentively.

"Where did you learn to whistle like that?" Tia hooked her hand through the crook of his arm. Ebenezer held the reins with his left hand and looked down at her. "My daddy taught me. He was a whistlin' man if ever there be one." He smiled and flicked the reins. "One day the slavers come take me away from him. I was fourteen years old. I never see my daddy again. But I always be rememberin' his whistle." He kept his eyes on the road. "You ever try it?"

"Oh, no. Never."

He took up whistling again as they drove toward the meadows on the grounds of Kindra Hall. She listened and smiled. Everything he did these days made her smile. It was when they were apart that her heart became solemn. She would sit in her room alone and think about her daughter lost somewhere in the world.

She missed Kindra terribly and had learned to pray to Ebenezer's God, Kindra's God, and now her God that He would bring Kindra home. But when she stood in Ebenezer's presence, he bestowed such assurance that God heard her prayers that her heart leapt with joy. She could believe God had heard her and was working everything out for good. She had to trust Him. She had to let go, and let God work things out to bring her daughter home.

Ebenezer changed his whistle to a slower tune and held the reins loosely in his hands. The wagon jiggled on the rough road. The sky filled with fluffy gray and white clouds but still showed plenty of blue in between. If they could get through the next few hours without a shower, she'd be grateful. Her eyes filled with happy tears. She was sitting beside the kindest man on Earth and they were going on a picnic.

Ebenezer pulled on the reins. "Whoa, there," he called gently as they rolled slowly beside a large oak tree in the meadow. "I think we've found the perfect spot." He set the brake and climbed down. He walked behind the wagon around to her side and held out his hand. "Easy now." He helped her down.

When her feet touched the ground, she ran her hands down the front her dress and looked around the meadow. In the distance a spray of flowers looked as if they were sprinkled on top of the green grass. Tamarind and oak trees stood tall here and there, and parrots and popinjays flew and landed on branches. They cocked their colorful heads as if curious at the people who occupied their neck of the woods. They began to caw and chatter, spreading their green and yellow wings as they flew over trees to chatter with other birds in the area.

"It didn't take long to get out here," Tia said.

"I been spyin' this tree fer a while, thinkin' you'd look real pretty sittin' under it, Miz Tia."

"I'm told that while we're out here, I should relax. Let's get the quilt out and do just that." She strode to the back of the wagon and pulled the quilt to her, while Ebenezer picked up the basket. In a matter of minutes, they spread the quilt over the soft carpet of grass, one side up against the trunk of the old oak.

Ebenezer lay on his back with his hands behind his head. Tia leaned against the trunk and closed her eyes. A soft breeze sailed about them as they lazed in silence. At the moment, they didn't feel the need to talk. Being together was enough.

Tia dreamed of the days she'd been in prison. Back then she couldn't wait to get out of the confines of the prison walls and find the emeralds. But now that she was out, she'd found something far more valuable than the gems. She'd found Ebenezer. It was almost heaven, sitting here listening to the bird's chattering overhead, feeling the soft stirring of the wind and being in the presence of this man.

“I’m gettin’ hungry.” Ebenezer broke the silence.

Tia’s eyes snapped open and she rolled onto her knees. “Well, let’s see what the cooks packed for us.” She removed the white tea towel, pulled out the food, and set the china plates on the blanket. Ebenezer poured the wine into the crystal glasses and grinned as he held his up in the air. “To us,” he said and clinked his glass with hers.

“To us,” Tia said. She sipped the tart wine and swirled the liquid as she gazed at him.

Ebenezer unwrapped the sandwiches from the cloth napkins. “Roast beef.” He handed her half a sandwich.

“It smells wonderful. Much better out here,” she said.

“Food always taste better outside.” They ate in silence. Tia set a plate of sliced mango before them and set aside two forks.

“Them cooks done us real good, I’d say.”

“You should have seen them when I came into the kitchen. It looked as if they had a conspiracy going on.”

“They good people,” he said.

“I know, Eb. They’ve treated me well since Kindra’s been gone.”

Ebenezer swallowed his last bite and dusted his hands. He leaned back and gazed at her. “Miz Tia, would you please stand up?”

“What?”

“Do me the honor and stand right here on the blanket.”

“What’s gotten into you?” Even though she was confounded by his request, Tia did as he asked.

Ebenezer rolled to one knee and took her hand. “I have to admit I feel a bit awkward, seein’ that I’m an overseer and you bein’ Massas’s mother-in-law. But Miz Tia—would you marry me?”

Tia’s heart swelled with love for this man. Hot tears brimmed her eyelids and she gave a little laugh.

Ebenezer’s ears turned a dark red. “Have I presumed too much to ask for yer hand?”

“No, my love. I’m just thinking how hard a life I made for Kindra and Denzel. She being the plantation owner’s daughter, and Denzel an overseer, and all because I thought he was too worthless in my eyes. I didn’t see in him what my daughter did. And here I am, all these years later, standing in her shoes."

Ebenezer looked more nervous than she'd ever seen him. It was as if his heart had fallen to his feet.

"But you showed me something, dear Eb. You showed me how wrong I was all those years ago. And you know something else? Denzel showed me the same thing. I was looking at a man by the money he made, not by the worth of his soul or by his own strength."

She squeezed his strong hands. "I'd be proud to be your wife, Ebenezer. What took you so long to ask me?" She smiled and kissed the top of his head.

He quickly stood and pulled her close. "You make me a happy man." He kissed her over and over, each time pulling away to look at her and smile. "Yes, sir! You make me a happy man!"

They laughed as they held each other. Distant thunder rolled in the sky. "We best get this stuff packed up and head back to the house. Them clouds sure ain't gonna wait for us no more."

"But they did wait for us to plan our future. Let's go home."

TWENTY-THREE

Ash Haven Plantation,
Charleston, South Carolina

KINDRA LOOKED OUT the window for the fourth time that morning. It was harvesting time at Ash Haven, and slaves spent from early morning to sundown picking that cotton. As she went about her housekeeping duties, she remembered back to the time she had to pick bolls of cotton in the cotton fields. She couldn't help but look out at the snow-white fields peppered with black slaves and remember the back-breaking work. Hundreds of acres of crops were ripe for picking. Each evening when she walked back to the shanties, Deborah, Abraham, and the others nearly fell into bed exhausted, their fingers cut and bleeding and their morale bruised.

That evening, Kindra helped Nelly and Mary in the kitchen and went back and forth to set the table with the Bridgers' fine china and to bring out the meal.

"It be different now that the mistress be eatin' her meals at the table again," Nelly said as she brushed past Kindra with a silver server of roast pork.

"What's more confusin' is the massa be joinin' her." Mary picked up a bowl of mashed potatoes. "Most times he don't be here during the supper hour."

"I can understand the mistress eating her meals in her room with those awful migraines, but why doesn't he eat in the dining room in the evenings?" Kindra threw the question over her shoulder as she nudged the kitchen door open with her hip to carry a plate of biscuits and butter to set on the table. Seeing the master seated at the head of the table, she quickly clamped her mouth shut and put the biscuits in front of him. He didn't act like he'd heard a word she said, and for that she was grateful.

"The harvesting is coming along slow but sure," Lawrence commented as he buttered a biscuit.

"I've been watching them from my bedroom window," Phoebe said, placing a starched white napkin on her lap.

"You should take the time to visit the workers in the fields. They might work faster if they see your face now and then." He forked a bite of pork roast.

"That's foolish talk, Lawrence Bridger, and you know it. That's what we hired Bart Odell for." She sat back as Nelly placed a cut of roast on her plate. "Besides, why haven't you gone to the fields the past few months? You spend an awful amount of time in the city these days."

"Don't sass me, Phoebe." He leaned back as Kindra poured wine in his crystal glass.

Kindra kept her eyes on the bottle as she moved to pour wine in Phoebe's glass. She'd learned at Whitestone that the masters talked freely in front of the servants, as if they were invisible. The Bridgers ate in silence, the tension in the air brisk.

"Cromwell bought a new cotton gin." Lawrence finally spoke. "The grids of that machine are closely spaced, making it hard for the seeds to pass through. It works better than ours." He forked a bite of greens. "The loose cotton brushes off better than our machine, too, and prevents the mechanism from jamming. He's thinking about hiring out his gin to other planters for extra profit. Smart man."

"We just purchased our cotton gin two years ago. Surely, we're not ready to purchase a new one." Phoebe held her crystal glass suspended and eyed him with raised brows.

Lawrence cleared his throat. "We need to keep up with our competition. Before, it took the slaves ten hours a day to separate a pound of fiber from the seeds. Since we bought the gin, a team of two or three slaves can produce fifty pounds of cotton a day. We've done well, expanding the production in bales considerably, but I've watched Cromwell's slaves. They're producing more than we are."

"I'm not concerned with keeping up with Cromwell's plantation. We were told we should get ten years out of our cotton gin." She took a sip of the dark wine and put her glass down. "I don't expect to buy a new gin before seven years, and then only if we need to."

"I wish you weren't so narrow-minded when it comes to expansion. If we bought this new model, we could buy more land and slaves. We could double our production."

Kindra set the last bowl of mixed fruit on the table. Lawrence scraped his knife on the plate and stared at Phoebe. She appeared to be only half listening to her husband.

Kindra heard all she wanted to before she went out the back door. The cool air refreshed her as she walked toward the dimly lit cabins. Night had fallen, and the slaves would finally get their rest. She cupped her elbows with her hands as she moved away from the Big House.

"Good evenin', Kindra."

Startled, she looked up to see Sammy, a field hand, coming toward her. He joined her strides toward the shanties. They walked in silence. The man wasn't a threat to her. She'd learned from Deborah that he was kind as the day was long. She had found this to be true. This wasn't the first time he'd waited beyond the house lawn to walk her to the cabins.

After they'd walked a few yards, Sammy asked, "You ever wonder what you'd do if you were free?"

"I am free," Kindra said with an amused smile. "I've just got to get word to my kin where I am so they can come and get me."

"You better not be talkin' like that 'round here. If word gets out to the massa, the overseer be too happy to string you up in a tree."

"Then why did you bring the subject up?"

"I don't know. Jist thinkin' it could happen someday."

Kindra's day had been a trying one. She was too tired to care what thoughts she shared. "I truly am free, Sammy. Just because you people don't know it doesn't make it not true." She clamped her hands tighter about her.

Sammy stared at her for a long moment. "That might be, but you best be keepin' that kind of talk to yerself." He slowed his steps as the cabins neared. "So, what you gonna do if you be free?"

Kindra dropped her hands to her sides and looked up at the darkening sky. "I'm going home to my man and children. I'm going home to my own plantation in Barbados, where I'm the mistress of that house."

He rolled his eyes and grinned. "You sho' got some imagination."

"There's no use talking to you, Sammy. You don't believe a word I say."

"Not when you go talkin' fanciful like that, I don't."

She changed the subject. "What would you do, Sammy, if you were free?"

"I'd build my own livery stable and hire it out for horse shoein'."

"That's a fine idea," she said. "Don't ever give up on your dream."

"You can bet I won't. I been playin' with this idea for a long time. And if you want to know the truth, I'd want you by my side."

Kindra's heart sank, and she stared down at her shoes. "You're a good man, Sammy. If I didn't already have a man of my own, I'd be tempted to share your dream. But my man's looking for me even as we speak. He's been looking for me night and day. And truth to tell, I can't wait to see him."

"How you know your man be lookin' fer you?" Sammy stopped walking and stepped in front of her.

"I've been told."

"By who?"

"The river captain."

Sammy hung his head and then looked at her.

Kindra repeated herself. "I'm going home to my husband and my children. They're waiting for me." A tear slid down her cheek, and she swallowed the salty tears in her throat. "My God's going to answer my prayers. He's going to deliver me from these chains of slavery."

Kindra entered the study with a broom in hand to find Phoebe kneeling on the floor, going through the bottom drawer of Lawrence's wooden filing cabinet. She held out an envelope and squinted at the scribbled writing.

"What have you found, Miss Phoebe?"

"I don't know. I've found nine letters hidden in this drawer. It looks like familiar handwriting, but I can't make out the words."

Kindra glanced at the name in the upper left corner. "Richard Goodman."

Phoebe's head jerked up. "That's my father." Her face blanched.

"Does he write often?"

"No—I don't know. I thought he quit writing years ago." She touched the envelope. "What is the date on this?"

"June fourteenth, eighteen forty-eight."

"Just this summer," Phoebe groaned. "I thought he gave up on me. Finding these hidden letters, I can't help but believe there are more." She frantically shuffled through the papers piled in the bottom of the drawer and pulled out a few more envelopes. She held them to her nose and tried to read the inscription. "The same writing. Oh, Kindra—I'm going to shoot my husband. He's been hiding these letters from me!"

"I'm sorry, Miss Phoebe."

"All this time I believed my father had turned his back on me for marrying Lawrence, and all this time he's tried to stay in contact."

"Should we look to see if there are more?"

"Yes! You look in that chest over there, I'm going to look in the other drawers here."

Kindra moved across the floor and opened the top drawer. She moved papers around but found nothing unusual. She stopped when she heard footsteps in the hallway and looked back at Phoebe, her brows raised.

Phoebe went to the door and glanced out. "Sophy. What are you doing here?"

"I'm done cleaning upstairs. I came looking for you."

"You're too nosy. If you're done cleaning upstairs, then go to the laundry room and help Tamar. She can certainly use your help."

"I ain't no laundry woman." Sophy shrank back.

"You're whatever I say you are. Now out to the washroom and leave me be."

Sophy let out a huff and turned down the hall. Kindra heard her stomping all the way out the back door. She stared at Phoebe, waiting.

"Go back to work. She's not coming back."

"Yes, Miss Phoebe."

Two drawers later, Kindra found several bundles of envelopes tied with twine. "Miss Phoebe." She held up one of the bundles. "I think I found the rest of your father's letters."

Phoebe stared at the mail, and she reddened as emotions washed over her. Her lips thinned. "I want all of them upstairs in my study." She took a handful of mail and left the rest for Kindra to gather and follow. Once they entered the upstairs study, they dropped the bundles on the desk.

Kindra looked up at the mistress, whose eyes spilled over with tears. "Oh, Miss Phoebe. This is an awful, and wonderful, moment."

Phoebe wiped at her eyes. "You're right. I don't think we're going to get a wink of sleep tonight." She laughed softly, and yet Kindra watched a tremor shake her.

They spent the next hour poring over the letters. When Kindra picked up another envelope and started to slit the waxed seal, Phoebe stopped her. "Wait. I've heard enough. I want to send my father a letter. I'm going to invite him and Mother to Ash Haven." She pulled out a fresh sheet of parchment and scooted it to Kindra. "I'll tell you what to write. When we're done, we're going to town to mail the letter."

Sitting in the coach, Phoebe turned to Kindra. "It's time I see an investigator. I know of a man who'll be discreet and do the job well. His name's Derrick Fisk." She looked out the window, her fist to her mouth, then eyed Kindra evenly. "You'll keep my affairs to yourself."

"Of course, Miss Phoebe."

The mistress closed her eyes as if the migraines had returned. "I need proof of Lawrence's affairs with that floozy, Candace Bigsby, and anything else he's been doing behind my back. Mister Fisk will give me the ammunition I need to rid *Master* Lawrence from the house." She brushed a tear away, and Phoebe shook her head. "Tell me about your past. Tell me about your life in Barbados when you were a mistress on your own plantation."

"Miss Phoebe." Kindra swallowed. "To my people back home, I'm still their mistress. They're waiting for me to return."

Phoebe drew back at Kindra's candid remark. She placed her hands on her lap and looked out the window again as the coach bounced along the busy road. "I've told you that won't be happening. You must put all thoughts of returning to Barbados out of your mind." She massaged her temples, her face pale.

"Yes, ma'am," Kindra said, her heart plunging to her feet. "I understand."

TWENTY-FOUR

KINDRA WATCHED TAMAR haul a large basket of clothes to the laundry room. The room was at the back of the house, down a long hall with a door that led to the backyard and the wash house. Kindra often found the old woman bent over the clothes and bedding, folding them neatly before delivering them to their proper destination—linens and bedding in the hall closets, clothes in the master's or mistress's dressing room.

Today, however, Tamar walked more slowly than usual and appeared flushed.

"Are you all right?" Kindra asked the old woman.

"I be fine, young lady. These tired bones o' mine jist feelin' a bit weak today." She shuffled to the laundry room, where she began folding and ironing more laundry.

"Why don't you fold the clothes, and I'll iron. I'm caught up enough that I can help you."

"Oh, that won't be necessary. You got yer hands full with the mistress's business when you ain't a-workin'."

Kindra's head went up. "What are you talking about?"

"Ain't no secret with the servants how you be hitched to the mistress's side these days. She don't come out of her room for nearly two years. You come along, and she is full of life and making more trips to the city than a bear to the woods."

Is it that obvious? "I don't know what to say. She seems to like my company."

"It's clear as daylight that's for sure."

"Goodness. I hadn't realized the mistress had hidden in her room that long. What came over her?"

"It be that Massa Bridger. He be making her life miserable, so miserable that those migraines be makin' the mistress sick day in and day out."

"I'm afraid she needs spectacles. Poor eyesight can cause migraines, too, but Miss Phoebe is adamant she won't be caught dead wearing them."

Tamar stopped folding the clothes and stood staring at Kindra.

"Did I say something wrong?"

"Nevah in my days have I heard a blackie talk so fine as you. Where you learn to talk like that?"

Kindra stoked the woodstove and then set the two flatirons on top to heat up. "I was brought up in the master's house. He insisted I learn to speak English like the rest of the members of the household." She thought it best not to tell the real truth. That she was the plantation owner's daughter might be too much for the old woman.

"So that's it. I be wonderin' 'bout that since you got here."

Kindra lifted a wrinkled pillowcase from Tamar's pile of clothes in the wicker basket and shook it. She draped the white material over the ironing board and began to press the wrinkles out. The two worked in silence for a while.

"You doin' real good with that flatiron. I be goin' out and wash another load if it be all right."

"Go on. I've got this." Kindra waved her away. Alone in the small room, she hummed a tune. The stove took the chill out of the cold room. She set the flatiron on the stove top and reached for the second iron. She kept up the rhythm of alternating the two irons while she worked and hummed the hour away. It wasn't long before standing still on the brick floor made her back ache. She had reached behind to massage the small of her back when she felt a presence in the room. She set the flatiron down and turned around. There stood Lawrence Bridger with an amused smile on his face.

"Master Bridger! I didn't hear you come in." Her stomach twisted.

"It's my house. I have the authority to come into any room or visit any servant I want." His eyes lit up, and he stepped closer, wrapping his arms around her waist.

"Don't!" Kindra pushed against him. "Get your hands off me!"

"You little devil! How dare you talk to me like that!" He pulled her closer in a vice grip and leaned to nuzzle her throat.

"Please don't!" Kindra tried to twist out of his arms.

"You want to take a trip to the whipping post?" His face grew red.

"No, sir. I don't." Kindra turned away.

"You think you're better than me!" Lawrence reached behind her and lifted the flatiron from the stove. He held it to her face, his eyes glaring down at her. "If you know what's good for you, you'll hold still while I take what's mine."

Backed up against the ironing board, she had nowhere to go. Kindra felt the intense heat nearly singe her skin. "Please don't," she whimpered.

"Then show me some respect, little missy!"

Kindra drew back, nearly tipping the ironing board over, the heat of the iron too close. Bridger held it a hair's distance from her skin. She closed her eyes and held her breath, expecting the scalding metal to burn her face. *God, no! Please help me!* Then she felt Bridger's hold loosen, and the air cooled around her face as he drew away. She heard the iron clink on the metal base and opened her eyes. He stood next to her, his fists clenched at his sides.

"Next time, you'd better treat me with respect!" He hissed and strode out of the room.

When she looked outside the door, she saw Phoebe at the back door in the dark hall. She stared at Kindra a moment, then turned and walked away.

Kindra let out the air she'd been holding. *Oh, Good God. Thank You for protecting me.* She turned to the flatiron sitting on the stove. *Lord, have mercy!* Shaken, she went back to work.

That evening, Kindra found Deborah on the front steps of the shanty, her shoulders slumped. "Good evening, Deborah. Are you all right?"

"No," Deborah whispered. She leaned her head against the post, her eyes welling with tears.

Kindra rushed to her side and sat down. "What's wrong, honey?"

"It be that overseer, Bart Odell."

Dread slicked up Kindra's back. "What about him? What happened?"

"He pulled me into the shed again. That's what happened." She pushed her skirt down to her ankles.

"Did he whip you?" Kindra glanced at the girl's arms, back, and face and found no signs of a whipping, but her arms were red as if she'd been roughened up. "Oh, Deborah." Kindra groaned. "Did he have his way with you?"

"Yes." She sniffled. "Jist like he always does."

"Oh, Deborah," Kindra said again. "I'm so sorry." She sat next to her and pulled the girl into her arms. Deborah's head fell to Kindra's shoulder, and she sobbed and sobbed.

After catching her breath, Deborah sat up and used the hem of her skirt for a handkerchief. "I sure hope you don't be called upon by Massa or Odell. They don't care iffen we don't want them to touch us. They do what they want." She paused to wipe her eyes. "Massa say I his property. He owns me."

Kindra recalled her encounter with Lawrence Bridger. She'd been spared his cruel intentions, but could she escape his illicit attempts again?

"How old are you, Deborah?"

"Sixteen, I'm guessin'. My parents were sold to another plantation when I was young. I don't know how old I be when that happened. I be old enough to know they ain't never comin' back. Old Katy done take care of me and the other children." She looked up at Kindra. "I don't look like a woman and I don't look like a child." She looked down at her worn shoes. "I been here some years."

Kindra's heart went out to the young girl. She needed to be protected from the master and the overseer. But could she truly help her? Was there a way?

Phoebe beat her pillow until it was fluffed up enough to lie her head down. She lay on her side and gazed at the moon outside her window. A multitude of thoughts raced through her mind as she thought of Lawrence and his shenanigans. Her eyes drooped and she yawned. She wished for sleep to put aside the mounting fears that ebbed her soul. Placing her hand under her cheek, she shut her eyes, purposing sleep to come. Sounds of the night crept to her ears. She listened intently as the floor creaked down the hall and a door closed softly.

Her eyes snapped open. She slid out of bed and tiptoed out of her room. The door to Lawrence's room was closed, as were the rest of the doors on the upper landing. She crept stealthily and listened at each door for muffled noise beyond. When she reached Sophy's door, she heard muted sounds. She bent to her knees and peeked through the keyhole. There in the light of the moon lay the silhouettes of two bodies. Lawrence and Sophy.

A hard rock settled into her stomach. She stood and crept to bed. She'd say nothing for now. She had lost Lawrence a long time ago. But Sophy? She needed to think this through. Maybe it was time to send the heathen to the fields. Perhaps it was time to bring in a new servant to take her place.

When Kindra stepped through the kitchen door the following morning, Nelly met her. "Mistress say for you to go to her quarters soon as you arrive."

Kindra's brows went up. "Whatever for?"

"Don't know. But you best be hoofin' it up them stairs and find out."

"All right." Kindra raised her chin and brushed the wrinkles out of her skirt as she ascended the stairs. She knocked lightly on Phoebe's door.

"Come in," a quiet voice called.

Kindra stepped in and found the mistress sitting on the edge of her bed, massaging her temples. "Have you a migraine again?"

"Yes. But that's not why I sent for you."

Kindra stood and waited.

Phoebe patted the bed beside her. "Come sit."

Kindra crept to the bedside and sat down, tucking her hands in the folds of her skirt.

"I'm moving you into the house," Phoebe announced. "There's a room at the end of the hall that is vacant. Would you like to see it now?"

Stunned, Kindra said, "Uh, of course." Her head began to spin with a million questions. What brought this on? Had her duties changed? Did Sophy have something to do with the mistress's decision? Her thoughts spiraled out of control.

She followed Phoebe down the west wing. Other than the mistress's chamber and study, Kindra hadn't seen the other upstairs rooms. A long window filled the end wall, lighting their path easily. When they reached the last door on the right, Phoebe turned the doorknob and pushed the door open.

Kindra stepped into a pleasant room that appeared to be a guest chamber. "Oh my, Miss Phoebe. Are you sure you want me to stay in this room?"

"I'm certain." Phoebe smiled, but it was clear her migraine persisted. Her usually pink cheeks looked ashen.

Kindra stepped farther into the beautifully decorated room. The walls were papered in pink and mauve roses. A double bed centered on one wall, a vanity against the next. A large round mirror hung over the dressing table. A wardrobe sat against the third wall next to a thin, long window that reached from the floor to the ceiling. White lace curtains covered the narrow window. A second window, equally long and thin, sat against the same wall as the vanity. There was another door next to the bed. Kindra stared at it questioningly.

"That's the servant's door." Phoebe opened it and stood aside.

Kindra peered out the door to see another door across a small landing. "Where does that lead?"

"My dressing room."

Kindra looked down a narrow staircase with steps so narrow between the two doors. At the base stood another long window. This was a side of the house she'd never seen. She stepped back inside the bedchamber and shut the door. "Have my duties changed?"

"They have. You're now my chambermaid. I'll be sending Sophy to the fields soon."

Kindra caught a glint of mischief in the mistress's eyes.

"She'll be sleeping in the shanty you've been sharing."

A thought rushed into Kindra's mind so fast she didn't know what to think. But she spat it out quickly before she lost courage. "Miss Phoebe . . . may I ask who'll take my post as downstairs' housekeeper?"

"I still haven't worked the details out. I'll think of someone."

"May I make a suggestion?"

"You may."

"There's a young girl who shares the cabin I sleep in. Her name's Deborah. I think she'd be a quick learner . . ."

Phoebe held her hand up. “I know the girl you speak of. Bring her to the house this evening.”

Relief washed over Kindra. “Yes, Miss Phoebe. One more thing, if I may.”

Phoebe’s brows raised, and her color darkened her cheeks.

“If you give Deborah the housekeeping job, can she share my room until the master is gone?”

Phoebe’s eyes widened, and her jaw firmed. “That’s quite an unusual request. I’d think you’d want the privacy of your own room.”

“I don’t mind. And besides, it would blindside his unwanted gestures, with two of us in the room.”

Phoebe nodded. “That it would. Bring the young girl to the house this evening. I hope you have no further requests.”

“Thank you, Miss Phoebe. I can’t think of anything else.”

“Then meet me in my dressing room in five minutes. I’m going to town and you’ll join me.”

“Yes, ma’am.” She watched Phoebe sail to her room with a lift to her shoulders. Then she spun around and her hand flew to her mouth. *Lord, You have given me favor in this house. Thank You for giving me this safe covering. I will praise You all the days of my life!*

TWENTY-FIVE

River Oak, Fields Landing, South Carolina

SNATCHING UP HER diary and The Ladies Companion magazine, Kit descended the stairs and went out the back door. Under a large oak, a square table and chairs sat. A lace cloth covered the center, with a small wire birdcage filled with cream-colored candles sitting on top. Kit smiled at the table decoration, remembering how her mother often found objects meant for one thing and put them to use for another.

Kit recalled the summer day she and her mother had gone into Fields Landing for an excursion. They'd come upon a shop full of used furniture and accessories. Grace had found the little cage and lifted it in the air. "Why, there's no room for a bird in this little cage." She had turned it around a few times before her green eyes sparkled, and Kit had known a brainstorm was coming on. Grace bit the inside of her cheek and puckered her lips as she squinted at the brown cage. "What do you think, Kit? Wouldn't this be darling on our garden table as a centerpiece?"

Kit eyed the birdcage and grinned. "I can see it now. Put a few candles in it and it'd look quite decorative in the evening."

Her mother's eyes widened. She picked up a larger, dark wicker cage sitting next to it and carried them both to the front of the store. "Write them up, please," she told the store clerk and then turned to Kit. "We'll hang the large one from the branch that drapes over the table. I'll have Gemma fill them both with candles."

Looking back, Kit remembered how much she had enjoyed that shopping trip with her mother. They often browsed second-hand stores when in town.

They had similar tastes in old relics and furniture, and with their heads together, they often came up with fresh ways to make old things seem new. Now, glancing at the other cage, Kit knew her mother had been right. The cages did invite one to sit outdoors.

She dropped the diary and magazine on the tabletop and gazed at the two gardeners busy trimming bushes for Saturday's celebration. The lawn stretched farther back, where another gate led to a stand of trees with a path to the stable. Bushes edged the yard's perimeter, and benches were placed along trails leading to the flower gardens.

Flopping unladylike onto the brown cane chair, Kit pored over The Ladies Companion for the hundredth time. Though the magazine was three years old, she never tired of reading the story "Young Love in the Old South" by Eliza Fisk Harwood.

Kit's party was only one week away. She wanted to brush up on the etiquette of a coming-out party. She'd been to several debut parties this fall, all packed with suitors and belles from the Low Country. The galas were splendid. She was looking forward to her own ball but couldn't help wondering whether the one man she dreamed of nightly would attend. Could Jackson make it to the party in time? He was out to sea, and to Kit, he may as well be on the other side of the world. The thought that he would miss her party taunted her every waking hour.

The garden gate creaked, and she turned to see Damaris sauntering up to her with a small basket of bread crumbs. "I'm going for a walk to the pond. Care to join me?"

Kit gazed at her beautiful cousin wearing a snow-white dress tied at the waist with a blue ribbon. Her caramel-colored skin accentuated the white muslin. Damaris's brows rose as if hopeful Kit would accept her invitation.

"I'll be along in a moment. I want to jot a note in my diary before I lose my train of thought."

"All right, I'll see you at the bridge." Damaris stepped away and went back through the gate. Kit dropped the magazine onto the table and picked up her diary. She had crammed the pages with endless reports of the parties she'd attended. What she considered her most important news was parties she'd recently been to and how she wanted her own ball to be.

The first gala she had attended was Charice Seward's. She was the daughter of Wendell Seward, Kit's father's most fierce competitor in rice production. For the women, however, there was no competition. They rolled their eyes at the men and hooked arms in a show of friendship. Kit was happy to attend Charice's coming-out ball. Her friend appeared a lovely belle from Kit's point of view. It was true, however, that Kit had danced so long she had worn a hole in her mauve satin shoes.

Her diary was filled with reports of belles and their beaus, rumored engagements, and her friends' weddings—but she often wondered, would she fill in reports of her own engagement? Her own wedding? She wrote about Jackson Harding, his good looks, his hazel eyes, and how he made her feel. The pages were filled with her hopes for the future.

Looking back, Kit realized he had pursued her love since her childhood. His quest for her had been constant during his every visit when he and his parents sailed across the Atlantic from Jamaica. Her memories were from as early as when he'd pulled her long braids as a child to when he had found her riding Scimitar this summer.

Today, she jotted down her wish for Jackson to attend her eighteenth birthday party, and, more so, her coming-out celebration. She tucked the diary in her pocket and went out the garden gate to find Damaris leaning against the bridge rail, tossing bread crumbs to the ducks. Kit walked briskly across the red-bricked path and joined her.

"You came," Damaris said softly, tossing another piece of bread into the water.

"I said I would." Kit reached for a few chunks and leaned over the rail, throwing bread to the waiting ducks.

Damaris seemed deep in thought.

"You're quiet today," Kit said.

"I know."

"Is it because you'll be leaving soon?"

"Yes. I'm going to miss you all."

"More than you'll miss Solomon?" Kit gave Damaris an amused grin.

"Now stop that, Katherine Bartholomew."

"Oh. I've hit a nerve."

"I'll miss him," Damaris said. "I don't know how I'll be able to leave him." She stared straight ahead.

"I'm glad you're here to celebrate our birthdays together, along with the coming-out party."

"Me too. The only thing is, I won't be able to dance with Solomon."

"I'll ask Father if he can come."

"I won't hold my breath." Damaris tossed the last chunk of bread into the water. Four ducks swam to retrieve it, and one plucked it out with its bill and swam quickly away.

"You never know. Father may surprise you."

Damaris shook her head. "Even if Uncle Camp said yes, my Solomon doesn't have fine clothes to wear. He won't come."

"I'm sorry," Kit said. She meant it with all her heart.

"Don't be. I'll see him anyway. I'll light the candle in the window."

The coming-out gala, only six short days away, took precedence over the usual routine. Grace made a hundred trips to the upstairs sitting room where the seamstress made last-minute changes to the girls' gowns.

She had called all the house slaves together that morning and instructed them to have the house shining before the end of the week. The company was common at River Oak; the servants knew what to do. This time, however, Aunt Katy would arrive a few days early to help Grace with last-minute details.

The Hardings were due to arrive by Friday. Kit's heart had raced at the prospect of Jackson staying at the house. That same heart hit the floor when Uncle Drew had declined. It was best, she supposed, since there were a thousand loose ends to be tied before the big day.

Today was the big day at River Oak. Everyone bailed out of bed and scurried in a hundred directions. The birthday party would be held at noon.

"You sit yourself down and eat those scrambled eggs, Miz Kit," Gemma said, carrying two plates to the table. She set one in front of Bella and the other in front of Piper. An inattentive Damaris sat across the table.

Kit didn't ask what could be on her cousin's mind. She knew.

Solomon spent the morning going in and out of the garden, setting up the tables and canvas awnings for the afternoon lawn party. All the while, Damaris found every excuse to be outside, helping with the white tablecloths or putting flowers in vases in the middle of the tables. There were slaves to do all this, but Kit knew Damaris wanted to watch as Solomon and two slaves carried tables and chairs and set things up. She could only imagine how long Solomon would drag out the work so that he and Damaris could steal a few moments together.

At least Damaris didn't have to wait until the afternoon to see him, Kit mused. She wouldn't see Jackson before the birthday party, and she hoped his family would arrive early. It had been weeks since the *Savannah Rose* had sailed away. Captain Harding had two stops to deliver merchandise, and then he'd sail to Jamaica to pick up Camille and the rest of his family before they returned.

The hour they'd been waiting for finally arrived. Kit looked out the window a dozen times and watched as the front drive filled quickly with buggies and carriages. All of her father's family arrived from Charleston. Her mother's cousins, Josephine and Peter, and their families paraded to the back yard. Sid and Lauren Sparrow arrived from upriver, bringing with them Adam, Rory, Florence, and Amy.

The back lawn was filled with a dozen round tables, each draped in white-starched tablecloths, with a vase of peonies in the center. A place setting of a crystal glass and a rose-patterned China plate sat before each chair. The sun dappled onto the guests and furniture, while the lawn was shadowed here and there by the great oak branches as they stretched their long arms over the tables and grounds. With fall in full swing, the sultry heat and humid air were long past, and a cool breeze softly ruffled the hems of women's skirts and tablecloths and the tendrils of black curls on Kit's forehead.

Nate and Zeek continued to escort the guests to the back lawn. With her family and Uncle Denzel's group, there were nearly seventy guests in attendance. Greeting them kept Kit on her toes. Still, she listened for one more carriage to arrive. Would the Hardings be here soon? Her eyes strayed to the garden gate time and again. But the afternoon dragged on.

Slaves came and went with trays of food and drinks, and after a noisy afternoon of fun and games, the cooks carried out the birthday cake. Grace instructed Kit and Damaris to stand on either side of the table. The large square cake had been beautifully decorated with cream-colored frosting. Eighteen small candles had been lit, and the tiny flames flickered in the afternoon breeze.

"All right, girls." Grace hovered over them. "Make a wish. At the count of three, you'll both blow out the candles."

Kit gazed at Damaris, seeing mischief in her cousin's eyes. Would she wish to marry Solomon? Kit found it challenging to concentrate on the merriment of the moment. She had trained her ears to hear another carriage coming up the lane, carrying the Hardings, but they hadn't come.

"Don't despair, Kit," her mother said. "Any number of things could have happened to delay them. They'll come."

With the party nearly over, she'd pretend to have fun. She half-heartedly looked forward to the evening celebration where she'd be presented to the community for her coming out. Now that she was eighteen, she officially was of marriageable age. She would get through the rest of the day, and when it ended, she would crawl into bed and cry herself to sleep.

Was this a taste of what a future with Jackson would be? Would he miss every critical occasion in their lives? The daunting thought created a rock in her heart. She closed her eyes at the same time Damaris did, squeezing them shut to ward off the tears that threatened to fall. *Please, Jackson . . . please come to the party tonight. I have to see you one more time.*

"Three, two, one!" the crowd called out.

Kit and Damaris opened their eyes and blew out the candles. The flames flickered out, and smoke filled the air.

Kit noticed Adam Sparrow standing a few feet away, his eyes hungrily watching her. She lifted her chin to acknowledge him. Did she have her heart set on the wrong man? Only weeks ago, Adam had reminded her he was here, while Jackson was out to sea. Now she watched as Adam smiled whimsically and nodded back, his hands in his pockets.

Hip! Hip! Hooray!" someone yelled. The crowd clapped, hugged the girls, and wished them many more birthdays.

Damaris stepped back with a soft smile on her lips and looked over her shoulder. Solomon stood beyond the gate, watching her. Kit saw his wide grin as he stood in the shadows. Damaris's shoulders lifted and her smile grew.

Gemma shoved her way to the table. "Step aside, folks, if you be wanting some cake." She picked up the cake knife and began cutting big squares of chocolate cake. She set each piece on a plate, and Penny passed them out.

"Birthday girls first," Penny said, handing a plate to Kit.

"Thank you, Penny." Kit tried to swallow the hole in her heart. She kept her eyes from straying to where Adam stood.

She heard a rustle beyond the tables and across the yard. She looked up to see Nate leading Ginger through the back gate; her black mane and tail brushed to a sheen. Nate's eyes shone bright as he led the filly past the crowd to where Kit stood.

"What's this?" Kit's hand flew to her mouth, and she looked to her parents. "Is she mine?"

"She's yours." Cameron threw his arm over Kit's shoulders. "But I think the two of you made that arrangement a long time ago." He smiled down at her.

"Thank you!" Kit hugged her father, then turned to Grace and threw her arms around her mother's neck. "This is the best birthday ever!" She walked over to where Nate stood holding the filly's reins. She hugged Ginger's neck and giggled. "Can you believe it?" She kissed the white star on Ginger's forehead and combed her mane with her fingers. "You're all mine, honey!"

The crowd laughed, and the party resumed with continuous noise throughout the afternoon. All the while, Kit's ears strained to hear another set of carriage wheels arriving in the front drive.

"We must get you girls inside to change your clothes. The rest of the guests will be arriving at six o'clock." Grace herded Damaris and Kit into the house.

"I'll see to the younger girls," Aunt Katy acted like a mother goose guiding her brood into the house behind them.

The air was filled with the delicious aroma of pigs roasting on the spits and a variety of foods cooking in the outer kitchens. Gemma, Penny, and Mama Jezelee had hurried back to the kitchens to resume their work.

Kit's stomach rumbled as she entered the house. She hadn't eaten a bite of food, so upset was she that Jackson hadn't come. Now the aromas wafting through the air sent her hunger pangs into motion. *Keep going!* She told herself as she made her way up the stairs.

"Hedy, I want you to attend to Kit and Damaris," Grace said.

Alice waited on the landing. "Alice, get me dressed, and Aunt Katy, could you help Beatrice with the younger girls?"

"I'm already ahead of you, darlin'. I've sent the girls to their rooms. I believe Beatrice has Bella sitting at the vanity."

"What would I do without you, Aunt Katy?"

"Plenty, dear. I've taken note of the way you've run this place like a well-oiled machine. I must say, you never cease to amaze me. When you set out to realize your dreams as a young girl, you never stop dreaming." Aunt Katy waved a hand in the air, and she looked around. "Look what you've done, honey. But I expect with all the commotion coming from that room down the hall, you could use some help." She winked and hurried farther down the west wing.

Grace looked at the ceiling. "All right, everyone. I want doors closed and everybody getting dressed." She gave Alice a look and summoned her to follow.

An hour later, Grace appeared with her auburn hair piled high in elegant curls. Her rust-colored gown flared out and swished as she moved down the hall. She stepped into Kit's bedchamber and gasped. "Oh, Damaris. You look absolutely charming."

Damaris came forward and held out her skirt with the tips of her fingers. "Do you think so, Aunt Grace?" The light in her dark eyes belied her question, and Grace stepped farther into the room. "I do. Turn around."

Damaris held out her skirt as she twirled around. The pink satin gown trimmed in white lace was beautiful. A second layer flowed from her waist and fanned out. The slender sleeves reached her elbows and then flared out. The hem of the skirt and sleeves were trimmed in delicate white lace. The front cut to just above her full breasts and was trimmed in matching lace.

Three pink baubles on her necklace posed as a choker, with pearl beads fanning out in a lace design. “Exquisite, darling. You look absolutely exquisite.”

A pleased look washed over Damaris’s face, and she clamped her hands before her. “Hedy’s just about done with Kit. Wait until you see her dress.” Damaris went to the vanity to watch Hedy finish Kit’s blue-black hair.

Hedy went to great lengths to dress Kit in her green-flowered gown. As the guests flowed into the downstairs ballroom, the grandfather clock struck six long tones. Finally, Hedy stood aside. “That's all you need, young lady. Let yer mama take a look at you.”

Kit swirled around on the stool and gazed up at her mother. Her slim, white throat was adorned with the opal necklace, whose colors revealed trace elements in its oval design and displayed multiple colors. Diamonds circled the stone. The matching earrings glistened on her lobes.

“Oh, Kit. Look at you.” Grace choked back a rush of tears.

Kit made a pretty picture. Her green-flowered taffeta dress spread its twelve yards of billowing material over her hoops and exactly matched the flat-heeled green slippers they’d recently purchased in Charleston. The dress set off Kit’s twenty-inch waist to perfection, and the tightly fitting basque showed a hint of breasts well matured for her eighteen years. But for all the modesty of her spreading skirts, the demureness of raven-black hair flowing to the middle of her back, her hands folded in her lap, Kit’s true emotions couldn’t be concealed. The smoldering gray eyes in her sweet face were turbulent, distinctly at variance with her demeanor. “I don’t think Jackson has arrived.” Kit glanced out the window, and her brows puckered. “Have you seen Camille yet?”

“No, honey. I can’t imagine what’s keeping them. I’m beginning to worry that something’s happened.” Grace wrung her hands and gazed at the three women in the room.

“Now, listen,” Hedy said. “You can’t go downstairs lookin’ all glum. Iffen I know one thing, that boy gonna be comin’. He won’t leave yer heart hangin’ on the moon.”

Music floated up the stairs from the hired orchestra below in the ballroom.

“Are we late?” Kit glanced in the mirror one last time.

"That be your cue, Miss Kit. You best git on out there," Hedy said.

A glance at the clock, and Grace motioned to the door. "It's time for you to make your appearance. We cannot delay this another moment. Chin up."

"Hedy's the reason I'm late," Kit snapped, her nerves in a ball.

"You'll be thankin' me later when all the fellas can't git their eyes off of you."

"Won't be a soul who gives a wit how I look." Kit glanced out the window for the Hardings' carriage one last time. *Jackson! Where are you?*

She left the window and spun around. When she did, the gown flared out. She imagined dancing in the arms of a particular golden-haired gentleman. Her cheeks flamed at the prospect. If he didn't arrive soon, the chances of dancing with the handsome ship merchant were nil.

"I'm going down to inform your father you're on the way. Don't delay." Grace kissed Kit on the cheek and fled the room. Damaris followed, with the girls from the other rooms quickly stepping past Kit's door.

Kit took a deep breath. With the slightest hint of a nod, she followed Hedy out the door and into the hall. Her heart pounded in her ears as she moved toward the top landing. She felt her throat clog with salty tears. *What could have kept the Hardings from coming?* She took a deep breath and lifted her face. She tried to shove her disappointment aside—in fact, she tried not to feel anything at all. The party must go on. How she would get through it, she didn't know, but she would.

She listened to the pleasant din of voices and laughter below. She walked to the top of the stairs and looked down where her father waited, looking up at her. Kit descended the stairs, her green taffeta gown swishing gracefully as she glided down.

As her foot hit the hardwood floor, her father's warm, approving eyes gleamed, and he crooked his right arm. "You look stunning, Katherine."

"Katherine?" Kit looked up at her father, brows raised.

"You look every inch a woman this evening. Your given name is befitting for the moment." He crooked his left elbow for Grace to join them.

"No, Camp. This is Kit's moment. I'm right behind you."

"All right. We mustn't keep the guests waiting. They're eager to see you." Cameron's smile remained as he escorted Kit down the hallway, accented with a dozen candles lighting the way to the ballroom.

Tonight was her night. She'd make the most of it. She'd brush all thoughts of Jackson from her mind if such a thing were possible.

The music stopped when they stood at the entrance to the ballroom. All eyes settled on Kit and her father. Grace moved up to stand next to them. Cameron cleared his throat and gave his daughter a proud look. "May I introduce my lovely daughter, Katherine Olivia Bartholomew." A round of applause resounded through the spacious ballroom, then quieted. He stood slightly away from Kit, his eyes shining. "I have invited all of you to share in the joy of her coming of age. Please take the time to congratulate her." He hooked an arm around Kit's waist and pulled her close.

The room thundered with applause again. When the noise abated, Cameron continued. "There are tables on the lawns with a bounty of food. Please help yourselves. Tonight, the band will strike up festive music, and we will resume the party in the ballroom. Now come, let's eat!"

TWENTY-SIX

KIT LISTENED TO the pleasant voices, the tinkle of glasses, the music in the background, and the swish of gowns as beautiful women danced or moved among guests. A slave in a stiff black coat, carrying a silver tray laden with glasses filled to the brim with red wine, threaded his way through the crowd. A neighbor decked out in bright jewels and a crinoline gown took one and held the elegant piece of finely etched crystal.

Zeek and Nate, dressed in refined white coats, stood at the stairs to assist the guests and direct them to the front door. Kit moved from the entrance to the table laden with punch bowls and refreshments. The floor was glossy, and the strains of a waltz filled her ears while all about her taffeta, satins, and crinolines swirled like so many colorful wings in a world of dragonflies. She glanced down at her own gown and pinched a fold as she glided across the floor.

African serving men moved about the floor, carrying heavy silver trays filled with an assortment of concoctions. Kit murmured her thanks and took a glass of punch from one tray and moved along the rim of the ballroom to stand by Damaris and Florence. Florence chatted excitedly as the tables were continuously restocked with punch and refreshments.

"I'm famished after the day's activities," Kit admitted to Damaris. "I didn't eat a bite of food. Care to join me outside to find something to eat?"

"Lead the way," Damaris said, smiling demurely.

They thoughtfully approached one of the tables, where a roasted pig sat in the center. There was so much food that it was impossible to eat it all. Kit recognized some of the meat: along with the roast pork, there was beef, mutton, and turkey. She watched the uniformed slaves offer food to guests from platters and bowls. Her parents had outdone themselves in the preparations for the party.

The girls sat at a table outside the tent. "I haven't seen the Hardings today," Damaris said as she glanced over the guests. "Do you suppose something has detained them?"

"I can't imagine they'd change their minds about coming. Captain Harding was adamant Camille had every intention of voyaging to Charleston." Kit lifted her hand and looked at it thoughtfully. "My party isn't the only reason she wanted to come. She and Mother are staunch friends, have been since the day Mama arrived in Jamaica as a young woman." She studied the crowd. "It's always possible something has held them up. I can't imagine what it would be."

"Jackson would be here if he had his way," Damaris assured her, her dark eyes gleaming.

"Maybe." Kit pushed thoughts of Jackson aside long enough to indulge in the delicious fare. She savored a bite of delicately seasoned greens, then cut into a slice of tender pork. After she swallowed the last of a biscuit, she ran a hand over her middle. "I feel better. I was beginning to get shaky."

People began to move up the lawn toward the piazza's bright lights. Kit stood. "We should go back to the ballroom. My parents will be looking for me."

The girls hooked arms as they strode back to the house. "It's too bad Solomon can't come to the party?" Kit said, tugging on Damaris's arm in a warm gesture.

"It's just as well. He wouldn't feel comfortable in a crowd of elites."

"That's true. It may very well be that neither of us will see our gents tonight."

"Gents?" Damaris's eyes flashed in amusement.

"Yes, of course." Kit held Damaris's hand and led her through the French doors. "Come on, silly."

As the girls entered the ballroom, it was obvious Cameron had been watching for them. "Ladies and Gentlemen," Cameron's voice boomed. "If you'll clear the floor, it is time for the father-daughter dance." He turned to the band. "Gentlemen."

The orchestra struck up a beautiful waltz.

Cameron crossed the floor, reached his hand to Kit, and bowed. She put her hand in his, and together they stepped onto the dance floor. The tempo of the music filled the air as they twirled around, Cameron proudly showing off his daughter, and Kit beaming in his arms.

As Cameron swung Kit in time to the waltz, Kit looked over the crowd and found her mother standing on the sidelines, biting her lip to keep from crying. Several minutes into the dance, father and daughter were joined on the floor by other couples. Within moments, they were surrounded by the crowd.

"You look lovely, Kit," Cameron said, a proud look in his eyes.

"Thank you, Daddy. You and Mother went to great lengths to make my coming-out ball everything I had wished for. I truly appreciate it."

They finished the waltz in silence, and Cameron ushered Kit back to the edge of the floor. He had barely released her when she was surrounded by admirers. Kit was gracious to the crowd of twenty or more young men surrounding her. Nevertheless, she searched for Jackson the rest of the evening, looking for his handsome face as she danced about with a dozen partners, each less adept at such practical steps than the one before—or perhaps it was simply a combination of the late hour and her own lack of enthusiasm for her partners.

At least six men were vying for Kit's immediate attention when a familiar face appeared on the fringe. She looked up into Adam's blue eyes and smiled at him. Many a heart turned over with roaring jealousy when they saw that private smile, and some simmered with anger when Adam extended a hand and Kit moved toward him without being asked.

"I was beginning to wonder if I'd get that dance you promised me," Adam said.

"I didn't promise a dance," Kit said coyly, relishing a moment to release the pent-up nerves that had been increasing all day. She let herself be led through the waltz and tried not to think of Jackson. He wasn't here. Adam held her at a respectful distance as he twirled her on the floor, but he looked down at her intently. "Have you given any thought to what we talked about?"

"No, Adam. I haven't. Too much has been going on."

"Or has someone else consumed your mind?"

"Both. I won't lie."

"Where is he now?" Adam raised his brows as he twirled her around.

"Don't taunt me, Adam. I haven't the foggiest idea." She straightened her arm to give them more distance.

"Come. I won't breathe another word of the beast." He pulled Kit into his arms. "Relax and enjoy the dance."

She allowed herself to be held in his strong arms. They stepped in time to the music as the room blurred. She tuned out everything: Adam, the band, and the people on the sidelines. The one person she'd waited for all afternoon and evening had not come. She lost herself in the strains of the music and tried not to think. At last, the violins faded, ending the waltz.

"Thank you, Kit, for allowing me this dance. Although I must say it felt one-sided." Adam's lips thinned as he guided her to the sidelines and stalked briskly away.

His quick exit stung. She cared for him in so many ways, just not the one he was looking for. She didn't love him. She couldn't fathom a future with him. But she wanted him happy. She had to remind herself she wasn't responsible for Adam's emotions.

Needing air, she slipped out the side door to the piazza. Once outside, she tilted her head up and breathed in the cool breeze. The night had brought on a coolness she embraced. Looking over her shoulder at the lit-up house, she slipped away to the gardens for a moment alone. She found a bench tucked between bushes and leaned back to kick off her shoes. "Oh, that feels good," she whispered and closed her eyes. *If I could only cease thinking of Jackson.* But visions of his handsome face haunted her. There was nowhere to hide, as thoughts of him consumed her every waking moment.

As the evening wore on and the guests milled about the property, Kit cast a glance toward the house. Aunt Katy and Cousin Josie were mingling with the guests. She searched the grounds for the Hardings, looking for Camille or Drew, and more importantly, Jackson. He was nowhere in sight.

Realizing she hadn't seen Damaris in the last hour, Kit went in search of her. She wanted to speak with her cousin before she went back into the house. As she threaded her way through the crowd, she could only guess where Damaris might be. Kit knew the event had lost her cousin's interest. Only one person tugged on her cousin's heartstrings, only one person held her thoughts captive day and night, and Kit was positive that person now held Damaris in his arms under an oak tree somewhere on the grounds. Damaris wouldn't be in the ballroom if she could be in Solomon's arms.

Smiling to herself, Kit neared the food tents and looked in. The lines at the food tables were dwindling as the ball continued. She roamed past the tables and glanced about, then headed back to the house.

She climbed the staircase and moved past the guest chambers used to hold wraps and bags, and where ladies could give final touches to their faces and hair. She quickly moved down the west wing and slipped into her bedchamber, lit by an oil lamp—and a candle in the window. The candle confirmed why she couldn't find Damaris.

When she descended the stairs and moved down the hall to the ballroom, she saw a familiar face. "Mrs. Cavendish, what a pleasant surprise. It is so nice to see you again." The old woman wore a gray gown of delicate Chinese silk and a necklace of sparkling diamonds.

"Ah, my dear Kit, it is a delight to see you. I apologize for arriving late." Mrs. Cavendish glanced around the room as if looking for someone in particular. "I know your mother is here somewhere."

"She is. She's still greeting the other guests. She'll be surprised to see you."

"No, she won't. She sent me an invitation, and I acknowledged that I'd be here." She tapped her cane on the floor. "She'd be more surprised if I didn't come." She scrutinized Kit up and down. "I hadn't realized you'd grown to be such a beautiful woman. I see a hint of dear Grace in you, but I have to admit, you've mostly taken after your father."

Agnes took Kit's arm, and the two proceeded around the rim of the floor. As they neared the refreshment table and Agnes leaned on her cane, Kit's father sailed across the room in their direction, well-fitted in his black jacket, white shirt, and black pants.

"Agnes Cavendish. So good to see you. Have you seen Grace yet?"

"I haven't seen hide nor hair of her. I expect she's busy with guests." Agnes shook her cane at him. "Look at you dressed to kill."

"I'll take that as a compliment." Cameron bowed low. "Now let me find my bride. She'll have my hide if she finds you're here and I haven't told her." Cameron escaped the hall. He'd seen Kit's disappointment at the Hardings' delay. Would they make it tonight? Or would Jackson break her heart?

TWENTY-SEVEN

JACKSON SAT STRAIGHT in the coach as the driver kept the horses going at a swift pace. He eyed his parents, dressed formally for the ball, and his brothers, fitted in suits and squirming uncomfortably. Twelve-year-old Rosamund wore a lavender dress. She looked like a blonde-haired miniature of her dark-haired mother.

Agitated that they were late, Jackson kept his thoughts to himself. The short glances sent his way told him the family knew he was in no mood for conversation.

The pounding of horses' hooves drummed on as the carriage flew through the main thoroughfare. The fall air was warm but not humid. He loosened his collar and stretched his neck as he kept his gaze on the scenery beyond. The trees blurred as the horses raced toward their destination. He splayed his fingers on his lap and clamped his knees. Would Kit be put out when he arrived? He'd promised to be there for her birthday. Not only had he missed her special event, it was nearing six o'clock, and they were nowhere close. The sun was lowering on the horizon, and here he was, confined to the blasted coach, miles from River Oak.

"We'll be there soon," Camille said, her eyes riveted on him.

"We've another hour, more like two." Jackson looked out the window, trying hard to calm his nerves.

"It's a shame we've missed the first half of the party. I hope Grace won't hold it against us." Camille went on.

"I've never known Grace to hold anything against you." Drew's calm voice filled the carriage.

Jackson's timing proved right, as it was nearly two hours later when the driver called out. "Whoa there, ladies! Take it easy up the drive." The carriage slowed as it turned off the main road and continued toward the Great House.

Jackson adjusted his smoky-gray jacket and let out a deep breath. The carriage rolled to a stop in front of the house, and a footman opened the door.

As Jackson stepped down to the graveled driveway, Zeek met the family at the base of the stairs. "The party be in the ballroom, suh," the trusted servant said softly. Jackson touched the butler's shoulder by way of thanks and took the steps on swift, silent feet.

The Great House was lit up at every turn as his boots clicked through the entryway and down the hall toward the direction of muffled music. Standing in the entrance to the ballroom, Jackson searched the crowd. He gazed at the women, ribbons and feathers in their coiffed hair, and wearing gowns more beautiful than he'd seen in some time. The men were equally bedecked in their finest suits. His heart thumped in his chest as he gazed at the guests roaming about the hall, some dancing, some moving in and out of the double doors across the floor, and some standing in circles in deep conversation.

As he scanned the large room, he found what he was looking for: beautiful raven-haired Kit danced in the arms of Adam Sparrow. His heart clenched as he gazed at her. She wore an elegant emerald-green gown with a stunning gold necklace. An opal stone surrounded by tiny diamonds rested on the slight rise of her chest, well below her bared throat. Jackson could feel his mouth go dry.

Nothing would deter him now. He wanted nothing more than to pull Kit into his arms, to hold her close to him and never let her go. He threaded his way past the dancing partners and tapped Adam's shoulder. "Pardon me," his deep voice cut in. "I've not danced with the guest of honor. You will excuse us?"

Adam stepped aside. "Of course. I've already danced with her twice. I don't think three times will be a charm." He stalked off with a spark of irritation.

Kit's gray eyes smoldered as she gazed up at Jackson. "You're late. What took you so long?" She gazed at his proffered hand. With as casual an air as she could manage, she placed her hand in his and let him twirl her onto the floor. They swayed for the first few moments, saying nothing, the air between them tense. Jackson held her at arm's length. She nearly missed a step, but he caught her from the blunder. Her steps rigid, she was clearly put out with him. Wishing for all the world he hadn't been late, and wanting to put an end to her frustration, his fingers tightened around her waist.

"Would you like a breath of air? —No, don't refuse." His mouth twisted lopsidedly. "I need it." Taking her arm, he steered her politely past the curious guests onto the veranda and down the flight of steep steps onto the flagstone patio.

Holding her skirts to keep from tripping, Kit cast a frantic glance ahead into the fragrant shadows as they walked toward the pond. "I can't disappear with you into the gardens! What will the guests say?"

"You're quite safe."

"From you or gossipy tongues?" Kit stepped away and massaged her arm.

Jackson felt her pull away and wondered whether it was because she was still irritated with him or because a slight chill had settled in the air.

"Kit, I need a word with you—alone." He pulled her under the giant oak that stood near the water. They could hear the distant splashes as fish surfaced.

The two stood in the night, an occasional laugh or shout faintly filling the silence. The music, now a more soothing waltz, gently flowed out to them. Kit wished she could get lost in the music, lanterns, and starry sky. But the look on Jackson's face made that impossible.

"I've missed you, Kit." He pulled her under a low-hanging branch, letting the shadows hide them from curious eyes. He felt her resistance at first, but then she relaxed and took a step closer.

Kit shuddered and looked up at him. "You never answered me."

"What's that?"

"What took you so long?"

"The blasted ship. The wind abandoned us in the middle of the voyage. With no trade winds blowing, the *Savannah Rose* sat still in the water. We waited hours for a breeze to pick up. Every hour kept me from getting closer to you. And every hour I worried you'd hold it against me."

Kit's eyes clung to his. "I don't hold it against you. You came." The music complemented the canopy of stars, the moonlight, and the blossoms. Jackson took her hand, and they swayed to the melody, both deep in thought. The strains of the violins came to an end, and Kit made to move away, but he didn't release her. "I think that's the last waltz," she said, meeting his gaze steadily. "Shouldn't we go in?"

"Is that what you want?"

She moved into his arms and pulled his chin down. "To be honest, *this* is what I want." He lowered his face to hers but didn't kiss her. The inches between them were maddening. She longed for the feel of his lips against hers. Involuntarily, she pulled him closer.

Jackson let his eyes roam her face until his gaze centered on her lips. Kit's mouth parted in anticipation, and indeed, Jackson would have kissed her had they not heard a noise from behind the tree.

Charice Seward was on the arm of Adam Sparrow as they wove through the garden and came into the light on the brick path. Kit watched Charice tilt her head up as Adam kissed her. After a brief moment, they moved on and disappeared into the shadows.

Kit smiled, looked up at Jackson, and stepped back into his arms.

Running his fingers underneath her jawline, Jackson tipped her face up toward his. Her heart thrummed so loudly she was sure he could hear it. *I haven't had nearly enough practice at this . . . .*

His lips met hers lightly, and Kit felt something inside melt. She closed her eyes and drank in the warmth, the nearness. His hand splayed in the small of her back and pulled her close. The kiss was strong, unhurried. The night around them felt unusually still. It was as if the world had paused.

Jackson broke away for air. "I've waited far too long for this, to taste your sweet lips."

Her knees shaking, Kit brought her arms up around his back and held on.

Jackson ran his fingers through her silky hair. "You're beautiful, Kit, inside and out." He brushed her hair away from her face and tucked it behind her ear.

She flinched and pulled back, but still, he gazed at her. She didn't see herself as beautiful, not with the scar that pierced her left eyebrow and the ugly disfigurement on her neck. *Could he see it in the dark?* "I remember when you used to pull my pigtails." She laughed softly, hoping to take his mind off her scars. "I wanted to punch you."

"And now?" came his deep voice.

"I miss those days. They seemed like they'd go on forever. Then you were gone. All these years you didn't come back, until this summer."

"My folks sent me to college. They wanted me to learn the business side of being a ship merchant. You couldn't have known I missed you, too."

"Did you?"

"I did."

"But you'll go away again." She stepped out of his arms.

"I don't know what to tell you, Kit. Except that I love you."

She loved the sound of her name on his lips. "Don't stop loving me, Jackson."

"I won't." He pulled her into his arms again and grazed her cheek with his chin.

"When do you leave again?" she whispered in his ear.

"You would ask." He pinned her to him, relishing the scent of rose water in her hair.

"Tell me." She planted her palms on his hard chest and pushed away.

He sighed. "We leave the day after tomorrow."

"So soon?"

"I don't have a choice. My father has a big delivery to make in Barbados. At this time in my life, I'm at his beck and call."

"I know, Jackson. And believe it or not, I understand. But I don't like it. I don't like not knowing when I'll see you again."

"Say a prayer for us." His brows knitted.

"What might I pray for?"

"Safety on the sea. This time of year, we're dodging hurricanes."

"Oh, Jackson!" Kit grabbed a fistful of his shirt in both her hands. "I can't bear knowing you're out there and in danger."

"Unfortunately, it comes with the territory of working on the high seas." He pulled her hands into his and clutched them in a sound grip. "You'll pray?"

"Of course I will." She squared her shoulders. "Every day."

"I'll write. I promise. You'll know when I'm coming." He held her upper arms to keep her in front of him. He was afraid she'd run back to the house with the weight of her disappointment. But he felt her relax in his hold and softened his grip.

Before he could kiss her again, Cameron stepped onto the piazza. "Kit, are you out here?"

Kit pushed Jackson farther into the shadows and walked out into the stream of light that spilled from the house. "I'm here."

"What are you doing out there? Your guests are looking for you."

"I needed air." She cupped her elbows and walked up the steps. She looked back in time to see Jackson step out onto the brick pathway. Before she slipped through the door, she gave him a fleeting look.

Jackson let out a deep breath and stepped away from the stand of trees. He sure didn't need to get Kit in trouble. He circled the house and went in through the front door. He wasn't about to leave her with the pack of wolves vying for her attention.

Damaris crept down the front steps and tiptoed stealthily to the side of the Great House. Looking back, she hoped no one would notice her absence. Eager to spend a moment alone with Solomon, she hurried past the outer kitchen and past the slave shanties in the colored district. No sooner had she passed a couple of cabins than she thought she heard steps behind her. She stopped and waited in the lane. She wondered who could be standing in the shadows behind her? A rustle in the branches of the tall oaks startled her, and she hugged herself. A loud shriek spilled through the air that sounded like, "Help!" Damaris jumped at the cry from the peacock perched above her. Trembling, she hurried past the tree and slipped into the rice barn. The large building was dark, and it took a moment to adjust her vision to the dimness. When it did, she found Solomon, tall and muscular, coming her way, a broad smile on his face.

She nearly ran into his arms. They stood just inside the large, double doors, the moonlight streaming in from the opening and casting shadows behind them as they held each other close. They only had a moment, aware that every second counted. Damaris gazed up at him rapturously.

He held her away to devour her with his eyes. "Did anyone see you come?"

"I'm not sure. I thought I was being followed, but apparently not. Everybody is absorbed in Kit's coming-out party. It was easy for me to leave." She glanced at the lane in front of the building. *Is somebody out there?*

Solomon's broad, calloused hands encircled her upper arms as he pulled her close to him again. "I count the hours until the moment you come to me. But I tremble at the thought of you getting caught."

"Don't talk, my darling. Just hold me." Damaris pressed her cheek against his hard chest.

"You look beautiful." His smile gleamed white against his dark skin.

Damaris stepped back and twirled around for him, showing off her pink, white lace-trimmed dress, and then looked up into his face. "I wish you could come to the ballroom and waltz with me." She swung around again, and her skirts flared out. Then she put her arms around his waist.

"I don't have fine clothes for somethin' like that." Solomon kissed her petite nose. "I hear the music, though." He pulled her close, put her hand in his, and began to sway. "You can show me how to waltz like them fancy folks up at the house."

Damaris smiled up at him and stepped away to arm's length. "Follow my lead." She moved two steps to the right and two steps forward, two steps to the left, and two steps back. They repeated the steps to the music that floated out to them. Solomon followed her lead, but his big feet moved clumsily, and after a moment she stopped. She touched his face and ran her finger along the crease beside his mouth.

"We've only a moment. I can't stay long." She cast a glance out over the vast interior of the building. "Someone might be spying on us."

Solomon threw his thick arm over her shoulder, pulled her close, and glanced over her head toward the road. "Who do you think be out there?"

"I don't know, but I think we're being watched."

Zeddie slipped inside the back door of the rice barn. He crept into the shadows and held his breath. He'd known of an interest brewing between Damaris and the field hand. He also knew that his father would work to keep them apart if he found out.

Now he watched Solomon pull Damaris against his massive chest and kiss her. She giggled when he let her go. Zeddie's heart beat loudly in his ears. He tried to stay inconspicuous, sure they didn't know he was there.

Solomon pulled Damaris into his arms again. She tipped her head and kissed his chin, his face in her small hands. She glanced toward the shadows of the barn. Zeddie watched her eyes stray to where he stood in the dark near the back entrance.

She stepped away and grabbed her skirt. "I must go!"

"Wait! Don't leave!" Solomon reached out to stop her.

With a last regretful glance back at the man she had fallen hopelessly in love with, Damaris fled the barn.

Solomon's large frame filled the entrance to the rice barn as he watched her race toward the Great House. He swung around with fire in his eyes. "Who's there?"

Zeddie stepped out of the shadows. "Sorry, Solomon. I didn't know she sensed I was here."

Solomon glanced back at the door, then at Zeddie, an irritated look on his face. "She don't trust a soul around here. She fears someone will tell your father."

"I won't."

"What are you doing here?" Solomon stared at Zeddie's blue eyes and held his fury. Still, he kicked a gunny sack across the floor and then swiveled back to stare at Zeddie again.

"It's dark out. She shouldn't be roaming the grounds alone at night." Zeddie stepped into the ray of silver light at the double-wide doors. "She should have confided in me that she wanted to see you. I'd have escorted her here and waited for her."

Solomon's arms glistened with sweat. His muscles flexed as he tightened his fists. Then he cleared his throat. "It ain't the first time she come see me. I watch the road."

"I don't like it, Solomon. She shouldn't be out here with you alone." Zeddie's eyes grew hard. "We'll be sailing soon. Until then, don't soil her reputation."

TWENTY-EIGHT

KIT GLANCED OUT the window to see dust rising behind a horse trotting up the long drive. "We've got company," she said, moving to the foyer and the front door.

"Who could it be?" Damaris followed, curiosity getting the best of her.

The horseman rode up the circular drive and called out, "Hullo! Postman here!"

Kit opened the door and stepped onto the front porch, Damaris quick on her heels. The two young women met the horseman on the drive.

"Hi, Johnny! You've got a letter for us?" Kit smiled brightly and held out her hand.

"Captain Kincade wants this given to Denzel Talmaze." The postman bent forward and gave the small letter to Kit. His eyes lit up as he watched her.

Kit's brows furrowed as she looked at the writing on the envelope. "I'll see that Uncle Denzel gets this." She looked back at Damaris and bit her bottom lip. "I suppose this means the *Sea Baron* is back."

Damaris felt her pulse pick up, and a tremor went through her body. She'd known that any day now the *Sea Baron* would arrive. But now that it had, she wasn't ready to leave. She looked up at Johnny, who hadn't taken his eyes off Kit. "Thank you for the delivery."

Johnny touched his hat and pulled back on the reins. His mount took a few steps back before he turned toward the carriage lane. "I'll be seeing you around. I've a few more posts to deliver before I head back to Charleston."

"The mail could have come on the *River Belle*. That was a long ride to deliver a few letters," Kit said.

"I didn't mind, Miss Kit. I was looking forward to delivering this post right into your hands."

Kit's face flushed. "You're quite forward, I might say." She swallowed visibly, and Johnny's face lit up again.

"At least you didn't disappoint me. It could have been Willie or one of the slaves who met me out here. I'm right glad to have the memory of your pretty face to follow me on the rest of the route." Johnny kneed his horse and touched the brim of his hat. "Good day."

"Well, of all the nerve!" Kit handed the letter to Damaris.

"You don't fool me one bit." Damaris hooked a hand in the crook of Kit's arm. "He just made your day."

Kit pulled back with a pout. "No, he didn't. I was hoping the letter was from Jackson. Instead, I have a terrible premonition it's news that you are all leaving for Barbados any day now." She took hold of Damaris's hand and swung it as they went up the steps. "I hate goodbyes."

After the two families settled at the long dinner table that evening, Denzel made the announcement the girls were dreading. "We'll be riding to Charleston tomorrow morning. The *Sea Baron* has arrived to take us home."

"Can't we stay a few more days?" Cyrus scowled and slumped in his chair.

"No, son. We've been gone for over four months. It's time we go home and check on the business of the tobacco fields and the plantation. I've left it all in Ebenezer's hands far too long."

"He knows what he's doing . . ."

"That's enough." Denzel gave Cyrus a stern look, and the room grew quiet.

"I'll have the servants help with the packing. It'll be ready by morning," Grace said.

"Thank you. I don't mean to make this a bad time. We've enjoyed ourselves immensely. But seeing as how we haven't found Kindra, I think it's wise to check on things back home." Denzel looked at Cameron. "You'll keep looking for her?" A wistfulness shadowed his countenance.

"Of course. We'll find her."

Anguish at the thought of leaving Solomon tore at Damaris's heart, and she set down her fork. She needed to see him. How could she leave him? She dropped her napkin on her plate. "May I be excused? I need to take a walk." She stood and turned quickly to escape the dining room.

"Damaris!" Denzel called.

"Let her go," Grace said. "It's their last night to say goodbye."

"So you knew?" Denzel's shoulders sagged.

Grace's lips curved upward. "I think we all did."

Damaris had heard enough. She fled out the front door, tears stinging her eyes. A cool breeze sailed about her as she ran down the steps. She hadn't put a candle in the window tonight. Solomon wouldn't be waiting for her. Her feet ate up the ground as she hurried toward the colored district. Was he in his cabin with his family? She surely couldn't just walk up and knock on his father's door. Fist to lips and tears streaming down her cheeks, she continued on. She passed several shanties before reaching the home of Solomon's family.

Before she could knock, the door opened and light spilled out onto the ground. Frozen in her steps, Damaris watched Cuffee step out.

"Good evenin', Miss Damaris. You out here all alone?" He walked over to where she stood. "You been cryin'. Somethin' wrong?"

"Y-yes. I'm looking for Solomon." She lowered her eyes and stared at Cuffee's worn shoes.

"He ain't here." Cuffee's finger lifted her chin. Kind eyes peered down at her. "You'll find him at the stable. Sometimes, he goes there when he's got a lot on his mind. He sure likes curryin' them horses. Helps him think. I 'spect he'd be pleased to see you 'bout now."

Damaris looked up at him. "Thank you, Cuffee."

"You shouldn't be out here all alone. It's not safe fer a young woman like you."

"I have to see Solomon." A shiver ran through her. "We leave for Barbados in the morning."

"I see. Well, like I said, Solomon's in that stable over there."

Damaris nodded and turned toward the narrow lane. She quickened her steps when she saw light filter out of the building she was looking for. At first, she didn't see Solomon when she entered the barn, but she heard his low voice as he talked to one of the mares in a stall.

Dust-coated lanterns, spaced at intervals to light the stable's interior, hung from sturdy wooden posts. A faint smell of hay and animal odors wafted through the area, muted by the evening air. Solomon's voice came from inside the rough structure. "Easy there."

Damaris heard the horse nicker in response.

Brush in hand, Solomon popped his head up when the stall door squeaked open. He just stared at her with his mouth open, but she ran into his arms.

"What are you doing here?" He set the brush on the ledge of the stall and placed both hands on her cheeks. "You've been crying. What happened?" His eyes searched hers, a flash of anger rushing to the fore.

"Oh, Solomon." She wiped the tears from her eyes and looked up into his rough-cut, handsome face. "We're leaving in the morning. I can't bear the thought of leaving you."

Solomon seemed at a loss for words. He stared at her for a long moment before he said, "I won't let you go." He wrapped his arms around her and kissed the top of her head. She smelled his strong scent in the sweat beneath his shirt. She felt his muscles protrude like steel through the thin material and allowed her hands to run behind his back, letting her head rest on his chest as she cried in anguish. They just stood in the stall, holding each other, not wanting to let go.

The horse stomped impatiently and swatted flies with her tail.

"Let's get out of here." Solomon pulled the stall door open for the two of them to step out. Taking Damaris's hand, he led her out onto the narrow road and looked toward the slave district. "Come on."

"I don't want to go back to the house."

"I just want to get you back there. We can talk under the oak."

"All right." Damaris clung to Solomon's hand as they walked the short distance to the Great House. They circled behind the kitchen garden and walked to the old oak where they'd spent many evenings. Moments later, his rough hand cupped her chin, and she looked up. He bent his head to claim her lips. She stood on tiptoe and clung to his neck. A groan escaped him.

Damaris came up for air. Their eyes held each other for the breath of a moment, and then she pulled his head down to her again.

After some time, Solomon pushed her gently away and said, "We must talk. There's so much I want to say to you and haven't, and here we've run out of time." He stared into her eyes. "Do you love me?"

"More than anything." She kissed the top of his hand.

"It does my heart good to hear you say that. Damaris . . . I want you. I've never said it, but I love you, too."

"But I'm leaving." Her throat clogged with tears.

"You'll be back. Am I right? You'll be back?"

"Yes. We have to sail to Barbados and check on the plantation. But Father said we're coming back."

"I don't have the right to ask you this. I'm a slave, and you—you're a plantation owner's daughter." He shook his head and looked up at the moon. Anguish ran across his rough jaw. "Will you save yourself for me, Damaris?"

"I want to. You know I do."

"But what?"

"Are you asking for my hand in marriage?"

"I am." He stood tall and looked down at her, his shoulders squared. "But I have nothing to offer you."

"I don't care."

"You should."

"But I don't."

His shoulders sagged. "Listen to us. What we want we can't have. When you sail away, you need to forget me. You need to find someone who can give you what I can't." He backed away and placed his hands on his hips, his chin to his chest.

"No! Don't say that. I will wait for you!"

"Stop it! We been foolin' ourselves. There will never be a future for us!" His hands went up as if to stop her from advancing toward him.

"Solomon!" She stepped forward, tears blinding her vision.

"Step away, Damaris."

"You don't mean it."

"I do."

"No!" She took another step and swallowed the hot tears in her throat.

"Go into the house." He turned and walked briskly toward the front of the Great House.

"Solomon!"

His hand went up, and he kept walking.

She fell to her knees and beat the dark earth. "Solomon," she cried. Sobs choked her until she couldn't think any longer. When she looked up, he was gone. "Why?" She pushed to her feet and hugged herself. "Why does life have to keep taking those I love away from me?" She cried out the words, but no one answered.

The silence consumed her. She lifted the hem of her skirt and wiped her eyes. Light from the house spilled onto the ground around her. Numb, Damaris entered the back door and went up to Kit's bedchamber. She stumbled into the room, crestfallen. Hedy was brushing Kit's hair, but seeing her enter, she stopped, hairbrush in hand. "What's wrong with you, child?"

Kit turned and gasped, "What's wrong, honey?"

"Oh, Kit!"

"Go on, Hedy. Leave us," Kit ordered.

Damaris flew into Kit's arms and sobbed. "It's over."

"What's over?" Kit gently pushed her back and looked into her eyes.

"Solomon and I."

"Oh, Damaris." Kit's chin went to the top of Damaris's head. "It's not over. Just you wait and see." She brushed her hand over Damaris's curls as she would a child. "Solomon loves you. That's as plain as the nose on my face. Maybe he's angry that you're going home, but he loves you."

"You weren't there. You didn't hear him. It's over, Kit." Fresh tears spilled down Damaris's cheeks.

The girls changed into their nightclothes, and Kit blew out the lantern before she slid in beside Damaris. They talked in the darkness well into the night. Damaris didn't know when she fell asleep. She only knew somewhere in the night that slumber numbed the ache in her heart.

Piper looked up at Damaris with a chagrined look on her face. "Why are we dressing up in these old rags?" She held out the course material as if she were about to curtsy.

"Because," Damaris lifted thirteen-year-old Piper's chin with an index finger. "We gots to be lookin' like them slaves in town." She held out her own brown, drab skirt and twirled.

Amos and Cato showed up at the entrance to the bedchamber. "Mastah Camp be sayin' we best git yer luggage down to the wagon."

"My trunk is against the wall. Piper and I can carry the bags." Damaris felt her heart fall to her stomach. She had anticipated seeing Solomon this morning, hoping he would be the one to carry her things to the wagon. She'd peered out the window more times than she could count but hadn't seen a glimpse of him all morning.

The two men picked up the heavy trunk and left the room.

"I'm going to miss this bedchamber. Kit and I have spent countless hours sharing our dreams here." She tried to swallow the lump that had taken up residence in her throat.

"Me, too. I'm sure going to miss Bella Grace, Sunny, and Maddie. River Oak is like our home away from home." Piper wiped at her cheeks, her lips pressed together. "We didn't find Mama." Then the real tears fell.

"Oh, Piper!" Damaris flew to her sister's side. "We didn't find her this time. But we can't give up. Daddy's so disappointed that I fear he can hardly think straight. We've got to be strong for him."

"I know." Piper pulled away and wiped her eyes with the back of her arm. "Come on. They're waiting for us."

The two girls grabbed a bag in each hand and descended the stairs. When they reached the foyer, they were met with a flurry of activity.

"You haven't eaten breakfast yet. You've got to get a bite before you leave." Grace gently pushed them into the dining room. "Gemma, see that they each get a fresh glass of orange juice. And see that they have plenty to eat. They'll be famished by the time they reach Charleston if they don't."

"Yes'm, Miss Grace. I'll see to it they eat plenty." Gemma patted Damaris's shoulder, a smile in her eyes. "We's gonna miss you fine girls when you be gone."

"What about us?" Cyrus asked as he and Zeddie slipped into chairs across from the girls.

"Don't you be thinkin' Aunt Gemma don't be missin' you fine boys. Now stay put while I bring out your food." She disappeared behind the swinging kitchen door, and the four Talmaze children stared at each other.

"Have you seen Father this morning?" Damaris asked her brothers.

"He's out walking the rice fields with Uncle Camp. They've been talking all morning," Zeddie said.

"I suppose they're making plans for Uncle Camp to keep looking for Mama." Damaris picked up the crystal glass of ice water and took a sip.

"Two horsemen showed up this morning. Aunt Grace said Uncle Camp hired them to search for Mother. They talked to Dad and Uncle Camp a long time before they rode off."

"Good. It helps to know the search will continue while we're gone." Damaris glanced at Piper. "See. Maybe we'll get word real soon and have to come right back to bring Mama home." She kissed Piper's cheek just as Gemma and Mama Jezelee paraded out with a fanfare of breakfast. Seeing the many bowls they carried to the table warmed Damaris's heart. The cooks had outdone themselves to send their family off with the best breakfast in all of the Low Country.

In the distance, Damaris heard the whistle of the *River Belle*. Many aspects of River Oak had seeped into her soul. She knew she'd miss this place for a long time to come. Yet her eyes wandered to the dining room window and the activity outside. There was no sign of Solomon. Would he let her go without saying goodbye?

TWENTY-NINE

RUFUS ENTERED THE sunroom with a silver tray in his hands. In the center sat a single envelope. He crossed the floor to where Phoebe sat in an armchair, sipping a cup of hot tea. Kindra sat in a hard chair beside her, an open ledger in her lap.

"A letter, ma'am." Rufus stood before Phoebe.

"Thank you, Rufus." Phoebe took the note off the tray and waved a hand. "You may go."

"Yes'm." Rufus left as silently as he had appeared.

"Now who could have sent this letter?" Phoebe didn't bother opening the cream-colored envelope. She handed it to Kindra and waited.

Setting the ledger aside, Kindra opened the envelope and read the note inside:

MASQUERADE BALL

Lawrence & Phoebe Bridger

ARE REQUESTED TO ATTEND THE BALL,
AT LITMAN HALL on SATURDAY,
10th of November current, at 4 o'clock p.m.
Zayn & Audrey Litman
Charleston, October 2, 1848

Phoebe's eyes lit up and she clamped her hands to her chest. "It's been years since we've attended a masquerade ball. I think it'll be delightful to attend the party, and I know just the shop that carries the best assortment of costumes and masks." Then she sank back against the chair, her brows furrowed and a frown darkening her face. "What am I thinking? I have yet to serve Lawrence with a divorce warrant, and here I am considering the masquerade ball." Tears rimmed her eyelids. She grabbed the invitation from Kindra's hands and tore it in two. "I'll not put on a charade that all is well when it's not." She stared at the vase on the round table before them.

A smile curved Kindra's lip. She'd seen Phoebe go through one heartache after another. "Why not?"

"Why not what?"

"Why not put on a charade that all is well? Isn't that what the masquerade ball is all about, a room full of people who have secrets? It's the one night you can give yourself the cloak of disguise, and Lawrence will never be the wiser."

Kindra watched a gleam come into Phoebe's eyes. "You're right. My life has been turned upside down. I'll give myself this one last dance before I turn his upside down—enough talk. Help me change. We're going into town."

Moments later, the two women were in the dressing room. Phoebe stepped out of her day dress and moved to where Kindra was waiting. She lifted her arms while Kindra slipped a burgundy satin gown over her head, taking care not to disturb her hair. She stood still as a post while Kindra's flying fingers latched all the buttons. When done, Kindra brushed the wrinkles out of her skirts. "You look beautiful, Miss Phoebe."

Phoebe glanced in the mirror at her reflection, then at Kindra. "Now tend to yourself. We'll be leaving directly." Phoebe's cheeks flushed brightly.

Kindra smiled to herself. Had she given the mistress good advice? She surely hoped so. There would be no backing out now.

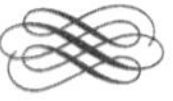

"I'll miss you." Kit bit her bottom lip.

"Oh, Kit, I'll miss you, too!" The two women hugged each other tightly.

The next few minutes were filled with goodbyes as the two families said their goodbyes, while trembling laughter filled the air.

"I do wish you didn't have to go." Grace wiped tears from her eyes. "And take good care of your father." She left Damaris's side and gave Denzel one more hug.

"Remember our talk," Cameron told Denzel.

"I will. And we'll be back before you know it."

"Sounds good." Cameron slapped his brother-in-law's shoulder and instructed his family to step back so the others could board the ship.

"Goodbye!" Denzel's family called out as they turned and climbed the gangplank.

"Goodbye! We'll see you soon!" came the cries from the Bartholomews.

A sailor retrieved the carpetbags sitting at their feet as Damaris and her family went to the rail. Damaris gazed down at her aunt and cousins standing on the wharf. They hooked arms and watched as she and Piper moved along the rail of the ship. Sailors waved goodbye to people below. The girls found an empty place and waved down at their family.

"I'm going to miss them." Piper's voice quavered.

"Me, too, honey." Damaris threw an arm over her sister's shoulder. Her heart swelled as she waved at Kit. The tears she'd been able to hold back until now slipped down her cheek as the Bartholomews waved back.

A long whistle blew from the boatswain's pipe, and the gangplank was raised from the dock's landing and up onto the ship's side. The vessel pulled away from shore. Damaris waved again and again. She could see her family waving back. They grew smaller as the ship crept away from the mooring. "Goodbye," she whispered.

A dull ache formed in her heart. Solomon had not come to say goodbye at River Oak. And now there was no way of seeing him until she returned. Would he forget her as he had threatened the night before?

Glancing out over the sparkling water, she waved one last time, knowing they could not see her. As the vessel picked up speed, the people on the dock appeared to be little more than dark spots on the shore. Damaris pulled Piper away from the rail. "Let's find our cabin. I want to get out of these rags."

As the vessel moved steadily into the Atlantic, Damaris's heart urged her to race back and find Solomon, but she could not; she was a captive on the ship for the next three weeks. She would put behind her what she could not change and, instead, look ahead to her future. They would return to River Oak again. Would their mother be waiting for them? Would the love of her life claim her lips once again? Be still, my heart! Be strong and vigilant for the family!

Damaris guided Piper down the steps below the quarterdeck. When they reached the bottom, the door above them was still open. She lifted her face to look out at the bright sky. *I will never give up.*

Phoebe instructed Matthias to drive them to the wharf. She had made numerous purchases for the coming ball, and the carriage was filled with a myriad of packages. Now she wanted to watch the ships come and go from the Cooper River.

"Do you ever wonder where all the people are going or where they're coming from?" Phoebe watched from the side of the road while the smells of dead fish and horse dung assailed them. Stevedores carried crates on their shoulders and went up the gangplanks with ease. Boatswains blew whistles as their ships moved out into the bay, and men shouted from wagons nearby.

All the commotion was familiar to Kindra as she eyed the names of the ships docked at the piers and hunted for the faces of her family. One ship moved away just to the right, and her heart stopped. The *Sea Baron*'s bell blew loud and clear as the ship moved beyond the last vessel in the harbor. Kindra leaned forward, trying for all she was worth to get a glimpse of the people standing at the rail. Was that Damaris? Two girls stood side by side, watching as the ship left port. Was that Piper standing beside Damaris? Kindra's heart pounded in her chest, and her head felt light. She could barely breathe as she struggled to keep herself from jumping from the carriage and running down the pier to cry out for the *Sea Baron* to stop, to wait for her!

Wagons rumbled by, and she gazed at each one with anticipation of seeing Cameron or Grace. Surely, they were here seeing her family off. Her eyes glistened and her soul crushed within her. *Did they give up on finding me?*

"Matthias," Phoebe's soft voice filled the air around them. "I'm ready to go home."

"Yes'm," the driver replied. He shook the reins, and the carriage rolled slowly away from the wharf. The sound of gravel crunching beneath the iron wheels echoed the wrenching sadness that claimed Kindra's heart. *Oh, Lord.*

Give me strength! I want to see my family. You said You would not give me more than I can bear. My heart is torn beyond comprehension. I need You now more than ever. How can I watch my family sail away without me? You must have a plan for me. But for now, my soul cries out. I need Your strength in my weakness.

THIRTY

Atlantic Ocean

DAMARIS HELPED PIPER settle into her cabin. "Let's get you changed out of those drab clothes." At thirteen, Piper's body was beginning to show signs of maturity.

"I hope I never have to wear these old rags again." Piper stepped out of her brown skirt and kicked it aside.

"Lift your hands." Damaris pulled Piper's tunic over her head and tossed it on the cot. "Unfortunately, we'll have to save these garments for the next trip. It's far better we put on a charade for the folks in town that we be po' slaves than to reap the rage of our betters. As far as they're concerned, even a free Negress can be strung up from a tree."

"I hate it when you talk like that. We've never been faced with any of the horrors you've talked about."

Damaris found a flowered dress and slipped it over her sister's head. "Well, it's true. Folks in the States have a low opinion of us darkies." She stepped back and frowned at the snug top.

"What happened to this dress? It fit fine before we left Barbados." Piper pulled at the bodice.

"I've a feeling you're going to need a new wardrobe when we arrive home. You've blossomed over the summer." Damaris went in search of another garment and found a loose-fitting, gauzy, floor-length dress. "That'll do. Now, if you don't mind, I want to get out of this thing and relax." Damaris held out the course skirt and looked down. She moved to the cabin door and opened it.

"I'm going to read. Don't worry about me." Piper picked up a small book and slid onto the cot.

"Damaris?"

"Yes, honey?"

"Thank you for looking out for me."

Damaris held the door in her hand and glanced back at her sister. "You're welcome." She started to step out when Piper stopped her once more.

"I wish someone could have helped Mama."

Damaris stepped back into the room and crossed the short distance to the cot. She brushed the curls from Piper's forehead. "Me, too." She kissed her sister's cheek and left the cabin. A rush of tears clogged her throat as she climbed the stairs and moved out onto the main deck. The breeze whipped at the hem of her skirt as she leaned over the ship's rail, but the cool salt air did little to assuage the deep hurt of not finding her mother.

At every turn, her heart ached. She ached for her mother. Would she ever see her again? She ached for her father, for the pain she saw in his face, and for Solomon. She gazed at the water that swirled behind them. She listened to the sounds of the sailors behind her, working the rigging, minding the sails, and mopping the deck. How could life go on when so much pain seemed to smother the life out of her?

She pushed away from the rail and went down the steps below the quarterdeck. Her cabin was small like Piper's. She didn't care. All she wanted was to lie down . . . to sleep away the minutes, the hours, the days. Instead, she sat up in bed and hugged her knees, trying desperately to remember the lines in Solomon's face, his thick lips, and broad nose. She tried to remember what it felt like to be held against his hard chest, rippling with hard-earned muscles, and to remember the feel of his rough hands when he cupped her chin. When she closed her eyes, she could almost smell the scent of his body, sweat from the days of work, and another smell . . . that could only be Solomon.

She listened to the water lapping against the ship's hull. The gentle rocking of the waves as they swayed the vessel was soothing, and tears slid down her cheeks.

Father, I need you right now. I need to feel Your presence. Your Word says You will hide us under the shadow of Your wings. Protect Mother.

Heal my father's wounds, and if it be Your will, change Solomon's heart. I love him, Lord. I don't want to lose him.

After three weeks at sea, Damaris peered up at the cloudless sky and watched the gulls flying in circles. Their broad grey wings flapped as they shrieked at the ship. In one more day, the *Sea Baron* would be landing on the island of Barbados. The birds were the lone sign that land was nearby. They were almost home!

Zeddie and Cyrus climbed the companionway to where she stood. Zeddie stood on the quarterdeck and leveled his telescope toward the island of Barbados, southwest of the Atlantic. The trade winds ruffled his black curls, and he peered a long moment before he handed the spyglass to Damaris. "Take a look."

Squinting, Damaris saw nothing. "I don't see land."

"You're holding the scope too high." He touched it gently and lowered it as she kept her eyes pinned to the lens. As she looked intently through the spyglass, she became aware of her father's presence. She backed away and held the telescope out to him. "Are we near?"

"I've come up here to inform you that the *Sea Baron* will be docking in the morning." Her father took the spyglass she offered. "You won't see the land yet. Maybe tonight when the city lights are on. But even then, that's far-fetched." He handed the telescope to Zeddie and grinned.

"You had me, Zeddie." She punched his shoulder playfully. "I was hoping to get a glimpse of land. If I don't see water for the rest of my life, that'll be fine with me." She whirled around and fled down the steps. When she looked up, it was to see her father and brothers gazing down at her with cheeky grins.

"Humph!"

Bridgetown, Barbados

The next morning, Damaris awoke to an odd sound. The swaying rhythm of the ship had stopped, and she realized that it was the ship's lack of motion that had awakened her. She listened again to the sounds outside her window. Voices shouting? Horses? Wagons? She rose to her knees and peeked out her porthole. A busy harbor met her eyes. They were back!

She flew out of bed and ran to Piper's cabin. The room was dark, and she crept carefully across the floor and shook her sister's shoulders. "Piper, wake up! We're here!"

"Wh-what?"

"The ship's docked. Get dressed, silly!"

Piper shoved the blanket off and stood. "Finally!" She pulled her carpetbags out from under the bed. She set them both on the coverlet and whirled around to face Damaris. "Are you packed?"

"No. I woke up and came straight in here. Carry on, and I'll do the same." Damaris scurried back to her cabin and pulled out her own carpetbags from beneath the bed. She soon had her personal belongings packed and her traveling clothes on. She was so excited to be home, she was sure she wouldn't be able to eat a bite at breakfast.

Piper rapped at her door. "Hurry. Daddy's going to hire a coach to take us home."

Footsteps sounded behind her. "We've docked and will be leaving soon." This came from Zeddie. "Give me your carpetbags and I'll carry them out for you."

"Thank you, Zeddie. Did you already get Piper's bags?"

"Cyrus has Piper's. Come on."

When Damaris stepped out onto the main deck, it was to find the crewmen had jumped ashore to tie the long ropes of the vessel to the heavy, iron stakes on the dock landing.

Damaris and Piper searched for their father as the crewmen's voices rose with their morale. Denzel stepped out of Captain Kincade's cabin. "There you are. Are you ready?"

"Yes. Cyrus and Zeddie are waiting by the gangplank."

"Then let's go." Denzel turned to Kincade. "We'll talk later. See me before you set sail."

"Will do," the captain said.

The family descended the gangplank together.

Touching her lavender hat with one hand to keep it from blowing away in the morning breeze, Damaris lifted her muslin skirts with the other and said to Piper, "Stay close by my side. You could get lost with so many strangers here." Together, the two of them ventured down the gangway ahead of their father and brothers. It wasn't long before people on the boardwalk filled in the space between them and their father, and they were shoved forward into the milling crowd.

"Are you glad to be home?" Damaris asked Piper.

"I didn't think I'd be happy to return without Mama. But now that we're here, I can't wait to see Gram and the rest of the household. And truth to tell, I can't wait to sleep in my own bed again."

Damaris's lips turned up in a wide grin. "Me, too." As the throng thinned, she watched her father shove his hat back off his forehead and glance over the area. "We're over here!" she called, waving her hand.

Denzel flashed a relieved smile and marched toward them, her brothers taking long strides to keep up. "I need to hire a carriage to get us to the plantation. Cyrus, you stay with the girls. Zeddie, come with me." Father and son turned back into the thick knot of people on the wharf and disappeared among the crowd.

Soon, a coachman helped Damaris and Piper into a rented carriage. Denzel and Zeddie stepped in next, and Cyrus climbed in last. He dropped into the leather seat and leaned back. "I can't wait to get home. It feels like we've been gone a hundred years." The carriage bumped along the cobbled road toward Bridgetown.

As the coach jerked through traffic, their father looked at all of them, weariness etched on his forehead. He opened his mouth to speak and then closed it.

"You tried, Father. You did what you could to find Mother." Damaris gave him a weak smile.

"I didn't give it all I had, or she would be in this coach with us." Tears rimmed his eyes.

Damaris reached for his hand and clamped it in hers. "Don't, Father.

Don't beat yourself up. Uncle Cameron has hired men to find her. They will, and we'll return to River Oak to bring her home."

Denzel nodded and heaved a deep sigh. "I miss her."

"We all miss her." Damaris glanced at her siblings.

They all nodded and watched their father with concern.

"We won't give up, Father." Zeddie squared his shoulders. "We're just returning to make sure the plantation is running right. We'll soon be back on the *Sea Baron* and headed to get Mama. We'll bring her home next time."

Damaris let his words soak in and soothe her. She wanted nothing more than to believe they would bring her mother home. She stared out the window and sighed. Tiny droplets of sweat beaded her upper lip and forehead. With the island's humidity, the coach was warm.

Would their grandmother be happy to see them? Or would Tia want to send them packing back to the States again?

THIRTY-ONE

Kindra Hall, Barbados

THE KITCHEN DOOR opened, and Ebenezer stepped in.

"Mornin', Eb," Louiza said.

"Mornin', Louiza. Is Tia up?"

"I'm sure she is. She jist ain't showed her face yet. Mayme's come downstairs, so I expect Tia to be in for breakfast real soon."

"All right." Ebenezer stood by the back door.

"Go on and sit down. Breakfast is almost ready." Clara moved to the shelf, pulled down a coffee mug, and stepped to the stove, where a pot of coffee was boiling. She filled the mug and handed it to him. "Here, take it with you. We'll only be a moment."

Louiza wiped her hands on her apron and watched the overseer move into the servants' dining quarters. "Massa and his children might be home today."

"Ebenezer been sayin' that fer a week. He's been sayin' they ought to be returnin' anytime now." Clara cracked eggs into the skillet.

"I find myself lookin' out that dinin' room window more times than I can count," Louiza said.

"That's not sayin' much. Since when did you learn to count?" Clara tossed her head back and laughed.

"Go on with you. I count all the time. How many eggs have you been crackin' this mornin'?"

"I don't know. I haven't been payin' much attention. I'd say enough to feed this bunch filin' to the table." She cracked another egg.

"You got a dozen eggs cookin' in that skillet." Louiza's brows went up as if she'd made a point.

"Truth is, I find myself lookin' out that window too. I be expectin' the family home soon." Clara picked up the wooden spoon and stirred the eggs in the cast-iron skillet.

Boaz came into the kitchen. "Mornin', ladies. That food sho' got my stomach roarin'. Be ready soon?"

"What you think? It be ready same time this mornin' as it is every mornin'. Sit yerself down and wait like a gentleman." Clara pointed the wooden spoon at him.

Boaz gave her a wide grin. "I sho' be doin' that." He went into the servants' quarters and pulled out a chair.

It wasn't long before the room filled with the rest of the servants. Clara set a bowl of scrambled eggs in front of Duncan. Corrie sat next to him. Ethel and Netty wandered in and took their seats.

Jasper and Mayme and their four children ate in the slave district. After tending to Tia, Mayme would go to their shanty and feed her family. When finished, Jasper and the children would go out to the fields to work, and Mayme would come to the Great House to lend a hand wherever she was needed.

The servants' dining room hummed as the slaves took their seats at the table. Clara and Louiza pushed through the kitchen door, bringing bowls of scrambled eggs and plates piled high with flapjacks.

"I'll pour the coffee." Corrie got up to help.

At long last, Louiza and Clara took their place at the table, and Ebenezer led everyone in bowing their heads. "Lord, for Your bounty we are grateful. Sustain us with Your grace. Amen."

"Good morning, everyone." Tia came into the room and looked around. "Breakfast smells good." She took a seat across from Ebenezer. "Now, do you suppose my family will arrive today?"

All eyes went to Tia. Dressed elegantly in a colorful dress, she folded her hands in her lap. She wore gold-hooped earrings that highlighted her skin tone. Her crystal-blue eyes glinted with kindness as she gazed back at them.

"We's jist been sayin' we think today be the day," Louiza said.

"I hope so. I miss them terribly." Tia dished scrambled eggs onto her plate.

"We all do. Why, we be cookin' like we expectin' an army of men to show up, just thinkin' they's gonna be here any minute." Louiza passed the biscuits.

Ebenezer kept his eyes on Tia. At last, she turned to him. "How are the tobacco fields coming along?"

"It be testy. We got the front hundred acres in good shape. But Jasper's found trouble on the north end of the property."

"Oh, no."

"That's what I said. We'll be headin' out to check those fields after breakfast. I'm thinkin' it's goin' to be a long day."

"The field hands?" Tia held her fork in midair.

"I've already got 'em out there pluckin' them devil hornworms off the plants. Sho' ain't gonna be good news for Denzel."

Louiza listened to the talk. Things were sure to get better when the Master Denzel returned.

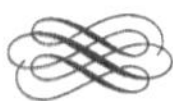

Louiza snapped the white-starched tablecloth open and let it flare over the mahogany dining table, then went to each corner to smooth out the wrinkles. She caught a glimpse of movement in the long drive and moved to the window. "Lord, have mercy!" She pushed the lace curtain aside. "I think they're here!" She set the fruit bowl in the center of the table and dashed to the kitchen. "Clara! They're here!"

"Goodness gracious me! We best be greetin' them!" Clara wiped her hands on her apron and straightened it.

Mayme pushed the curtains aside in the sitting room. "It's them!" She stood at the base of the stairs. "Come downstairs," she called to the maids.

A rustle of feet filled the hallway above. Moments later, the servants moved to the front porch as the carriage rolled to a stop.

"Welcome home!"

Damaris gazed out the coach window as the rig rolled in front of the porch. The Great House seemed larger than she remembered, and grander. Her heart skipped a beat, and she didn't wait for the carriage driver to assist her. Instead, she pushed the door open, alighted on the graveled driveway, and opened her arms wide, for there were all of the house slaves, standing and waving, broad smiles on their faces. "We're back!" she cried.

The servants ran forward as everyone scrambled out of the carriage to greet them. Much noise and laughter filled the air, so much so that, in the distance at the curing barn, field hands came to the entrance to see what all the commotion was about.

With them was Tia. She pushed through the workers with a basket hooked over her arm, and stopped and looked as if to see for herself that the family was truly here. "You've returned!" Her face lit up and she turned back into the curing barn. "Ebenezer, they're home!" She didn't wait for him. She dropped the basket and ran to close the distance between her and her family.

Damaris looked up at her father. "Gram's happy to see us."

"I see that." He started toward Tia. When the two met, Tia stepped back and looked Denzel over from head to foot. Then she clutched his arms and broke into a delightful smile. "It's so good to have you back!"

Damaris and her siblings looked at each other, frozen to the ground. They weren't accustomed to their grandmother showing kindness to their father. When they left for the States, she had been brash and cruel. What happened to her while they were gone?

"Why, you've been gone far too long," Tia continued. "We've been watching for all of you every day for the past week. I began to wonder if you'd decided to stay in the States."

Denzel stared down at her, seeming to have lost his tongue. When he gave no immediate response, she asked, "Are you all right?"

The servants stood with the children as they watched Tia and Denzel.

"I . . . I'd half expected you'd ask about Kindra." His voice was low, hardly audible.

Tia looked at the carriage and then at the children. Her eyes settled on each one. Damaris watched as her grandmother's eyes moved to her. They held each other's gaze for a breath of a moment before Tia turned and looked up at Denzel and patted his arm.

"Son, I wanted . . . I hoped with all my heart that you'd bring my daughter home. I pray to God every day that He keeps her and sustains her, but truth to tell, I didn't think she'd come home this time." She continued to pat Denzel's arm and then squeezed both of his hands. "He's going to bring that girl home. He's going to hand my daughter over to you. It's just not the right time now."

Denzel slowly nodded, his face flushed. "As much as it kills my heart to accept your words, I know that be the truth. We tried. We tried to find her. We almost did . . . but as you see, she's not with us."

The somber moment froze the crowd. They waited to see what would happen next. Denzel didn't step away from Tia; instead, he planted his big hands on her slim shoulders and gazed down at her. "Something's different about you."

Tia's face lit up in a bright smile.

Just then, Ebenezer strode up to the two of them. Damaris had noticed the overseer watching at a respectful distance, but at the mention of Tia's countenance, it seemed he had something to say.

Denzel looked over. "Eb!"

"Denzel!" The two men hugged. "'Bout time you set your feet on this tobacco plantation." They clapped each other's shoulders and stood back.

Ebenezer moved to Tia's side and slipped his arm over her shoulder. He turned her toward the small party that watched them. When the children gasped and looked at each other, he announced, "We've been waiting for the family to return to make an important announcement." He dropped his arm to take Tia's hand. "Denzel, I've asked Tia to be my wife, and she graciously said, 'Yes.' We'd be honored if you'd permit us to make this union official in your eyes."

Ebenezer couldn't have looked prouder to have Tia at his side. He seemed at peace with himself. Holding Tia's hand seemed like the most natural thing in the world.

Damaris watched them with mixed emotions. Had her grandmother changed so much that Ebenezer would want her for his wife? And had she heard Tia correctly? Had she been praying every day for her mother's return? What happened while they were gone?

Cyrus and Piper broke away from the crowd to hug their grandmother.

Damaris held back and looked up at her father. There was hope in his eyes. Whatever had happened to Gram, he seemed to welcome the change. Damaris, on the other hand, couldn't. She still remembered the night she'd heard her grandmother confess to stealing the emeralds and admitting that it was why the marauders had taken Kindra. From that day on, Damaris kept a distance from Tia. How could she forgive her?

Mayme slipped her arm around Damaris's waist. "We're glad you had a good trip."

The house slaves broke out into laughter and moved to each member of the family. Hugs aplenty went around. It wasn't long before Damaris felt tears of joy at seeing their beautiful faces.

"I've missed every one of you." Damaris took Louiza's hand and squeezed it. "And we're famished!"

"Land sakes alive! We'd best feed these people!" Louiza looked to Clara, who'd just let go of Piper. "We'd best make them a feast!" The two cooks went back into the house with jaunty steps.

Duncan, Jasper, and Boaz strode to the coach and began unloading the luggage.

In all the raucous banter, Damaris hadn't noticed that her grandmother had left Ebenezer's side. She now stood beside her, beaming.

"Gram?" Damaris hesitated.

"Come here, young lady. I swear you've become a woman in your absence."

Damaris obediently went into her grandmother's arms. She let Tia hug her but felt her own body stiffen in her hold.

Tia stood back and looked into Damaris's eyes. "Are you all right, honey?"

"Y-yes. I'm fine."

She knew she hadn't fooled Tia. Her grandmother gently clasped Damaris's shoulders. "We'll talk later. Something's bothering you. I feel it."

Damaris stepped away and looked down at her white kid leather boots.

Tia's finger lifted Damaris's chin, and Damaris saw genuine concern in her eyes. "Whatever's bothering you . . . You can come to me. We'll pray about it."

There it was again. Her grandmother had used the word "prayer". For as long as Damaris could remember, Tia had believed in witch doctors and dark spirits. Damaris remembered wondering why her grandmother believed in such foolish things. But now there was a stark contrast to Tia's past. There was a renewed countenance in her face . . . a glint of joy in her eyes. What had happened while they were gone?

Mayme moved to Damaris's side. When she did, Tia brushed soft fingers along Damaris's chin and moved away. The gesture was kind, so unlike her grandmother. Damaris looked at Mayme, glad for the interruption. "Mayme. It's so good to be home. As much as I loved seeing Aunt Grace and Kit and the others, I'm happy to be back at Kindra Hall."

"You were missed. This place isn't the same without you." She held Damaris at arm's length. "If I didn't know better, you done found love while you were gone."

Damaris's head jerked up, and a flood of tears spilled from her eyes. "Oh, Mayme. I miss him." She flew into the woman's arms and cried.

For a long moment, Mayme held her. "It's going to be all right, Miss Damaris." She patted her back and crooned. "I don't suppose you want to tell Aunt Mayme all about him?"

Damaris pulled back. "I should be having this talk with Mama, but since she's not here," she hiccupped, "I need to talk to someone."

"Come into the house. Let's get your bags unpacked, and you can tell me all about it."

Kindra Hall, Barbados

The morning rain lasted only minutes. Grateful the world wouldn't be too wet, Tia sat still as Mayme put the finishing touches to her long, ebony hair. She tucked a spray of white jasmine in the layers that had been combed up on one side of her head and pinned with gold pins.

Mayme stood back and examined her handiwork. "Miss Tia, you be the prettiest bride today."

Tia looked at Mayme's reflection in the mirror and smiled warmly. "I don't care what I look like to anyone except Ebenezer. Looking at my reflection in the mirror reminds me of how much that man has done for me. I used to be a vile and conceited woman."

Mayme placed her hands on Tia's shoulders and hunched down to put her cheek against the bride-to-be. "Miss Tia, when God changes our hearts, He changes us inside out. I've never seen that evidenced more in anyone than I've seen in you."

"That's the nicest compliment anyone's ever given me. Thank you."

Mayme glanced out the window to see the sun cutting through the gray clouds. "Enough talk. Denzel's waiting downstairs to escort you to your groom."

Tia's hands flew to her chest, and she closed her eyes. When she opened them, she said, "I do wish Kindra could see what is happening this very moment. Life is so ironic at times."

"Why, Miz Tia, what do you mean?" Mayme gave Tia her full attention.

"I fought Kindra with all I had to keep her from marrying Denzel. In fact, I made their lives pretty miserable. And all because he was an overseer on the plantation and I wanted more for her." She looked down at her hands in her lap. "And yet, today, that same man is going to walk me down the aisle to my beloved Ebenezer, who is also an overseer on a plantation. My Kindra would never believe the changes I've made in my life. And in part, she is responsible for these changes. It took the devil taking her away for God to find me."

"God always knew where you were, Tia. He was waiting for you to find Him." Mayme held out her hand. "Now, come. You have two men waiting for you."

The tables on the lawn were filled to the brim with food. People wandered about, laughing and calling in merriment during the wedding reception. On the porch, a half-dozen slaves loudly played their violins, flutes, and a banjo, setting the tempo.

Denzel's family and slaves alike danced to the music. Ebenezer swung a smiling Tia around and kicked his heels. A large circle of slaves had formed a ring around the couple and clapped their hands while Tia and Ebenezer danced.

"They look happy," Denzel observed as he walked up to Damaris.

"You think?" She gave her father a cheeky grin.

"You're not dancing." It was a statement Damaris knew her father wanted an answer to.

"Now, who would I dance with, Zeddie?"

"Several of the field hands have stepped up."

"I know. I don't feel like dancing."

"Solomon's not here. You can't waste your life away waiting for him."

"Now you sound like him."

"Meaning?"

"He told me not to wait for him, to find somebody more suitable and richer." Her throat constricted and began to clog with tears.

"Maybe you should listen to him."

"Don't, Father. Not today."

"Solomon's a field hand. He'll never be able to provide the kind of life you're used to."

"With all respect, I'd like to end this conversation."

"All right." Her father started to walk away.

"Father."

"Yes."

"Wasn't Mama the plantation owner's daughter . . . and you—you were the overseer?"

"I didn't have anything to offer your mother. When I married her, I guess you could say I got to enjoy the inheritance your grandfather, Phillip Cooper, gave her. There's not a day that goes by that I'm not grateful things turned out the way they did. I loved her fiercely—and I still do."

"Hmmm. Life is full of surprises, isn't it?" She looked out at Ebenezer bowing to Tia as the music ended.

"It is." He held out his hand. "May I have this dance?"

Damaris curtsied. "You may."

Lord, will I ever have a wedding dance with Solomon? If it's Your will. I'd be forever grateful.

THIRTY-TWO

Atlantic Ocean

THE WAVES CRASHED against the hull, and the pounding sea rolled sailors across the main deck. Pulling himself up, Jackson sprang toward the railing and held on as the ship plunged first one direction then the other. A river of water surged over the deck, carrying Corky in its tide. Jackson reached out just in time to save the sailor from plummeting into the raging waters.

"Get a hold of the rail!" Jackson called through the roaring wind as he grabbed a fistful of Corky's shirt and dragged him to the ship's side. They no sooner grabbed onto the rail than the swells rose high above the ship in a vast bowl, sending the *Savannah Rose* sliding down its side and up against the next cruel wave that pinned them in. The ship had just begun its ascent up the crushing wave when the water slammed into the hull and tossed the massive vessel to the bottom of the valley; the roiling water pushed the merchant ship up the other side once again.

Jackson swallowed and felt the blood drain from his face. Were they going to sink in the middle of the sea? The slick, salty water worked against his grip on the rail, and he was thrown into a group of sailors who fought to find something to grab ahold of as they slid across the deck, sloshing with seawater. He tried to steer clear of the floating debris of barrels and tack that swished back and forth. Two of the masts had broken during the storm, and the men cried out as they collided with the rigging and yardarms that now lay strewn about the deck.

He peered up at the remaining yardarms, stripped of their sails, that cut through the black sky. The broken rigging pierced through the air, snapped with a resounding crack, and shot like a deadly spear. A crewman dove to the deck, barely avoiding being plunged through by the pole. It slammed to the deck, sending water cascading every which way. The pole rolled with the tilt of the ship as the next swell sucked the *Savannah Rose* into a trough again. The crewman staggered to his knees and collided into Corky, who threw his arms around the man and pulled him to the side.

Captain Harding leapt to the middle of the churning deck and cried, "I want every man tied to a rope!" His panicked eyes searched the faces of the men until they landed on Jackson. "What are you doing here?" He furiously demanded. "I told you to stay below in the cabin with your mother and the family!"

"I'm needed out here!" Jackson yelled over the screeching wind. "Woodrow's looking after them!"

Drew's face flushed with anger, and he yelled something into the air, but the wind carried it away. Jackson clung to the rigging and tried to steady his feet. He pushed away and took giant steps to avoid debris swirling in the water.

When he finally reached his father's side, he shouted to make himself heard. "What would you have me do, sir? I won't go below. I'm needed here with the rest of the men." His voice boomed in the wayward wind, and he braced himself for his father's command.

"We've got to get the *Savannah Rose* to safe harbor before it becomes a carcass of a ship," his father ordered. "We've lives to save." He looked around wildly. "Not all the masts are shattered. Strike the lower yards and top masts. We're going to beat this devil of a hurricane!"

Jackson slapped his palm on his father's shoulder. "Aye, aye, sir!" He stepped back and was slammed to the deck by the force of the wind. He clawed his way to the below-decks companionway, shouting orders to the crew.

The sea tossed the ship over the next mountainous wave, and he looked up at the charred clouds. Lightning carved a bright dagger into the black sky, followed by a clap of thunder. The ship rocked with a monstrous moan that sent chills through him. "Oh, God almighty!" He cried out as he clung to the companionway rail. "If you would silence the winds and give calm to the seas, I would be forever grateful. Save my family. Save these brave men, and if it be Your will, save the *Savannah Rose*!"

Jackson stomped across the sodden deck, bracing himself against the death pitch. He watched the black clouds roiling over and over as if a giant hand were kneading bread. He half expected to see the clouds' part and send forth a silver lining. He so believed God would hear his cry that he stood spellbound in the midst of the strong winds.

The saltwater stung his eyes, and he wiped his face, clinging with all his might to the rail and watching the men climb the ratlines to detach sections of the masts. Then they could hoist the storm sails on the lower gallants and acquire some mobility in the angry sea. The wind howled and roared as the ship tilted and tossed the men on the ratlines, making it difficult for them to maneuver. But they were made for the sea and scrambled to the task. They jumped down to the deck and tied the rigging to iron hooks. Jackson let out a deep sigh, grateful to be among men who had worked this ship long before he was born.

The squall went on for hours, and then all at once the sea quieted.

Soaked and chilled, Drew and Jackson stood by the helmsman as he guided the *Savannah Rose* to shore to assess her damage.

"Everybody out of the cabins. You're going ashore," Captain Harding boomed.

A shaky Camille crawled out of her room and summoned Rosamund to her side.

"Mother's pale as a ghost," Jackson said, holding the door to the quarterdeck wide as his family climbed one by one to the watery deck.

"We need to get her on solid ground. She's never experienced a voyage like this."

A longboat bobbed in the water next to the hull. A rope ladder hung over the side for the crewmen to climb down and assist the passengers. Corky and three men manned the oars. They helped his mother and sister into the rocky boat. Spencer and Woodrow were next.

A second longboat waited for the older crewmen and the cook, who had taken a beating in the squall. Both boats rowed to the sandy white beach.

Every muscle in Jackson's body ached as he watched his family glide across the water safely away from the wretched ship.

"The rest of you will stay on the vessel and get to work. We'll not sail to Jamaica until we mend the rigging and repair this blasted ship!" said Captain Harding.

A roar went up as the sailors nodded and began the repairs. Jackson felt eyes on him as he looked over the devastating wreck. His father watched him with a measured gaze. Jackson pushed his wide-brimmed hat off his forehead, squared his shoulders, and reached down for a thick rope. There was work to do. He'd do his part like a man. He'd never make a good merchant captain until he joined the crew in the worst of times as well as the best. He threw the rigging over his shoulder and sloshed his way over to Charlie. "Let's check out this rope. Grab the other end."

When he glanced up again, his father's eyes glinted with pride. Jackson nodded and looked away. He pulled the rope over the wooden planks until it stretched across the deck. He and Charlie checked every inch of it and noted its condition, knowing they might need some of it for the repairs. When Jackson looked up again, his father was gone, probably to the hold to see what damage had been done there. Water would need to be bailed out. *Lord, give us the wisdom to repair this ship and get back onto the sea.*

Thirteen days later, the *Savannah Rose* limped into port at Riverbend, Jamaica. The morale of the crewmen was high.

"Grab the aft line, Woodrow," Jackson called.

The ship moved close to the dock as Woodrow wound the rope around the cleat and tied her off.

"Corky could have done that, but Dad wants us to throw our shoulders into the work." Jackson slapped his brother's back, glad to be home on solid ground.

He watched his father approach his mother and take her arm. Drew led his wife down the gangplank to the waiting carriage. He settled her and Rosamund into the coach and then strode back to the main deck. "Leave this for the crew. We're riding out to Yarabee Hall."

"You sure?" Jackson dropped the rope against the ship's side.

"Your mother's eager to get home and make preparations for the holiday. And she wants all her family home."

"All right." Jackson turned to his brothers, who worked near the stern. "Woodrow. Spencer. Let's go."

The boys dropped the jute ropes and strode over to their father.

"Climb into the carriage. We're going home."

"Whooie!" the boys hollered and nearly ran down the ramp.

"It'll be good to see Yarabee Hall again. I feel like a wet rat!" Jackson slapped his hat against his thigh.

"Get used to it if you want to be a merchant captain." Drew clamped Jackson's shoulder. "You did good, son."

"Thank you, sir."

"Now let's get down there. Your mother will strangle me if I don't get her out of town and on the road home."

"I'm ready. Home sounds mighty fine to me."

As the carriage jerked away from the wharf, Jackson glanced out the window at the massive ship. He was grateful to be on dry land once more, but he had one more wish. He'd give anything to have Kit by his side. He'd be on the island a few days before they headed east to Barbados to unload the shipment. After that, they'd sail to Charleston, where he had left his heart. He had a black-haired southern belle waiting for him, and he'd do whatever it took to get her back into his arms.

THIRTY-THREE

River Oak, Fields Landing

CAMERON AND KIT trotted their horses to River Oak. After an hour riding in the frothy waves along the beach, they needed to get back to the plantation. Cameron's mind rambled in a dozen directions, making plans for the new rice barn and the upgrades for new equipment after the harvest ended. Times had been hard— it always was on a rice plantation— but they'd done well. He breathed in deeply and felt a sense of pride for what he and his family had accomplished.

They rode the half mile from the beach to the home stretch. The Taney River babbled beyond and wound its way toward the Atlantic Ocean in a slow-moving motion. The river created a current that enabled rice to be grown.

Cameron and Kit came up to the backside of the rice fields, where hundreds of slaves were bent over and hard at work.

Cameron leaned forward and breathed in deeply again. All of a sudden, he noticed the air felt cooler. He wrinkled his brow and glanced around. Everything seemed normal, but he still felt a sense of warning and tensed. The breeze worried him. It felt unsettling, shifting in a calm, steady movement, like a mighty, silent hand pushing the air from behind and forcing it to the shore.

He shielded his eyes and squinted toward the ocean. The clouds, charred a dark gray, moved faster overhead. It spread from the south toward the north in an ominous quiet.

"What's going on, Father? You seem worried." Kit glanced at Cameron, her face flushed.

"I think we need to recheck the fields." They'd been drained of all water for the last ten days. Nearly three hundred field hands slaved away, their rice hooks busy hacking down the sheaves. A third group would pick up the dried stems and tie them together, making ricks in the carts some seven feet wide and twenty feet long. Tungo saw to it that the men stacked them in the barn in piles as high as the tallest men could stack them.

Cameron spotted Cuffee working a row between Cabeto and Solomon. *It's good to see him out in the fields with his sons,* he thought. Cuffee stopped chopping the sheaves and glanced up at the sky, and Cameron knew he felt the change in the air, too. The wind had changed direction many times since the ride back from the shore, and the air seemed heavy, like a harbinger warning of trouble ahead.

"Let's take a ride over to the river." He pulled his reins to the left and began trotting Scimitar toward the banks beyond the fields.

"What are you thinking? Is something wrong?"

"Might be. It's too quiet. Something's not right."

"What do you think it is?"

He kept his intuitions to himself for the moment. Several of the workers nodded at them as they passed, but Cameron paid no attention. His mind set, they reached the river in little time, and he stepped down to the bank. The horses nickered and shook their bridles as if they sensed danger ahead. Mud sucked at Cameron's boots as he neared the edge of the stream. He looked back at Kit, who had leaned forward to watch him. He put a hand up to warn her as he bent to watch the water flow. It should be running north and south toward the ocean. He stepped back and searched the ground near the stand of trees on the bank.

"What are you looking for?" Kit started to dismount.

"I'm looking for a twig."

"What for?"

"Just watch." He picked up a thin stick and tossed it into the water. The cottonwood twig floated away in the lingering current, slower than usual, it seemed. It continued flowing south. Cameron shoved his hat off his forehead and watched the stick ease toward the bend in the river.

Kit strode up beside him as he kept his eye on the stick. Together, the two walked several hundred yards to where the river turned and widened. The twig flowed to the curve, and they followed it.

"What are you looking for?" Kit asked again as she eyed the murky water.

Cameron didn't answer; instead, he walked slowly, keeping pace with the flow of the river. Just past the bend, the twig slowed and then stopped. Cameron crouched at the bank and saw that the current had nearly stopped. Alarmed, he stood and turned to Kit. "I think we're in for it."

"In for what?" Her face flushed as if she were about to scream. "Would you please explain what this is all about?"

"I didn't realize it earlier, but now I see. It's been building all afternoon."

Kit folded her arms across her chest and waited.

"I think there's a blower headed our way."

"A hurricane?" Kit looked out over the water and up at the trees.

"This isn't the time of year for it. The season has passed." Cameron watched the stick float on the water, knowing it should be flowing along at a steady pace. "But I've an eerie feeling we have a freak hurricane heading our way."

"We haven't had anything like that for the past five years. Hopefully, you're wrong. Maybe it'll just be strong winds and rain." She touched his arm in a firm grip. "Dad, think about it, these storms generally pass us up. Every time we think we're in for it, they ride on past us and hit further north."

Cameron patted her shoulder. "You're probably right. I hate to ignore the signs, but you can't predict Mother Nature, you know that." He strode back to his horse and mounted the animal. "Let's ride back to the beach."

"We just came from there," Kit said, but did as he asked. She lifted herself into the saddle and reined Ginger to ride alongside him.

"I just want to check the flow to the shore." Cameron put Scimitar into a gallop. Together, they rode toward the beach. The tide had moved up farther than usual for that time of day. He shoved his hat off his forehead for the second time. "Look at those dark clouds."

Kit's hair blew behind her as she leaned into the ride.

"The wind's blowing stronger! And it's coming from the southeast!" Cameron looked over his shoulder as the horses thundered over the white sands. "That means the storms running in from the ocean, straight for us!"

The sand sliced the air and nicked his face. The sea swirled, in an ugly, dull gray, and the swells were topped with high, forming whitecaps that rushed toward them in a sudsy foam.

"The air's warmer here. That's concerning," Kit said.

Cameron watched her visibly swallow.

"If this storm you're predicting is coming from the ocean, I fear for Jackson. The *Savannah Rose* is out there."

"That's true."

"I hope he and his family didn't get caught in it."

"That makes two of us. We won't know until we get word from them."

"Father! I couldn't stand it if anything bad happened to Jackson. I must see him again!"

"Kit, pull yourself together. I think we've got a strong one coming," yelled Cameron. He spun his horse around and started back toward River Oak. "We don't have a moment to lose. I've got to warn Tungo to shore up the dikes!"

Cameron and Kit spurred their horses back the way they had come, each in their own thoughts. Every planter in the lowlands knew that a hurricane could destroy a rice crop in any given year and prayed none would ever hit their property. Three sinister things plagued a planter's thoughts, three vicious things they had no control over: the outbreak of malaria, typhus, and, more than anything, hurricanes.

When they reached River Oak and thundered to the barn, Cameron jumped off his mount, and Kit did the same. The wind here, although crisper than usual, wasn't as strong as they'd experienced at the beach.

"We've got to warn Tungo," Cameron said. "He'll need to get the field hands and their families to safety." He handed the reins to both horses to Nate and started out of the stable, but turned back to Kit to say, "We've got to tell your mother to get things in place at the Great House."

Together, father and daughter strode at a fast clip. When they reached the house, all was quiet except for distant sounds in the kitchen. Cameron and Kit looked at each other.

"Where is everybody?" Cameron asked.

"The girls are probably in their rooms. I'll bring them down." Kit started up the stairs while her father poked his head into the sitting room and dining room before heading down the hall toward the library and study. A glance showed Grace wasn't anywhere. "Where's my wife?" he muttered to himself. He went farther, back to the sunroom and ballroom, certain he wouldn't find her there. He was right. There was no sign of her. When he reached the foyer, Kit met him at the base of the stairs.

"The girls are upstairs in their rooms, but I didn't see any sign of Mother."

"Well, where in tarnation is she?"

"She could be down at the slave district. She often helps there if there's a problem." Kit clutched her skirts, waiting for him to tell her what to do.

Cameron stomped to the porch and gazed out over the grounds. Already the wind had picked up. "I'm going to look for her. We need to get everybody into the cellar and quick!"

Kit called back to him. "I'll get the girls and house servants to the cellar, but don't make us wait too long for you."

Cameron watched his daughter stride into the house at a fast clip, relieved he could count on her to keep a level head in times of trouble. Taking the steps two at a time, he rushed back to the stable, his hand over his eyes to protect them from the gritty air. "Have you seen Grace?" he called to Nate.

"No. She's not at the house?"

"Not that I saw."

"I best be checkin' on the horses." Nate waited for orders.

"Bring Scimitar, I'm going out to the fields."

"Right away, suh!" Nate led the black Arabian to the entrance of the stable.

Cameron mounted and reined the horse toward the slave district. "See to it the rest of the horses are in their stalls, then get back here as fast as you can!"

Nate ran off, while Cameron remembered the storm of '31. It had beached ships in Charleston, shattered houses, and killed hundreds of people. The tide surge had pushed saltwater nearly three miles up the freshwater rivers and flooded rice fields with the killing ocean water.

Glancing frantically toward the shanties, he didn't know where to begin. Grace could be behind the door of any one of them. Slaves stood on their doorsteps, hands shading their eyes and glancing about as danger lurked in the air.

"You seen Mistress Grace?" he asked as he passed the old women.

They shook their heads, their eyes wide. "Not today, Massa."

He looked up at the sky and saw the dark clouds roiling. He continued toward the rice fields, where hundreds of workers bent over the rice. He spotted Tungo coming toward him and kneed Scimitar toward the overseer. When the two men met, he gave orders. "We've got a blower coming in! We've got to get these people out of the fields and into safety."

Tungo lifted his hat off and looked up at the sky. "I do that right now!"

Cameron helped the overseer round up the field hands. Years back, he'd seen to it that they built shelters of brick and mortar on higher ground, farther up the hill behind the slave district. The shelters served two purposes at all times. Food was stored in the cooler temperatures, but when the blowers came, the people huddled there and stayed until the threat passed.

The men rode down the long lanes between fields and hollered instructions to the field hands. "Get to the shelters! We've a blower coming in!"

The slaves pounded the ground as they rushed to look for their families and scramble for safe shelter. The wind picked up, and now and again dirt flew in gusts and swirled around. It wouldn't be long before the rains fell.

Cameron still hadn't seen Grace. He left the slave district and rode in haste to find her. He reached the house just in time to see Bella Grace run out to the porch with Maddie and Sunny right behind her. Kit joined them, her hair blowing in the wind.

"I thought I told you to get down in the cellar!" He felt a renewed sense of frustration.

"We've looked everywhere. We can't find Mother!"

"I haven't seen her either!" Cameron pulled off his wide-brimmed hat and slapped it against his pant leg. "I'm going back to look for her. Where's William?"

"Gemma said he went down to the fields."

"I was just there. I didn't see him. What in thunderation am I going to do with all of you! Get down into the cellar. I'll find your mother and Will." His horse backed up and whinnied, ears pricked. "Do as I say—now!"

Kit pushed the girls back into the house and turned back to him. "Find Mother!"

THIRTY-FOUR

GRACE BRUSHED THE damp curls off a young slave woman's face. "Your baby boy is beautiful. Now rest. You've been up half the night, bringing this little one into the world." She touched the infant's tiny hand. "I'll come back and check on you later today."

"Thank you, Miss Grace. You always be too kind." The tired mother kissed her baby son's ebony curls and closed her eyes peacefully.

"The mothah be a healthy woman," Moab said. "She be fine."

"Make sure she gets plenty of rest."

"Yes, Miss Grace." Moab towered over her as she opened the door to the shanty. "You be needin' a bit of rest yerself."

Grace stepped outside the cabin with a smile on her face. She didn't mind helping Moab deliver the babies on the plantation. Helping to bring a new babe into the world felt rewarding. But Moab was right. She'd spent much of the evening sitting by the slave woman's side. She'd told the woman's husband to send for her when his wife's hour came. He'd reluctantly pounded on their door while the stars were still out, and Hedy sleepily rustled Grace awake.

Now she looked forward to an afternoon nap. She hadn't taken too many steps when she noticed the shift in the air and the clouds, gathered low and ominous. She clutched her skirts and set out to the Great House, but paused when she saw Cameron riding his horse toward her. Was that concern on his face? She looked up at the sky again and hurried toward him.

"Where have you been?" He slid off his horse and stormed over to her.

"I've been helping Moab with Elsie's baby." She gazed at the darkening clouds. "I think we're in for rain."

"We've a blower coming! Can't you see?" He waved his hands wildly at the trees rattling around them.

Dust kicked up in the air, and Grace pulled her skirt to her nose and peered up at Cameron. "I was inside the cabin. I had no idea. We've got to get the children and the servants into the cellar!"

"Kit's working on that as we speak."

Moab stood behind them, taking in all the confusion.

"Get that family to safety, and you too!" Cameron ordered.

"Yes, suh. I be doin' that right now." Moab ran back into the shanty while Cameron reached his hand out to Grace. "Grab hold of my hand. We don't have a moment to waste!"

Grace threw up her hand, and Cameron hoisted her up behind him. He reined Scimitar toward the house, while Grace clutched his waist with both arms.

"This isn't the right time of year for a hurricane," she said.

"You're right. We didn't see it coming." Cameron stopped his horse in front of the porch steps. "Go in and get down to the cellar. I'll be there shortly."

"Where are you going?"

"Willie's out in the field. I'm going after him."

Grace felt the color drain from her face. Her son was out in the fields? Would Cameron find him in time?

"Go in, Grace!"

She grabbed her skirts and hurried up the steps.

When Grace opened the door, she found Kit barking orders at the servants. "You're next, Gemma. And I won't hear another word about it!"

Gemma looked over in time to see Grace come into the sitting room. "Thank goodness you be here. I 'bout had a heart attack, worryin' you wouldn't make it."

"I'm here. Listen to Kit, and get down into the cellar." Grace gazed at her daughter. "Who all is down there?"

"The girls and the servants. Gemma's last." Kit searched her mother's face. "Where were you?"

"Get down in the cellar, young lady. We'll talk there."

"You first," Kit said, stepping back.

"You're not in charge anymore, but I'll go." Grace stepped down onto the first step into the cellar. She heard the muffled sounds of the others who'd already found seats below. When she reached the bottom, she searched the faces of everyone there. Only Willie and Camp were missing, and they'd be here soon. She looked up at Kit. "Come down and close the door. Your father and Willie will be here soon."

Kit glanced toward the window of the sitting room and bit her bottom lip. "All right. We don't know how long they'll be." She climbed down a ways before she grabbed the short rope of the trapdoor to close it.

Once the door was closed, the cellar darkened. As their eyes adjusted to the dimness, Grace realized an anemic glow gave some light in the dim room.

"Where are the matches?" she mumbled to herself. "We don't have to sit in the dark." She moved objects on the shelf, found the wooden matches, and lifted the glass on the kerosene lamp. The fire flittered and danced and swayed, then settled into a rhythmic pulse that lit the room. She covered the base with the glass dome and set the lamp in the middle of the shelf. With that done, she gazed around the party, sitting against the walls.

Maddie's eyes were wide. "Mama, where's Daddy and Willie?"

"They're coming, honey. Come sit by me."

Maddie quickly got up and scooted next to Grace.

"I'm coming too." Sunny moved across the floor and waited for others to scoot over so she could sit next to her mother.

The servants huddled together and spoke in low tones. Grace touched Maddie's lap to comfort her. "Sit still." She noticed Penny and Hedy's worried faces as they drew their children close to them. Their hushed tones continued.

"Hedy, are you all right?" Grace asked.

"No, ma'am. I'm worried about my man," Hedy answered honestly.

Grace looked at Penny, who seemed near tears. "You too?"

"Yes, ma'am."

"Tungo and Camp are working on getting everybody to the shelters. I'm sure they'll be fine." Grace wished she knew that to be true. But she wouldn't utter anything negative to these women. As it was, she was beginning to wonder when Camp and Willie would arrive and be seated in the cellar with them. Her stomach churned like the roiling clouds.

Gemma crooned to the women. "Don't fret about your men. My Nate be out there with them. We gots to trust the Good Lawd will protect them all."

Grace clamped her fingers around Maddie's and Sunny's wrists as she closed her eyes and prayed.

Objects slammed against the house, along with the undeniable sound of tree limbs and branches peppering the roof. Loud thumps and clangs were heard above as if chunks of debris were being thrown down the chimney.

"Lord, have mercy!" Grace breathed. "Where's your father and Willie?" She knew leaving the cellar now was foolishness, but that didn't stop her desire to climb the stairs and hunt for them. She clung to the girls and pinned her eyes on Kit.

Kit clasped her hands in her lap. Bella Grace leaned her head on Kit's shoulder and squeezed her eyes shut. Kit patted her lap and then clamped her hands together again. "I'm sure Father's all right. He's probably in the shelter with the field hands," she said with a shaky voice.

"He should be here with us," Maddie wailed. "How do you know Daddy didn't blow away?"

"We don't," Sunny said. "He should have joined us in the cellar!"

"He would have if he could have," Grace said, her stomach twisting in a knot. She kept her voice calm for the girls' sake, but she wouldn't know a moment's peace until she saw her husband's face. Willie's too. "We don't know what happened before the storm hit. He'll come," Grace said.

The noises continued, and the rain thrummed the roof. They all huddled together, looking at each other for assurance, and waited.

It seemed like an insurmountable time before the quiet grew. Finally, the long-awaited sound Grace had been waiting for came. Boots scraped the floor above them, and the trapdoor flew open. Cameron called down, "Is everybody all right?"

"Daddy!" Maddie cried out.

"Yes, we're all right," Grace breathed in relief. "Is Willie with you?"

"He's right here. You can come up now." The sound of her husband's voice sent peace to Grace's soul.

"All right. Let's get out of here." Grace stood aside to let her daughters ascend the stairs.

"No, Mama," Kit said, holding her sisters back. "You first."

"All right." She was eager to make sure Camp and Willie were unharmed. Once she was back up the stairs, she rushed into Cameron's embrace. "Where were you?" It wasn't until then that she realized his clothes were soaked.

"We got caught in the storm, and then the rains came. We had to take shelter with the field hands," Cameron said.

"You look no worse for wear, but we heard terrible sounds while we were down there." Grace inspected Willie, who stood back, his clothes soaked as well.

"Come on up, girls," Cameron said, looking down through the trapdoor.

Crawling from the cellar, their eyes wide, each of them looked about to see the devastation the hurricane had wrought.

The cooks and housemaids climbed out and looked around the room, as Gemma was the first to speak. "I didn't know what to expect when we come up here. But seeing there's still a roof over our heads, I be thinking that Someone upstairs be watching over us." She looked at Mama Jezelee and Penny. "If the kitchen is still there, we be putting a meal together d'reckly."

"Willie, go upstairs and see what havoc has been done there. The rest of you stand with me. We'll wait," Grace said.

Cameron went from one room to the next, inspecting the downstairs. He came back with a strained smile. "I don't understand it, but the house seems to have escaped major damage. There are several windows broken, but we can deal with that. For now, we'll board them up." He kissed Grace's forehead. "I'm going outside to assess the loss. I'm afraid the slave district didn't fare as well."

"All right." Cupping her palms over her elbows, Grace tried to calm the tremors that shuddered through her. She needed to be strong for her children. Looking now into the faces of her loved ones, tears brimmed in her eyes. "The Lord heard our prayers. We are all safe."

Grace pulled Maddie into one arm and Sunny into the other, and waved Bella, Grace, and Kit to her. "Come here, all of you."

"Oh, Mama!" Bella Grace cried. "I was so frightened!"

"Me, too," Maddie snuggled closer.

"I know, girls. But we're safe now. No harm has come upon us." She touched each one to assure them all was well.

Willie appeared at the top of the stairs. "There are a few broken windows, but the blow didn't rip off the roof." He smiled brightly and skipped down the stairs. "I'm going out to find Dad."

Grace released the girls and turned to Willie. "You'll probably find him in the slave district. I'm afraid to hear the verdict on how the shanties have fared." Her brows raised in concern.

"I'm going with Willie." Kit started across the living room floor.

"You'll do no such thing, Katherine Olivia. You'll stay right here with us," Grace ordered.

"Mama . . ."

"No back talk. We don't know what destruction has been done out there. You'll remain in the house until I'm confident it's safe."

Kit rolled her eyes. "All right." She went to the window to look outside as Willie escaped the room. The front door slammed behind him.

"There are broken limbs scattered around the front lawn," Kit said.

"I hope that's only the worst of it," Grace said, joining her. She pushed the curtain aside and looked out. Broken limbs lay all over the lawn and down to the river. The water had risen, and branches floated downstream.

"The boat's gone," Kit said.

"It'll be days before we realize the extent of this hurricane." Grace dropped the curtain and turned to the housemaids. "Go to each room and give me an accounting of the damage. We'll need to make a list."

"Right away, Miss Grace," Alice said as she started for the stairs.

Martha crouched and looked into the fireplace. "There be a lot of banging around the chimney while we be below." She pulled the gold screen away from the hearth. "For heaven's sake! There be a branch in here!"

"Let me see!" Maddie hurried to Martha's side. She looked into the dark hole, then whirled around to face her family. "There *is* a branch in the fireplace!"

It took days to assess the devastation to River Oak. When Cameron went out to the first section of rice fields, he feared what he might find. Dread filled him at the thought they might have lost the crop. Tungo and Willie joined him as he walked down the middle of the road between fields. Mud sucked their boots, and puddles of water lay everywhere. Cameron looked out over the fields, and his breath caught. As far as he could see, the fields were flooded. The storm's rain had pushed the river over its banks and into the fields of mature rice. The harsh winds had snapped the stalks, leaving them limp in the water.

He took off his hat and slapped it against his leg. "Looks bad. Real bad."

"Let's check the water. We might be able to save some of it," Tungo said.

They stepped into the field and waded into a row. Muddy water reached halfway up their boots. Cameron bent, cupped a handful of water, and took a drink. He spit it out and shook his head.

"No good?" Tungo asked.

Cameron shook his head. "Too salty."

"What we gonna do, suh?"

Cameron's hands went to his hips as he observed the fields farther out. "We might salvage some of the crop. But the repairs for all the damage the hurricane caused will eat up this year's profits. With repairs to the dikes and canals, the shanties and the barns, we can count this year's crops a loss." Disheartened, he headed toward the Great House. "I won't be entering the annual rice contest this year."

"If it looks bad for us, it's likely bad for the other plantations," Willie said. "Maybe the blow hit the Sewards' plantation worse than ours."

"Don't go there, son. I don't wish this on anyone." Cameron stopped walking and looked down at his muddy boots. "We have no control over Mother Nature. It's a reminder we should be grateful for the good years. There's work to do. A lot of clean up and repairs to be made. Thank God we have the manpower to get it done."

"I know which men be good for rebuildin'," Tungo said.

"I'm counting on you for that." Cameron slapped the overseer on the back.

Night after night, Cameron sat in his study, going over the logbooks and ledgers, his gut torn in two. He'd grown quiet around the family and didn't know what to tell them. They looked hopeful that everything would be all right. The truth was, he'd had to spend most of their savings to keep River Oak afloat. This was the first year that had really tested his faith. As he crunched the numbers and went over the books again, he leaned his head in his hands. He'd make it work somehow. The crop would be better next year. He had to believe that.

A few weeks later, a letter arrived at the Great House. Wendell Seward was making an offer for River Oak. Cameron wasn't surprised; as a matter of fact, he had half expected the letter to come sooner. Seward was offering a handsome price for the land, but Negroes were cheap after the devastating hurricane, and his offer was below market price. Cameron ripped the letter in two and threw it in the trash. He hadn't built up River Oak to sell it off to his fiercest competitor. His children had been born here. This was their land. God's land. He wouldn't let his family down. *Dear Lord, I've always asked You to partner with us in all that we set our hands to. I'm asking You now that, what the devil meant for bad, You turn around for good.*

THIRTY-FIVE

PHOEBE AWOKE AT the first crack of dawn as pain pulsed at the base of her skull and worked its way to her temples. Though she lay in the richness of a soft bed, with sheets of lace and silk, she wasn't spared the anguish of pain.

Lying there, she stared out the window at the morning sky. A patchwork of thunderheads spread across the expanse in muted shades of gray, the colors dull, just like her soul. A glow limned the horizon, tinting the mists in soft hues, and the sun, as it rose, played hide-and-seek with the fog. *Would it rain again today?* she wondered, for the charred clouds lingered, threatening another downpour.

The throb in her head kept time with the old clock on the wall. She closed her eyes and clenched her fists. How long would she endure such pain? Was she destined to live out her years in suffering? Taunting thoughts chased each other through her mind, reminding her of the truth. *I'm a vain woman. I endure this pain rather than seek help for my tired eyes.*

The truth alarmed her, and Phoebe opened her eyes again. She gazed out the window to where life pulsated. She had become a prisoner to her own vanity, hiding from her husband's scathing eyes.

Moments later, the world awakened with a yellow-and-scarlet ball bursting from the east, splitting through the gray and forcing the drab clouds to dissipate. Staring out the thick lead glass at the awakening world, her heart leapt with hope. Could she change the direction her life was going?

A rooster crowed, and the sound split through her head. Lying beneath the plush blankets, she fought the urge to rise and cross to the water closet. Yet, slowly, she swung her legs over the side of the bed. When her feet touched the floor, the room began to spin. *Oh,* she moaned. *Not again.* She waited for the walls to stand still. A short distance from the bed was a cold hearth where the embers were quickly dying, and the room was chilly.

Phoebe stumbled to the window and touched the cold panes as she looked at the grounds below. Slaves were already working in the fields. *If only the room would stop swirling,* she thought as the throb in her head pulsated with each beat of her heart. She leaned her forehead against the cool pane and felt darkness closing in on her. Before she could turn back to her bed, her legs gave way and she crumpled to the floor.

On her way down, she heard a gasp, followed by quick footsteps and a female calling her name. The voice seemed to come and go, then a murky darkness descended over her like an ocean wave.

Kindra smiled at the sound of the rooster crowing. Like clockwork, the sun rose, the rooster crowed, and she stepped out of her room, ready to meet the day. Brushing the wrinkles out of her skirts, she made her way to the east wing to Phoebe's bedchamber.

She had long since given up on giving a courteous rap before she entered the room, as Phoebe had reprimanded her for doing so more than a dozen times. Kindra silently pushed the door open and stepped into the rose-colored sitting room. At first glance, she found the coverlet turned down, but Phoebe was nowhere in sight.

Turning toward the water closet and standing at the closed door, Kindra quietly asked, "Miss Phoebe, do you need assistance?"

No answer.

It was then she spotted Phoebe lying face down on the tapestry rug, just below the window.

"Phoebe!" Kindra rushed to Phoebe's side and dropped to her knees. "Miss Phoebe!" She gently shook Phoebe's shoulders, turned her over, and stared at the mistress's pale face. Phoebe didn't stir.

"Phoebe, wake up! Miss Phoebe!" Kindra started to rise and run for help, but stopped when she heard a faint moan escape the mistress and her eyes flutter open.

"W . . . what happened?" Phoebe pushed herself into a sitting position. "Oh, Kindra . . . my head!"

"Let me help you up." Kindra gently pulled Phoebe to her feet and led her to the edge of the bed.

Phoebe pointed to the brown bottle on the nightstand. “I need my medicine.”

Kindra stepped to the table and picked up the bottle. *Laudanum*. She poured the reddish-brown liquid into a silver spoon and offered it to Phoebe.

After she swallowed the medicine, Phoebe pressed her fingertips against her forehead and closed her eyes. When she opened them again, Kindra was watching her with concern. “Would you like to lie down and rest some more?”

“No, I would not,” Phoebe said adamantly. “I have plans to go to town to see Lawrence’s lawyer.”

Kindra was dismayed. “I may be out of line, Miss Phoebe. But you’re pale as a white handkerchief and in no condition to go anywhere.”

“You *are* out of line,” Phoebe lashed out. “I don’t need you telling me what I can do or can’t do.” She continued to rub her temples, looking paler by the minute.

Kindra took a step back, set the laudanum on the table, and looked down at her shoes, not wanting the mistress to see her distress. When she looked up, Phoebe was pinching the bridge of her nose as if to will her headache away.

“I have too much responsibility to attend to. I cannot afford to be wracked by this pain that imprisons me.” She reached out her hand. “I’m sorry I spoke so harshly.”

Kindra took Phoebe’s hand with uncertainty. “Are you feeling any relief from the medicine?”

“The laudanum is beginning to work.” Phoebe pulled her hand back and ran it down the front of her nightgown. “Has Lawrence left the house yet this morning?”

“He left hours ago,” Kindra said.

“Of course he did. We don’t talk anymore. We are just two people in this big, old house, living isolated lives.” She brushed a tendril from her forehead with a look of discouragement. “It’s just as well. We’ve already gone separate ways in our hearts.” Her face began to get some color back and she looked at Kindra. “Am I wrong?”

“Who am I to say, Miss Phoebe?” Kindra looked at her hands.

“Tell me. What should I do?” Phoebe pressed.

Kindra didn't want to interfere with their personal lives. "I wish you would see an eye doctor."

"You've said that since you've arrived at Ash Haven." Phoebe's hand went up.

"You could be rid of these horrendous migraines if you were to get glasses."

"The headaches *have* increased, and I believe you're right. It is my bad eyesight that is causing the headaches to grow." She shook her head vehemently. "I'll not be confined to my bedchamber because of it. It's time to relieve myself of this vain and debilitating curse."

Kindra couldn't believe her ears. "Then you'll have your eyes checked?"

"Yes. It's time." Phoebe smiled wanly at Kindra. "Get me dressed. The morning is wasting away."

The carriage stopped on the side of King Street. The sign on the office door read, Benjamin Russell, OD, Optometrist. Phoebe fingered her reticule nervously and gazed out of the window at the red-bricked building. "Well." She sighed heavily and hesitated to accept the driver's hand, as if doing so solidified the reason she was here. She lifted her chin and moved out of the carriage. Her shoulders rigid, she turned to Kindra. "Come inside."

"Are you sure, Miss Phoebe?"

"Of course, I'm sure. Don't dawdle."

The driver had stepped away from the coach door, and Kindra stepped down to the street unattended. She, too, held her shoulders rigid, but for a different reason. No matter how many years had gone by since she'd been kidnapped from Kindra Hall, she still found it difficult to accept society looking down on her as if she were less than human. She heard the carriage door close behind her, but she kept her head up. The driver was no better than she, as he was hired at Ash Haven, too. She clutched her skirt and walked up the sidewalk to join the mistress.

Phoebe opened the door, and the two of them stepped inside a small waiting room furnished with a couple of visitors' chairs. A slender woman met them right away. "I'm Dr. Russell's receptionist. How may we help you?" The middle-aged woman kept her gaze on Phoebe.

"Would Dr. Russell have an opening this morning to ch . . . check my eyes?"

"He's with a patient at the moment. I'll let him know you're here. Your name?"

"Phoebe Bridger." It seemed to Kindra that Phoebe's shoulders went up a little higher, as if she'd tensed some more.

The receptionist barely glanced Kindra's way. When she did, Kindra didn't miss the hard cut of her gaze. "You may be seated while you wait, Mrs. Bridger."

"Thank you." Phoebe took a seat and glanced at Kindra. "Sit."

"Your slave woman can wait outside." The woman's lips thinned as she went to the door and opened it wide.

"She'll remain with me," Phoebe said, standing.

A dark look came over the receptionist's face. "Then stand against the wall. The chairs are for patients." She didn't wait to see if Kindra heeded her command. She disappeared into another room and closed the door.

Phoebe shook her head. "People!"

A half hour later, the door opened and a man appeared. He touched his hat as he looked at Phoebe and went out onto the street, shutting the door quietly behind him.

Kindra noted that doctors' offices had a way of seeming somber. It didn't matter who visited the physicians' buildings; all patients whispered as if there was an unspoken respect for the establishment.

"Mrs. Bridger." The optometrist came to the waiting room and held out his hand. He was a tall, elderly man with thinning gray hair combed back from his forehead, wearing round, wire-rimmed spectacles. He gazed at Kindra. "It'll take a while to test your eyes. Your servant girl can wait outside." He placed a hand on Phoebe's back to guide her through the door as if his statement was final.

Phoebe stopped and looked back at Kindra. "As I told your receptionist, she'll come with me."

"That's highly unusual, Mrs.—"

"I insist!" Phoebe didn't move.

The doctor cleared his throat and turned several shades of red. Finally, he looked at Kindra. "Come along."

She followed them to a room down the hall and stood by the door as Dr. Russell went through the tests for Phoebe's eyes.

When they were completed, the doctor smiled kindly at Phoebe. "You are long overdue for a pair of glasses, Mrs. Bridger. Have you experienced any headaches recently?"

"Every day, Dr. Russell." Phoebe glanced at Kindra.

Kindra didn't move. She wanted nothing more than to step outside this stuffy office and breathe in the fresh winter air. Still, she kept a straight face and waited.

"It's not uncommon for women to put off wearing glasses. I assure you, once you've worn them for a week, you'll wonder why you waited so long." He stretched out his hand and Phoebe took it.

For the first time this morning, her shoulders dropped as if relieved. "How long will it take for my spectacles to be ready?"

"It'll be a good two weeks, ma'am. We'll send a post when we have them here in the office."

"Good enough." Phoebe turned to Kindra. "Let's go. We've more errands to make before the noon hour."

When the two women reached the coach, the driver asked, "Where to, Mrs. Bridger?"

"Dougherty Street. Baxter and Steward's office."

The driver's brows nearly stretched to his hairline. "Very good, ma'am." He handed Phoebe into the rig and strode to the front of the carriage while unaided Kindra climbed in and shut the door.

The horses' hooves clattered over the cobbled streets as the carriage rumbled through the streets. Minutes later, the coach rolled to a stop in front of the attorney's office. Phoebe leaned forward and looked out the window, her attention intense. Kindra casually looked out, too. The sign hung precariously from one chain above the boardwalk. "Baxter & Steward." It wobbled in the breeze as pedestrians walked along. The words were faded and in need of a fresh coat of paint. The door to the establishment was in no better shape. Blue paint had chipped away long ago, exposing the bare wood. And the small window, centered in the upper portion of the door, had a crack.

Phoebe's lips curved up in a smile. She looked at Kindra. "If these men are representing my husband in our court case, I find it difficult to believe he has a leg to stand on. It looks to me as if they're barely standing on their own two feet." She leaned back on the leather seat and rapped on the ceiling, "Let's go home, Matthias."

Kindra had just finished the last touches to Phoebe's hair when the sound of carriage wheels crunching on the carriage lane below drew her attention.

"We've got company!" Phoebe glanced in the mirror and pinched her cheeks, then glided across the floor to the bedchamber door. "Come. I want you to meet my parents."

"Your parents?" Kindra could hardly keep up with Phoebe as she sailed down the stairs.

"Yes. Remember, we posted a letter to my father a while back. I sent him and mother an invitation to come to Ash Haven." The words were barely out of her mouth when she reached the landing, and Rufus opened the front door. Phoebe flew onto the porch; her arms open wide as two elderly people stepped out of the coach.

Kindra watched Mister Goodman smile brightly as he approached Phoebe. It was easy to see he was happy to see her, but Mrs. Goodman beat him to Phoebe's side. "Let me look at you!" Phoebe's mother's arms stretched wide, and she embraced her daughter. "It has been too many years since we've seen you . . . and you're wearing glasses."

Phoebe cleared her throat, looked back at Kindra, and gave a little smile. The wind kicked up, sending leaves rattling across the drive. "Come inside before you're blown away," Phoebe kissed her mother's cheek, then turned to her father. "Welcome to Ash Haven." She pushed her spectacles up the bridge of her nose.

Kindra watched them, happy for Phoebe that her parents were back in her life. How long they'd be at Ash Haven, she didn't know, but with the New Year coming, and half of Charleston invited for the Bridgers' New Year's celebration, she thought the timing was just right.

Rufus carried two large pieces of luggage up the steps as he followed the Goodmans into the house.

"Take their suitcases to the west wing, second door to the left," Phoebe instructed.

"Yes'm." Rufus climbed the stairs and disappeared on the upper landing.

Kindra felt out of place knowing Phoebe needed to speak with her parents. She glanced up the stairs, eager for a moment alone. She started to slip away when she heard Phoebe's lilting voice. "Kindra!"

Kindra turned and clamped her hands together.

"Come. I want you to meet my parents."

Mister Goodman's brows went up at his daughter's request. Mrs. Goodman's frown spoke volumes.

"Your mother's weary after the long travel. I believe she'd like to rest and freshen up before dinner." Mister Goodman's hand went to his wife's back.

"Father, I'd like you to meet my newest slave. This is Kindra." Phoebe pushed Kindra forward.

Kindra felt her skin prickle with embarrassment. Didn't Phoebe understand her parents wouldn't be impressed with the new slave? And why was Phoebe so obsessed with her?

Mister Goodman looked down at her with the eyes of a slave owner. "Did Lawrence buy her?"

"Of course he did. He buys all of our slaves." Phoebe's shoulders stiffened. She looked at Kindra apologetically. "You may take the rest of the day for yourself, but I'll need you to help me change for supper."

"Yes, Miss Phoebe." Kindra was glad to escape Mister Goodman. She needed time alone to figure out what was going on with Phoebe. It was as if she clung to her slave for moral support. That wasn't normal. A mistress didn't treat her slave like she was her best friend, yet that was precisely how Phoebe treated her.

"She's a beautiful slave," Kindra heard Mrs. Goodman say as she neared the top landing. "Has she produced any stock for you since she's been here?"

Their voices faded as Kindra rushed to the end of the west wing and threw open the door to her bedroom. The words stung her heart. *I want to go home, Lord. How long before I see my husband and children again? How long!*

Two weeks after the new year, the Goodmans climbed into their coach and rode away. Kindra thought their visit had done Miss Phoebe's heart a world of good. Mister Bridger, on the other hand, had become even more contentious. The surprise visit had nearly been his undoing. Now that they were gone, Kindra had an ominous feeling that sparks were going to fly.

THIRTY-SIX

Kindra Hall, Barbados

DAMARIS STARED AT the calendar on the wall and wondered where all the time had gone. It seemed only yesterday that she and her family had arrived home at Kindra Hall. And yet nearly six months had passed, with the family adjusting to the disappointment of not bringing Kindra home with them.

As Damaris drew a line through the day, anticipation for the upcoming trip to River Oak sent a thrill through her. Yes, she was looking forward to seeing Kit and the rest of her family, but more than that, she hoped to see Solomon again.

From the first day she stepped onto the *Sea Baron* to sail home, to this moment, standing in the Great House, her every waking thought and heartbeat centered on returning to River Oak to see the rough-cut features of Solomon's handsome face. She yearned to feel his touch and to kiss his lips once again.

Yet worry had worked its way into her soul. She had seen him walk away, his back straight, his shoulders rigid, as he reconciled himself to the idea that he could never have a future with her.

How many nights had she drowned in her tears? How many mornings had she awakened with a sense of despair? How many hours had she yearned for that first kiss and to hear the words "I love you" once again? Damaris had lost count.

Solomon was her world, a world she'd lost, a world she could never have, as they lived two different lives, one a slave, the other the daughter of a wealthy plantation owner. If only she had not searched him out. If only she had not tasted that first kiss. And if only she hadn't surrendered the only heart she had to a man who couldn't keep it.

The sound of laughter and pans rattling in the kitchen tore her eyes from the calendar, and she laid the pencil on the table. Having checked off another day brought her closer to the day she would voyage across the sea and, hopefully, fill the hole in her heart.

Before breakfast, she wanted to walk to the gardens and pick fresh flowers for the house. Placing a straw hat on her dark curls and picking up a long-handled basket, Damaris passed through the bustling kitchen as if she were on a mission. "Morning!" she said as she headed for the back door.

"Where you be goin' like a butterfly flittin' out the door?"

Damaris stopped and turned to see Louiza, hands on her hips, and Clara wiping her hands on her soiled apron. Both had raised brows and Damaris's full attention. "If you must know, I'm headed for the garden to pick some flowers for Mother's vases. I won't be long." Her hand went up as she waved at them and slipped out the back door.

She could hear the cook's voices sail out to the walkway beyond the kitchen. "She sho' bring a splash o' sunshine to dis' ole house," Louiza said.

"Yes, and we be missin' her when the family be leavin' in a few more days."

That would be Clara's voice, Damaris thought. As much as she looked forward to the voyage to River Oak, she would miss the cooks.

In early April, spring sprouted across the island, not that the tropical weather didn't keep the plantation in bloom year-round, for it did. But the freshness in the spring air made everything feel new. Reveling in the morning sunshine, Damaris collected sprigs of pink frangipani, then swung around to the front of the house and walked toward the long drive. Orange and yellow hibiscus covered the grounds along each side of the lane. Coucou and flying fish blooms battled for attention, their tall green growth and yellow and red flowers bursting with color, and nearly a dozen long, red, needle-like prongs flying from the center of each bloom and swaying in the breeze. These flowers were the pride of Barbados and brightened the lush green foliage.

It wasn't long before she realized she wasn't alone. Colorful parrots and popinjays squawked in trees, making it difficult to ignore them. She enjoyed watching their loud antics as they turned their heads every which way as if watching her below. Damaris went to work cutting long-stemmed coucous and hibiscus and filled her basket. The scents perfumed the air, and she closed her eyes as she breathed in the fragrance of the island.

"There you are." Piper walked up, dressed in a blue day dress. "Breakfast is ready. Father's come in to join us and wants to fill us in on details of the trip."

"Really?" Damaris tucked one more hibiscus stem into the basket and turned toward the house. "I hope nothing has changed. I'm ready to go back to River Oak. What about you?"

"So am I." Piper glanced back at the beautiful flowers lining the drive and waved her hand. "I wish Mother could see how beautiful all of this is."

"Me, too." Damaris hooked her free hand in the crook of Piper's arm. "We'll bring Mother home this time. I feel it in my bones."

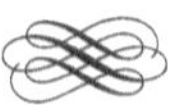

Damaris started for the stairs to go over her wardrobe, but Tia intercepted her before her foot touched the first step. "There you are."

Damaris turned and gazed into her grandmother's gentle face. It had been six months since she'd been home, and still, it caught her by surprise to see the rough edges of Tia's personality replaced by a warm and friendly attitude. Still, Damaris held back. She was standing at the very staircase on which she'd hidden as a child and listened to the private conversation between her grandmother and Ebenezer when Tia had confessed to being to blame for Kindra's abduction. Damaris knew she hadn't heard everything her grandmother had said, but somewhere in the conversation, Tia had admitted to stealing emeralds from a man who, in turn, captured her mother and carried her away. Gram had cried in shame that long-ago night, but Damaris's heart had become cold. How could she ever forgive her?

"You wanted to see me?" Damaris took a step back before her grandmother touched her shoulder. She could see the movement was not lost on Tia, as a look of hurt fell over her grandmother's countenance.

"Damaris," Tia began. "Can we talk?"

Damaris wanted to run, to escape this inevitable moment, but she couldn't run forever. "Of course," she said and glanced out to the front porch. "Would you like to sit outside? The breeze is refreshing right now."

"That sounds like a grand idea." Tia smiled with uncertainty.

The large porch was surrounded by hanging ferns spaced every few feet along the railing, and thick plants and ferns were placed in stone pots that rimmed the outer edge and lined the walls. White wicker chairs were placed strategically among the greenery, and they each took a seat.

Damaris placed her hands in her lap and waited. "How can I help you, Gram?"

"You can help me by explaining what is bothering you." Tia came straight to the point.

Taken aback and feeling heat lick up her neck, Damaris cleared her throat. "Nothing is bothering me, Gram. Why would you assume such a thing?" She swallowed, feeling wickedly wrong in her answer. But she'd never before encountered a confrontation with her grandmother.

"Don't play coy with me, young lady. You forget who you are talking to. I can see right through you. You've been avoiding me, and I want to know why." Tia held Damaris's gaze and continued, "Now fess up. What's wrong?"

Damaris was undoubtedly in a hot spot, but she had no intention of telling her grandmother the truth. What could she say? She leaned forward and took her grandmother's hand. Doing so surprised Tia, but she continued. "Gram, sometimes life has a way of knocking us off our feet. Mother's kidnapping has taken a toll on me in more ways than I had expected." She swallowed to control the tears that wanted to spill. "I have to deal with the loss of my mother in my own way. My answer isn't what you hoped to hear, I fear, but I have nothing more to say."

Tia sat back and closed her eyes. She stayed that way for a long moment, so long that Damaris began to think she was praying. When Tia opened her crystal blue eyes, she gazed deeply at Damaris. Her hand reached out and covered Damaris's own. "I'll accept your answer, honey. Somehow, I think there is more, but I won't press you for it." She stood. "You have some packing to do. Go ahead. I think I'll go in search of my husband."

Damaris watched as her grandmother gracefully crossed the wooden porch to the steps. Tia stopped and turned around with a contented smile and bright eyes. "Don't you just love the smell of that tangy tobacco?" Tia stepped to the ground, waved, and walked away.

Damaris didn't move. The constant smell of cured tobacco hung in the air, tangy and spicy. Yes, she loved that smell. It was the smell of home.

She went back into the house and climbed the stairs in search of Mayme. It was time to plan her wardrobe for the upcoming voyage to River Oak. The chambermaid was always a great help when it came to packing.

Again, thoughts of a muscular black man with a rough-cut handsomeness filled her thoughts. *Oh, Solomon,* she groaned. *Please wait for me. Please love me again as you did before I left.*

Damaris passed her grandmother's bedchamber and saw that her door was ajar. She stepped back and grasped the brass doorknob, intending to close the door, but before she closed it, she noticed a hardbound book lying at the foot of the bed. Curious, Damaris slipped into the room and gazed down at the plain gray book.

"What's this?" she half-whispered to herself. Thumbing through the worn pages, she soon realized it was her grandmother's diary. Damaris read snippets of her grandmother's dreams and aspirations in her early years. Toward the middle of the book, she read about her mother's birth. This warmed her heart, and she was eager to read some more. She walked to the French doors, where there was more light.

She combed through the pages, skipping many passages, as she knew she had no business snooping into her grandmother's personal belongings. But she couldn't help herself. Page after page revealed accounts of Tia's daily life.

Hearing sounds below and fearing she'd be found red-handed, Damaris started to move out of the room. She quickly set the diary on the bed, hoping to replace it where she found it.

Voices grew louder, and she needed to escape Gram's room or she would have some explaining to do. She took a step away from the bed, then stopped. She snatched the journal up, closed the door, and hurried to her room, her heart thrumming in her chest. *I'll just read it tonight,* she reasoned, *and take it back in the morning.* Wanting to learn more about her grandmother, she quickly shoved the book under her pillow and went in search of Mayme.

Later that evening, Damaris started at the beginning and read page after page of the gray journal, tears streaming down her cheeks. Every line described the woman who had first arrived at Kindra Hall, a woman who was mean-spirited and deceitful. Damaris's mind went to the image of her grandmother today. These days, it seemed as though Tia grew more kind, graceful, and delightful with every passing day. But reading about her made Damaris more aware of how much she missed her mother. Life continued, but they were living it without Kindra.

A breeze sent the lace curtains rippling inward, inviting Damaris to take an evening walk outside. She set the journal aside and sailed down the hall toward the stairs.

"Where are you going in such a hurry?" Piper asked as Damaris flew past her to the porch. Damaris eyed the long drive and ran onto the dirt road, casting reddish-brown dust beneath her shoes and soiling the hem of her white cotton dress in her haste to escape the family and the journal.

Her family's daily life had become convoluted, with too many twists and turns in her grandmother's past, her father's search for his wife, and the children caught in the web of it all. *God . . . are You out there? Do You care what we're going through?*

Only silence.

The stars twinkled brightly in a black canvas of sky. Damaris stopped and stood in the middle of the road . . . alone. "Mama," she called among the tropical forest that lined the road. "We're coming after you! We're going to bring you home."

The breeze rattled the fronds of the palm trees, and the leaves glistened in the light of the moon. Looking up at the vast sky, she realized one thing was sure and certain: God was in control. The moon and stars were always there, and the sun always rose. The Universe continued without a hitch. Something about that gave Damaris's hope.

She turned back to Kindra Hall with a sense of encouragement. The journal had revealed her mother's past, along with Gram's. Having read so few pages, she had an urge to finish it. Though her grandmother would surely miss the diary, Damaris decided to take it with her on the trip. She wanted to know everything—the good and the bad—no more secrets.

Her mind set on the trip, and her heart resolved to find her mother, she walked up the long drive toward the Great House. Light shone on the grounds from several windows. Her home looked inviting in the dark of night.

We'll bring you home, Mother. This time we'll bring you home.

Denzel rode along in the wagon with Ebenezer by his side. The two men were headed to the wharf to make sure the tobacco crates were numbered and ready for shipment. They'd spent the morning walking the grounds and checking the tobacco fields for hornworms. It seemed the overseer had gotten a handle on the devils, and the crops looked good.

Denzel was happy for Tia and Ebenezer. They made a good team. If only Kindra could see her mother now.

The wagon rolled to a stop in front of the warehouse where their shipment was stored. While Ebenezer checked on the tobacco crates, Denzel strode up the gangway to the *Sea Baron*. When he reached the main deck, he found Captain Kincade going over the ship's manifest.

"When do you plan to sail?" Denzel asked and leaned against the ship's rail.

"Day after tomorrow. We've a large cargo of sugar going this time. Mister Hadding meant to deliver it today, but they had some trouble. He sent his slave boy with a message this morning, explaining they'd send the barrels on the wagons tomorrow afternoon." Kincade shoved his hat off his forehead. "Why do you ask?"

Denzel stared at his boots and kicked an idea around in his head. He pushed away from the rail and gazed out at the sparkling waters. "I want to go to the other side of the island." He glanced up to see Kincade pin his gaze on him. Denzel looked away, a heaviness in his chest.

"Bathsheba?" Kincade's low voice broke the silence.

"Yes. I'd like to go in the morning."

"That can be arranged. Like I said, Hadding won't bring his freight until after noon. If we leave early, we can be back in plenty of time."

"All right. I'll be here bright and early." Denzel shook the captain's hand

and strode down the gangplank. He went in search of Ebenezer, his heart feeling a bit lighter.

The *Sea Baron* sat in the bay as Barnabas and Denzel rowed the longboat to shore. The oars splashed the deep turquoise waters and moved the boat closer to the narrow white-sand beach that fringed the thick green vegetation. Although the jungle hid its base, the top of a tall hill covered with exotic trees could be seen some distance from the shore. Strangely shaped coral rocks, some as large as a shack, littered the shallow water near the beach.

It felt strange, rowing to these shores eight years later. An eeriness filled the air. More than once, Barnabas looked over his shoulder with wide eyes. They neared the shore and climbed out, pulling the boat with them, and wading in waters waist high as they sloshed to the beach. When they finally waded out of the foamy waves, they threw the oars inside the boat and began to trudge through the sand. Palm and banana trees grew thick along the shore. Denzel remembered where the worn path had cut through the dense growth. He looked for it now, glancing back now and then to make sure Barnabas was behind him.

"I think there's a path up to the right over there," Denzel said, slogging through the clinging sand that seemed to want to hold him back.

The cool breeze was a godsend. It not only made the trek through the jungle more bearable, but it also kept the mosquitoes at bay. Insects buzzed around them, but they seemed more interested in the plant life than the two men who worked their way through the tropical foliage.

The men stumbled along the trail, stomping through dried banana leaves and various dead foliage. Even with the cool breeze, sweat trickled down Denzel's neck, and his shirt began to cling to him.

After a couple of hundred feet, they came to a clearing with round huts circling a fire pit. The sight slugged Denzel in the gut, and raw feelings of despair crawled into his heart. He couldn't talk. He couldn't breathe. Eight years of agony slammed him in the solar plexus. This place represented the last time he'd seen his wife's beautiful face, the last time he'd heard her lilting voice, and the last time he'd had a good night's sleep.

"You all right, Denzel?" Barnabas stood over him, his eyes cast down in respect.

"I'm all right. I just had to come here to remember why I can't stop looking for my wife."

"Yes, suh." Barnabas' eyes went to the circle of huts. "She be a brave woman."

"Yes. I know of no woman any braver than my wife." Denzel swallowed the ache in his throat. He strode to the cell that Kindra had been thrown into. He walked inside the mud hut and gazed around for some sign that his wife might have left behind. He looked out the door toward the cell that once was his. He closed his eyes and remembered Kindra's sweet voice when she called his name. All at once, he dropped to his knees and wept. He pounded the ground and cried out, "Why, God?" He rocked back and forth. "Why did they take my Kindra away?" He tore at his shirt and clenched his jaw. He couldn't stand the thought that his Kindra had been thrown into this cell and then sold as a slave. When he grew still, he prayed. *Give me favor to find my wife, Dear God. Help me find her.*

A long while later, he came out of the hut and found Barnabas sitting on a log. Barnabas looked up and nodded. "You got it all worked out wit the Lawd?"

"Yes, Barnabas. When you get back from this next merchant run, I'm going to find my wife."

"That sounds real good, Massa." Barnabas smiled widely and led the way out of the jungle. "That sure be soundin' real good."

THIRTY-SEVEN

Cooper River, Charleston

THE MORNING SUN rose and streamed across Jackson's face as he stood on the deck of the *Savannah Rose,* his eyes intent on the shoreline. The water slapped against the hull as he called out, "Lower the sails and heave to!"

They'd soon move into their dock on the Cooper River, and he'd soon head out to River Oak. It had been six long months since he'd last seen Kit. Every movement he'd made this morning aided his agenda of getting off the vessel and pulling his girl into his arms.

From his angle, he could see a small slice of the main docks. The pier looked like a hive of bees as merchants and stevedores swarmed across the wooden planks, loading and unloading goods from the longboats rowed in from ships anchored in the bay.

Before long, the *Savannah Rose* jolted as it slid alongside their mooring.

"Grab the aft line, Corky," Jackson called out. He joined the sailor and watched as the boat slid along the dock. Corky wound the rope around the cleat and tied it off.

Morale was high as the sound of boots clomped across the main deck and crewmen lowered the gangplank and began the process of unloading crates and barrels to the street below.

Standing at the rail, his heart thumping in his chest, Jackson's mind raced to the woman who consumed his thoughts day and night. He visualized her dark gray eyes, her pert nose, and her long raven hair. He intended to ride out to River Oak within the hour. He wanted nothing more than to hold her tight.

He heard steps coming down from the quarterdeck and swung back to see his father wearing his wide-brimmed hat and white captain's suit. "As soon as we're finished here, we need to go over the next shipment before we set sail again," Drew said. He held the ship's manifest in his hand.

Jackson strode to the quarterdeck. "Before we set sail . . .? I thought we were going to be in the harbor a few days."

"We'll be in town for the next two days, then we'll ride out to River Oak," Drew said.

Jackson felt heat rise to his neck. Frustration strangled him. Just when he thought he'd escape the blasted ship and be on the road to Fields Landing, he learned he'd be delayed from seeing Kit. "What's so important about our next shipment that it can't wait until after we get back from River Oak?"

"We have an unusually large lumber order going out. We've got to make sure it is all accounted for and stacked in the hold before the rest of the freight is loaded." Drew's eyes went to the manifest in his hands. "This is going to be a larger load than normal. We need time for the men to get it loaded and make room for the rest of the shipment. I'm putting you in charge of the lumber. See to it that Corky mans that detail. He's familiar with stacking lumber."

"All right," Jackson said and squinted in the bright sunlight at the dock loaders. "When do you want the lumber brought onto the ship?"

"Tomorrow. The lumber will be delivered to Tobago Island, and then we'll sail to Jamaica." His father's eyes sparkled. "I'll get a full two weeks with your mother before we make the next run." He removed his hat and ran his fingers through his hair. He stood for a moment thinking, the wind stirring his hair. "I'm ready to relax on dry ground for a while."

"Is the sea losing its charm?" Jackson had to ask. This last trip out was the most extended voyage he'd been on. It had been too much water for him. He'd spent many a night with his mind wandering to River Oak and Kit. The longer he sailed the sea, the more he realized he wasn't cut out to be a sea captain. And yet he wracked his brain for a line of work that would suit him. He wouldn't quit sailing until he found something more fulfilling. He'd gone to college to learn the business side of being a merchant captain, but now that he could be taking over the *Savannah Rose* in a few short years, he didn't want it.

"No," Drew responded. "The sea's not getting the best of me, but not seeing your mother is. The business of being a ship merchant has robbed us of many good years together." He put his hat back on. "We'd better get to work. The morning's wasting away."

Drew walked over to his first mate, Jamie, and showed him the manifest while Jackson strode to the rail and looked down at the pedestrians on the wharf. He didn't need to see her smoldering gray eyes to know the raven-haired beauty who stood below was Kit. Her white-gloved hand was held over her forehead as she looked out over the bay.

She was dressed in a pale-green gown with a dark-green ivy pattern on the overskirt and the underskirt, which peeked just below the overskirt hem. Double layers of pink eyelet embroidery set off the low, dropped-shoulder neckline, and pink bows trimmed the short sleeves. A matching pale-green ribbon pulled back her ebony hair to one side, revealing the cream-colored skin of her shoulders. He gulped. "Kit," he said to himself, willing her to look up at him.

As if on cue, she glanced up at the *Savannah Rose* and her eyes lit up. A smile split her lips, and she waved at him.

Surprise at seeing her at the pier reminded him of the first time he'd seen her standing there a year ago. Was she looking for him, or was it time for Damaris and her family to return from Barbados?

He waved back and pointed to the gangplank at the side of the ship. He cupped his mouth and called, "I'm coming down!"

Kit nodded and turned to someone at her side. It took him a moment to realize the lovely young girl was Bella Grace. Six months had matured her. Bella looked up and waved, and then followed closely on Kit's heels.

Jackson threaded his way between the sailors on the deck and strode down the gangplank. By the time he reached the bottom, Kit and Bella were waiting for him. One look at Kit, and he couldn't restrain himself. He picked her up and whirled her around. When he set her feet on the ground, he gazed down at her smoky gray eyes and asked, "How did you know we were in port?"

Kit's cheeks flushed a dark red, and she gazed back at him. "I didn't. What took you so long?" Her arms went around his neck, and Bella gasped. "Kit Bartholomew!"

No longer caring where they stood, Jackson pulled Kit into his arms. She didn't resist, and feeling her yield to his touch, Jackson tilted her head to meet his ardent kiss. He touched her lips gently at first, then more insistently. He held her tightly, and although he felt her momentarily melt against him, he could also sense her begin to tense and push away.

He knew he had to let her go, but it was the last thing he wanted to do. Loosening his hold, he allowed Kit to slip from his arms.

Bella groaned. "I sure don't think this is the time and place for this. Father's going to have your hide if he sees you manhandling Kit like that."

Kit ignored her sister's protest, but she pushed away from Jackson, nevertheless. She stared up into his face as if wanting another kiss, but when he pulled her close and bent his head down, she turned away breathlessly. "Please, stop this minute! Propriety demands that we wait until we're alone. We can't make a spectacle of ourselves in front of the whole world." She stepped back and brushed her hand down the front of her bodice and skirt, her cheeks flaming.

"All right, Kit. If we must." Jackson turned to Bella. "You've grown into a very pretty young woman these past six months."

Bella smiled and stepped forward to kiss his cheek. "Thank you, Jackson. I'll take that as a compliment. She leaned back, placed a hand over her eyes, and squinted up at the vessel. "Did Woodrow sail with you?"

"Not this time. The overseer is teaching him the ropes of the sugar plantation."

"I see. I had hoped to see him." She frowned and puffed out a breath of air, blowing the curls off her forehead.

Jackson looked around. "Where's your father?"

"He's with Captain Wilder on the *Valiant*. They're checking the rice shipment. He'll be happy to see the *Savannah Rose* is in port." Kit looked at him, and Jackson thought she might run back into his arms. "How long will you be here?"

It was all he could do to keep his distance. "We'll be here a week."

"Then you'll come for supper tonight?"

"Not tonight. I had every intention of coming out, but we have business to attend to here in Charleston for the next couple of days." He watched her cheeks inflame. "Kit, I'd come this minute if I could."

She lowered her eyes. "I know." She feigned a smile. "I'll expect you at River Oak the day after tomorrow." She grabbed his shirt and gave him a slow grin. "Don't disappoint me."

He wanted to pull her to his chest, but he didn't move. "I won't, Kit. I'll be there."

She stepped away and looked over the wharf. "We've come to meet Damaris and the family. They should arrive today."

"I figured as much. How long will they be here?"

"Until they find Aunt Kindra. My father hired a couple of men to search for her. They rode out a few days ago and said they've finally got a lead. Father and Uncle Denzel will surely check it out right away."

"That's good news. I hope they find her." Jackson looked up at the ship's rail to see his father signaling him to return. "I've work to do." He hurried toward the gangplank, then turned and waved goodbye. "I'll see you in a few days," he called.

He ascended the gangplank, his steps lighter. "Oh, how I love that girl. I'm going to marry her if it's the last thing I do," he breathed with a husky growl. *But I'm not going to leave her. I don't know what I'm going to do, but I'm staying on dry land.*

"Let's go into town and get a meal." Drew threw his arm over Jackson's shoulder.

"I'm all for that. My stomach's been growling up a storm the past hour." Jackson dropped the jute rope and wiped his hands on his pants.

They strode the short distance from the docks to the row of buildings that lined Cooper River. In this part of town, the businesses lined one side of a long road that paralleled the river. "I've never understood this part of town," Drew said, keeping up a steady gait as they walked with the flow of people along the strip.

"What makes you say that?" Jackson gave his father a sidelong glance.

"There's only two eating houses on the riverfront, yet look at all the people. First thing in the mornings, the customers are vying for tables."

Jackson brushed his tawny hair off his forehead. He listened with interest as they walked past the storefronts. He eyed each business with curiosity. "I hadn't noticed it was limited to two cafes. I did notice there's only one bakery shop, but there's no place to sit."

When the two men entered the King's Inn, the restaurant was full. It was clear they would have to wait until a table was available. Jackson's stomach growled again as the aroma of food wafted throughout the establishment. "We could walk over to the Crab House. They serve breakfast there."

"We're already here. A table will be freed up in a couple of minutes." Drew held his hat in his hand and leaned against the wall.

"Would you gentlemen like a cup of coffee while you wait?" A waitress hurried over as quickly as her girth would allow, a coffee pot in one hand and a couple of mugs in the other.

"We'll wait," Drew said.

"Suit yourself." She moved to the first table on the floor and began filling half-empty cups.

"It's too bad there are no coffeehouses on the strip," Jackson mused in a low voice.

Drew cocked his head toward the dining room. "This is considered a coffeehouse." He no sooner replied to Jackson than the waitress walked up to them with menus in hand. "Folks are getting ready to leave that table across the room." She dropped coins in her apron pocket, dipped a dishrag into a bucket of water, and wrung it out. As the party walked out, she stacked the plates and ran the wet cloth over the table. "Have a seat. I'll be back for the mugs."

Jackson grinned and pushed the four mugs to the edge. "The wait wasn't bad."

Drew picked up the menu and glanced over it with no response.

The waitress flew back, holding a small pad and pencil. "What'll you fellas have?" When she took their order, she swept the four mugs off the table and disappeared into the kitchen.

Forty-five minutes later, and well fed, Jackson and his father stepped outside. "Good food," Jackson said. He kept his eyes on the establishments on their way back to the *Savannah Rose.* Other than the two cafes and the bakery shop, there were no more eating houses on this side of the Cooper River. "Have you noticed how many coffeehouses there are on the Caribbean coast?"

Drew rolled his eyes. "I'm sorry I brought it up, son. You seem fixated on the lack of eating houses on the strip." He led them across the road, dodging the traffic of wagons and carts.

Jackson didn't respond. A thought was brewing in his mind. He straightened his jacket and continued to the ship.

"That was the most miserable and hottest ride to River Oak I can ever remember," Damaris said as she tossed her straw hat onto the bed.

"I have to agree with you." Kit removed her hat as well and set it on the hat stand. "What would you like to do first?" She raised the windows in her room.

The air was thick and warm, and a sultry spring breeze wafted in. Kit gazed out at the sparkling river flowing lazily downstream and drank in the smells of the plantation: the damp, loamy scent of the rice fields, the dried veils of moss hanging low in the oak trees, mixed with the intoxicating scent of the magnolias. Hundreds of camellia specimens were flowering along the path to the pond, while many others of her favorite blooms were still sleeping. The ruffled blossoms had burst into shades of pink, white, and red. Kit felt a surge of love for her birthplace, her home. She couldn't imagine ever wanting to leave River Oak, and yet, for one man who sailed the sea, she would leave it all to bask in his love. She turned back to see her cousin on the edge of the bed, a wistful look in her eyes.

"Are you all right?" Kit joined Damaris and put an arm around her cousin's waist.

"Do you think the men Uncle Camp hired have found my mother?"

Kit saw Damaris's face alight with unexpected hope. "I certainly hope so. Father seemed to think they had a strong lead."

"I've had a premonition we'll bring Mother home this time." Damaris paused and closed her eyes. When she opened them, she said, "Sometimes, I have a hard time remembering Mother's face. Will I recognize her when she comes home?"

"Oh, honey," Kit consoled. "Of course you will." She gave her cousin a reassuring smile. "She'll be just as beautiful as she was the day she left." Kit knelt, fanning her skirts about her, and looked up into Damaris's face. "Your mother had the most beautiful green eyes and silky black hair, and I loved her honey-colored skin."

Tears welled in Damaris's eyes, and she laughed softly. "She was the prettiest angel in the world to me. She had such a gentle touch . . ." The tears spilled then, and Damaris wiped them away.

"They'll find her, Damaris. We mustn't lose hope."

"I know." Damaris smiled sadly. I'm not giving up." She retrieved her hankie from her pocket. "Solomon didn't come to the house to help bring up the trunks." She looked at Kit with despair in her eyes. "Do you suppose he'll stay away?"

"I don't know, hon. To tell the truth, I haven't seen much of him at the house since you've been gone. It seems he's thrown himself into his work." Kit smiled. "I've seen him at the stables, though. Nate's been showing him how to groom and care for the horses."

Damaris clamped her hands together and rubbed her thumb over her knuckles. "That's where I found him the last night I was here. He was in a stall, brushing down a horse. I think he has a way with them. He's patient."

"He still oversees much of the packaging of the rice. I go down to the fields sometimes, just to watch the slaves work. Father doesn't like it. He thinks it's no place for a lady. But how will I ever learn to be a good plantation mistress if I don't know how things are run from top to bottom?" She grabbed Damaris's hand. "Come on. Gemma's got supper waiting for us."

As the girls went downstairs, Kit thought about her cousin's dilemma. Would Aunt Kindra come home soon? And would Solomon stay away? *Please, Lord, come to Damaris's aid. I couldn't bear to see her heart broken.*

THIRTY-EIGHT

DAMARIS LOOKED OUT the window to see Uncle Camp and her father ride up the drive to River Oak. They'd stayed in Charleston after she and her siblings drove to the plantation. Seeing her mother wasn't in the wagon, her heart plummeted. *What went wrong? Why isn't Mother with them?* She flew out the door and ran down the graveled lane. "Where's Mother?" she asked as she neared the horses.

The look on her father's face said it all. His dull eyes and his countenance clearly showed his defeat. He climbed down and trudged to where she stood. "The hired men were on a wild rabbit chase. The woman they thought was your mother was someone else." He slapped his hat against his pant leg. "We'll be going to Charleston the day after tomorrow." He looked up at Camp, still sitting on the wagon bench. "Your Uncle Camp has things that need attention before we ride out again."

Damaris felt her anger rise like the tide. She couldn't hold her tongue. "You should have stayed in Charleston! You're never going to find Mother out here!"

"That's enough, Damaris. Go into the house!" Denzel's voice boomed over the drive, and his dark eyes smoldered like black coals.

Defiant, Damaris lifted her skirts and marched to the colored district with determined steps. Where she was going, she didn't know, but she couldn't go back into the house, simmering like a hot teakettle. She needed to walk off her anger.

The slave women watched as she passed them with fire in her eyes. She kept going, feeling as if smoke were coming out of her ears. *Would they ever find her mother?* She stomped past the rice buildings and sheds and beelined it to the rice fields, where hundreds of slaves bent over their work.

She kept walking, ignoring the heads that popped up in curiosity to watch the daintily-dressed black woman storm past them as if she were a freight train heading toward a cliff. Her eyes blurred as disappointment held her prisoner. *How long, Lord? How long before You give Mother back to us?* She continued doggedly down the long dirt road, fury her only companion.

All at once, she stopped. She had walked farther from the house than she'd ever gone before. When she stopped, the workers near the road gazed at her. All the pent-up anger began to dissipate, and a rush of despair claimed her heart. As she looked out over the fields at the curious onlookers, a hard lump filled her throat, and salty tears streamed down her face. She didn't care that the field hands watched her as silent tears spilled down her cheeks. Her body shuddered with discouragement.

She hugged herself, felt the spring breeze flutter the curls on her forehead, and closed her eyes. It was then she felt Solomon's presence behind her. Even with her eyes closed, she knew it was him. She knew the scent of the man she loved, and she opened her eyes. When she turned, he stood before her, tall and muscular and looking as if he wanted to pull her into his embrace. Instead, he stepped away and his jaw clamped tight. His hands hung at his sides as if he didn't know what to do. Did he want to pull her into his arms, or did he want to walk away?

"Solomon," she said, a shudder running through her.

"I'm here." He hung his head then looked up, his eyes riveted on her. "Why you runnin' out here? It ain't safe."

"I don't care." Her bottom lip quivered.

"What's wrong?"

"Everything. You. Me. Mother." She trembled again, hating her weakness.

"I heard the massa say he goin' after yer mother," Solomon said and looked out over the fields. "They didn't find her." It was a statement full of lead.

"No. They didn't find her." Tears welled in her eyes again.

He stepped forward and pulled her into his arms. He let her cry herself out. When she was done, she looked up into his rough-cut features. "You didn't come to the house when I arrived." Her words sliced the air between them.

"No. I didn't." He took a step back. "I be workin' when you come." His hands clenched and his forearms flexed. He looked out over the fields as if looking farther ahead than the scene before them.

"I thought about all the things you said before I left," Damaris said. "Do you still feel that way?" She had to know where he stood. Her heartbeat pulsed in her neck in a staccato rhythm.

Solomon looked down at his boots, and he kicked the loose soil. "Yes. I still mean them. You know and I know there ain't no future fer us. There's no point in hopin' fer somethin' that ain't never gonna happen." His eyes hardened as he looked down at her. "You know that's true."

"No. I don't know if that's true. I haven't given up on *us*!"

Dust rose in the distance as a horse galloped toward them. When the rider grew near, they could see it was Zeddie. The horse trotted to where Solomon and Damaris stood.

"Father sent me out to bring you back to the house." Zeddie gave Solomon a stern glare.

"I don't ride," Damaris said, looking up at her brother as if the horse's back were a mile high.

"I've got the reins, Sis." He reached a hand down to her. "Just hang on to me."

Damaris's chin rose. "I'll walk." She turned around and took two steps toward the house. Before she could take another step, she felt herself being lifted off the ground and settled onto the back of the Arabian. She quickly clung to Zeddie's waist and looked down at Solomon. "Of all the nerve!"

Zeddie reined the gelding until he faced back toward the house. When he did, Solomon slapped the horse's rump. The steed whinnied and took off at a run.

"Stop this horse!" Damaris cried out.

"No!" Zeddie called back.

When Damaris looked over her shoulder, she saw Solomon's hands on his hips and his head thrown back as he laughed at their ridiculous sight. She clung to her brother. "Solomon's going to pay for this. Just you wait and see!"

Kit blew out the lamp, and she and Damaris climbed into bed. The moon was high and bright in the clear night sky, and silver light shimmered across the floor, lighting the foot of the bed. Lying next to Damaris in the silent hours of the night, Kit was wide awake.

After several moments, Damaris broke the silence. "Mother's been gone eight long years." She let out a long breath. "I've done a very bad thing."

Kit raised onto her elbow. "What did you do?"

"I took Gram's journal. I found it lying on her bed, and I took it before we sailed."

"Why'd you do such a thing? She's going to have your neck when you get back!"

Damaris put a finger to her lips. "Shhh! You'll wake the whole house." She turned and faced Kit. "I did it because of what Gram said one night a long time ago."

"Now you've got my undivided attention. What did she say?"

"One evening, when I was a child, I couldn't sleep. I crept out of my room and went down the stairs, but when I got halfway down, I heard voices in the sitting room." She paused. "It was Gram and Ebenezer. I don't know why, but I stopped right there and crouched low and listened."

"And?"

"Gram was crying . . . I had never seen her cry before. It kind of scared me. So I sat really still and listened to what they were saying."

Damaris paused for a long moment, and Kit began to think she'd fallen asleep.

"Gram confessed that it was her fault that the raiders came and took Mother away." She was silent again, then said, "She said something about jewels. But I couldn't hear everything."

"Oh, no," Kit said.

"I know. I went to bed with a rock in my stomach," Damaris whispered. "I always wanted to know more."

"And you've kept this secret to yourself all these years?"

"Yes. I hated Gram for the longest time."

"I can understand that. Did you confront her about it?"

"No. She seemed so ashamed, I didn't have the heart to let her know I knew."

"So what now?"

"Well, for one thing, I'm going to read her journal. See if it reveals what she did."

Kit's heart beat in her chest as she listened to Damaris. She couldn't keep the map and the journal a secret any longer. "I have a secret, too." She felt Damaris's eyes on her.

"Really? What is it?"

Kit put a finger to her lips, crept to the bedchamber door, and listened for sounds beyond. "I don't want anyone to hear this." She crossed the room and opened the bottom drawer of her armoire. She fumbled through the heap of winter undergarments until her fingers touched what she was looking for. Carefully, she lifted out the treasure map and carried it to the bed. She proceeded to unfold the map and spread it open on top of the coverlet where the moon lit the foot of the bed.

"I found this seven years ago," she said nervously. "And look at the date on the map. It was made eighteen years ago, just before Aunt Tia was taken to prison."

"Where did you find this?" Damaris's dark eyes went wide.

"The bluebird's cage is in the sitting room. There's a false bottom in the cage, and it fell open one day while I was feeding the birds. This map and a small journal fell out onto the floor."

"But . . . why was this in the bluebird's cage?"

"Someone hid them there." Kit waited a beat, then she told the story of the marauders who'd come and raided their plantation.

"Wait." Damaris climbed out of bed and fished around for something in her travel bag.

"What are you doing?" Kit asked.

Damaris put a finger to her lips and brought a book back to the bed. "This is Gram's journal."

Kit stared at the plain gray book in awe. "Well, open it. Maybe there's a clue about the map in the journal." She slipped out of bed and relit the kerosene lamp.

Damaris read snippets from the passages, each recorded in Tia's own handwriting. She stopped often to glance at Kit, stunned by her grandmother's actions. The hour was spent with oohs and aahs as she continued to read. All at once, Damaris slammed the book onto the bed, her palm resting on top of the current page. Horror filled her eyes. "I found what we're looking for."

Kit could hardly contain her excitement, yet from the look on her cousin's face, she refrained from sounding too hopeful. "What does it say?"

"My grandmother admits to stealing emeralds from a man named Jule Spade. Listen to this. *'I hid the jewels on the Savannah Rose in the first cabin beneath the bunk. When the timing is right, I'll go back and reclaim them. The world doesn't know it yet, but I'm one of the richest women in the world, and it serves Phillip Cooper right.*' "

"That's our grandfather," Damaris said.

"What else does it say?" Kit tried to read over Damaris's shoulder.

Damaris read on, turning several pages, then stopped. *"'The emeralds are gone. Someone has found where I hid them.'"* She pored over the pages before she put the book down again, her face pale.

"What is it, Damaris?" Kit picked up the book and read: *"Jule Spade has been riding out to Kindra Hall, requiring me to return the jewels. I tell him that I don't have them. But he won't let up. He has threatened to take Kindra if I don't produce the emeralds. My selfish deeds have caught up with me. It may cost me my daughter if I don't find the jewels."*

Kit swallowed the hard knot in her throat and stared down at the map on the bed.

"Do you suppose that map tells where the jewels are?" Damaris asked.

"I don't know. There's a journal that came with it. I hid it."

Damaris's voice quivered when she spoke. "Gram was right. It's because of her that my mother was taken away."

"She stole the emeralds eighteen years ago." Kit let out a discouraged sigh. "All that happened before Aunt Tia went to prison. How can we hope to find the jewels now?"

"I don't know, but if we found them, we could return them to their rightful owner and just maybe he would return my mother to us."

Kit couldn't sit any longer. She rose and paced the chamber floor, all the while tapping her chin with her forefinger. "I hid the journal in the barn. It might give us more clues to finding where the emeralds are."

Damaris closed the journal and hugged it to her chest. "What are you thinking, Kit?"

"I'm thinking . . . we have to find the jewels."

THIRTY-NINE

"WHERE YOU GIRLS goin' all dressed up in yer fine ridin' clothes?" Mama Jezelee set two bowls of oatmeal on the table.

"I'm not riding," Damaris said, giving Kit a nervous glance. "Kit insisted I wear her skirt."

"Well, *I* am." Kit dipped her silver spoon into the sugar bowl, scooped out two servings, and sprinkled them over her steaming oatmeal. "Damaris is just coming to watch how I saddle Ginger." She picked up the rose-patterned creamer, poured a little milk into her bowl, and stirred the mixture together.

Damaris did the same, keeping her eyes on the creamer as she said, "I don't care to ride, but I think it's fascinating that you not only ride, but you saddle a horse as well."

"Not always," Kit said, blowing on the steamy oatmeal on her spoon. "Sometimes, Nate does it. I did, however, send word to him this morning that I'm in the mood to do it myself."

Gemma set a glass of orange juice in front of each woman. "You gals be getting up late this morning. Everybody else has eaten and gone about their business. You musta have talked the night away." Her midriff jiggled as she laughed. "I remember those days when I was young. Sleep wasn't so important then. Nowadays, I need all the sleep I can get. That ole sun sure be coming up mighty early." She poured fresh coffee into their cups and then disappeared through the swinging door.

Damaris kept her eyes on the steaming bowl of oatmeal. She looked as if she thought the whole world knew what they were up to.

"Relax," Kit said under her breath, gently kicking Damaris's foot under the table.

"I can't." Damaris took a bite of toast and stared at Kit. "What if we get caught?"

"We won't. Nate's expecting us to show up at the stables. He doesn't have any reason to believe we're there for anything more than saddling up my horse."

Damaris nodded and kept eating. After breakfast, the girls slipped into the dusty stable and listened for sounds of Nate.

"Take it easy," came Nate's voice outside the opposite side of the stable, where the double doors led to a corral.

"Good. He's busy. We can't waste any time." Kit hurried to the small tack room off the end of the aisle. She knelt on the dirt floor, scraped open the bottom drawer, and reached her hand to the back. She felt around the bulky items until she felt the journal nestled safely where she'd hidden it.

When she pulled the book out, Damaris leaned in to take a look. "It's beautiful! You didn't tell me it had a picture of a peacock on the cover." She took the book from Kit's hand and ran her finger over the green stone covering the peacock's eye. "Is this real?"

"Surely not," Kit said, giving the stone a closer look.

"It looks real." Damaris held the book up to the light that filtered in through an upper window. Dust motes floated lazily in the air, but even so, the gem sparkled richly, and the girls looked at each other with raised brows.

A thrill ran through Kit as she examined the stone with renewed interest. "I forgot how beautiful this is. I was only ten when I found it." She took the journal from Damaris and moved it this way and that. "This is one of the emeralds!" She whispered loudly.

They both cocked their heads, listening for Nate's voice as he worked with the horses.

"Now ain't you somethin'," Nate said as the sound of clopping hooves circled the corral, sending a cloud of dust into the stable.

"We'd better go back." Kit slipped the book under her black vest, and the two girls strode through the stable yard and hurried into the house. Standing in the foyer, they looked at each other and listened again for sounds of activity around them. "Where is everybody?" Kit hadn't remembered her mother talking about any plans for the day, but it seemed time was on their side. She was eager to ascend the stairs and get to her room. When she reached the top, she nearly collided with Alice.

"Where you goin' like a scared rabbit?" The maid eyed Kit with disdain.

"We're going to my room and we're not to be disturbed." Kit took a few steps down the west wing and turned around. Alice stood at the top landing, leaning against the broom, a suspicious glint in her eyes. "Get back to work, Alice."

"Yes'm." Alice stormed down the east wing and began sweeping the tapestry rug with a vengeance.

"Kit?" Damaris said, her brows raised.

"Come on." Kit led her cousin into the bedchamber and shut the door.

"You were rather harsh on the maid," Damaris said. "Not that it's any of my business, but I've never seen you act like that with any of the servants."

Kit's shoulders sagged, and she plopped down on the bed. "It's different with that woman. She's disrespectful, and we've gone toe to toe."

"But why?"

Kit held up the peacock journal. "Because she rummaged through my things and stole this book and the treasure map." Kit breathed in deeply, feeling her cheeks flush.

Damaris's mouth opened to an "O" and her eyes grew round. "Sh . . . she knows about the journal and the map?"

"Alice is the reason I hid the book in the barn. The map was easy enough to hide in my room, but make no mistake, I gave Alice a piece of my mind, and I threatened to have her sold if she breathed a word of my secret."

"I think I'm going to be ill." Damaris sat on the edge of the bed.

"Don't be silly. We're fine. Now let's see what the journal has to say." Kit opened the book and saw there were only a few lines of information. The first entry was dated July 7, 1841. Under that, and printed in large letters, were the words "Tobago Island." Then there was an assortment of drawings similar to the map, but here each drawing had an explanation: an old sign with an arrow, two palms crossing, three huts, and a village. The journal seemed to be a report of the date and location of the treasures. The owner of this book had written a list of treasures he had buried.

Kit read the list. "Pieces-of-eight gold coins, ivory elephant head pendant with diamond eye, ivory heart pendant, and emerald stones." She paused.

"The last thing on the list is the eye of the peacock." She looked up at Damaris. "This must be a clue to the cover of the journal. One of the emeralds has been sitting out in front all along!" Kit felt her heart flutter.

"Maybe . . . if we find the rest of the jewels and return them to Jule Spade, he might know where Mother is and return her to us." Damaris jumped to her feet. "I know where Tobago Island is. It's just south of Barbados."

Kit felt dread at her remark. "You just got here. And you're talking about a three-week voyage across the Atlantic."

"I know, but if it means finding Mother, we have to try."

"What are you thinking?"

"I'm thinking we should go back to Charleston and talk Captain Kincade into sailing to Tobago."

"He won't do it." Kit shook her head vehemently. "He won't risk losing his job."

"He'll do it for me. He knows this trip is all about finding Mother. He'll do it if it means bringing Mother home." Damaris fell to her knees, her eyes brimming with tears. "Please, Kit. We have the map and journal. We can show it to him. He'll do it. If we find the jewels . . . only then do we have a chance to bring Mother home."

Against her better judgment, Kit relented. "All right, we'll try. But first we must put together a plan."

"Oh, thank you!" Damaris threw her arms around Kit's neck. "

"Jackson and his father are supposed to arrive soon. We can't do anything before they leave."

Damaris clamped her hands to her chest. "We'll get my mother back. I know we will."

Jake started up a barrage of barking, and Kit ran to the window. She pulled back the lace curtains to see their black-and-white collie running around two horsemen trotting up the lane. It didn't take long to recognize Jackson. He looked altogether handsome, sitting tall in the saddle in his white shirt and his sun-browned features. His sinewy fingers gripped the reins.

"They're here," Kit said, gliding to the door.

"Wait . . . what do we do with this?" Damaris held up the peacock journal, the emerald sparkling in the afternoon sunlight.

"We'll hide it in your travel bag for now." Kit snatched the book from her cousin's hand and stuffed it alongside Tia's diary.

"Kit." Damaris touched her arm. "When do you think we can sail out to search for the treasure?"

Kit bit her lip. "I don't know. I suspect Captain Harding and Jackson will be here a day or two. Until then, we'll have to lie low. In the meantime, you'd better come up with a convincing story to tell Captain Kincade if you want this to work."

"All right." Damaris's expression was pinched. "I suppose I can wait a little longer, but I fear Father and Uncle Camp will return, making it impossible to leave."

"They won't come home today. Not only are they searching for your mother, but Father has plans to see Captain Wilder on the *Valiant*. They've a large shipment going out. By the time they come home, we'll be gone."

FORTY

KIT AND JACKSON strolled quietly along the garden path leading to the pond. Once they were out of earshot of the house, Jackson broke the silence. "You've hardly said two words since I arrived."

"I have a million things to say, but I don't know where to begin." Kit stepped away, needing to put some space between them. Could she continue to wait months at a time for Jackson? Is this how life would be if she committed herself to him?

"Waiting for my return has been hard on you. I can see it in your eyes."

Kit lowered her eyes. "What you said is true, Jackson. Each time you leave, it is longer before you return."

He shook his head. "I can't keep putting you through this." He was silent for a long while, and Kit swallowed. When he finally spoke, his voice was low and taut. "I've run our circumstances through my mind a thousand times." His hazel eyes darkened, and he led her off the path. Once they were behind a camellia bush, he pulled her into his arms. "Kit, I want you for the rest of my life, but I won't make you wait for me the way I've watched Mother wait for my father."

"What are you saying?" She gave him a full look, seeing the raw strength in his sun-browned features and seeing uncertainty in his eyes.

"The sea is uncertain. Too many things happen at the mercy of the sea. Ships fail and storms come." He recalled the last storm when he had wondered if he'd ever see Kit again. He put his hands on her waist, drew her nearer, and looked down at her steel-gray eyes, which at the moment were smoldering.

"Are you saying you don't want me?" Kit pushed away from Jackson's hard chest.

"I want you more than anything," Jackson assured her. "You're in my thoughts every waking hour. Not a moment goes by that I don't see your raven hair and your lovely face." He drew her back to him. "I've been working on a plan that I think will work for us. In a few weeks, I'll know if it will solve our problem."

"You are talking in riddles." Kit kissed his chin, drew his head down, and tasted his lips.

Jackson groaned and pulled her tight. He savored her full lips, never wanting to let her go. When he pulled back, he knew the thoughts brewing in his mind the last couple of days would somehow have to work. "What if I told you I've changed my mind about being a merchant captain?"

"No, Jackson. You're not giving up your dream for me." Kit stepped away from him and held up her hand as if to keep him at a distance.

"I'm not giving up my dream because of you." He gave her a weary smile. "I've grown tired of sailing. I want to stay on land."

Her gaze was sharp with curiosity, but she didn't say a word.

"I think there's a future in coffee."

"Coffee? It's been around forever." Kit's brows rose questioningly.

"I'm not talking about growing it. I'm talking about opening coffeehouses along the coast. Not just a restaurant, but a coffeehouse that serves only desserts, pastries, and baguettes. The customers could buy a cup of coffee and be on their way, or they could sit and enjoy a piece of pie."

"You've really thought this through." Kit took a step forward.

"There are plenty of eating houses in Charleston, but few coffeehouses. I found one on the riverfront, but was hard-put to find a seat. The place overflowed with men wanting a cup of java before they went on their way. All at once, the idea hit me like a rock. There is a way to stay on land and make a decent living." He grasped Kit's hands and gazed into her eyes. "Could you marry a coffee proprietor?"

"I don't know." Her brows creased teasingly.

"I want to open a chain of coffeehouses along the coast, Savannah, Edisto Island, and Beaufort. In time, we could own a dozen coffeehouses, but there's more."

Kit stared at him in wonderment. "There's more?"

With both of our fathers owning their own merchant ships, I want to become a major coffee bean supplier along the coast as well. We could supply coffee all the way up to New York."

Kit's mind swirled with his excitement. Could they make a go of it? "There are already merchants buying coffee from suppliers. Why would they want to buy yours?"

"Because I'll find supreme beans, and I'll advertise them as the king of the crop. Columbia grows the best there is. I think we can make this work."

"Hmmm." Kit tapped her chin with her forefinger. "Although I'd have to travel, I'd be home more than sailing the seas as a merchant captain."

"With that handsome head of yours full of all these ideas, have you come up with a name for your enterprise?"

Jackson smiled down at her with a sheepish grin. "I have."

"You have?"

"Harding's Brew & Leaf Café." He gave her a broad smile. "Serving tea would invite women into the establishment as well, but rather than serving a full meal, this would invite businessmen and housewives alike to sit a short spell for a quick cup of coffee or tea and a pastry, and then they can be on their way."

Kit walked back into his arms and cupped his face in her hands. "Jackson Harding, you've thought of everything." She kissed him soundly. "And if this works?"

"I want you as my lifelong partner." He brushed the curls aside and kissed her forehead, then her nose, and then her lips. "Marry me, Kit."

"I will marry you, Jackson, but you must ask Father for my hand."

"When will he be home?" He looked back at the house.

"Not for a couple of days. Enough time for you to investigate your idea. And one more thing."

"Go on."

"You're going to have to convince your father of your change in plans."

"I intend on telling him tonight."

"Do you think he has a clue?"

"After the last two days, I think he might."

"Harding's Brew & Leaf Café. I like it. Let's hope your father will, too."

Kit and Jackson knew their time together on this trip would be limited. They clung to each other and talked endlessly of his new enterprise. When the time came for him to return to Charleston, he pulled her aside. "We sail in a couple of days, but I'll ride out to see you before we leavc." He pushed his hat back and gave her one last kiss. "When I come back, I'll be asking your father for your hand."

"I'll be waiting for you." Kit's mind reeled, and guilt plagued her heart. Jackson had just introduced his plan to start a coffee enterprise, and here she had plans of riding out to find the jewels. Would he be waiting for her when she came back?

Jackson mounted his horse and gave her one last look. Drew started his horse down the graveled drive, and Jackson followed.

Kit waited for the appointed hour. In a few hours, it would be dark. She and Damaris would slip out of the house at midnight and take her father's wagon into Charleston. As crazy as it sounded, the escapade had her heart pounding. Would they be safe on the road? Would they encounter her father before they reached Charleston? A knot filled her stomach, and she turned to Damaris. "We'd better say goodnight if we're to pull this off. Go on in. I'll be there in a moment."

"Yes, you're right. Goodnight," Damaris said. She slipped inside the house and gently shut the door.

Kit strode to the stable and looked for Nate. He was nowhere in sight. *Good.* She hitched two horses to the wagon. That done, she tied their reins to the hitching post and strode back to the house.

Fully dressed, Kit and Damaris lay in bed and waited for the sounds in the house to settle.

Kit's stomach was in a knot.

Dear God, I ask for protection as we set out for this journey. I ask for the courage to see it through. And God . . . work it out so that Aunt Kindra can come home.

She stared at the ceiling for a long time, watching the shadows of tree limbs sway in the breeze. The moon cast a pale light, creating an eerie feeling in Kit's mind. *Don't think!* she scolded herself. *This is all for Aunt Kindra.* A long while later, she started to doze. The house grew quiet as the night closed in.

"Wake up!" Damaris whispered. "It's time to go."

"I'm awake." Kit tossed aside the covers and rose. She brushed the wrinkles out of her skirts and glanced around the room. She didn't know how long it would be before she returned. Could they accomplish their mission and make it home unscathed? She was about to embark on uncharted territory. She had never gone on a treasure hunt on an island where she'd never been. Yet for Aunt Kindra, she had to try. "All right, let's go."

Kit led Damaris down the stairs and through the house with goose bumps on her arms. It seemed that every step they took was amplified in the dark house.

Damaris bumped into a dining room chair, and it scraped loudly on the polished floor.

"Shhh!" Kit gave her cousin a warning look. "They'll hear us."

Damaris nodded. "Which way are we going?"

Kit raised her finger to her lips with a stern look. Sounds of the night met her ears as the house creaked and groaned in ways she'd never noticed before. She tiptoed to the kitchen and threaded her way past the large work table to the outside door.

The moon cast slivers of light across the walkway that divided the outer kitchen and the house. The girls walked past buildings to the stable, where the wagon and horses waited.

"Get in!" Kit ordered as she climbed up. Untying the reins from the brake, she slowly guided the horses away from the stable and out to the long drive. The wheels crunched loudly on the gravel road, and the low-hanging Spanish moss in the oaks looked ominous, with its dark fingers reaching out as the girls passed.

Kit looked back a dozen times to see if lights were being lit in the house or if Nate had discovered they'd taken the rig. The first thing he'd do would be to alert Mother that they had left in the middle of the night. But every time she looked back, all was still. They were soon rolling down the main thoroughfare that led to Fields Landing, the moon casting shadows through the large oaks that lined the lane.

"I don't know why I let you talk me into this," Kit said, sitting straight as a post.

"It's our only chance to get Mother back," Damaris said with a quiver in her voice.

"Are you scared?"

"I'm petrified."

They didn't talk for the next while as the sounds of creatures hidden in the dark shadows of the woods sent chills up their spines. Then Kit heard another sound behind them. Was that the sound of horse hooves? She glanced over her shoulder and shook the reins to speed up the team. The wagon wheels rattled loudly, and Kit swallowed. She looked back again and again, each time feeling as if they were being followed. But each time she saw nothing but the empty lane behind them.

They'd gone a few miles when Damaris asked, "Is someone following us?"

"I think so." Kit's fingers clenched the leather reins, fear licking up her neck. They were nearing a thick forest, the trees arching over the road like a tunnel and shutting out the last glint of the moon. In utter darkness, they rode on.

Damaris reached a hand and touched Kit's arm. Kit pulled on the reins and slowed the wagon to a stop. Owls hooted in the distance. The hair on Kit's neck stirred. "I think we should go back," Kit said.

"No!" Damaris whispered loudly.

"We're being followed. Someone's been keeping up with us for a long while. It's not safe."

"We've gone this far, keep going," came a third voice.

Kit and Damaris turned to see Bella Grace pushing her head out from under a canvas cover in the wagon bed.

Kit gasped. "What are you doing here?"

"You didn't think you'd set out on this adventure without me, did you?"

Bella pouted and then smiled. "Of course, you did. That's why I hid." Kit and Damaris exchanged a look of near panic.

Bella looked like an angel with her long blonde hair flowing in the dark of night.

"How did you know we were sneaking out of the house to ride to Charleston?" Kit's mind was racing.

"I heard everything you said earlier tonight."

"You what?" Kit felt anger rise like a tide. "You were eavesdropping on us?"

"I didn't mean to. I went to your door to come and talk when I heard you two talking." Bella shrugged. "So, I sat on the floor outside your room and listened."

Dumbfounded, Kit gave Bella a dry look but caught the gleam in her sister's eyes. "You had no right to invade my privacy!"

"Don't give me that look, Kit. You're not the only one who likes to go on mysterious treasure hunts. If you kick me off this wagon, I'll go straight to Mother and tell her what you're up to. You won't get far."

A twig snapped loudly in the woods. The three of them held their tongues. The black trees appeared like giant men, looming tall in the dark, ominous forest. Someone was out there. They could feel it.

After a long while, Kit whispered, "It's going to be hard enough convincing Captain Kincade to take the two of us across the ocean. Now we have you to contend with." She huffed and continued, "Mother is going to have a fit once she discovers Damaris and me are gone. I left her a note explaining where we're going, but you . . . she'll not know you came along too."

"Yes, she will. I left my own note. Now let's get going before we get caught."

FORTY-ONE

SOLOMON WAS OUT in the stable, brushing down his favorite horse, when he saw Kit lead two mares to the wagon and hitch them up. He knew this was odd, so he hid in the barn and watched her. When done, Kit turned back to the house and slipped inside. Something wasn't right. He fought the urge to tell Mistress Grace that her daughter was planning a late-night journey. But he couldn't make that claim; he didn't know what was going on. So, he waited.

The minutes went by slowly, every noise in the barn pronounced. After a long while, he heard quick footsteps. As he watched, Bella climbed into the back of the wagon and pulled the canvas tarp over her. *Now why would she do a fool thing like that?* He stood and stared at the wagon a long time, making sure to stay in the shadows. Being black had its advantages; he melded into the night as if he were a part of it.

Soon after, Kit and Damaris made their way to the barn. Solomon hung back and watched the women climb into the wagon and drive out the long drive. *What them ladies up to?* Curiosity got the better of him and he quickly saddled a horse. He kept his black steed far behind the wagon but close enough to keep his eyes on the women. The dense forest blocked the light from the moon, but he could still see the wagon up ahead. He followed slowly. He wanted to see where the women were going, but he didn't want them to know he was following them.

Was Damaris leaving? Had she given up on him? It pained him to see the hurt in her eyes, but the truth was he had nothing to offer her except this. He could follow and make sure they were safe. Strangers lurked on the roads at night. If anyone approached the women, he would be there to protect them.

He kept his eyes on the wagon, wishing for all the world they were safe at home and in bed. When the wagon slowed to a stop, he reined his horse off the road and hid behind a tree. *What are they doing now?*

Jackson couldn't sleep. A balmy breeze wafted in his cabin as the sea purling against the hull rocked the ship in a gentle lull. He needed to see Kit again before her father returned from Charleston. He wanted to be there to ask Cameron for her hand in hopes that Mister Bartholomew would give them his blessings.

But images of the southern beauty kept him awake. Earlier that afternoon she had looked smart in her white top and riding skirt, her black vest and black felt hat sitting pert upon her black tresses. How could a man resist her?

They wouldn't have much time together the next time he rode out to River Oak. His father had warned this was a short trip. They would be sailing soon. The more he thought about it, the more he couldn't lie on his bunk and wait till morning. He slipped out of his cabin and went into town to saddle up his rented horse. Before long he was on his way to River Oak. He wouldn't get much sleep tonight, but if he had to, once he reached the plantation, he'd sleep in the hay loft until morning. He sat tall in the saddle, knowing he was on his way to see his girl. It was going to be a long and lonely night, but it would be worth it when he saw Kit's lovely face in the morning.

Kit kept her eyes on the lane as the wagon rumbled along. It seemed that the road grew longer by the minute in the black of night. She still sensed they were being followed, but whoever was following them had not shown himself. The tense muscles in her neck began to ease.

It was all she could do to sit straight and guide the horses on the dark road with Damaris's head lying on her shoulder. Damaris and Bella had long since fallen asleep, leaving Kit responsible for getting them to Charleston and to the *Sea Baron* in the dead of night. She could imagine Captain Kincade's reaction when he learned he had three crusaders needing his assistance to rescue her aunt.

The wagon rolled endlessly on, the rattling wheels and the clopping of hooves her only company. Up ahead she saw a break in the trees where moonlight shone on the lonely road. Kit drove toward the light, relishing its glow. All at once a dark shadow loomed ahead as a horse and rider drew near. She pulled up on the reins and called out, "Who goes there!" She wished she'd brought along her father's ten-inch musket.

"Say that again?" The dark form asked as he trotted his horse toward the wagon.

"Wh . . . who goes . . . Jackson?" Her voice faded away.

"Kit?"

Damaris rustled awake and Bella flew out from under the canvas tarp to peer over the wagon bench.

"What are you doing out here?" Jackson came to the clearing and rode up to the wagon, a look of bewilderment on his face.

"I could ask you the same thing, Jackson Harding."

A twig snapped on the side of the road behind them and a horse snorted.

"Hold it right there!" Jackson pulled out a musket and pointed it as the dark figure rode up behind the wagon.

"Don't shoot.,"

"Solomon?" Damaris stood in the rig and looked back.

Solomon walked his horse to the side of the wagon and looked down at them. Kit felt her body go limp. "Solomon, you gave us a fright! What are *you* doing here?"

"I been followin' you ever since you ride out of River Oak." He smiled wearily at them.

Jackson aligned his horse with Solomon's. "What are you women up to?" His low voice reverberated over the dark road.

Kit's shoulders slumped. "We're on our way to the *Sea Baron.*"

Jackson dismounted and walked over to where she sat and looked up at her with an amused grin. "Why, may I ask, are you riding to the Cooper River docks in the dead of night?"

Kit lifted her chin and squared her shoulders. "We're going to ask Captain Kincade to take us to Tobago Island." As she said it, the words sounded foolish. She was glad it was dark. At least Jackson wouldn't see the rush of red creeping up to her scalp. She felt hot as a coal stove in December.

Jackson pushed his wide-brimmed hat off his forehead and stared at her in disbelief. "It may be none of my business, Kit, but why in tarnation would you want to go and do a fool thing like that?"

"We're going to find the treasure so we can get my mother back," Damaris cut in.

Jackson looked over at Solomon. "Do you know what these women are talking about?"

"No, suh. But somethin' be tellin' me these ladies ain't thought this thing through." He jumped to the ground and went to Damaris's side of the wagon. "What you talkin' about? What kind of treasure you lookin' for?"

Damaris folded her arms across her chest and jutted her chin. "Kit and I discovered why Mother's been kidnapped." She stared down at Solomon. "We have proof of it."

Solomon looked to Jackson.

"Would someone please make sense of all of this?" Jackson gazed at Kit.

Kit pulled the peacock journal out of Damaris's bag that sat between them. The emerald stone glittered in the moonlight that slanted through the trees.

Jackson reached out a hand. "Let me take a look at that."

Kit handed the book to him. "It appears that some eighteen years ago, Aunt Tia stole emeralds from a man named Jule Spade. She hid them in your father's ship before she went to prison. Unknowingly, someone saw her do it and he found the jewels. He buried them in a secret place on Tobago Island." Kit took the book from Jackson and then pulled out her aunt's journal and waved both books in the air. "It's all here." She set the books on the wooden bench between her and Damaris and pulled an old piece of rag out of her pocket. "And then there's this." She shook it open for all to see. "It's a map." She heard Bella gasp behind them but no one said a word.

"Kit . . ." Jackson tried. He cleared his throat. "This is the darndest story I've ever heard. And I have to admit it's mighty convincing. But Kincade will never agree to sailing across the Atlantic with Denzel's daughter and niece without previous permission." He pulled his hat forward. "It isn't going to happen." His voice was firm but gentle.

"But . . ." Damaris bent her head and began to sob. "It's the only way we'll ever get Mother back." Her shoulders shook as the tears fell.

Solomon reached up and scooped Damaris into his arms and cradled her. "Shhh . . . don't cry." He set her on her feet.

Damaris's head fell to his chest and she let the river of tears flow. "I've lost my . . . my . . . mother . . . and I've lost you." She sobbed.

Solomon's broad hands caressed her back and then he began to run them over her long black tresses. "You haven't lost me, my love. I'm right here," he soothed. He kissed the top of her head.

She looked up with wet cheeks. "Do you mean it?"

"With alla my heart." His dark eyes claimed hers as the rest of them looked on. "I don't know how we gonna do it, but I want you for my wife."

Damaris pulled his face down and unabashedly kissed him soundly. "I will marry you, Solomon. Nobody will keep us apart."

"Can we go home now?" Bella yawned. "I've seen and heard all I need to for one night." Her voice echoed over the dirt road.

The party of night owls laughed. But when they became quiet, Kit asked Jackson, "And what are you doing on the road in the middle of the night?"

He touched the brim of his hat in mock salute and grinned. "I was on my way to see you."

"Well, since you and Solomon are here, you can escort us back to River Oak."

Solomon handed Damaris back onto the wooden bench. She looked at the others. "We've done all of this for nothing. I guess we'll never find Mother now." She sounded so defeated.

"Don't give up hope," Jackson said as he mounted his horse. "You have to keep the faith." He waited for Kit to turn the wagon around, and then he rode up alongside it. "There's redemption in keeping the faith." He looked over at them. "You understand what I'm saying?"

Damaris swallowed. "No. Tell me."

"The Good Book says, 'Faith is the substance of things hoped for, and the evidence of things not seen.' You've been believing your Mama would come home all these years. You've never given up hope. Keep the faith, Damaris. Don't give up. She's coming home." Jackson gave Kit a warm smile and kneed his horse to ride in front of the wagon while Solomon took up the rear.

Kit had loved the man before tonight, but with his words of wisdom, she saw a side of him she'd never known, and she loved him even more. She flipped the reins. "Git up there!" She would follow Jackson all the way back to River Oak, and she would follow him through life. She nudged Damaris and said, "It looks like there may be a double wedding coming up in the near future."

"Now wouldn't that be something," Damaris said. "I'm going to put my faith in that, too. I don't ever want to let Solomon out of my sight again." She paused. "And I'm taking Jackson's advice, Kit. I'm believing Mother will be there to witness our wedding."

FORTY-TWO

Ash Haven, Charleston, South Carolina
May 12, 1849

"FIRE!" THE SCREAM came from a downstairs servant.

Phoebe jumped up from her seat and dashed to look out a window. Smoke billowed from the barn near the slave quarters. "Lord help us!" She went to the base of the stairs. "Everybody, outside! Form a bucket crew . . . now!" She flew out of the house toward the stables and called out to the slaves who watched the flames in horror. "Get the horses out of the stable! Get the children up to the house!"

Pandemonium broke loose as old women rushed children to the Great House, and old men ran to the barn and swung the doors wide open. Dark, billowing smoke filled the sky.

Phoebe hiked her skirts, ran to the edge of the cotton fields, and cupped her mouth. "Get out of the fields and to the barnyard now!"

Kindra ran up behind her. "A horseman just rode down the drive with a torch in his hands!"

"What did you say?" Bart Odell rode up on his steed, a whip in one hand, pulling on the reins with the other.

Kindra pointed to the carriage lane. "There's a stranger headed to the west fields with a torch in his hands!"

Odell kicked the horse's flank. Dirt shot out from the horse's hooves as he galloped after the unknown arsonist.

Fire crackled and snapped as the flames licked through the slats of the barn. "The cotton gin is in there!" Phoebe ran farther down the road between the fields. "Drop your tools! I need every hand back to the yard! Grab buckets of water!"

The field hands flew out of the rows like fire ants from their holes. Men, women, and teenagers ran to the clearing. Men drew water from the iron pump in the yard to fill buckets as fast as they could, while other men ran to the well at the edge of the colored district. They dropped buckets into the water. Slaves formed long lines and passed water buckets to the next in line until the one in front sloshed water onto the angry flames and tossed the bucket aside, reaching for the next full bucket.

Horses whinnied and ran toward the main thoroughfare once they were freed. Slaves yelled directions at each other as they fought the infernal flames and watched with terror as sparks flew through the air and drifted toward the cotton fields.

"Thank goodness the fields are in the planting stage," Phoebe called to Kindra, " and not in the picking stage." She watched the barn burn, defeat in her heart. The pungent smoke sailed out across the fields as the slaves fought the flames.

Odell rode back to the clearing, his musket in hand. "He's dead," he scowled.

"The torch?" Phoebe asked, afraid to know the truth.

"I shot him on the road. He never got a chance to set the fields on fire."

"Oh, thank God." She looked back to see the slaves still frantically fighting the fire with their water buckets.

Hours later, embers glowed in the twilight. The stable lay in rubbles of hot coals. The charred cotton gin stood like a giant black omen. *Someone intended to do harm*, Phoebe thought. *And who was that stranger?*

In the days that followed, Lawrence disappeared. Mister Fisk, Phoebe's private investigator, identified the man Odell had killed as Eldon McClure, whom Lawrence had hired. Mister Fisk reported a list of mischief her husband had engaged in, some of which Phoebe had long since known. His affairs with lewd women, gambling her money away, and now the unsavory announcement that Eldon McClure had been hired to not only burn down the barn, but the Great House and the cotton fields.

Phoebe sent word for her father to come. Lawrence was absent, but she feared he wasn't done. Two days later, Richard Goodman sat in Phoebe's study with the original deed to Ash Haven. "The deed I signed on your wedding day isn't legal."

"What?" Phoebe stared at her father. "How could he lie to me?"

"I was afraid Lawrence would pull a stunt like this someday. Hearing that he hired a man to set the barn on fire doesn't surprise me."

"Me neither, Father." She felt heat rush to her face. "Still, it's quite unsettling that he would actually follow through." She held her father's eyes. "But the deed you signed truly isn't legal?"

"No. I signed the real deed to the plantation over to your mother. That paper you hold in your hand is bogus." He gave her a wry smile.

"So Lawrence could never have gotten his hands on the property anyway." What her father had done began to sink in. She felt intense relief. The property was protected from Lawrence.

"That's right. I knew that even though I signed the deed to you, Lawrence would have legal control of the plantation."

Phoebe sighed. "None of this is mine?"

"I'm sorry I deceived you, but none of this is yours."

"What of the slaves?"

"They belong to the owner of Ash Haven."

"Mother owns everything?"

"That's correct." Her father held her eyes. "What do you want to do?"

Her head swimming, Phoebe removed her glasses and rubbed the bridge of her nose. "I want to divorce Lawrence and move to the city. I'm tired of plantation life. I don't want to deal with it anymore."

"All right." Richard Goodman leaned forward. "I'll help you find a townhouse in Charleston." He stopped. "I assume that's where you'll want to live?"

"Yes. I want to find a charming place in the city. No more sitting out here away from society."

Her father stood. "I need to go into town and telegraph your mother. I'm sure she'd like to join you in your search for a new place to live."

"What will you do with all of this?" Phoebe waved her hands in the air.

"Sell it. Cottons in its prime. This plantation will bring in a handsome price."

As her father stood to leave, Phoebe rang the bell.

Deborah appeared at the door. "Yes, Miss Phoebe?"

"Tell Kindra to come downstairs. We're going to town."

Stunned that Phoebe had been gifted with the ammunition she needed to win her divorce and had plans to move from Ash Haven, Kindra rode along with the mistress as she delivered the valid deed to her attorney. Her mind whirled. How much longer would Phoebe require her company? Would she be sold right along with the rest of the slaves and be forced to start all over again with new owners?

"I'm ready to spread my wings," Phoebe said as she snapped her fan open and stirred the thick, humid air. "I miss my mother. We have a lot of catching up to do. With you as my traveling companion, we can take the train to New York and visit as often as we'd like." She smiled, mischief in her eyes. "Let's travel around the world. There's nothing to stop us now."

Let's? Kindra's bewildering thoughts grew. "You want me to move to the city with you?"

"Of course. You're everything I need in a chambermaid. I couldn't bear to leave you behind."

Kindra felt a sense of hope rising at the suggestion that she'd live in Charleston with Phoebe. Might she run into Denzel, Cameron, or Grace on the streets of the city?

Once they arrived at the office of Phoebe's attorney, Phoebe handed him the deed. After examining the document, the attorney set it on his desk. "It seems your parents pulled the wool over your eyes as well as your husband's."

"And rightly so, Mister Croft. My father saw Lawrence for what he is: an evil, conniving man. Lawrence had hoped to get rid of me and bring in the woman he's been having an affair with. It appears I was never the mistress of Ash Haven, nor will the little snippet, Candace Bigsby, be either."

"As a rule, you being a woman makes filing for a divorce almost impossible. But given the recent fire at Ash Haven, and with the reports from your investigator that your husband meant to do harm, I see no reason why the judge would rule against you.

"Your court case should be swift, Mrs. Bridger, seeing as how neither you nor Lawrence has any legal hold on the plantation. I will submit a copy of the document immediately. Your divorce should be final in two years."

"That long?" Phoebe's brows creased, and she bit her bottom lip.

"The judge may request to extend the time." He stood and removed his spectacles. "I see you've finally given up the fight."

"No, sir. I have never given up."

"I'm not speaking about Lawrence, Mrs. Bridger." He pointed to her glasses with his own. "Have the migraines gone away?"

Phoebe smiled and pushed her eyeglasses up her nose. "Yes. The headaches are a thing of the past."

He looked over at Kindra sitting next to Phoebe and frowned. "I'll be in touch with you, Mrs. Bridger. Good day."

Phoebe sailed out of the courtroom a free woman. "It'll be two years before I receive papers that I'm truly free. But I shant marry again. Who would marry a divorced woman?" She placed her gloved hand to her lips and smiled. "I don't care. I'm free of Lawrence Bridger."

Lawrence stomped out of the courtroom and shook his fist. "You've tricked me, Phoebe! I'll never forgive you for that."

"My parents tricked us both," Phoebe said calmly. "And I will forever be grateful to them." She turned to Kindra. "Come. Let's go home. My first order of business will be to fire Bart Odell, that wicked overseer, and until the plantation is sold, I'll put Abraham in charge."

That evening, Kindra read a passage from Isaiah in the Bible: Behold, the Lord's hand is not shortened, that it cannot save; neither his ear heavy, that it cannot hear. She left her bed and looked out at the moon and stars. *Lord, hear my prayer. Please take care of my children. And for Denzel, I ask*

that You give him the strength he needs to carry on. And if it wouldn't be too much to ask, would You show me the way to his side? I want to see my Denzel again.

"I see you're back, Mrs. Bridger." Mrs. Anderson glanced over at Kindra for a long second with a look as if Kindra standing in her store would grow poison oak on her floors. She turned back to Phoebe. I have your material ready. Tell your slave to take them out." She looked in Kindra's direction once more.

Phoebe looked over. "Take these things out to the buggy."

"Of course, Phoebe," Kindra took a step forward.

Mrs. Anderson spun around with fire in her eyes and glared at Kindra. "Watch how you speak to your betters, girl!" Her voice rose. "You are to call her Mistress Bridger or Miss Phoebe."

"Yes'm." Kindra nodded, embarrassed that she'd forgotten something so simple.

A moment later, she walked back into the dry goods store and picked up the last of the five packages wrapped in brown paper. She and Phoebe left the shop together. She was conscious of Mrs. Anderson's scowl as they walked out to the street. *Goodness!* Thought Kindra as she stowed the bags under the seat. *Must Mrs. Anderson be so mean?*

"Let's go to the bakery down the street," Phoebe said, seeming to ignore the shopkeeper's crassness.

As they passed a hat store, two ladies were coming out. Kindra half-smiled at them as she walked by. The women raised their brows and moved to the other side of the walkway.

There were other people on the walkway as Phoebe and Kindra window-shopped. Most of them acted the same, either whispering or moving to the other side of the sidewalk to avoid getting too close. Kindra pretended not to notice and kept walking, but it stung to hear the cruel words they were saying.

Phoebe noticed the mean-spirited actions of the afternoon shoppers. "Pay them no mind, Kindra. They're little people with little minds."

But by mid-afternoon, Kindra had had enough of the rude actions of the city people. Phoebe had one more stop to make—at a high-end dry goods shop—before going home.

"Why don't I just wait in the coach, Miss Phoebe?" Kindra suggested. "I don't think they'll like the idea of a colored girl going in there."

Phoebe laid a hand on her shoulder. "You've been a perfect soldier today with all the assaults coming your way. I've never seen so many haughty women in my life. You can sit in the buggy and wait. I'll only be a moment."

Glad for the relief, Kindra sat in the buggy and rested her feet. Her mind went to her family, Denzel, and the children. *Wouldn't it be heaven to see them again?*

Phoebe finally stepped out of the shop. "They didn't have the gloves I needed. But the store clerk said they have them on the next block. Walk with me. Do you mind?"

Kindra stepped down and rejoined her mistress.

Denzel and Cameron stepped out of the hotel café and turned down King Street. "We've spent the last three days following false leads. I don't know what to make of it." Denzel felt a knot in his stomach. He truly believed he'd find his wife on this trip. But every day they followed a lead; they returned to the hotel with nothing to show for it.

He searched the faces of the black people who walked toward him, something that had become second nature these days. Could he find his wife on the streets of Charleston?

"I think we should ride out to Ash Haven," Cameron said, sticking a toothpick in the corner of his mouth. "Mister Croft seems to think your wife is their slave."

"He seemed pretty convincing," Denzel shook his head. "But he didn't know the name of Bridger's slave woman." He kept pace with Cameron.

"That's true, but his description of the woman who worked for them sure did resemble Kindra. I think we should check it out." Cameron elbowed him.

"You're right. Let's check it out." Determination set Denzel's jaw. He wouldn't pass up any chance of finding his wife. They still had three blocks to go before they came to the livery where their horses were stabled. *Would he find his wife today?*

The afternoon breeze picked up, ruffling their skirts. Kindra held onto hers as she threaded her way along the walkway, careful to keep close to the store buildings and not touch a pedestrian. Phoebe found the store she was looking for, and they went in. They quickly found the gloves Phoebe wanted and were soon back on the walkway, Kindra holding the package.

"Why are there so many people out today?" Kindra asked.

"It's the weekend. It always brings the shoppers out. And with the society parties coming this summer, the dry goods stores are busy."

Kindra, dressed in her simple day dress, carried the new packages for Phoebe. It was all she could do to keep out of the way of pedestrians, and she nearly fumbled into the wall, avoiding them. As she struggled to regain her balance, she looked up. *Could it be?* The man walking toward her looked like an older version of the Cameron she remembered. And there, next to him, the man she loved . . . her beloved Denzel! "Is it you?" she whispered, unable to voice her question for anyone else to hear. She felt the blood drain from her face, and her head felt light.

"Are you all right?" Phoebe touched her arm.

Kindra kept her eyes on her man, straight ahead. At the same time, Denzel saw her. She shoved the packages into Phoebe's arms.

"Kindra!" Phoebe rebuked her.

But Kindra didn't wait. She started toward Denzel, not caring who she touched. She lifted her skirts and ran to the man of her dreams.

"Kindra!" This time, the voice was her husband's. He swooped her up and swung her around. Without letting her go, he set her down and looked deep into her eyes. "I can't believe I've found you!" He looked up into the sky and laughed. "Thank You, Lord!" He cupped her face to hold her steady. "Is it you?"

"It's me," Kindra cried. Her eyes blurred as she looked into his wonderful face. Tears streamed down her cheeks as she kept her eyes on him. She felt his hands clutch her arms, and she didn't want him to let her go. The world swirled around them. She was aware that people stared, but she didn't care. Nothing mattered now except the man who stood before her.

"Kindra!" Phoebe's stern voice carried over the crowd.

Kindra clutched Denzel's hand and turned toward the mistress, who had threaded her way toward them and now stood a mere five feet away. Phoebe stared at Kindra and then Denzel, her eyes wide. "Is this him?"

"Yes, Miss Phoebe. This is my husband, Denzel."

Cameron stood next to Phoebe, looking on with a beaming smile. He turned to her. "I'm Cameron Bartholomew, ma'am. This woman who accompanies you today is my sister-in-law, Kindra." He threw an arm around Kindra's shoulders, and she smiled up at him.

"Yes, well . . . she is also my chambermaid." Phoebe seemed to be at a loss for words. Her face blanched, and she held the packages as if her life depended on them. People moved around them as they continued on their way. The four stood frozen among the busy crowd, and Denzel kept his hand on Kindra's arm.

The driver rode up and parked the rig by the curb.

"Get in the coach, Kindra."

"Miss Phoebe?"

"You heard me, get in the coach."

Kindra's heart hit the boardwalk, and she looked up at Denzel. Could this be happening? She heard Denzel's strained voice cry, "She's my wife!" Tears blurred her vision as she pulled her arm out of his hold and backed away toward the carriage.

"Kindra! No!" Denzel called out.

She looked longingly at him before she stepped into the rig. "I'm not a free woman."

"I've been searching for my wife for eight long years!" Denzel pleaded with Phoebe. "Cameron, tell her!"

Kindra heard the shaking in his voice. She shivered from head to toe. *Lord! We need Your help . . . now!*

"Good day, gentlemen." Phoebe started for the coach.

"Ma'am!" Cameron stopped her.

Kindra watched as Phoebe halted and glanced back. Her world was quickly shattering.

"We're done, gentlemen." Phoebe placed her foot on the step, but then she stopped. She eyed Kindra as tears welled in her eyes. They looked at each other for a long moment.

Kindra held her breath.

Phoebe squeezed her eyes and shook her head.

"Phoebe?" Kindra reached a hand to her.

"Get out!"

"What?"

"Get out right now!"

"Miss Phoebe?"

"You heard me. Get out of my coach." Phoebe backed away and stood aside.

Kindra stood on wobbly legs and stepped out of the coach. She looked at Denzel with uncertainty, then back to Phoebe for reassurance.

Phoebe waved her on.

"Kindra." Denzel gasped.

She held Phoebe's eyes. "Thank you, Miss Phoebe."

"Don't thank me, Kindra. If you want your man, you better go to him now before I change my mind."

Kindra spun around and ran into Denzel's arms. "You found me!" The tears she'd held back for so long were released and now spilled down her cheeks.

"I sure did!" He held her tightly.

Kindra looked over to see Phoebe standing at the coach door, sadness in her eyes.

"Ma'am," Denzel said, turning Kindra toward Phoebe, his arm over her shoulder. "Thank you." Kindra felt Denzel's body trembling. "I've prayed every day that the Good Lord would bring her back to me."

Phoebe's shoulders dropped. "Your wife is a jewel. She's been of invaluable help in my time of need." Her voice quivered. "Your wife stood by my side in my darkest hours."

Kindra held her breath as Phoebe spoke.

"She's been a gift to me." Phoebe let go of the carriage door and walked up to them. She took Kindra's hand and put it in Denzel's. "Now I give her as a gift to you."

Kindra's knees went weak. She threw her arms around Phoebe's neck. "Thank you for everything."

"You're welcome, my friend." Phoebe pulled away. "You'd better go before I change my mind."

Kindra turned back to Denzel, wanting nothing more than to be held in his arms, to kiss his lips and talk to him for hours. But all of this would have to wait, as they were still on the boardwalk with a flurry of curious onlookers passing by. She could only imagine what was going through their minds as she saw their looks. Here she and Denzel were, two darkies carrying on as if they were regular white folks on the streets of Charleston.

He pulled Kindra against his side. "I can't believe it. It's been too long since I've looked into those beautiful green eyes."

When Kindra looked back, Phoebe was climbing into the coach. The rig slowly jogged into traffic and rolled down the street. She was gone.

"Let's go home," Cameron said, a contented smile on his face.

"Home," Kindra said, clinging to Denzel's side. "The most beautiful word I've ever heard." She put her hand in Denzel's, and the two of them followed Cameron up the street.

Thank you, Lord! I'm going home!

FORTY-THREE

River Oak, Fields Landing

THE SUN HAD not yet set, and a slight, cooling breeze drifted in from the lazy river, bringing with it the scents of swamp rose mallow and jessamine. Damaris sat on the porch and sipped tea with Grace, while Kit and Jackson rode their horses. Bella sat on the top step and leaned against the white pillar.

"How I slept through your escapade last night, I'll never know." Grace looked as if she were trying to look stern.

But Damaris caught the gleam in her eye and relaxed. "It was our last attempt to find Mother."

"But to ride out in the middle of the night . . ."

"It was the most exciting night of my life," Bella said, resting her head dreamily against the post.

"You've always had a desire for excitement, my dear. You're going to give your father and me gray hairs long before our time."

Bella looked up. "Father's already graying." She gave her mother a cheeky grin.

"Four daughters will do it." Grace held the peacock journal in her hands. "I can't believe Kit kept this and the map a secret all these years."

"She comes by it honestly," Damaris said. "I've heard stories about your adventures and how Aunt Olivia hid Grandfather Phillip's letters in her trunk." She leaned back, her heart sinking. "At least you were able to sail to Jamaica to look for him. My search for the jewels to save Mother fell flat."

Grace set the book down and squeezed Damaris's hand. "I don't think you would have found those emeralds. They've been hidden for too many years. Goodness knows, time and weather change the lay of the land."

"Who's to say Scoot Sweeny didn't go back and dig the treasure up?" Bella broke in. "Still, it would have been fun to try."

Damaris listened to their back-and-forth what-ifs. None of it mattered now. From her vantage point, she could see the slave district. The field hands were filing back to the community from a long day's work. She watched for one particular, tall, ruggedly handsome man, and her heart picked up speed when she saw him. Solomon had promised to come and see her after the supper hour.

On that breezy evening, while the three women sat lazily talking, Damaris heard the sound of three loud whistles as the *River Belle* steamed slowly upstream. Instead of going past River Oak as expected, the steamboat slowed to a stop in front of the Bartholomews' boat ramp and bumped the pier.

Damaris leaned forward to see who might be stepping off the boat. To her surprise, Uncle Cameron walked onto the ramp, a smile on his face as he turned back as if waiting for someone. Behind him came a woman with honey-colored skin and long, black hair.

Damaris slowly rose and held her breath, her hands going to her chest. "Mother?" She flew down the stairs and ran across the lawn. "Mother!"

Kindra picked up her skirts as she stepped off the ramp. She ran up the lawn, her arms outstretched. "Damaris!"

Mother and daughter collided in a rush of tears and babbling words no one understood. Their tears flowed, and soft laughter abounded.

"Mother!" Damaris said again, her eyes blurring. "You're home . . .You're really home!" She threw her arms around her mother's neck, feeling as if this were all a dream.

"Let me look at you," Kindra said, stepping away to arm's length. She looked Damaris over head to toe, tears brimming in her eyes. "You've grown into a woman, a beautiful, beautiful woman." She drew Damaris back into her arms. "We have so much catching up to do."

At a distance, Grace waited, a desperate yearning in her eyes and a smile lighting her face. Damaris reluctantly let her mother go and watched her fly into Grace's embrace. "Oh, my, Grace. It's so good to see you. Just look at you. You're just as lovely as the day we last saw each other." The sisters hugged and cried. There was so much to say, but tears needed to come first.

The spell was broken when a band of boys and girls flew out of the house, whooping and hollering as they ran down the lawn. "She's home! Mama's home!"

Piper flew into her mother's arms, weeping and talking as she hugged her. Kindra broke out into tears again. "You're a young woman, my baby!" They hugged, and kissed, and laughed, and then Kindra looked over at Zeddie and Cyrus.

Her hands flew to her lips. "Let me look at my boys." She opened her arms wide as Zeddie stepped to one side and Cyrus the other. She pulled them both to her and kissed their cheeks.

Kindra looked up at Denzel with a warm smile. "My children have all grown. Damaris and Zeddie are young adults, and Piper is a beautiful young lady. And my baby . . . Cyrus . . . has grown so tall." She laughed softly. She kissed her youngest son and let the tears flow. She closed her eyes for a long moment, and Damaris felt peace wash over her soul. Kindra opened her eyes and said, "The Lord has brought me home to my family."

The crowd said a silent Amen, and then laughter broke out as Kindra circled the group for more hugs and tears. "It's so good to see all of you!"

News of Kindra's return must have spread like bees from a broken hive, for the village of slaves stood at the entrance of the colored district. One man came forward, a woman by his side, and grown children followed him. As they came closer, Kindra could make out who this man was. Just when she thought she'd cried herself out, Cuffee strode up with his wife, Tabitha.

"Welcome home, Kindra," he said with a glint in his eyes. "I see you're finally free."

"I am." She swallowed. "And you're home with your family." She looked over at his wife.

"You remember Tabitha?" Cuffee gently pushed his wife forward.

"Yes, I do." Kindra took her hand. "You must be happy to have your husband home."

"Yes, ma'am, I am." Tabitha slipped her arm around Cuffee's waist and pulled him forward.

Kindra stared into Cuffee's eyes for a long moment. The memories of days gone by, days they had shared, were firmly behind them but would be imprinted on their hearts forever. Kindra watched Cuffee swallow.

"I'm happy to see you with your family again. God heard your prayers."

"And yours," Kindra said. "We've seen some hard times . . . but it's all behind us now."

Her family and the Bartholomews watched reverently as the two greeted each other.

Cuffee looked at Denzel. "This woman never give up on seein' you. She prayed every night that the Good Lord bring her home."

Denzel slipped his hand around Kindra's waist. "As long as I live, I'll never stop thanking Him for bringing her home."

Kindra saw the love in his eyes, and the family shifted and laughed. She looked over at Damaris, knowing they had so much to say, but it would have to wait. There were too many family members to talk to. But when she gazed at her daughter, she found Damaris's eyes had traveled to the tall, rugged man who had left Cuffee's side and now stood beside her daughter. *Who might he be? Is my daughter in love?*

Kindra's heart sank. Having been gone so long, she hadn't watched her daughter grow up. Damaris wasn't a child anymore. She was a woman. And from what she could tell, the man holding her eyes had discovered the same thing.

As Kindra's eyes strayed to her daughter, Cuffee spoke up. "Solomon."

The man broke his gaze from Damaris and looked over at them.

"Come meet Damaris's mother," Cuffee said.

Kindra hadn't missed Damaris taking the young man's hand as they walked up. "Mother, this is Solomon, Cuffee's son." The proud look in her daughter's eyes spoke volumes.

"It's nice to meet you, Solomon. The last time I saw you, you were this high." Kindra held her hand to her chest.

The family laughed and shuffled again.

Kindra looked at everybody. Then she looked beyond to the house, the grounds, and the pond. "I feel like I'm floating in a dream. I've waited so long for this day . . ."

The sound of horses' hooves pounded up the drive. Kindra turned to see Kit and a handsome man come flying up the carriage lane.

"Aunt Kindra!" Kit cried as she slid off the horse. "You're home!"

FORTY-FOUR

"MOTHER?"

Kindra looked out the sitting room window in time to see the *River Belle* stop in front of River Oak.

Grace appeared at the entrance. "Kindra, your mother . . ."

"I saw her. How did she know I was here?"

"I haven't the foggiest idea," Grace said, her brows raised.

When they stepped onto the front porch, they saw Tia on the boat ramp, looking toward the front lawn, a broad smile on her lips. She looked up at the house and appeared to spot them. "Kindra?" came her faint cry. "Is that you?"

"Mama!" Kindra left Grace's side and flew down the steps. She ran to her mother, who looked years older with graying hair. When she reached Tia's side, Kindra threw her arms around her neck. "How did you know I was here?"

"I didn't." Tia stepped back, a confused but excited look on her face. "How? When? I didn't expect to see you!" She held her arms open wide. "The Good Lord has heard my prayers!" She pulled Kindra into a warm embrace.

Kindra felt as if a jolt of lightning had struck her. "What did you say?" She stepped out of her mother's arms and searched her face.

"The Good Lord . . ." Tia stopped, and tears brimmed in her eyes. "Honey, we have a lot of catching up to do. I'm not only surprised you showed up at River Oak . . ." She laid soft hands on Kindra's cheeks. "I have good news for you."

Kindra waited, every nerve in her body alert.

"You've always wanted me to serve your God." Tia smiled warmly. "When Jule Spade took you away, my whole world crumbled. It wasn't long before I realized the gods I depended on had failed me." She waved her left hand in the air. Kindra didn't miss the gold band on her mother's ring finger. "Ebenezer, the patient man that he is, helped me to see you were right all along. God is the only One who could hear my prayers." Tears glistened on Tia's cheeks, yet her eyes shone brightly, and a smile lit her face.

"You gave your heart to Jesus?" Kindra had to know if this was what her mother was saying. "You gave up the witch doctors?"

"Yes, my girl, I did. No more evil spirits for me."

Kindra felt unspeakable joy. She knew Grace stood just behind them and had heard everything. Kindra turned to her. "Can you see it? Can you see the change in Mother?"

Grace hugged Tia. "Yes, Kindra, I see the wonderful change." She gently pushed Tia back. "What are you doing here? How did you know where to find us?"

"Can we go up to the house? My old feet are worn out after standing at the rail of the riverboat. There was too much beauty in the countryside to sit down."

Kindra waved at the steam captain as the *River Belle's* whistle blew and the steamboat chugged away from the bank. Tia's luggage sat on the boat ramp.

Cries of joy filled the air as Piper and Cyrus ran down the lawn. After a round of hugs, Kindra pointed. "Cyrus, bring your grandmother's things up to the house."

"Yes, Mama." Cyrus's eyes lit up. "It's good to see Grandmother. We're all together now."

"I'll help." Piper hefted a bag and lugged it off the ramp.

They didn't get far before Amos and Cato strode down the lawn. "We'll take those," Amos said as they relieved them both of the bags.

"Where you wantin' the luggage?" Cato asked.

"The west wing next to Kindra and Denzel's room." Grace lifted her skirts.

Kindra hooked her arm through her mother's. "Let's sit on the porch. You have a lot of explaining to do. How is it you showed up at River Oak?"

Tia patted her arm as they trudged up the yard. "You think I've got some explaining to do." She raised her brows. "You're the last person I expected to see when I stepped off that riverboat."

"You're just in time for tonight's party," Grace said, a mischievous smile on her lips.

"What are you celebrating?" Tia asked.

"Two wedding engagements," Kindra said, placing an arm around Damaris's waist.

Kit walked up and sat next to Grace.

"What?" Tia laughed. "Both of the girls are getting married?"

"Yes," Grace pulled Kit to her side. "You've arrived just in time for their weddings."

"Well, who are the lucky men?"

"Gram? Do you remember when I returned to Bridgetown, how I could hardly wait to return to the States?"

"I do. I've never seen such a moody soul. It was all we could do to get you to unpack your clothes. So who is the lucky fellow?"

"Solomon. You'll meet him tonight."

"Is he coming out of town?"

"No." Damaris paused. "He's coming in from the fields."

"The fields?" Tia grew silent and gave Damaris a sober look. "I assume you've thought this through."

"I have, Gram. I'll not change my mind."

Tia slowly nodded her head. "Then love him and don't look back."

Damaris threw her arms around Tia's neck. "Thank you for understanding."

Tia turned to Kit. "And you've grown into a beautiful woman. Who is the lucky man in *your* life?"

Kit stepped away from Grace. "I believe you already know him, Aunt Tia."

"Really? Try me."

"Jackson Harding." Kit's cheeks flushed.

"Captain Harding's son?"

"One and the same." Kit's eyes lit up.

"But isn't he going to be a sea captain like his father?"

"No. His career choices have changed. He'll be launching his first coffeehouse this summer."

"A coffeehouse? But why?"

"Because he wants to stay on dry land . . . and with me," Kit said. "We'll build our family with him at home instead of abroad."

"That makes perfect sense. I'm sure you've thought it through also." Tia sighed.

"We have. That's just the beginning. There's so much more to it."

Tia looked around at all of them. "Do you need a hand with your party tonight? I don't have a thing to stop me from helping." She gazed at the two families, love filling her heart.

"We've got it all under control, Tia," Grace said. "You being here will top off the evening wonderfully!"

That evening, Kindra welcomed the men when they came in from the fields. Cameron looked unsettled when he first saw Kindra's mother, but Kindra quickly worked to put his concern to rest. "Mother isn't the same woman you knew years ago," she said in a low tone and winked at her mother.

Standing nearby, Denzel said, "I could have told you as much." He put an arm over his mother-in-law's shoulders. "I'm just wondering if she's told you the rest of her story?"

Kindra raised her brows and gazed at her mother.

Tia raised her ring finger and smiled.

"Your mother's a married woman." Denzel gave her a wry grin.

"I did notice the ring." Kindra held her mother's hand and gazed at the simple gold band. "Tell me, who is it?"

"Really, Kindra. You have to ask?"

"Ebenezer?"

"He's a fine man. He's taught me so much." Tia smiled solemnly. "I've never met anyone so good and kind."

"Now, isn't that ironic?" Denzel asked.

"To say the least. You fought so hard to keep us from marrying, and all because Denzel was an overseer . . . and now, *you* married an overseer."

The family fell into laughter, and the room buzzed. When they settled down, Tia spoke. "I've heard it said, 'God works in mysterious ways. I'm proof that is true. I've never been happier than I am today. And now you're home . . ." She held Kindra's hand. "My joy is complete."

The sound of shuffling feet interrupted the small party. Kindra looked back to see Cuffee and his family standing in the foyer. Cuffee looked appalled as he gazed at Tia. Kindra cleared her throat. "You've come just in time to greet Mother. She arrived less than an hour ago." *Will it take an act of God to bring these two people together?*

Cuffee stepped forward. "It be a long time since we last seen each other." His hands hung at his sides. "You be the last person I ever wanted to see on this earth . . . But life has played a trick on us . . . You'll be my grandchildren's great-grandmother." His eyes grew dark.

"Cuffee!" Kindra felt heat slide up her neck and over her scalp.

Tia laid a hand on her arm. "I owe this man an apology." She stood. "I used you badly, Cuffee. I demanded you do unthinkable things. I'll regret that for the rest of my life."

"Because of you," he said, "I spent years away from my family." His lip quivered. It seemed he just couldn't let it go.

"I'm sorry, Cuffee. I'm asking you for a hard thing, but can you forgive me?" She held her chin up, not with pride, Kindra felt, but as a woman who'd faced much adversity in her life and would face this now with humility.

A painful silence hung over them like a dense fog. Only the ticking of the grandfather clock filled the air.

Cuffee stared at Tia, and Kindra saw his jaw tense. He glanced at Tabitha, and his wife nodded, a sad smile on her face.

Kindra held her breath.

"I forgive you, Tia." Cuffee's shoulders sagged. "I want my heart and mind free from hate.

Tia held out her hand, and Cuffee took it. "Friends?" she asked.

"Yes. After today, we be friends."

The room burst into loud sighs, and Kindra's hand flew to her heart. "Now we can celebrate!"

Jule Spade slid off his mount and hid behind the trees at the bank of the river. He crept slowly to the boat ramp and peered up at the Great House. It was all lit up as if a special event were taking place inside. He looked up the long drive. Only a couple of coaches were parked outside. He didn't dare go to the house. He'd waited a long time for Tia to make her move. He could wait a little longer.

He had hired a spy to keep tabs on her. The man had watched her every move when she was on the streets of Bridgetown. Always the scout returned with a negative response; it seemed Tia had no inclination to leave the island.

When Jule Spade first kidnapped her daughter, he had hoped Tia would give up the emeralds. But time went by, one year, then two. She had more patience than he'd given her credit for—it was apparent she was in no hurry to make her move.

Now, eight years later, his man reported Tia had been seen in Bridgetown, talking to Captain Billy Picoult of *Intrepid,* one of Cameron Bartholomew's merchant fleet. His spy had overheard the woman making plans to sail to Charleston, South Carolina. Jule remembered that day. He had been so satisfied with the report that he had paid the man double, along with a promise to triple the payment if he procured the date of Tia's travel plans.

In the meantime, Spade prepared the *Caribbean King* to sail at a moment's notice. He still believed the journal and map Scoot Sweeny had made were hidden at River Oak. If Tia had plans to sail to Charleston, it could be for only one reason. She was finally going after the treasure map.

After three weeks at sea, and with his spyglass pointed toward the *Intrepid*, he had finally found himself outside the Bartholomew home, waiting for the right moment to make his move. He pulled out his knife and held it in the moonlight. He ran his thumb over the blade. Razor sharp, he snapped his hand back. The metallic taste of blood met his tongue as he licked his thumb. *What a fool I am*, he thought, and swore under his breath. He stepped into the saddle. He would return in the morning. Maybe then he could corner the panther.

Grace instructed the house slaves to have the house shining before the end of the week. The double wedding would be held at River Oak.

"I can hardly believe the day after tomorrow will be the wedding." Grace sat down at the table with Kindra and Tia.

"Are the girls still sleeping?" Tia asked.

"I believe so. They were up for hours, talking." Kindra smiled. "It was music to my ears. Ah, Grace. I have to pinch myself a dozen times a day to believe I'm really here with all of you." She reached one hand to her mother and the other to Grace.

"You're not the only one. That you are sitting at my table is a dream come true." Grace sipped her tea.

Denzel and Cameron strode into the room with muskets in their hands.

"Goodness! What are you up to?" Grace asked.

"We have a wedding coming up, don't we?" Cameron asked.

"Well, yes. But what does that have to do with you two gallivanting through the house with muskets?"

"The cooks need fresh meat for the reception. We'll be back later this morning with a hind quarter of beef and a pig. Mama Jezelee's already dressing out a turkey."

"Wonderful." Grace turned to Kindra. "We need to go over the list of food for the party. It's just our family and close friends, but I don't want to run short of anything."

Tia stood. "While you work on your list, I want to take a stroll around River Oak. I've only seen the front lawn and the house. I'm sure there's much more to see." She excused herself and went out the front door.

Grace and Kindra bent over the list of preparations. The big day would come all too soon.

Jule Spade hunkered low behind the camellia bushes and watched as Tia walked along the path to the pond. Just when he would have lunged for her, the brat, Kit Bartholomew, rode up on her mount.

"Good morning, Aunt Tia. Are you enjoying your walk?" She slid off her horse, holding the reins as she talked.

"Your parents have done a remarkable job with the layout of River Oak."

"Thank you. Mama loves working in the gardens. If she's not pruning flowers, she's sitting for hours, sketching what she sees."

"I would have thought you'd be in the house, preparing for your wedding, instead of out riding." Tia pointed to the horse.

"Come in with me. I'll show you my wedding dress." Kit tugged on her arm.

"I'd be honored. I thought you'd still be asleep." Tia turned back to the house.

"Damaris is still in bed. I'm so keyed up about the wedding that I couldn't sleep any longer. Just imagine, in two days I'll be Mrs. Jackson Harding."

"That has a nice ring to it. Lead the way."

Jule swore under his breath. Why did that girl have to get in the way? He sank low behind the bush as the women walked by. He simmered. *I don't have all day! I've got to get that map before the morning's gone!*

The house grew quiet as the girls were in their rooms, and Kindra took a nap. Grace didn't know where the boys had gone, but she was glad to have this time to herself. She went downstairs to check on the cooks' preparations. When she reached the bottom, she heard a man's low voice coming from the sitting room. Curious, she crept to the entrance to find a stranger with his back to her, Tia in his grip.

Alarmed, Grace stepped back into the foyer and leaned against the wall. *Who is he, and what is he doing with Tia?*

"Where's the map?" Grace heard cold fury in the man's voice. Stunned, she leaned against the casing and glanced at her foil hanging above the fireplace. Could she reach it before he saw her?

"Let me go, Jule! Haven't you done enough?" Tia struggled against him.

"Get me that treasure map!"

"I don't know what you're talking about!"

Grace moved stealthily toward the mantle and slid the thin sword off its hooks.

"Don't lie to me," the man growled. "Nothing gets past you. That map is here, and frankly, I find it fascinating that you've shown up here too." His contemptuous voice lashed at her.

"You've got it all wrong, Jule. I don't care about the emeralds anymore. I gave up on them before you dragged my girl away!"

"Shut up!" he hissed. He tightened his grip and held a blade to Tia's throat. "I don't mind slicing that selfish little neck of yours. Now, where are the jewels?"

Grace stepped forward and pushed her blade against the man's neck. "Drop the knife, mister!"

Jule stiffened, but he kept the blade against Tia's neck.

Tia gasped.

"I said drop it." Grace pushed the point of her blade into his flesh. She saw blood trickle down his neck.

"You don't have the nerve, lady!" Jule pushed Tia away and swung around, his blade raised in the air.

Boom! The air immediately filled with smoke.

Terror filled Jule's eyes as he dropped the knife and grabbed his chest. He fell to the floor with a sickening thud.

Grace turned to see Cameron holding a smoking musket. "Thank God you came!" The foil clanged to the floor as she rushed into his arms.

"He's dead," Tia said, her voice dull.

Cameron set the gun against the doorframe and pulled Grace tightly against him.

A scuffle of footsteps and cries flooded the stairs as the family and guests raced to the room. "What happened?" Bella asked. They all stopped when they saw the stranger lying face down on the floor in a pool of blood.

Denzel stormed through the front door and pulled Kindra to his side.

"Who is that?" Sunny gasped, her face pale.

"That's Jule Spade," Kindra said. "The man who kidnapped me."

"He won't be bothering you or anybody else anymore," Denzel said. He buried Kindra's face into his chest.

The cooks had come from the kitchen and now stood at the back of the crowd. "Is everybody all right?" Gemma asked.

"We're fine, Gemma," Cameron said. "Tell Cato and Amos to get this worthless piece of hide out of my house. I'll meet them outside." He massaged Grace's back. "You all right?"

"I'm fine."

He tipped her chin up and smiled down at her. "You still have a knack with that foil." He kissed her forehead.

"And you have a knack for showing up at the right time."

Kindra stood before her daughter, admiring her in her wedding dress. Tears brimmed in her eyes. "You look lovely, my baby."

"Oh, Mama! I've waited all these years for you to come, and now you'll sail home without me."

"Are you having any doubts?" Kindra looked into her daughter's eyes.

"I love him, Mama."

"But?"

"But it will be hard to see you go."

Tia came to the door, her face flushed. "Kit's ready to go down. Are you?"

Kindra drew Damaris to her. "You'll be fine, my darling."

Damaris nodded and sniffed.

Kindra pulled out her handkerchief and dabbed at her daughter's eyes. "Ready?"

"I'm ready."

Cameron and Denzel waited at the base of the stairs, elbowing each other.

Kit and Damaris hugged. "I'm proud to be sharing my wedding day with you," Kit said and kissed Damaris's cheek. The two women picked their way down the stairs in their stunning white gowns. When they reached the bottom, Denzel stepped forward and claimed Damaris.

Cameron's eyes shimmered with a hint of tears as he smiled at Kit. "I remember the day you were born. You were so tiny, and your mother gave you such a big name. But I knew right then you were my kitten."

"I love you, Daddy!" Kit wrapped her arms around his neck.

Kindra and Grace laughed softly.

"I think we're ready," Kindra said. She and Grace went to the front door, where Zeddie and Willie waited to escort them to their chairs on the lawn. The orchestra struck up the music and everybody stood. Denzel led Damaris down one side of the steps, and Cameron led Kit down the other.

Solomon and Jackson waited with expectant gazes. All could see that the two men were ready to receive their brides. At last, the women stood beside their men, and the fathers took their seats.

The minister went through their vows.

"Do you, Kit, take this man . . .?"

"I do." Kit looked longingly up into Jackson's eyes.

Jackson gazed back at her, his eyes moist.

The minister turned to Damaris and Solomon. "Do you, Solomon, take this woman . . .?"

"I do." Solomon trembled. "I don't want to give up this woman, but she's givin' up her rich life for me."

Damaris felt as if the day floated in a dream. Soon her parents would be leaving for Barbados, and she would stay behind with the man she loved. *Where he leads, I will follow, Lord, even if it means living in the slave district.*

"I now pronounce you man and wife." The minister nodded to both couples.

Jackson beamed and drew Kit into a long kiss.

The guests roared and clapped.

Tungo stepped forward and laid a broom on the ground. Solomon and Damaris looked at each other, held hands, and jumped over it.

Cheers and whistles pierced the air.

Solomon pulled Damaris into his arms and kissed her soundly. He turned her to face the audience on the lawn. "This be my bride. I will love her as long as I live."

Approving cries went up again.

Damaris's vision blurred as she looked out at her family. *Enjoy this day,* she told herself. *This is what you wanted.*

When the vows were completed, the musicians picked up their stringed instruments and filled the air with the strains of a waltz.

"Dance with me, Kit." Jackson led his bride onto the makeshift dance floor. He bowed low and looked up, his hazel eyes shining. Then he took her into his arms and twirled her around.

Solomon held Damaris to the side and looked at her wistfully. "I don't know how to dance."

"Come, my love. I'll lead." Damaris felt giddy as she led her big, handsome husband to the dance floor. She curtsied gracefully and glanced up at him with so much love. Then she took his hand and placed it at her waist. Keeping her eyes on Solomon, she led him through a waltz. He clumsily followed, but she didn't care. They would dance through life together.

When the music ended, the couples sat at the head table for their wedding meal. Cameron picked up a crystal glass and clinked a spoon against it. "It is time to give the couples a toast." He looked lovingly at Kit and smiled at Jackson. "We've known Jackson's family, it seems, forever. We go a long way back. I met his father, Drew Harding, when we lived on Cooper's Landing in Jamaica. Drew became my best friend." Cameron looked over the table at Drew and Camille.

"His wife, Camille, became Grace's good friend during Grace's early days on the plantation. Through the years, we've shared many happy memories." Tears clogged his throat, and he swallowed. "We never imagined the day would come when we would share in the joy of our children marrying each other. It can only bring many more shared memories in years to come." Cameron raised his glass and looked down at Grace, whose eyes glistened with tears.

The guests raised their glasses, drank to the toasts, then broke out into a modest wave of applause and polite hurrahs.

Cameron cleared his throat. "I have an announcement to make." He looked down at Solomon and Damaris. "Solomon, as a gift to you and your bride, I now declare you a free man. You can sail with your bride to Barbados."

"What?" Damaris flew out of her chair and threw her arms around Cameron's neck. "Oh, thank you, Uncle Cameron!" Tears filled her eyes as she looked at the man she loved and then out to her mother. "We're *all* going home!"

The guests roared and raised their glasses.

Tears swam in Kindra's eyes as she looked at her daughter and son-in-law, then to her husband. She swiped her glistening cheeks. Denzel smiled and squeezed her shoulder. She let out a contented sigh and looked back to Damaris before lifting her eyes upward. "My heart is full of happiness and so very thankful for God's promise."

Weeping endures for a night, but joy comes in the morning!

The Winds of Love Series

Hearts of Home Series

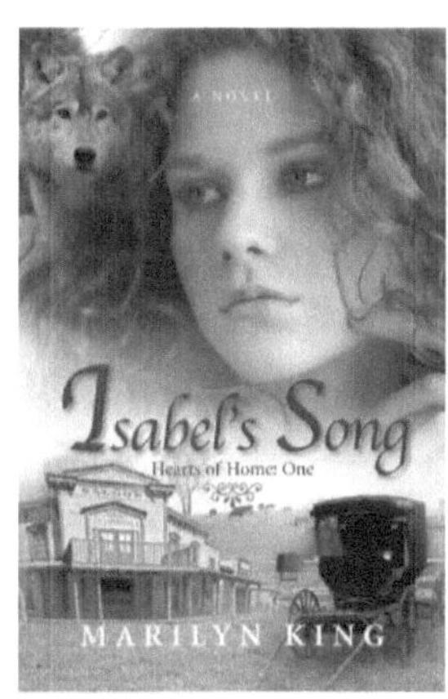

The Call of the West Series

www.ingramcontent.com/pod-product-compliance
Lightning Source LLC
Chambersburg PA
CBHW051322250626
47155CB00007B/2413

* 9 7 8 0 9 9 6 7 2 5 8 1 1 *